Jove titles by Clare Coleman

DAUGHTER OF THE REEF
SISTER OF THE SUN

CHILD OF THE DAWN

CLARE COLEMAN

JOVE BOOKS, NEW YORK

CHILD OF THE DAWN

A Jove Book / published by arrangement with
the authors

PRINTING HISTORY
Jove edition / March 1994

All rights reserved.
Copyright © 1994 by Clare Bell and M. Coleman Easton.
This book may not be reproduced in whole or in part,
by mimeograph or any other means, without permission.
For information address: The Berkley Publishing Group,
200 Madison Avenue, New York, New York 10016.

ISBN: 0-515-11334-4

A JOVE BOOK®
Jove Books are published by The Berkley Publishing Group,
200 Madison Avenue, New York, New York 10016.
JOVE and the "J" design are trademarks belonging to
Jove Publications, Inc.

PRINTED IN THE UNITED STATES OF AMERICA

10 9 8 7 6 5 4 3 2 1

PRONUNCIATION

The vowels of the language of Tahiti are pronounced as follows:

> *a* as the "a" in "father"
> *e* as the "a" in "say"
> *i* as the "e" in "me"
> *o* as the "o" in "so"
> *u* as the "u" in "rule"

When two vowels are adjacent in a word, each is pronounced as a separate sound. The accent on a word usually falls on the next-to-last syllable. The presence of an apostrophe in a word indicates a break or glottal stop.

NOTE: A glossary of unfamiliar terms appears in the back of this book.

ACKNOWLEDGMENTS

For their help, I would like to thank:

The members of the Wordshop: Kevin J. Anderson, Michael Berch, Michael Meltzer, Dan'l Danehy-Oakes, Avis Minger, Gary Schockley, and Lori Ann White, for reading and critiques.

Dorothy Wall, for critical insight.

Dorothy Bradley, for help with proofreading.

Halau Hula 'O Malieikekainalu—its members, and Kumu-hula Malie Rosare, Hawaiian dance and language teacher.

City of San Jose Library, especially the Santa Teresa Branch, for providing space for our "Making of a Book" exhibit.

University of Santa Clara Library, for access to a 1773 edition of Hawkesworth's *Voyages*.

The Clark Library at San Jose State University.

CHILD OF THE DAWN

ONE

Under a clouded sky, a two-hulled voyaging canoe approached its island destination. As the sailing craft neared landfall, cries rang out from everyone aboard—praises to the canoe-master for his skill, to the gods for providing safe passage. Along the shore ahead, black sand beaches spread beneath stands of coconut palm. Inland, mountain slopes rose steeply, vanishing into mist.

A shaft of sunlight broke through the overcast, tinting the feathery clouds that topped the peaks. At last the travelers understood the name of this fabled island—Great-Tahiti-of-the-golden-haze. A robe of green in an infinity of depths and shades covered her flanks. Her colors were strange to the newcomers—mist-softened, lush, yet in places so fierce that it hurt the eyes to gaze too long.

The double-hulled canoe, the *pahi*, had come from the swarm of coral islands far to the east. Its hulls were pieced together from small wooden sections sewn with tough cord twisted from coconut-husk fiber. A platform of lashed planks for carrying passengers and cargo bridged the hulls. The two mat sails were plaited from strips of pandanus leaf.

Most of the men aboard—warriors, craftsmen, paddlers— had never seen the soaring peaks of a high island. Tugging at their sparse beards, or fingering the sturdy fiber of their loincloths, they spoke to each other with awe.

One of the female passengers, however, knew Tahiti well. Tepua-mua, a highborn woman of the atolls, gave a soft

1

sigh. She remembered how long it had taken her to get used to this new country—the valleys that cut so deeply into the hillsides, the still, moisture-laden air that seemed heavy to someone from the windswept coral islands.

Now Tepua was returning to her adopted land after an extended stay with her family. Accompanying her was her cousin Maukiri, a sturdy atoll girl with a plump face and a fondness for mischief. Maukiri was stockier than Tepua, pleasant in appearance but not striking. Her youthful buoyancy and spirit more than made up for any lack of physical charms. Tepua, on the other hand, had a wild atoll beauty that suggested her ancestors' struggles against wind and sea.

Dressed in a skirt and cape of finely plaited pandanus leaf, Tepua stood as tall as many men. Though she had the figure of full womanhood, her training as a dancer had kept her as slender and supple as an atoll palm. Lustrous black hair with tints of blue tumbled down her back. Her skin was a luminous bronze, clear and smooth. She had a high forehead, an oval face with wide cheekbones, and a square jawline that came to a point at the chin. Her eyes were large, almond-shaped, and fringed with black lashes.

Tepua and Maukiri watched eagerly as the canoe approached the frothing line of surf, where the Sea of the Moon beat against the submerged barrier reef. Plumes of sea-foam spewed into the air, raining down as fine spray that wet their skin, salted their lips.

A gap in the arc of white surf marked the pass, where ocean swells rolled through into the lagoon. The canoe-master shouted orders as the double-hull approached. Tepua and her fellow passengers clutched anything they could hold on to as the *pahi* rose on the back of a long wave. For an instant it held there, the twin bows surging upward like two birds about to fly. Then the bows dropped as the wave gave the *pahi* a tremendous push that sent it hurtling through the pass.

Tepua leaned to one side as the double-hull turned in response to the helmsman's powerful pull on the steering oar. Veering out of the wave just as it started to break, the *pahi* emerged into the glassy turquoise of the lagoon.

The crew took down mast and sails and began to paddle.

Soon a stray land breeze enveloped the canoe with the island's warm breath. It was rich with fruit and floral aromas, laden with moist perfume.

Tepua's thoughts turned to Matopahu, a nobleman of Tahiti who had once meant much to her. His house in the high chief's compound lay just ahead; she hoped she would find him nearby. How she longed to be ashore!

Yet something out there was amiss. Among the delightful aromas, she sensed a discordant note. The harsh tang of burning wood could not be hidden by anything else. *Cooking fires?* Had she forgotten how much smoke the many pit ovens of Tahiti produced?

Curious, Tepua searched for an explanation. She saw many canoes drawn up on the beach, and none in the water. Surely some great occasion must be keeping everyone ashore. In the distance, above the coconut palms, smoke rose in a dark plume.

Maukiri turned, sniffing the breeze. "Someone is cooking a big feast. I hope they invite us to share it!"

Tepua eyed the smoke. Something about it seemed menacing, although she didn't know why. As the canoe drew closer to the source of the fire, she began pointing out details along the shore to her cousin.

"That mountain is sacred to the high chief," she said. "And over there is his point of land—a place you must never go." Far ahead, where the shoreline jutted out, stood a majestic grove of Tahitian chestnut. In the deep shade lay the high chief's sacred courtyard, his *marae,* the site of rituals forbidden to women.

The view brought memories that made Tepua shiver. The *marae* was a somber and terrifying place. In its shadows, the gods alighted in the form of birds, eating the carcasses laid on the offering platforms, sacrifices of pigs, dogs, and— when the gods demanded—men.

Putting those thoughts aside, she gestured at the pleasant scenes before her, clusters of thatched roofs shaded by coconut palms or breadfruit trees. "All the people of our atoll could live in one district of Tahiti," she said as Maukiri's eyes grew round. Tepua, too, had once been astonished at the sight of so many dwellings.

Just beyond the houses, the coastal plain ended and foothills began. Some dwellings were perched on the lower slopes, others at the mouths of narrow valleys that slashed like adze-cuts into the foothills, extending as far inland as the eye could see.

Though a rush of joy came over Tepua at the sight, she could not forget that she was giving up much to return to Tahiti. At home, by virtue of her birth as well as her service to her people, she was the foremost woman of the island. Here in Tahiti she would be treated with far less respect. She was returning to her life as a dancer in one of the lower ranks of the Arioi Society. Long ago she had pledged herself to serve their patron god, Oro-of-the-laid-down-spear.

While Maukiri gaped at the sights around her, Tepua went aft to where a bamboo cage was lashed to the deck. Inside sat a beautiful white dog with gentle eyes, upright ears, and a plumed tail. Her name was Te Kurevareva, Atoll Cuckoo. Tepua gave the dog fresh water in a coconut shell. She put her hand through a gap and stroked the animal. The plumed tail wagged against the bamboo canes, and a wet nose poked out to nuzzle Tepua's face. She had brought this rare and valuable animal as a gift to the Arioi chiefs, though now she did not want to give the dog up.

Maukiri crouched beside Tepua. "Stop playing with your dog and tell me where we are going," said her cousin in an exasperated voice.

"You will see soon enough," said Tepua, straightening up. She wanted to leave a few surprises for her cousin. What would Maukiri say when she discovered such common Tahitian sights as rivers of fresh water flowing to the sea? At home, fresh water was found only in cisterns and a few brackish pools. What would Maukiri think of bananas, breadfruit, and a host of other foods she had never tasted?

"Then tell me about the people we will visit first," begged Maukiri, her brown eyes alight with anticipation.

"I have many friends," Tepua answered. She did not know where she would find a place for Maukiri, but the question did not bother her now. Tahitians welcomed guests, especially if they had good tales to tell. Some prominent family would take Maukiri in.

Eventually the two cousins would have to separate. Tepua would live with the performers and dancers of her Arioi lodge. Maukiri would have to find other accommodations. "I will make arrangements for you," Tepua promised.

The younger girl turned, sniffing the breeze. "I'm not worried, cousin. Your friends must know how hungry we are. Smell the food!"

Again Tepua eyed the ashy haze that hung over the trees. Could all that have come from cooking?

"Feasting! Dancing!" Maukiri crowed. "What a good day to arrive."

The canoe made its way along the coast. Now the source of the smoke was much closer. Gray billows boiled into the sky with such violence that Tepua felt an upsurge of alarm. "That is no cooking fire!"

Her cry drew the gaze of everyone on the *pahi*. The men began to shout and gesture.

Tepua shaded her eyes, squinting hard at the shore. In the shadows of the palm groves she saw figures scurrying. An orange ribbon of flame shot above the treetops.

"*Aue!* Something tall is burning." She clenched her fists as the realization swept over her. The only large structure in this area was the great high-roofed theater where the Arioi acted and danced. "*Aue, aue!*" she cried, her voice breaking.

The commotion grew aboard the *pahi*. The paddlers lost their rhythm, and the twin bows swung off course. "Head for shore!" Tepua shouted at the canoe-master.

She turned as a tall, tattooed atoll warrior left his place and came to her. This man was the captain of her escort guard, charged with bringing her safely to Tahiti.

"There may be trouble here," he warned. He stood beside her, arms folded, eyes narrowed.

"Maybe someone was careless with a torch." Tepua knew, even before the warrior scowled, that her suggestion was foolish. Who would use a torch in daylight? And cooking was done far from the performance house. No spark from the pit ovens could have set off this blaze.

"We will see," said the escort captain. He was the best warrior her brother could spare to accompany her. Though slender, he was powerful, and he had five good men with him. Yet none of them had ever traveled this far from home. None knew the ways of high islanders.

Tepua heard screams from shore as more people, men as well as women, fled the fire. They wore wreaths of flowers and festive dress, but their celebration had been interrupted. As the people ran, their flower-crowns fell off and were trampled. Broken palm fronds and blossoms scattered to the breeze.

Maukiri began to moan softly. Tepua held her cousin's hand, but the words of reassurance she tried to say died on her tongue. The white dog whined from inside her cage.

Tepua felt Maukiri start to shiver. "It is a bad omen. The gods must be angry," the girl wailed.

"Men have done this, not gods," Tepua answered firmly. She studied the growing turmoil on the beach. What had happened? Invasion? War? "You stay here," she said in a low voice. "I will see what the trouble is."

"Hold in the shallows," she heard the warrior captain order the paddlers. Still a good way from shore, he clutched a long double-ended spear, leaped out of the *pahi,* and splashed ashore. Tepua took a spear from another warrior and jumped down into water that rose to her thighs. The men of her escort guard followed.

When she caught up with her captain, he tried to dissuade her, saying that he would investigate the trouble. Tepua refused his offer, but allowed him and two of his men to follow as she plunged into the trees toward the site of the fire.

Then she saw people wearing distinctive garlands of yellow mountain plantain, sweet-scented ginger, or the sacred red-and-purple *ti* plant. Their tattoos were familiar, for she bore some of the same. These people were her fellow Arioi, members of Wind-driving Lodge.

With a shock, she realized that the Arioi had been in the midst of performing, their faces smeared with red sap and their bodies blackened with charcoal. Some were hampered by oversized loincloths and other ridiculous costumes used in satires. Her jaw tightened with rage even as her mind reeled with disbelief. What evil had interrupted the devotees of Oro in their celebration?

She looked for people she knew but could not recognize anyone under the face paint and costumes. "What is happening?" she called. The fleeing performers were too panic-stricken to stop or answer.

She heard the harsh crackling of burning thatch. The smoke caught in her throat and made her gag. Then she was close enough to see the performance house ablaze, its high roof completely enveloped in flame. She groaned aloud in anguish. This was where the god Oro had inspired her, making her dance with such a frenzy that the Arioi asked her to join them. And now this great work of polished wood pillars and pandanus thatch was doomed!

As Tepua fought her way through the rolling clouds of smoke, worry for her fellow Arioi performers filled her thoughts. Where was her friend, Curling-leaf? And Aitofa, the chief of the women's lodge?

At last Tepua emerged from the drifting haze and could see the scene clearly. Now she understood why no one had tried to put out the fire at its start. Warriors bearing unfamiliar tattoos stood about the site, brandishing clubs and shark-toothed swords, threatening anyone who dared come close. No onlookers braved these fierce sentries. She saw Arioi and common folk watching with horror from the shadows.

"Tepua! Tepua! Is it really you?" The cry made her spin around. There stood another painted figure, as difficult to recognize as the others. She knew the voice. Curling-leaf!

Before the escort captain could prevent her, Tepua rushed into her friend's arms. "I am back. Oh, it has been so long!" Curling-leaf's embrace was strong, but Tepua felt the young Arioi woman quivering with rage and fright. "Who did this?" Tepua asked, searching her friend's eyes. "Who are those warriors? Why don't you have any weapons?"

Her own three guards clustered close about her, but she waved them aside. What could this handful do against so many others?

She turned back to Curling-leaf. "Tell me what happened."

"There is no time!" wailed her friend. "Everything has changed since you left. The high chief was cast down."

Cast down! Tepua stared at her friend, unable to make sense of the words. When she left Tahiti, Knotted-cord had been high chief over this district and several others. She remembered him as petty and irascible, but not arrogant enough to overreach himself. The only threat to his rule had been the popularity of his brother, Matopahu.

His brother! She closed her eyes, remembering Matopahu's ambitions as well as what he had meant to her. Had Knotted-cord been pushed aside in favor of his reckless sibling? She forced herself to ask.

"No." Curling-leaf's answer made Tepua heave a relieved sigh, but the next words gave her a chill. "The chief's brother had to flee."

"But Matopahu was not hurt. He is alive, isn't he?" She clutched at her friend's arm, demanding an answer. It was for Matopahu as well as the Arioi that she had returned to Tahiti.

Curling-leaf looked regretful. "He is, but that's all I know. Someone told me he has gone to live in Eimeo."

"Praise the gods, he is alive." Tepua's pulse began slowing and she felt steadier on her feet. "But who is the new chief, and why this outrage?"

Her friend glanced apprehensively at the line of guards around the burning performance house. They were starting to notice the two women. Curling-leaf headed in the opposite direction, tugging Tepua after her. "We can't stay. The new chief wants to destroy us." As Curling-leaf spoke, several other Arioi women emerged from the smoke, their garlands and costumes in disarray, flowers falling from their tangled hair. They rallied around Tepua.

"Go to my *pahi*," Tepua told them. "Straight through the trees and down the beach." She ordered one of her warriors to see that they got aboard safely. Ignoring the escort captain's pleas that she go with the departing women, Tepua plunged ahead with Curling-leaf and began to search for others who needed help.

She felt Curling-leaf take her hand, and this time the grip was firm and steady. The spirit had come back into

Curling-leaf's eyes. Now she looked more like an Arioi, despite her shredded garlands and the soot smudges over the red sap on her face.

"The others are hiding," Curling-leaf said. "We have to find them." She beckoned Tepua through a grove of breadfruit trees. Overhead, waxy leaves of deep green hue spread a thick canopy.

"Arioi? Hiding? Why aren't any of them fighting?"

"With what?" Curling-leaf answered angrily. "Our weapons are gone! While the whole troupe was performing, the creature who calls himself high chief had them stolen."

"Who is this man?"

"He was a minor chief. After you left, he led a rebellion against Knotted-cord. Now he takes the name of Land-crab and rules as high chief."

Tepua, bewildered, followed her friend across the leaf-carpeted grove. It surprised her that an unexpected rival had risen against the former high chief. And this Land-crab had done something far worse, something unheard of. Arioi were under the protection of their patron god and immune from attack, even during outbreaks of war. A covenant of peace reigned at all Arioi performances; this was a tradition that the most exalted chief had never violated. Until now.

"The usurper chose a good name," said Curling-leaf bitterly. "He sits on us like a fat crab on a heap of coconuts, and tears us apart with his claws."

Well, this Land-crab would see what it was to anger Oro, Tepua thought, clenching her fists.

"Look! More of our friends," cried Curling-leaf. Tepua gathered another group of Arioi refugees and sent them to her *pahi*. She and Curling-leaf continued searching, finally reaching the smaller thatched houses of the Arioi women's compound. The neatly swept yards surrounding them were empty. Not even a stray chicken appeared in the shadows beneath the breadfruit trees.

Tepua saw daylight glimmering through the latticework walls of the houses. Clutching the spear in her damp fist, she approached the one house where she thought she heard rustling. "Who is in there?" she demanded, but got no answer. She edged closer, toward the hanging mat that half-covered the doorway. Again she spoke a challenge, and this time heard another sound, a scraping. Or was it weeping?

With her spear-tip, she thrust aside the mat and looked inside. A lithe female figure wearing a red-dyed sash sprang to meet her. The woman had an eel-jawed knife clenched in one fist. Her unpainted face was twisted in rage. Tepua knew the features and lowered her spear even as the other checked her attack.

"Aitofa!" Tepua cried as she realized that she had burst in on the chief woman of her Arioi lodge. Then she saw the bright smear of blood on Aitofa's arm and the clumsy, loose bandage that she had been trying to tie around the wound with one hand.

Tepua threw down her weapon and ran to help Aitofa. The lodge leader looked as hard and stern as ever, but there was a certain weary despair in her eyes. She was a slender woman, heavily tattooed, her legs entirely black from ankle to thigh.

"You returned at an evil time," said Aitofa while Tepua retied the bark-cloth bandage. "We had no chance against Land-crab's treachery."

"But why did he do this? I have never heard of such—"

"We mocked him in our performance."

"That is our privilege!" Tepua was outraged. It was the right and even the duty of the Arioi to restrain chiefs by use of satire.

"He either does not understand that or chooses to ignore it," said Aitofa, with a return of her usual acerbic tone.

"Did we insult him?"

"We poked fun at his greed for power, but we have been harder on other chiefs."

"Then he had no right to steal our spears and burn our playhouse."

"Well, he didn't see it that way. When he learned what we were planning to present, he called us disloyal. We put the play on anyway, and this"—Aitofa opened her hands, palms up—"is the result."

"What can we do now? Who will help us?"

"As of yet, I do not know." Acting as if she had forgotten

her wound, Aitofa picked up a short club and headed for the door.

"I have a large *pahi*," Tepua offered, quickly explaining how she had been gathering other Arioi and sending them to safety. "I can take a few more passengers."

"Good. We can use your help. The water today is too rough for smaller craft."

"But where are we going?"

Outside, Aitofa pointed between the trees toward the glimmer of gray water. "North along the coast—to Matavai Bay," she said. "If our friends there haven't deserted us, we will be safe."

When Tepua returned to the beach, she found a crowd of disheveled Arioi, mostly women, waiting for her. They were all trained warriors as well as performers, but without weapons they could not stand up to Land-crab's forces. Still wearing their paint and the remains of their costumes, they stood in groups, talking grimly.

Tepua's warriors, some arguing among themselves, watched from the *pahi* or the shallows. "You cannot take everyone," cried Curling-leaf when she saw the size of the crowd waiting to board.

Tepua looked at the deck that bridged the hulls of her double canoe. The thatched cabin, the dog's cage, the water bottles and supplies took up needed passenger space. She waded out to the canoe-master. He was a veteran of many journeys, with a bush of wiry hair that held a shock of gray. "We must take these people to Matavai Bay," she told him. "Remove the shelter and make as much room as you can."

"What about my other passengers?" asked the canoe-master. He opened his hand at the group of artisans who had left home at the request of a chief of Porapora. After delivering Tepua to Tahiti, the *pahi* was to take the craftsmen to Porapora and wait there while they finished the chief's work. Then the men would sail home, taking in trade for their services a wealth of Poraporan goods.

Tepua answered, "The others can stay here until you return for them."

The canoe-master and the artisans glowered at her, but she ignored their reactions.

"You are in no danger," she said to the craftsmen. "If the chief here challenges you, offer to build him something. Maybe he needs an altar for one of his sacred canoes."

She glanced at distant whitecaps as she felt the harsh wind blow against her cheek. To reach Matavai, the *pahi* would have to go out through the reef, sail the rough Sea of the Moon, and come in through another pass before darkness fell.

The canoe-master seemed aware of the need for haste; he gave sharp orders. Quickly the crew dismantled the deck cabin and carried it ashore. Tepua watched as they carefully unloaded Te Kurevareva's cage and set it beneath a palm tree.

Atoll Cuckoo had a gentle and patient nature, making it easy to grow fond of her. Tepua originally had intended to offer the precious white dog, possibly the only one of its kind in Tahiti, as a gift to the Arioi leaders. During the journey, she had found it increasingly difficult to think about parting with Te Kurevareva. Now the troubles here had completely upset her plans.

She couldn't worry about the white dog now. Her Arioi friends needed her help. "I will be back for you," Tepua said, scratching Atoll Cuckoo behind the ears and accepting a lick on her hand. Then she went to see how many women could be crowded onto the deck of the *pahi*.

"Tepua, this is foolhardy," said the warrior captain, who had brought his men up behind her. "I have a duty to your brother to keep you safe. You owe nothing to these Tahitian players. Come with us now to Porapora. We will bring you back here when the trouble is over."

Tepua took a deep breath and stared into his dark eyes. "These Tahitians are now my people. I cannot dessert them."

He gestured toward his warriors. "Then we must escort you to Matavai Bay."

"There is no room!"

The captain stared back with equal resolution. His men did not move from her path.

"If you insist on protecting me," Tepua answered, "then I will stay here, with the craftsmen, while my Arioi friends go to safety. Let me give the orders."

At last, the warriors let her pass. She found Maukiri standing to one side, trembling. Tepua tried to comfort her. "Don't send me away," Maukiri insisted. "I can help you here. I can look after Te Kurevareva."

"Then take her out of her cage and hide her somewhere," said Tepua. Maukiri seemed glad to have something to do. She went off to fill a coconut shell with fresh water for the dog.

In a short while, all the costumed Arioi managed to crowd onto Tepua's vessel. At her insistence, Curling-leaf joined them. Aitofa had not returned, but Tepua could wait no longer. She told the canoe-master to depart.

The warriors and craftsmen, with their equipment and supplies, remained behind on the beach. A crosswind was blowing, making the canoe-master's task even more difficult. Tepua watched nervously as the sails were raised and the laden craft set out.

The lagoon was choppy, the sea beyond, heaving and gray, but the sturdy *pahi* had faced far worse. Tepua stood watching its departure as the sails grew smaller, rising and falling on distant swells. Gusts of wind tore at her hair and stung her face.

"Who are these invaders?" came a challenging voice from behind. She whirled, seeing that her guards had already brought up their spears. A turbaned Tahitian warrior was approaching at the head of his own group of men. Land-crab's guards had finally discovered their visitors!

Tepua strode forward, wishing she could find a single familiar face among the high chief's warriors. The leader of the canoe-builders began to speak, though the softer dialect of Tahiti sounded awkward on his tongue. He proudly proclaimed his coral island origin and the skills of his men.

The high chief's captain looked at him skeptically, then barked an order that sent a messenger running along the beach. The captain glanced at the armed visitors. "Savages," he muttered to the man beside him. "Atoll dwellers." Then, in a loud voice, he demanded, "Show us the rest of your weapons."

The master canoe-builder pointed to the heap of adzes, tools with wooden hafts and heads of shaped black stone or shell. "We cut wood, not men," he answered.

"A sharp answer!" replied the warrior, laughing at his own wit. Then he waited silently for his messenger to return from the compound of the high chief, which lay above the beach near his sacred point of land. Tepua saw a runner coming from that direction, and then another. Even from this distance, she could hear the resonant note of the conch-trumpet being blown.

The warning cry of a herald rose over the fading echoes of the conch. "The high chief comes! From his home in the sky, he flies like the sea eagle to challenge the invaders. The high chief comes!"

A crowd of turbaned warriors ran out from the compound, lined themselves on either side of the high chief's path, and held up their spears. Land-crab came, riding the shoulders of his bearer, his appearance regal, his gaze fixed straight ahead. Tepua waited with curiosity as well as distaste for her first close look at the usurper.

The Tahitians who were wearing cloaks and wraps loosened their garments and bared their bodies to the waist. Seeing this unusual gesture of respect for the arriving chief, Tepua reluctantly removed her own cape. She watched the lead warrior hurry to meet Land-crab, then turn to walk beside his bearer.

Land-crab was a sizable man, Tepua saw; unlike many chiefs, he was not grossly huge. Beneath his painted cape of fine bark-cloth she saw hints of a warrior's body—broad in the chest and amply muscled. To compare him with a sea eagle seemed appropriate, for his nose was a great beak curving down his face, and his eyes were large and glossy.

Tepua bit her lip in fury as she saw the usurper approach in all his undeserved grandeur. His expression was cold as he gazed down from the neck of his sweating bearer. In one hand he carried a fly-flap, a tuft of feathers attached to a long wooden handle that bore a scowling carved figure. "So you are canoe-builders?" he said to the men who faced him.

"I have my own. And strangers on my shore can only bring trouble. How did you get here?"

"By *pahi*," said the master craftsman humbly. "But we have lent the boat to someone who needed it. Noble chief, we ask only your permission to stay here for the night. In the morning, before you wake, we will be gone."

"Gone where? To build canoes for my enemies?" He shook the fly-flap impatiently.

"To Porapora," the craftsman answered.

Land-crab tossed his head. "Then your work is not likely to trouble me. Even so, I have little reason to grant your request. You land without permission. . . . You invade my shores. . . . Why not feed you to the sharks?"

There was a sudden commotion to the side. Tepua heard Maukiri shouting and then saw two warriors dragging her, a third leading an unwilling Te Kurevareva by a tether about the neck. A soft cry spilled from Tepua's lips. Maukiri had tried to hide the animal under the trees. . . .

"What is this?" asked Land-crab, his face suddenly alive with interest. Tepua stifled a groan. With a single glance, Land-crab had grasped the significance of Te Kurevareva. "What is this animal doing here?"

She did not want to give up Atoll Cuckoo, and surely did not want the usurper to have her. But how could she avoid it when everyone stood in danger? Land-crab would have what he wished in any case. Yet she had to force out the words. "This fine dog is a gift for the high chief," she called loudly. "We offer you this as our token of respect."

Murmurs of astonishment spread through the crowd of warriors, but Land-crab did not answer at once. Everyone knew how precious were the long white hairs of this animal, used to fringe fine garments for chiefs and priests. The dog would be a prized possession to a man like Land-crab.

Tepua imagined what was running through his thoughts. Now that she had announced the gift, accepting it would put him under an obligation. If he did not respond with generosity, then he would be scorned as the stingiest chief in all of Tahiti. But hospitality to atoll dwellers would do nothing for his reputation.

At last, Land-crab replied, "I accept your gift with pleasure. I did not realize that such distinguished visitors as yourselves had arrived on my shore. Please forgive the poor manners of my men. I will leave *them* to sleep out under the weather while you fine people have food, entertainment, and comfortable mats under a roof. Come. All of you. Today you are guests of the mighty Land-crab."

Tepua walked with Maukiri as they followed the men along the beach. Streaks of tears ran down Maukiri's face.

"Do not fret, cousin," Tepua whispered. "He will not harm Atoll Cuckoo. She is too valuable."

"I . . . do not trust . . . this Land-crab."

"He has taken our gift, so he is obliged to treat us well," Tepua answered with an angry toss of her head. With disgust, she added, "Even though he is my enemy, I must pretend to be pleased by his hospitality." She paused, crouched, and ripped up a length of beach vine. "Help me cover my Arioi tattoos," she added. "The new people here do not know me. Let them think I am just a canoe-builder's woman."

As the two walked, they plaited simple garlands. Maukiri helped Tepua drape one around each ankle, to hide the tattoos that marked her rank of Seasoned-bamboo. They made wreaths for their hair as well, trying to maintain the appearance of a festive mood.

"Everything here is so strange to me, even the plants," Maukiri said as they entered a wooded path, where stands of *ti* raised spear-shaped leaves splashed with violet and veined in yellow. Whorls of periwinkle flowers, as white as coconut cream, with crimson centers, blossomed from glossy foliage. Tepua recalled her own first impressions of Tahiti, how she had been overwhelmed by the profusion of new flowers and scents. But today her thoughts did not linger on these pleasures. She kept wondering what Matopahu was doing, and how she would find him.

As they reached the fence of bamboo canes that surrounded the high chief's compound, Tepua once again found herself searching in vain for familiar faces. The sentries she had known were gone. The ones who stood now, spears firmly in hand, eyed her with disdain. And there were so many! In the past, the posting of guards had been a formality. No one would have dared intrude on the high chief's compound.

Once inside the gate, she did not see a single servant that she recognized. Apparently Land-crab had made a clean sweep, replacing Knotted-cord's people with his own. Tepua had to bear the icy gaze of the female attendant who met her and Maukiri, then escorted them to a small guest house for women.

The compound of the high chief, with its thatched houses and shady breadfruit trees, had changed little since Tepua had last seen it. Yet life here was not the same. No longer did children of the court attendants run freely about the yard. The flock of roaming chickens was gone; the pigs were confined to one corner by a small pen.

When Tepua reached her quarters, she found them shabby, the roof thatch rotting, the floor mats worn and ragged.

"What are we going to do?" Maukiri asked with a sigh.

"Learn everything we can about this troublemaker," said Tepua. "But first there is something more important. We have neglected the gods who watched over our journey. Come. There's a shrine nearby where women bring offerings. Then we will wash and make ourselves presentable."

A crier called the guests together for the start of Land-crab's welcoming ceremony. Warily, Tepua and Maukiri joined the others, taking seats on mats that surrounded a bare, open space in the compound. Land-crab sat on his high stool, flanked by attendants. One man held up the huge, carved staff of office. Two more stood by with long feather-tipped sticks, making certain that no flies disturbed their chief.

Land-crab's best dancers and performers, his Arioi, had fled. Tepua wondered how he planned to present an entertainment. She watched two young drummers come forward, their faces damp with sweat. These boys were so nervous that they almost dropped the drums they were carrying.

The pair took their positions, one with a round skin-head

drum, the other with a drum of the hollow slit-log variety called *toere*. When they began to pound out a rhythm, three dancers crept into the clearing.

Tepua almost laughed at the absurdity of the scene. The dancers were young girls, beginners, who kept glancing at each other for cues. Only the one in the center seemed to know the order of the steps. As they labored through their performance Tepua remembered Small-foot, her dancing pupil of long ago. With proper teaching, she thought, these girls would someday be worth watching. Now they were merely an embarrassment to their host.

As soon as they were done, the girls ran from the circle and out through the compound gate. Tepua wondered if Land-crab would punish them for their poor showing. She sighed and waited as another group of dancers, warriors from the high chief's compound, came forward.

At last Land-crab seemed to tire of the entertainment. His bearer lifted him, and he advanced toward his guests. The harsh, beaked face looked down impassively as his orator, standing at his side, began to speak.

The heavyset orator began with effusive praises, lauding his chief as if the man were a god. He went on to inform the guests of their immense good fortune. "You, who sit with us today, will have tales to tell your grandchildren. Think of their looks of amazement when you speak of the great man whose company you shared." The orator went on, enlarging on the exploits of Land-crab, until it seemed that he had conquered all of Tahiti.

Then the chief's bearer carried him a step forward, and Land-crab himself began to speak. "Here is what you must know of the one who rules this land," the chief said. "I am the strong north wind that flattens the grass. I am the wave that washes over the beach. The god of war is the one I serve, not the god of peace.

"Each season my power and my territory increase. Soon, even you of the distant atolls will bring me tribute. . . ."

Later, after the boastful speech was done, Tepua and Maukiri sat waiting for the meal to begin. In her anger at her host, Tepua wished that she could refuse his hospitality. Yet she dared not bring attention to herself. What if he realized that she was an Arioi?

During the entertainment, Tepua had occasionally glanced in the direction of the high chief's cookhouses, where large pit ovens lay under roofs of thatch. She had seen few servants coming and going, and little evidence of preparations. Now she began to wonder how Land-crab would deliver the promised feast.

Suddenly a parade of servants appeared bearing baskets of steaming food. Most of these bearers headed for the large party of men, a few coming to Tepua and Maukiri and the women of the chief's household. Tepua watched her cousin's look of astonishment as the portions were handed out. Here were foods that Maukiri had never tasted—breadfruit, wild plantains, freshwater fish—all flavored by the exotic leaves used to wrap them for baking.

Tepua did not stop to introduce these delicacies to Maukiri. Despite all that had happened she was hungry, especially after so many days of scanty rations while traveling. To her delight she found that the plantain was rich and smoky, of the ruddy mountain variety called *fe'i*. The breadfruit—so pleasant to the tooth—was perfectly baked. How had Land-crab managed, with so little apparent effort, to produce such a magnificent meal?

Tepua paused to look around. Following custom, the guests sat slightly apart from each other, men and women in separate parties. Each had his or her own place setting on a banana leaf, with cups of salt water and coconut sauce for dipping, fresh water for washing the fingers. Land-crab sat in a high place of honor, his four-legged stool elevating him above everyone else. Two servants knelt beside him, each feeding him in turn from a polished bowl. A man who claimed that his touch was sacred, Tepua noted sourly, did not feed himself—lest his hands overburden his stomach with *mana*.

She glanced at the other travelers from her atoll and saw beaming faces as they dipped into a meal far better than any chief at home could command. Her gaze turned to the servers, and she followed their path back to the gate. . . .

The food had been prepared elsewhere, she realized. But

where? Suddenly the morsel in her mouth grew as cold as a river stone.

The Arioi feast! Of course! The big ovens near the performance house had been baking a meal for the players. Now the performers were gone, scattered by Land-crab's treachery. *And this was their stolen meal.*

Tepua's throat tightened and she had to force herself to swallow. She looked at the rest of her portion and found that her appetite had fled. The others guests did not care. What did it mean to them that Land-crab had defied the peace of Oro, destroying the work of the god's servants?

Suddenly Tepua stood up. "Stay here," she managed to whisper to Maukiri. "Say that I'm unwell, if anyone asks." Then she ran out of the compound, to the shore, and along the stretch of gritty beach until she was alone.

"I will avenge this wrong," she shouted across the water, hoping that somehow Oro would hear her. "We will come back—all of us—and bring you the honor you deserve. Land-crab will suffer for his crimes."

: TWO
. . . .

Matopahu, brother of the deposed chief, dreamed that he stood in the sacred courtyard, under leafy, dark trees, shrouded by night. He knew this place of worship and sacrifice by the gleam of torchlight on damp paving stones, by the chill at the back of his neck from the breath of the gods. . . .

In the flickering light, hands moved with a slow, menacing rhythm. Solemn chanting filled the air. Flame-lit figures of priests hovered over a body that lay on a wooden platform. The corpse's legs and feet were drawn up, the arms clasped about the shoulders.

A spike of ironwood had been driven through the crown of the head, another through the ears. The dead man's head was thrust back and the mouth cried out silently. It was the face of Knotted-cord, Matopahu's brother!

Now the eye of the dream moved closer, and Matopahu saw that the moving hands held sennit, the golden cord made from coconut-husk fiber. It was long, finely made sennit, anchored to the wood spike that protruded from the top of his brother's skull. With each hypnotic movement the hands drew it over the face, wrapping the forehead, binding the eyes, coiling down over the bridge of the nose. The cord wrapped around the spike that transfixed the ears. It wove back and forth, covering the features and making the head a faceless mask.

The low throb of the chant grew louder as the offering was made to the gods.

> Here is your fish
> O great Ta'aroa
> Whose curse is death.
>
> Here is your fish
> Caught from the great waters. . . .

With a gasp, Matopahu woke from the nightmare and found himself in his place of exile—on the shore of the island of Eimeo. He was soaked with sweat and huddled up on his side, his body so tightly curled that for an instant his muscles did not unlock. The dream's terror carried over into waking; a shudder went through him, suddenly freeing his legs. Then he heard a comforting voice beside him.

"*Aue!* You have had another bad dream."

Matopahu turned to see the plump face of his companion, Eye-to-heaven, who squatted beside him. Overhead hung the palm-leaf thatch of their simple shelter, and Matopahu could smell a fresh breeze from the sea. Bright sunlight danced on the water only a few steps away.

"It was the same dream?" asked Eye-to-heaven, the stocky priest who had fled with him to exile after the overthrow of Knotted-cord. Eye-to-heaven was Matopahu's *taio,* his sworn friend, closer than a brother.

"The same," Matopahu groaned. Feeling his pounding heart slow, he crawled out into the shade beneath the needles of an ironwood tree. He sat up cautiously, waiting for his head to clear.

"I have slept too long," said Matopahu, glancing at the morning shadows. He stood up and gazed at the water, past the lagoon and foaming breakers, across empty open sea. From this side of the island of Eimeo, neighboring Tahiti lay out of sight. He was glad not to be facing in that direction. Every glimpse of the distant peaks brought back painful memories of what he had lost.

Matopahu was tall and powerfully built, a renowned warrior of the *ari'i* or chief's class. He had a handsome, strong-featured face, intense eyes, and wavy black hair that tumbled from beneath a ragged bark-cloth headband. Here in exile he possessed none of the fine garments or head-pieces from his life at his brother's court. He wore a simple *maro,* a strip of bark-cloth wound about his narrow hips and between his legs. On this warm morning he did not bother to retrieve his only other garment, a tattered cape of bark-cloth that lay inside his shelter.

For a moment longer Matopahu stood listening to the quiet washing of waves against the pebbled shore. He had been living here for almost a month, ever since his brother's fall. In disguise he had made several forays home, but each time had found Land-crab firmly in control. Last night he had learned of the latest outrage. . . .

He turned to his friend, who seemed wide-awake and full of energy. "You were up early. Have you heard more about the Arioi?"

It was Eye-to-heaven's habit to gather news every morning from fishermen and traders and share it with his friend. Today, however, he seemed to be holding something back. "Is there something else?" the *ari'i* persisted.

The priest sighed. "My *taio,* I do not know if this will bring you joy or pain. Tepua-mua has come back. She was seen near yesterday's fire."

"What happened to her?" Matopahu asked anxiously. "Where is she now?"

"Last night she was one of Land-crab's guests," the priest continued in a low voice. "He invited her entire party into his compound."

"Guest?" Matopahu stiffened in outrage. Why would she seek friendship with his greatest enemy?

"I do not understand that," said Eye-to-heaven. "But I do know that someone must talk to her and explain what has happened to you."

"It is better if she thinks me dead." Matopahu felt a stinging in his eyes and tried to blame it on a gust of wind. He had been expecting her return to Tahiti for a long time. Why did she have to appear *now*? Whatever Tepua had been to him no longer mattered. Land-crab's priests had ruined all his hopes. Again, in his mind, he heard the chanting from his dream, the words of the *aha-tu* prayer over his brother.

> Take this fish
> O great gods.
> Take this fish
> As your offering.
> May all his family die
> And none be spared.

Matopahu knew that the grim ritual from his dream had been carried out, his brother's corpse wrapped tightly in cord and given to the gods. The resulting curse fell on himself, the last of his line. Once, long ago, he had hoped that Tepua would be the mother of his children. Now Matopahu's own life was in grave danger. There certainly would be no children.

"I do have some encouraging news, my *taio*," said the priest. "This morning I did more than squat on my heels and trade banter with fishermen. I found Imo, the healer I have been looking for. He lives in a valley not far from here."

"And what will this *tahu'a* do for us?" Matopahu asked skeptically. For many days, Eye-to-heaven had been searching for a means of lifting the curse from Matopahu. Most people took this to be impossible, expecting that the *ari'i* would soon fall ill and die. Eye-to-heaven had refused to accept such gloomy views and had suggested prayers. But he needed a generous offering for the altar. He had asked that Matopahu provide ten fine pigs and as many white chickens—a difficult task for someone who possessed nothing.

In his days as brother of the high chief, the *ari'i* could have gone to any man of substance, asked for whatever he needed, and had his request granted at once. He would have been obliged, of course, to return a similar favor eventually. Now, because of the curse, people scorned him as a living corpse. Why waste good pigs, they said openly, on a man who is doomed?

"I think this Imo can help us," Eye-to-heaven insisted. "I have invited him to join us for a meal."

"He will eat with us?" Matopahu said in surprise. Most men viewed him as so tainted by his curse that they shunned all forms of contact.

"He is protected by his tattoos and his rituals," the priest answered. "He has no qualms about joining us. But we need something worthy to offer such a man." With these words Eye-to-heaven gestured subtly toward a ball of line that lay behind him. Matopahu understood. It was unwise to speak directly of fishing before setting out, lest some spirit overhear and warn the fish away.

As much as Matopahu enjoyed his friend's company, the effects of the nightmare made him hesitate. Perhaps Eye-to-heaven would fare better alone. He met the priest's gaze, but the words he felt he should say would not come.

"Let us get moving," said Eye-to-heaven, looking at him steadily. "I hear your stomach growling." The *ari'i* saw that his friend had obtained several young red mullet for bait. The priest picked up the green palm-leaf basket that held the fish.

Matopahu felt an odd tightness in his chest at his friend's loyalty. He lifted his head. If Eye-to-heaven needed him, he would go. He took the fish club and line, then followed his companion along the shore to his beached outrigger canoe.

During the month of exile, Eye-to-heaven had proved his friendship time and again. Formerly high priest to Matopahu's brother, Eye-to-heaven seemed to be enjoying his new rootless existence, free from the duties of the priesthood.

After the overthrow of Knotted-cord, the two men had sought refuge in several districts. No chief had welcomed them to his household. But Eye-to-heaven had a relative in this district of Eimeo who grudgingly gave them permission to fish his waters and sleep on his land. Matopahu had known he would find no better hospitality elsewhere, and so had settled here until he could find some way out of his predicament. If there *was* a way out . . .

Matopahu's outrigger canoe already had some equipment in the bottom—stone sinkers, paddles, extra fishhooks, and a shell knife. The men added what they were carrying, then carried the vessel down the beach and into the shallows. Wading into deeper water, the two climbed aboard.

The day was calm, with little offshore current—good conditions for deep-line fishing. Small waves were breaking against the barrier reef, making a long line of whitecaps that paralleled the shore. Both men paddled the canoe out through a pass, into blue-black water that was only mildly choppy.

Feeling more cheerful, Matopahu scanned the sea, noting several fishing canoes in a cluster. The men aboard were working one of the well-known albacore "holes," where such fish could most easily be caught. Because the exiles were not permitted to approach these places, their task was doubly hard.

The restriction did not seem to bother the priest. "I like the look of the water over there," said Eye-to-heaven. He dug his paddle deep, sending the light craft arrowing across the swell. Soon both men set aside their paddles. With a shell knife, Eye-to-heaven sliced open a pair of mullet. Laying a fillet on each side of the barbless hook, he tied these on with thin fishline, leaving the tails to dangle invitingly behind.

Using a fisherman's hitch, he attached a stone sinker and more pieces of fish, as chum, to the line. Then he dropped the baited hook overboard. As he let out line from the inside of the ball, he measured its length against his arm. When the right number of lengths had gone out, he stopped and made a knot for reference.

"See how you fare," he said, handing the line to Matopahu. The *ari'i* was surprised at this offer. Was the priest trying to prove the gods had not all turned away from his friend? Matopahu hesitated, but Eye-to-heaven put the line into his hand. Then both men intoned prayers for success.

With his right hand, Matopahu gave an upward jerk to release the special knot that held both chum and sinker to the hook. He felt the tension in the line slacken as the hook came free. The warm sun on his back and a fresh sea breeze in his face relaxed Matopahu as he moved the line to attract fish. Noticing that the canoe was starting to drift, he picked up his paddle in his left hand, braced the shaft under his left

shoulder, and began to stroke gently against the weak
current.

"Good," said Eye-to-heaven, dipping his own paddle.
"The line is standing well."

For some time they continued this way, paddling gently.
Meanwhile, Matopahu saw the other canoes going in. Their
crews had come early and were done. Or perhaps they
sensed that the "hole" was fished out for the day.

"You try," said Matopahu, offering to hand the line back
to his friend.

"Not yet." The priest waved him away.

Suddenly the line shivered and grew taut in Matopahu's
hands. Something had taken the bait! He answered the pull
with a steady tension, letting the fish hook itself. A sudden
jerk would pull the hook loose, but a steady pull would set
the barbless point deeper into the fish's jaw.

Quivering, the line angled out as the albacore surfaced
and made a run away from the canoe. From the fish's wake
and the tension on the line, Matopahu could tell that it was
a big one.

As he gripped the line, he felt an onset of troubling
sensations that had grown familiar of late. His fingers
slowly turned numb, his face cold. He gritted his teeth as his
vision clouded and his head spun with dizziness. The canoe
seemed to be tilting, or was it his own body that was falling
toward the water?

Similar attacks had troubled him since the night of the
aha-tu ceremony. Perhaps this showed that the gods wanted
him to die. . . .

Matopahu's first impulse was to let everything go and
collapse in the bottom of the canoe. What did it matter if he
abandoned his grip on the line? The fish would be lost
anyway. It was folly to think that the gods would allow this
magnificent albacore to be caught by such an ill-fated man.

Yet the angry part of him, the part that refused to think of
himself as a sacrifice to any god, now made him stiffen his
back, clench his teeth, and fight the spell of sickness.

The line in his hand came alive, slicing in zigzags through
the water. Now he could see the shadowy blue of the

albacore's back, the silver-yellow shimmer of its flanks as it turned. This fish would make a fine meal to offer his guest.

Matopahu saw his *taio* watching him as he played the albacore close to the canoe. Each time he brought it in, the fish broke and ran, stretching the line until it sang and burned between his fingers.

"You have hooked an *aahi araroa*! And on the first cast!" the priest crowed.

An *araroa*! A man-sized fish! Matopahu's excitement faded as he noticed his dizziness return again, his vision clouding, his fingers growing stiff and clumsy. But he had gotten this close to landing the albacore. He could not quit now, even if he had to defy the gods.

Once more his fury rose. He drew in his breath, braced his feet against the sides of the canoe, and waited while the line whipped about in his hand. Slowly, strength returned to his arms and clarity to his vision.

He glanced at Eye-to-heaven, wondering if he had noticed any lapses, but the priest was absorbed in watching the albacore. "A fighter!" he exclaimed, his eyes never leaving the silver wake that cut through the blue water around the boat. Most albacore would exhaust themselves in two or three runs, but this one had taken more than that and was still strong.

The sea erupted in a shower of sparkling spray as the fish leaped. Its long pectoral fins spread like wings; rainbows flashed from its back.

"*Aue!* He is indeed the length of a man," the priest exclaimed.

This time the albacore headed shoreward, toward the reef. With a shout, Matopahu hauled back on his quarry, realizing that the fish might snag and break the line on the sharp coral. Again he played the albacore to the canoe, but just as it was almost close enough to be clubbed, the fish revived. It dove straight down, nearly pulling him over the side.

It came up on the opposite side, between the canoe's hull and the outrigger float, thrashing and churning. With a quiver of the beating tail, it writhed over the float, then dove once again.

Eye-to-heaven plunged his hand into the sea, trying to

free the line, but Matopahu saw that he was too late. The cord was hopelessly tangled about the canoe. Now if the albacore turned back, it might throw the hook and escape.

The fine fish . . . lost! Were the gods punishing Matopahu for daring to rise above his fate? The thought blazed into anger. This *araroa* was his!

With a roar that startled Eye-to-heaven, Matopahu grabbed the fish-club. With a quick look for lurking sharks, he flung himself out of the canoe and over the outrigger toward the struggling fish. Opening his eyelids underwater, he ignored the salt sting in his eyes and grabbed the line that was snaking past. Wrapping it around his fist, he gave a heave, yanking the albacore toward him.

The albacore thrashed, beating the sea into foam with its stiff crescent-shaped tail. Its long pectoral fins spread out like wings and the gills pumped wildly as he hauled it closer. The fish mouth opened and closed, showing the small but thorn-sharp teeth in the bony jaw.

He lifted the fish-club and struck down at its head. Water cushioned the blow and he only knocked off a few scales. Raising his head from the water for a quick gasp, he aimed the club once more. The albacore shuddered and went rigid briefly before it began thrashing again.

Spines raked Matopahu's wrist, drawing blood. The pain and the fish's refusal to die unleashed his fury and he struck again and again at the silvery head, the round staring eyes, the snapping jaws. The sea swirled in red as the fish-club became a weapon of war. He was no longer striking just at the albacore, but at a foe who sought his death. . . .

A hand fastened on his upraised arm and held against his struggles to jerk free. Suddenly Matopahu was no longer on the battlefield, but immersed again in the sea. The enemy before him was just a fish, now quivering helplessly, its head bruised and discolored by the beating.

Matopahu looked up and saw Eye-to-heaven's face, now solemn. A mixture of pride and shame flushed Matopahu's face as he flung back his brine-soaked hair.

"Enough, my friend," Eye-to-heaven said quietly, still leaning far out of the canoe and bracing himself on the outrigger to hold Matopahu's arm. "The *araroa* is yours."

The great albacore gave one last shudder and grew still, starting to sink. Matopahu helped Eye-to-heaven wrestle it into the canoe. When the *ari'i* hauled himself aboard, he stared down at his prize. The fish's size made it a worthy catch indeed. If only he had not disfigured the head.

Eye-to-heaven sensed his thoughts. "A few blemishes do not ruin a fish like this! We are not offering it at the *marae*. We are going to eat it." With a cry of triumph he picked up his paddle and headed in.

When they carried the huge albacore ashore, Matopahu saw a crowd of men watching. "We have plenty to share," he called out, still feeling the flush of victory.

"That is your fish. Eat it and grow strong," said a young man who seemed to speak for the others.

Matopahu knew there was no point in arguing. He had previously tried to share his catches. People thought him so tainted by his brother's disgrace that they would not eat anything he had touched. Eye-to-heaven, protected by prayers, remained his only companion. Today, at least, there would be one more.

Soon Eye-to-heaven crouched over the small round pit that they used for cooking. He uncovered some buried coals preserved from the previous fire, brought dry coconut fiber for tinder, and got a new blaze started. He added wood and old coconut shells for fuel. While the heavy black stones within the pit grew hot, he busied himself cutting up the fish into chunks and wrapping them in hibiscus leaves. Matopahu joined him, turning his thoughts from his troubles to the meal he would soon be enjoying.

"The stones are ready," said Eye-to-heaven after a while. When the packets of fish had been placed between the stones, and the oven covered with layers of palm leaf, Matopahu went off to hunt for fallen coconuts. The chief of this district had forbidden him to climb trees, but allowed him to take anything he found on the ground.

Most fallen nuts had already been ruined by coconut crabs, which cracked them open with huge claws and left empty shells behind. Whenever Matopahu did spot an oblong husk that looked freshly fallen, he thumped the greenish-brown side to see if it was rotten. Now and again he found one worth keeping.

Finally the *ari'i* returned to the campsite with his last load of coconuts. He saw Eye-to-heaven sitting with a stranger, a wizened elder with a wisp of gray beard and tattoos over most of his body. Beside the stranger lay a bunch of ripe bananas—his contribution to the meal. Here at last was Imo, the mysterious healer whom the priest put so much faith in.

The *tahu'a* greeted Matopahu with a suspicious gaze. Does he also think of me as already dead? the *ari'i* wondered darkly. Yet Imo was an expert at removing evil influences. Matopahu wanted to know how his friend had found this man, and what he expected to learn from him, but he sensed there would be no talk until after the meal.

The men opened the oven, took their portions aside, and ate silently. The fish was excellent, thought Matopahu, though he had only seawater in a coconut shell for sauce. The bananas would have been better had they been cooked, but he did not complain.

After the meal the men buried their leavings deep within a thicket, since anything in intimate contact with a person might be used against him in sorcery. "I must be more careful than most people," the healer said. "I have enemies everywhere. When I help someone, I often anger someone else."

At last the three took seats by the shore. A comforting breeze rattled the fronds of the nearby palm trees.

"I am familiar with your woes," said Imo to Matopahu. He nodded his head gravely and stroked his small, sparse beard. "Your father was a great chief. It does not please me to see what has happened to his sons."

"Have you ever known the *aha-tu* curse to be lifted?" asked Matopahu uneasily.

Imo paused to glance at Eye-to-heaven, then stroked his beard again. "It is something for the gods to decide."

"Then it is possible?" asked the *ari'i*.

The healer gave a faint smile. "I can promise nothing. But you are a strong young man. If you follow my instructions—"

"It will not be easy to get the chickens and pigs—"

"Pigs?" Imo glanced again at Eye-to-heaven and then turned back to the *ari'i.* "Do not think that you can merely bring an offering and sit watching while priests chant prayers. You will gain nothing that way."

"Nothing? But—"

Eye-to-heaven looked surprised. "I thought I had a way to help you, my friend, but Imo's plan is far better. You will need a strong infusion of *mana* to free yourself from this curse, and he offers a way."

Matopahu listened with widened eyes as the *tahu'a* described a source of spiritual power. Imo knew of an ancient shrine, long neglected, that lay high in the hills. He wanted Matopahu to restore this *marae,* cleaning out the weeds and debris, resetting the stones. Then he must learn the consecration ritual and carry it out flawlessly in a night-long vigil.

"There is great *mana* in that place," said Imo, speaking of the sacred power. "If you fulfill your duties, the gods will surely hear you. They may even grant your plea."

"But there is a risk," cautioned Eye-to-heaven. "Remember how ancient this *marae* is. Few men would dare touch such sacred stones—"

"Can I be worse off than I am now?" Matopahu asked with a forced laugh.

The *tahu'a* only looked at him and did not answer.

THREE

Noon had almost arrived by the time Tepua's canoe brought the atoll travelers into Matavai Bay. Her warrior captain continued to plead with her as they headed across the vast expanse of water toward a crescent-shaped shore. "How will I explain this change of plans to your brother?" he kept asking.

"Don't start worrying until you see how I am greeted," she replied. "If the other Arioi are safe, then you'll know that you can leave me here."

"I saw no great welcome when I brought your companions yesterday," he reminded her.

Tepua felt deeply troubled over the turn of events, but held to her resolve. "We are friendly with the ruling chief of this district," she explained. "We have performed for him often. If he sent no welcoming party, it was only because the visit was unexpected."

She tried to take cheer from the pleasant scene, enjoying the warm sunlight on her face and the gentle rocking of the canoe. Yesterday's clouds had blown away, leaving only azure sky above the island's tall central peaks. In stark black and green, the mountains rose over folds of spur ridges and deep valleys. Her gaze followed the verdant tumble of the land from hills down to the coastal plain.

Everything would be different now, she knew. The life she had looked forward to resuming was gone. Yet the discomfort of her exile would be small compared with what others had to suffer.

She thought of the people of Matopahu's district, the unfortunate new subjects of Land-crab. These people had long enjoyed the presence of their Arioi lodge, one of the best known in all the islands. Now who would perform the great legends and teach the ways of worshiping Oro? The religious ceremonies would grow lifeless, reduced to the cryptic mutterings of priests. Soon the gods would turn away.

No. Tepua was not willing to abandon the good people her troupe had served for so long. She had already heard suggestions that her lodge seek a new district willing to give it a permanent home. She would oppose that move if there was any hope of returning to Matopahu's ancestral lands.

As for Matopahu himself . . . She clenched her jaw with frustration. He had vanished into exile. Somehow she would have to find him.

At last Tepua's canoe approached the shore. On the gently sloping beach, Aitofa, the chiefess of the women's lodge, stood waiting with a few companions from Wind-driving Lodge. Wearing a fresh cape and a garland of flowers, Aitofa looked her former self again. "You see," Tepua said with satisfaction to her atoll captain. "All is well here. Go on to Porapora and do not worry about me."

She turned to Maukiri, who was gazing with a furrowed brow at the beach ahead. "Cousin, you can go to Porapora, and then home if you want," she whispered. "Perhaps Tahiti is not for you after all." Maukiri, however, clutched Tepua's hand and insisted that she would stay with her.

The warrior captain accompanied the women ashore and looked about in all directions, as if expecting an imminent attack. Yet the scene appeared peaceful, with children playing at the edge of the water and fishermen mending their nets under the dangling needles of ironwood trees. The warrior peered into the shadows and walked close to a hut that stood above the black sand beach. Then, seemingly satisfied with his inspection, he listened while Aitofa informed him that this district was ruled by the great chief, Tutaha i Tarahoi, who had offered her Arioi his hospitality.

"I will bring your brother news of your safe arrival," the

guard captain said finally to Tepua. She shouted words of parting as he returned to the double-hulled canoe. Then, with an unsettled Maukiri beside her, she walked along the shore of the district that would be their temporary home.

On every side lay signs of prosperity. The feathery tops of coconut palms arched out over the water. In the breadfruit groves, fat yellow globes hung in clusters of twos or threes, some so high that a pole could not reach them. Outrigger canoes in great numbers were pulled up on the beach. Highborn men swaggered about, wrapped in voluminous cloaks of *tapa,* the excellent bark-cloth used for Tahitian garments.

With a glance at Maukiri, Tepua turned to Aitofa. "I had hoped that my cousin—"

"I understand," the chiefess interrupted. "There is a place for her, if she is willing to work. We left most of our attendants behind."

Maukiri brightened. "I can stay with the troupe?"

"Yours will not be an easy life," Tepua warned her. Attendants took care of most tedious chores, leaving the players free to practice or to simply amuse themselves. Maukiri might find the demands too heavy. But for now, her cousin had no alternative.

Aitofa hailed a passing novice and sent Maukiri with her to find the other attendants. Then the chiefess, who held the coveted Blackleg rank, the foremost in the Arioi hierarchy, led Tepua on a walk along the beach.

Tepua felt that she owed much to this woman. On several occasions, Aitofa had stood up for her against Head-lifted, the chief of the men's lodge. She had accepted Tepua as a novice in the troupe despite his objections. Later, when Tepua made a foolish mistake, Aitofa had protected her from dismissal. Now Tepua looked at her for guidance through the trials ahead.

"Our position is difficult," Aitofa confided as they went. "You and I must talk, but not here. Do you know the path up Taharaa Hill?"

Tepua turned to gaze at one of the most striking features of the shoreline. Taharaa Hill jutted out into the water, its steep face of red clay rising to a crest sparsely covered with trees. "I have been up the trail," Tepua said, recalling earlier visits.

"Good. Then meet me at the top. When the sun is over there." She gestured at a point about halfway down the sky. "But do not tell anyone where you are going."

They continued along the beach, soon reaching the guest houses that the host chief, Tutaha, had set aside for his visitors. Two rows of neatly thatched dwellings, some with cane walls and some fully open to the breeze, stood in a breadfruit grove. A brook nearby flowed quietly into the lagoon. A huge, gnarled ironwood tree grew by the shore, its needles hissing softly as they tossed in the wind.

The houses were deserted. Tepua heard drumming in the distance. "The other dancers are practicing," Aitofa explained. "We have to keep Tutaha amused if we want to stay. I hope you have lost none of your skills."

"So do I," said Tepua. At one time she had been hailed as the best dancer in the troupe. Now, after so much time away, she felt stiff and awkward. She glanced down at her body.

The atoll garments she wore, of finely plaited pandanus-leaf matting, had served her well on the voyage, but were not suited to Tahiti. Aitofa seemed to understand. She beckoned Tepua inside one of the houses and handed her a length of painted bark-cloth.

Putting the mat skirt and cape aside, Tepua wrapped herself in the *tapa* cloth. The feel of the soft and pliant material against her skin made an immediate difference. She was almost a Tahitian again. The sound of drumming began to call her.

"Go," said Aitofa. Tepua happily raced out to plait a garland of beach vines and flowers. When she heard the pounding of the music, she could almost forget the difficulties ahead.

From afar, Aitofa saw the stocky figure of Head-lifted, the men's-lodge chief, coming from the direction of Tutaha's compound. As he drew closer she saw that his face was severe, his body taut with anger. "Our host will not keep us here long," Head-lifted told her. "And we have nowhere else to go. This is what your scheming has brought us!"

"I have heard enough accusations from you," Aitofa replied. He had agreed to perform the satire that angered the usurper, but now seemed to be trying to push all responsibility for the outcome onto her.

"We could have been more subtle," he went on. "We could have waited awhile before ridiculing the man."

"That is not the Arioi way."

"And what kind of Arioi can we be now?" he retorted.

Aitofa stood up to him. "We have a task ahead of us—a message to spread. We will perform the same satire for Tutaha, and for any other chief who invites us to his district. Before we are done, Land-crab will be the laughingstock of Tahiti."

"That is what we will *not* do," he answered.

"The troupe thinks otherwise. Have you forgotten that a lodge chief can be replaced?"

Head-lifted's face was livid. The veins in his neck stood out as he glared at her. "Do not speak words you will regret, Aitofa. This is not *my* command. Our host, Tutaha i Tarahoi, forbids us to perform any satire. We will stick to the classical legends or find ourselves all in the lagoon."

Then Tutaha needs to be mocked as well, Aitofa thought. Yet what could she do? It would be folly to insult one's host or go against his wishes. Her plans would have to wait.

In midafternoon, Tepua took a steep trail, heading up the flank of Taharaa Hill. She had obeyed Aitofa's instructions, slipping away without telling anyone her plans. As she walked, she kept looking back to make sure that no one was following her.

The climb was exhausting, an ascent over trails worn deeply into the red clay of the hillside. She did not know why Aitofa had insisted on such a distant place for the meeting. Perhaps there were more enemies down below than she realized.

At last, when she reached the top, she gazed on a vast panorama of water and land. Her old fear of heights had never left her, but the view of Matavai Bay was so commanding that she stood firm. A sheer drop lay below her. To the right stretched open sea. To the left, the coastline was cut deeply, curving in a great arc. On the gleaming waters of the bay she saw outrigger canoes that appeared no larger than a fingernail, their tiny sails stretching before the breeze.

Tepua sat quietly for a time and contemplated the view. Then she heard footsteps, turned, and saw Aitofa coming up the wooded trail. "Now we are free to talk," the Blackleg said, slightly out of breath, as she gazed at the scene below. "From here, Tutaha and Head-lifted and all the other men who trouble us are like tiny crabs on the beach."

"More worries?" Tepua frowned.

"Look at all this," said Aitofa. "The bay and the land around it are all under Tutaha's control. We dare not anger such a powerful chief."

"But what have we done to him?"

"Nothing. Yet. But we have been warned." Aitofa explained the restrictions that Tutaha had imposed on the visitors.

"Does this mean that he supports Land-crab?" Tepua asked when she heard that the satire had been banned.

"He says nothing one way or the other."

"I saw Tutaha's canoe sheds," Tepua said bitterly. "And many war canoes. If this chief took up our cause, he could destroy Land-crab in a day."

"If he had enough encouragement, he might."

"Then we must encourage him!"

"Do not be too eager, Tepua. Tutaha is ambitious—for himself and for his son. He has all this land and wants more. His family could take our district for themselves, and then we would be no better off than now."

"Then we should not look to him for help?"

"We should hope that he stays out of the conflict. For now, we must try to keep Tutaha's friendship and make no requests he cannot meet."

Tepua sighed. "And what of Matopahu? Why is he not also a guest of Tutaha?"

Aitofa's expression froze. Tepua felt that she had something more to say but was holding it back.

"You have heard something?" Tepua pressed.

"He is safe from his enemies in Eimeo. You may not see him for a while."

Tepua felt her throat tighten. Matopahu had been foremost in her thoughts throughout the journey. Now that she was back here, how could she bear the separation?

Aitofa pressed her hand, trying to offer some comfort. "Tepua, there is something you can do for both of us. You have a gift. Pray to the gods. Perhaps they will show you an answer to our predicament. And to Matopahu's as well."

Tepua tried to gather her thoughts. She looked out at the bay, where two large sailing canoes appeared to be having a race. One was pulling up rapidly from behind.

"Ask the gods. . . ."

She knew what Aitofa wanted. Tepua had a prophetic gift, but one she had long tried to keep secret. In Tahiti, she had told only Matopahu about it. She wondered what had made him reveal it to Aitofa.

Once more she looked at the pair of canoes far below. She had been mistaken, she realized. One was not in pursuit of the other; they were sailing off in different directions. *One carries my hopes, and the other, my life.* Perhaps it was too late to change course.

She balled her fist. "I will . . . try," she answered hoarsely. "But I need a quiet place. No one must disturb me."

"Good. I will arrange for whatever you need. You will not return to the troupe tonight."

Aitofa led Tepua on a different route down, coming to a settlement at the base of the hill. The Arioi chiefess had family ties here; and she and Tepua were made welcome by a local underchief. After a pleasant meal with the women of the household, the Blackleg showed Tepua to the small guest house that she was to occupy alone.

"Meet me in early morning," said Aitofa as they were about to part. "Behind the compound is a bathing pool in the brook. Go upstream until you see three large rocks in a row."

Aitofa hurried off so that she could return to the troupe before dark. Tepua was left alone under a thatched roof—to deal with the troubling request that her leader had made. Plaited mats covered the floor, cushioned by a layer of freshly cut grass. The slanting sunlight of late afternoon filtered through openings between the canes that walled the little house.

In Tepua's lap lay a long loop of cord, the kind used by children for making string figures. She stared at the cord, hesitating to take it between her fingers. The art of *fai,* string figures, was popular on Tahiti as well as the atolls. To most people it was only a game. But when Tepua worked with string she sometimes entered a trance, seeing in the patterns the answer to a difficult question.

Of course, there were others with prophetic gifts, men who fell into fits and spoke in distorted voices. Long ago, Matopahu had been such an oracle, seized sometimes by a god whose voice was high-pitched and difficult to comprehend. But such oracles were not always trustworthy. Tepua understood why Aitofa was relying on her for this delicate task.

Tepua had always been cautious with her gift, asking the gods for a vision only in times of need. Now, with all the difficulties surrounding her, the need appeared sufficiently great. In a soft voice, she began to chant, calling on the spirit of her ancestress, Tapahi-roro-ariki, who had helped her through so many trials. When the initial chanting was done, Tepua wrapped the cord once around each hand.

Her start was the classic one; she slipped her left middle finger beneath the string crossing her right palm, then picked up the string on the left palm in the opposite way. Trying a variation of the usual opening, she lifted a loop from the back of one hand, slipped it over her fingers, and dropped it across the strings that stretched between her hands. Repeating with the other side, she went on to pick up strings from her little fingers and pull them across her palms.

Then her inspiration failed, and she sat staring at the cord. The pattern suggested the beginning of a figure called Running Away. Who was fleeing? she wondered. Was it the usurper Land-crab or her own Arioi troupe?

She tried picking up the cross-palm string of each hand

with the middle finger of the other, a classic move. This merely threw the whole into a tangle. Disconsolately, she let her hands fall into her lap.

Several more attempts brought her only half-seen suggestions in incomplete figures. The daylight filtering through the cane walls faded until she could no longer see the strings. With a sigh, she accepted the fact that the gods had ignored her pleas. Or perhaps she was just too weary to grasp what they had shown her. The morning of dancing and the climb up the hill had exhausted her.

She unsnarled the cord, hung it carefully on the center-post of the guest house, and went to sleep.

Tepua came violently awake as if she had been shaken. A sound echoed in her head although everything outside was quiet. The noise was the bone-jarring crunch of wood against coral.

She shivered against the night's chill, huddling with her *tapa* cape drawn closely around her. What had she heard?

"A dream," she muttered to herself, but this one had been too strange to dismiss. It had carried no images, only sounds. She remembered more. The crash of waves, whipped by a landward-blowing wind. The hoarse cries of men.

Had some great canoe met its end on the barrier reef during the night? She was too distant from the lagoon for the sounds of shipwreck to reach her. Had her guardian spirit somehow brought the sound into her dreams?

Hastily she dressed herself in the wrap and bark-cloth cape that Aitofa had provided. The best vantage point would be the top of Taharaa Hill. If there was truly a wreck on the reef, she could see it in the moonlight and run for help.

She hesitated. Thoughts of spirits and demons chilled her more than the night wind. She stared up at the waxing moon and tried to put her fears aside. This was not a night when ghosts walked.

Yet, as she started out of the guest house, she wondered what she was doing. Why, of all the sleepers, had she been summoned for this task? She could not answer, yet she felt the spirit of her ancestress guiding her as she turned back to snatch the looped cord from its hook.

Outside, the cool air chilled her beneath the cape. She began chanting a prayer of protection, just in case some rogue spirit had chosen the wrong night for wandering. The trail to Taharaa Hill was no easier to climb than in daylight, but the exertion soon warmed her.

At last she stood atop the sheer cliff that plunged into Matavai Bay. The water below lay calm, rippling with moonlight. The line of surf marking the outer reef shone in ghostly green and white. No wrecked craft struggled in the breakers. She listened, trying to catch any sound besides the muted thunder of the ocean against the reef. There was nothing.

Puzzled, she retreated from the precipice and took a seat near the tallest of several coral-flower trees that stood at the brow of the hill. Looking up, she saw tufted branches, black against the sky.

Then her thoughts returned to the sennit cord about her arm. Perhaps now the strings were ready to yield answers. She unwound the loop, draped it across her hands.

Her fingers gleamed faintly in the silvery light as she began. Her palms moved together and apart in rhythm to the chants that accompanied each finger. She went from simple figures into more difficult ones. Canoes, houses, mountains, men. All formed between her fingers, yet none drew her into a vision as they had so many times before.

The moon was starting to set. Soon she would have no light. She had failed once at this, and now she thought she would fail again. . . .

Without knowing why, she suddenly found herself making the first in a series of figures about the demigod Hiro, famed as a great navigator as well as a trickster. What had this legendary canoe-builder to do with her situation? Only her fingers knew.

A simple but elegant triangular pattern called the Reclining Seat of Hiro grew between her fingertips. It transformed itself quickly into the House of Hiro. More of Hiro's possessions followed in quick succession. The *Marae* Stones, the Swing, the Mountain, and the Canoe Cabin.

The strings merged, separated, interwove. She released her thumbs from the loops and spread the four running diamonds of Hiro's Net between the index and little finger of both hands.

This was the last figure of the series, yet she could not let it slide from her hands and begin anew. She held up Hiro's Net to the moonlight. The strings glinted in silver and gray, like the weave of a spiderweb. Hiro used his net to catch spirits. What would she catch?

Her thumbs began to move, crossing her palms, hooking into the triangles around each little finger. Entranced, she watched her hands. This was not a figure she had ever made before. Her thumbs returned, bringing the little finger strings.

There were no figures beyond Hiro's Net, yet she was making one. Without knowing why, she released the strings from her index fingers, then inserted them into the thumb loops from above, pulled the strings taut.

She half expected a confusing tangle, but the pattern lay before her, as clear as any she had yet formed. She stared at it. Three long strings ran parallel between her hands. Woven across the three was a pattern that suggested an underwater coral head with a spiked point.

"Hiro's Rock," she murmured, naming her figure after a well-known submerged reef in the waters that lay close by. And as she gazed at it, the strings became the jagged gray-and-white surface of coral, looming up from the dim greenness of the ocean.

The vision drew her in until she was no longer sitting on Taharaa Hill, gazing at images in the strings. Now the vision surrounded her, plunging her into the sea beside the infamous underwater reef.

This has never happened before, she thought in amazement. Before her lay Hiro's Rock, a massive, jagged, welling up of coral from the barrier reef. Its spike did not break the ocean's surface, but lay waiting just beneath the long ocean swells. The coral shelf from which it grew lay deep enough so that the waves passed over without breaking. No pounding surf would warn away a canoe whose master mistakenly took the stretch of open water for a pass into the lagoon.

Suddenly Tepua saw the underside of a huge shadowy

hull plowing through the sea. It struck the great bank, breaking off chunks of coral and shedding splinters. The entire reef and the sea itself seemed to shudder. A terrifyingly familiar sound came again, louder than ever, the agonized grating of planking against stone.

Now totally immersed in the vision, Tepua felt herself rising to the surface. She heard not the muffled undersea roar, but the cries of seabirds overhead, the splash of canoe paddles, the voices of men. A bright blur grew, resolving itself into a scene of water and sky.

Yes, she discovered. A vessel *had* struck the reef. Now she was looking at the craft from above the waterline. A strange tickle of awe and fear began. What filled her vision looked at first like the base of a painted cliff rising from the water. Whitecaps broke against a towering mass, but one that rose and fell on the long ocean swells.

She stared harder and realized that the great side was made not of rock but of wood—planks painted black at the waterline, then the yellow of parakeet feathers, then bright red toward the top. And high up, far higher than any deck should be, stood masts that were taller than trees. The sails that flew from these reached toward the sky like billowing wings.

A floating island with white wings . . . Tepua had heard of such vessels, but had never seen one. Neither Tahiti nor any other island she knew could have produced this wooden beast. It must have come from beyond, from strange lands far over the horizon.

A few sailors from distant lands had visited her atoll in a much smaller craft. She knew little more than what those men had told her. Yet she had often heard a prophecy that one day a monstrous vessel such as this, floating upright with no need of an outrigger, would come to Tahiti and cause great upheavals.

Now the impossible wings hovered over her, filling the air with their sound. She listened with dread to the drawn-out creaking and groaning of timbers mixed with the clank and rattle of strange ropes made from links of stone. She could not doubt that this was the ship of the prophecy. Somehow it had come to grief on Hiro's Rock.

Glancing around her quickly, she saw the familiar landmarks of Matavai Bay. And she saw, too, that the arrival of the ship had not gone unnoticed. Approaching from several directions were double-hull war canoes, their upturned prows bearing likenesses of gods. Feather pennants flew from the carved posts that stood high above each upward-curving stern. Painted banners of *tapa* billowed between each pair of sternposts.

On the raised deck of the grandest canoe of all rode a war chief wrapped in a long feathered cape. His wicker headpiece, covered with feathers and shells, almost brushed the roof of the canopy that shaded him. Both cape and headpiece were decorated in brilliant feathers of scarlet and yellow gold, the colors flickering and shifting, as if made of flame.

Other vessels carried grim-faced warriors—common men dressed simply in turbans and loincloths, or men of high rank wearing feather headdresses and stiff half-circle gorgets. She saw that the bilges of these canoes were filled with round, water-smoothed stones used for slinging.

Once more Tepua was startled by the sound of wood grinding against coral. She also heard the anguished cries of the men aboard the stranded vessel, sensing their fear that they would die in the thundering water if the onshore wind did not break. Perhaps this would be for the best, she thought. If the ship broke up on the reef and the crew drowned, there would be no need for a battle.

Tepua knew, from experience on her home island, about the terrible weapons that these winged ships carried. She could not bear the thought of what might happen if the Tahitians provoked a fight. As she hung above the vessel, she looked away from the faces of the threatened crew, wishing to forget that they were people, and not just invaders.

A sudden cry rang out from one of the war canoes. "The wind is turning!" Even as she heard these words, the strong onshore wind was faltering. Gradually it died and a breeze from the land sprang up.

Shouts of jubilation came from the stranded ship as its crew sensed the possibility of salvation. Hearing the outcry,

Tepua felt a mixture of relief and despair. Had the gods chosen to save these strangers after all?

The seaward breeze filled the huge sails and the ship's bow swung free of the reef. Afloat in deep water, the vessel slowly turned. As the ship gathered speed, a cheer went up from the warriors aboard the canoes. The gods had defended the land. The intruders were leaving without a fight.

Tepua was less sure of the victory as she watched the course of the ship. It was not heading out to sea, but working its way along the seaward side of the reef, apparently searching for a pass. At last it found a way through the coral.

The excited chatter of warriors faded to silence as they watched the form of the vessel grow once again, finally coming to rest near the mouth of a freshwater river. The canoe fleet gathered around, still keeping a cautious distance.

For the first time, Tepua looked closely at the men aboard the great ship. They seemed dwarfed between the towering white of their sails and the massive bulk of the hull. She remembered the dress of foreigners from her earlier experience, and was only briefly taken aback by the strange coverings over their arms and the odd flaps and ruffles that distorted their figures.

Her attention went to their faces, some bearded, some not. Some were pale, others swarthy, still others pink and ruddy-cheeked. The crew was lined up along the ship's railing, staring at the warriors in canoes, who stared back at them in equal bewilderment.

One figure stood apart from the rest, on a raised portion of the deck. Although not tall, he carried himself with dignity, and wore a headpiece that was grander than the others—blue, three-cornered, and decorated with glitter. She guessed that he was the master of the ship.

How she wished that the gods might grant her some way to speak with him! She knew that these men from afar could be kind or cruel, just like her own people. They might be persuaded to go away.

She saw a canoe arrowing in under the great ship's stern, people aboard holding aloft fowls, fruit, and trussed pigs.

Perhaps the Tahitian war chief had decided to be sensible, and was seeking peace. Or perhaps he merely hoped to distract the enemy so that the war canoes could attack.

Other laden craft followed, and soon a lively commerce began. Tepua caught glimpses of reflections from shiny trinkets and strings of beads. More canoes approached, bringing pigs and other foodstuffs in exchange. Yet she sensed the mood in other canoes was less than friendly.

Slowly the commanding *pahi* drifted closer to the ship. The war canoes closed in, their bilges heavy with sling stones. Yet the foreigners seemed not to notice, distracted as they were by the trading and by naked young woman who swam around the ship, holding their *tapa* garments in bundles above the water.

Then came another large double-hull bearing a man cloaked in black and white, and wearing the tall headdress of a priest of Oro. As this *pahi* approached the ship, the trading canoes withdrew.

Tepua wondered what the priest intended, and a small hope grew. Perhaps he would offer hospitality to the foreigners. Allowing the ship's crew ashore might be risky, but better than the alternative of battle. The slender hulls of the *pahi* drifted alongside the foreign vessel. The priest of Oro came forward. Reaching up, he gave something to one of the men on the ship.

Tepua could not make out the object, which shimmered with red and yellow as it passed from hand to hand among the foreigners. Finally it reached the man who commanded the vessel. As he lifted the present, Tepua saw that it was a tuft of sacred red-and-yellow feathers. Instantly she knew that it was a talisman of war, meant to direct Oro's wrath against an enemy.

Unwary, the captain accepted the feathers and seemed eager to give something in return. But Tepua knew that the priest would accept nothing. The foreigner watched with evident astonishment as the priest's *pahi* was paddled away.

Then, with a shout, the priest raised the frond of a coconut palm whose leaflets had been tied in a peculiar pattern. What signal was this? Tepua wondered. An answering roar came from many throats. Slings whirled, releasing a rain of stones on the ship.

Most of the missiles fell harmlessly onto the awnings that the foreigners had rigged to shade themselves. There was a flurry of activity on the ship. Defenders pointed long, clublike weapons at the attacking canoes. Tepua knew what was coming next and screamed a warning that she alone could hear.

If only she could hold off this moment. The foreigners seemed uncertain. They looked to their leaders for a signal.

Then the dreaded thunder came, both from the hand weapons and from two black snouts that poked out of the hull from beneath the ship's railing. Feather pennants fell from shattered sternposts. Capes and helmets were torn away. Smoke drifted over the attacking canoes.

Crimson welled and ran over bronze skin, orange body-paint and blue-black tattoos. Warriors screamed in rage and disbelief, clutching their bodies where terrible wounds had been bored by things unseen. Crazed by fear and pain, some people leaped overboard. The surface of the lagoon broke into chop, as if stirred by a storm.

In confused disarray, the war canoes backed off, their paddlers pale and sweating. Tepua saw the war chief fold his arms, a grim expression hardening his features.

Surely he knew now the nature of his enemy. To press on could only bring disaster. Yet the chief gave a hoarse yell, commanding his craft into the fray. While the bulk of the force turned to attack the foreigners at their stern, his *pahi* made a course for the bow. Several war canoes flanked it, slings and stones ready.

Men chanting defiantly, paddle blades flashing, the double hull shot forward. Another rain of stones flew. Tepua could see that some hit their marks, invaders reeling under the onslaught.

Then came a flash as sudden and dazzling as a lightning strike, and a roar that could have drowned out a hurricane. The *pahi* bucked violently. The platform disappeared in a cloud of flying splinters. In a burst of horror, Tepua realized that the noble Tahitian commander was gone. She saw only a fragment of a scarlet-and-yellow-feathered cloak that drifted outward on the backwash from his sinking war canoe.

Tepua emerged from the trance and found herself sitting tensely upright. The string figure of Hiro's Rock was still stretched tightly between her fingers, in front of her wide-open eyes. Streams of tears wet her cheeks; she felt drained, exhausted.

She turned her head, feeling her hair tumble about her face. The night was quiet, heavy, still. The setting moon still hung where she had last seen it. Had nothing actually changed?

The rollers broke with distant thunder against the outer reef. But no lost foreign ship showed its form against the moonlit ripples of the bay. The terror of invasion was suddenly, miraculously, gone.

For a long time she stared out at the water, overwhelmed by what she had seen. Then she rose, stiff from sitting so long, and made her way wearily down the hill. The night was gone. Aitofa would be looking for her.

The stream was still in deep shadow when Tepua found the place that Aitofa had described, the black rocks beyond the bathing pool. She gritted her teeth and plunged in. The cold water helped her come alive again. When she looked up, she saw the chiefess waiting.

Quickly Tepua emerged and wound herself in her barkcloth wrap. Then, with great hesitation, she related what she had seen. As she spoke, Aitofa's expression grew bleak.

"You aren't the first to bring a warning like this," Aitofa said when Tepua was done. "I've heard about foreign ships. But never in such frightening detail."

"Should we tell Tutaha?"

Aitofa frowned. "How can we get anyone to listen? You have no standing with the priests. No one will believe you." She looked away, fell into thought for a moment. "Tell me, Tepua. How soon do you feel this invasion will come?"

Tepua wondered how she could answer. In the attacking canoes, she had seen many faces, but none looked familiar. She had also glanced around Matavai Bay, with particular attention to Taharaa Hill. Had anything been different? The trees?

"*Aue!* There was something strange," Tepua shouted. The memory remained vivid. She had noticed how the peak of the hill was crowded with onlookers. And the familiar grove on top had changed. In the vision, a huge coral-flower tree stood alone, its high branches shading the people below. How long would it take, she wondered, for a tree to grow so high?

"Aitofa, I think that many seasons must pass before this terrible day arrives. You and I and Tutaha may not live to see it."

"That gives me little comfort," the chiefess answered. "Yet it means we need do nothing for now."

"Then why did the gods show me this? I wish I had not seen it."

Aitofa gave her hand a reassuring squeeze. "Somehow these troubles yet to come are tied to our own. I cannot say how. You are the gifted one. In time the gods will tell you."

"And meanwhile, I must live with the memory of these horrors."

"Tepua, I am sorry. It was my idea for you to seek this vision. If I can help ease your pain . . ." Her eyes widened. "Perhaps there is something. I will speak to Eye-to-heaven."

Tepua's pulse jumped. "Eye-to-heaven is here?" The stocky priest was her own friend as well as Matopahu's *taio*. If nothing else, she might hear some news from him.

"He isn't here, but we may see him soon. Tutaha has asked us to leave his district. An Arioi lodge on Eimeo invited us to stay with them awhile."

"Matopahu—"

"Perhaps you can find him. We'll talk to the priest first. There is something he will have to explain."

Tepua did not know what to make of this last pronouncement. But she was glad to be leaving Matavai Bay, a place that now carried such harsh memories. Remnants of the vision lingered as she followed Aitofa along the stream's bank and onto the path that led to shore.

FOUR

The morning after Tepua's vision at Taharaa Hill, a flotilla of double-hulled canoes ferried her troupe across the Sea of the Moon. She knew only that another Arioi troupe—the members of Chipped-rock Lodge—had invited hers to the neighboring island of Eimeo. She had never met these people before, but Arioi of different lodges often helped each other.

As Tepua sat on a pitching deck and watched the shark-toothed peaks of Eimeo grow large, she listened to the chatter of her companions. "Tutaha wanted to get rid of us," some said. "We are better off away from Tahiti," replied others. Though Tepua was glad to leave Matavai Bay, she felt she was abandoning the people of her district. When they learned that their Arioi had been forced to move again, they would lose all hope of regaining the troupe.

Yet she took some encouragement from the fact that the Chipped-rock Lodge was offering assistance. Her own lodge, Wind-driving, had fallen into desperate straits. With no place to live, the players would soon disperse, probably never to gather again. Now, if they all worked together, they could preserve their long traditions.

Not only would they serve Oro. Soon, Tepua hoped, they would have a chance to ridicule Land-crab again, gathering allies wherever they performed. But to do so required many items they did not have.

The Arioi of Wind-driving Lodge had left everything

behind when they fled Land-crab. To perform before an
audience they would need costumes, paints, adornments,
musical instruments. The troupe had borrowed what it
needed to entertain Tutaha, but now was empty-handed
again. With help from Chipped-rock Lodge the leaders
could properly outfit the troupe.

At last the canoes came around to the western side of
Eimeo. Here, several sandy islets stood close to the main
shore. The flotilla entered the quiet waters that separated the
islets from Eimeo itself.

"That reminds me of home," said Maukiri wistfully to
Tepua as they gazed at the closest islet. This *motu* was
heavily forested and overgrown by jungle vines. Tepua
could not see past the coconut palms along its shore. Yes,
she thought, at first glance it did remind her of the islets that
made up the ring of her home atoll, but the dense undergrowth gave it a wild, uninhabited look.

To everyone's surprise, the Arioi canoes did not head
toward the beach of Eimeo. The boatmen halted in the
shallows close to one end of the *motu*. "We will make a
home here," Head-lifted announced. People began climbing
down from the canoes and wading ashore.

Some playful members of the troupe decided to have a
swim. Tepua watched as they splashed out, modestly
keeping their bark-cloth garments about their hips. When
they reached deeper water, the swimmers whipped off the
clothes and quickly submerged. Some bundled the *tapa*
garments and held them above water with one arm while
stroking with the other. Others tossed their clothes to their
friends before plunging in.

Tepua did not join them. Curiously, she gazed at the *motu*
ahead and wondered how the troupe would live there.
Nowhere did she see any signs of habitation; the tangle of
forest nearly reached the water's edge. The Arioi would
have to work for days just to clear space for shelters and
pit-ovens.

There was a reason, Tepua thought, that no people lived
here. Ghosts? As she studied the overgrown islet, she
shivered and drew her cape more tightly around her shoulders.

"Why are you just standing there, cousin?" asked Maukiri brightly. Wasting little time on modesty, she unwrapped herself and plunged into the water. Maukiri's arms swept gracefully as she swam across the transparent lagoon. Suddenly there came another splash as a young man dove after her.

"Your cousin already has an admirer," said Curling-leaf, coming up behind Tepua on the deck.

"She will have more," said Tepua, feeling a faint pang of envy. Only one man occupied her own thoughts. Aitofa had promised to help her find Matopahu, but Eimeo was a large island, with many districts. She grimaced in frustration.

Another splash. "That makes two," said Tepua's friend, with a touch of envy in her own voice. Poor Curling-leaf, with her pleasant but plain face, had never gotten the attention from men that Tepua thought she deserved. "I think your cousin can outswim them!"

"Only if she wants to," Tepua replied.

"She is more than just a good swimmer," said Curling-leaf. "She learns quickly. She speaks so well—"

"Yes," Tepua answered, gratified that her efforts showed. During the voyage she had insisted that Maukiri use the Tahitian dialect, dropping the hard "k" and "ng" sounds of atoll speech. Tepua had also taught her many words that only Tahitians used. Her cousin was doing remarkably well in adjusting to this new life—far better than Tepua herself had done.

"You two! Come!" Head-lifted, the men's chief, stood beckoning on the shore. All the other passengers had disembarked. Tepua jumped down into the water, which reached to her knees. With reluctance as well as curiosity she headed for the beach.

This was a low islet, barely above water, yet she could see that no storm had recently washed over it. Hibiscus and trumpet vine covered the sand beneath the coconut palms, leaving no pathways. A party was already at work hacking its way inland. Tepua watched the men swinging their stone-headed adzes. Then she joined the women who were walking toward the other end of the *motu*.

The grainy black-and-white sand felt harsh beneath her

feet. Chunks of broken coral lay scattered everywhere. In places along the shore, the underlying black rocks were exposed. Tepua wondered if, long ago, an angry spirit had thrown these rocks down from the mountaintops.

From the dense interior came a whiff of steamy air, bringing the moldy scent of decaying vegetation. Unseen birds screamed. Underfoot, tiny crabs darted into their holes.

"Look," said Tepua as they reached the end of the *motu*. The beach widened here, where a brisk wind was blowing across a point of land. Above the beach, the forest thinned to scrub. "We can clear a space," she said, thinking of the open practice area needed for rehearsals.

"I want to stay here," declared Curling-leaf. "The sea breeze is good. It will keep off the flies."

"Then we'll build our shelter over there," said Tepua. She and Curling-leaf climbed the gentle slope to the edge of the forest, then turned to gaze back at Eimeo's curving shore-line. Matopahu was somewhere on the other side, across the narrow stretch of water. Tepua intended to find him.

In the following days, the Arioi of Wind-driving Lodge struggled to establish their settlement in exile. To every-one's dismay, the Chipped-rock Arioi who had brought them here offered no other assistance. Despite promises, the visitors were left to fend for themselves.

"Was this a trick?" some people began to mutter. "Ar-ranged by Land-crab to get us away from Tahiti?" But most of the exiles seemed determined to make the best of what they had.

Tepua's group made small clearings along the shore, put up shelters of sticks and palm fronds tied crudely with vines. Meanwhile, old gray-brown coconut husks had been left to soak in the lagoon for several days. When the fibers were soft, Arioi men sat and rolled handfuls on their thighs, making a tough and durable three-ply cord. Using lengths of this sennit, everyone retied the bindings that held their simple shelters together.

The women divided their work, collecting shellfish and coconuts, gathering fuel for the cookfires, or hacking away underbrush. Tepua joined the group clearing the women's practice area.

At the end of each morning's labor Tepua would stagger wearily into the lagoon for a cooling dip, then fall onto the spread of palm fronds that served as her bed. Only when she had eaten the main meal, in midafternoon, did she let her thoughts return to Matopahu. She spoke to Aitofa every day, but the chiefess could give her no news of him.

Now that Maukiri had decided to serve the Arioi, Tepua felt a need to educate her cousin on subjects she had never raised before. In spare moments the two women sat in a shady spot and talked about the followers of Oro.

"I've seen the way you look at the high-ranking Arioi," Tepua told her cousin. "Do not be too hasty with your admiration."

"I think they are the best people in the islands," Maukiri replied.

"Some are. Others—some in the highest ranks—disgrace us by doing nothing to help the troupe."

"How can that be? After spending years mastering the chants and learning to perform—"

"That is where you are wrong, cousin. Those of high enough birth often skip the rigorous training. They join us, then settle at once into a life of pleasure."

"But you are of high birth," Maukiri said, "and you began as a novice."

"When I arrived in Tahiti, I was taken for a savage!" Tepua reminded her. "It was enough that the Arioi let me in at all. Even now that they know who I am, many people resent having an atoll woman in the lodge."

"Then you do not think that I . . ." Her cousin's voice trailed off.

"Maukiri! Are you already thinking about joining? Look at the trouble we are in!"

Her cousin kicked the coarse sand with her heel. "You know my dancing. I am not as good as you, but almost. . . ."

"It takes more than skill at dancing. The god must seize

you. If that happens, then everyone will know that you must be one of us."

"*Aue!* Is that all?"

"No. The rules are strict. Have you heard them?"

Maukiri repeated what she had learned from other conversations. The Arioi were dedicated to pleasing their patron god through dance, chant, and mime. They instructed the people, retelling the legends of the great Oro, who presided over peace as well as war. They carried out essential rituals, including those that assured abundant food.

"There is one thing you have not mentioned," said Tepua. "We Arioi swear to remain childless. Do you understand that?"

"I wonder how you can manage it," Maukiri said. "The men and women certainly enjoy each other—at every opportunity."

"And sometimes a child is born," Tepua continued, "despite our efforts to keep it from happening."

"Then the women is sent away?"

"Not if she does what she must. Before the child draws its first breath."

"*Aue!*"

"Yes. I thought that might trouble you, Maukiri. I have never heard you say no to a chance for *hanihani*. At home you didn't worry."

"There was no reason."

Indeed, Tepua knew that if unwed Maukiri bore a child at home, it would be quickly adopted by one of her relatives. If she joined the Arioi, however, any child of hers would be suffocated at the moment of its birth. "Think about this awhile," Tepua cautioned. "Do not be too eager."

Early one morning, the company gathered at an assembly ground that had been cleared from the atoll forest. Rumors had been flying, and now they were confirmed. Chipped-rock Lodge had not abandoned the exiles after all. Tepua's troupe had been invited for a visit, to participate in a ceremony of friendship. Wind-driving Lodge would soon be performing again!

The air was charged with excitement as the players of

lower rank sat on the ground, the others finding makeshift seats. *A new performance.* At last the troupe had some hope of returning to its former way of life.

Many Arioi formalities had been abandoned in exile. Gone were the high stools of the lodge chiefs, and their elaborate fans and high-plumed headdresses. Aitofa sat on a palm log, her dark curly hair adorned only by a wreath of orange beach vine. Head-lifted, the men's chief, sat beside her on a similar log, the gray fringe around his bald spot decorated by a single yellow feather. These two were the only members of the lodge holding the coveted Blackleg rank. The tattoos that covered their legs from ankle to thigh showed that they had reached the pinnacle of their lodge.

As Tepua waited for the leaders to begin, she noticed that a third seat in front of the crowd sat empty. She could not help wondering if some person of importance was expected. But the seat remained empty as the meeting began, the leaders discussing which dances and plays would be best for the coming occasion. Groups formed and duties were assigned. At last the gathering began to disperse.

Just as Tepua stood up to leave, a visitor appeared— perhaps the one who had been expected. At first glance Tepua saw a bedraggled figure dressed only in a *maro*. Suddenly she recognized the man. Eye-to-heaven!

She felt a warm shock spread through her, and her stomach jumped. The priest would certainly know where to find Matopahu. Trembling in her eagerness, she threaded her way through the crowd of her fellow performers.

Impatiently she stood waiting while Eye-to-heaven conferred with the lodge leaders. Straining to hear the conversation, she gathered that he had come to offer his assistance. The players needed many things that their hosts had not provided. They lacked bark-cloth for fresh clothing, but no trees on the *motu* were suitable for making it. They needed certain leaves and berries for face paints and cloth dyes, as well as bamboo for making nose flutes. Seeing the priest's ragged appearance, Tepua wondered how he could help.

She shifted her weight from one foot to the other, nearly dancing in her frantic wish to speak to him. For the moment, her troupe's problems seemed unimportant. All that mattered was Matopahu.

Eye-to-heaven saw her and subtly acknowledged her presence with a sideways glance, but his discussion with the lodge leaders went on. At last, when Head-lifted invited him for refreshments, the priest briefly turned aside. "I must talk to an old friend first," he said loudly, beckoning Tepua.

Then she was alone with Eye-to-heaven, with no one else interrupting. She wished, with sudden fierceness, that the man before her was Matopahu. How she would fling herself into his arms. . . .

She wiped her stinging eyes with the back of her hand. She had to be careful not to want too much. Eye-to-heaven was a start. Yet she felt her stomach sink at the troubled look on his face. "I am sorry that my *taio* could not welcome you back," the priest said.

Uncertainty made her discomfort worse. She had heard whispers about the fate of the high chief who was Matopahu's brother, but no one had explained what had happened to Matopahu himself. Was he sunk so deep in anger over his brother's overthrow, and his own change in fortune, that he could not face anyone?

Impatiently she flung back her hair. "If it is Matopahu's pride that is keeping him from me, tell him to cast it away."

"There is pride, but that is not all," said the priest. Tepua did not like the note of caution in his voice.

"I have known Matopahu too long to be turned away easily, Eye-to-heaven. I have had enough of mysteries. Is he sick? Tell me!"

The priest hesitated. "He is holding up better than I expected."

"If you won't say what is weighing him down," said Tepua, exasperated, "then let me help lift his burden."

The priest frowned. "What he has to do now, he must do alone. When I see him—"

"Let me come with you!"

Eye-to-heaven sighed. "He is stubborn. And perhaps foolish. If I bring you to him, I do not know what he will do."

She felt coldness seep through her insides at his words.

Had Matopahu gone so deeply into mourning that he would not want to see her? She had been away a long time, but that could not have changed things so much.

Clenching her fist by her side, she said, "Show me the way. He need not know how I found him."

The priest sighed. "My *taio* does not always know what is best for him. Seeing you may help him through his difficult trial. Can you leave your duties?"

Tepua straightened herself and turned toward Aitofa. Asking permission to leave was not easy, Tepua realized. The time away from here had changed her. On her home atoll she had been the one who gave orders.

Yet her high birth meant little to the Arioi of Tahiti. If she disobeyed Aitofa, she knew that she could be dismissed from the troupe. The position she had worked so hard to attain would be lost, her service to Oro ended.

The lodge chiefess finished her conversation with Head-lifted and came to Tepua. "Go with the priest, if you must," she said quickly. "But be cautious, Tepua. Listen to what Eye-to-heaven tells you. Only a priest understands what has happened. I do not know if you should touch Matopahu or even go close to him."

"Touch him . . . Not if it is *tapu*." Tepua blinked away a tear. "I . . . understand," she said, though she did not, and backed away.

Matopahu's sharp stone adze bit deep into a stalk of giant bamboo as thick as his forearm. Another stroke nearly severed the cane, but a few tough fibers held. He twisted the stem in his sweat-grimed hands, wrenching it loose and throwing it aside.

He knew that his mood was hardly the proper one for this task. Clearing a path to an abandoned *marae* should be done in a spirit of awe and reverence, not impatience. He lifted his adze and felt a wave of dizziness that dropped him to his knees.

Oh, gods and ancestors, not again! He tried to lift the adze but it slipped from his fingers. Around him the bamboo canes seemed to crowd in, like warriors about to take him prisoner. He fought to get to his feet, but his legs had become clumsy and nerveless.

The sun in this clearing had beat too long on his head, he tried to tell himself. But the pounding pain of a headache became the pounding of drums, and the throb of a low chant that grew louder. . . .

> Here is your fish
> O great Ta'aroa. . . .

Matopahu clapped his hands over his face. The memory of the dream filled his mind. The disembodied, fire-lit hands wound cord about the corpse of his brother. . . .

While the drums beat, the dead arms were lifted and the sennit passed around. The folded legs were lifted and the sennit passed around. It bound the calves to the thighs, the knees to the chest, the elbows to the sides. The cord wound ever tighter until the wrapping became a solid mass about the body.

The sennit mask of the face grew dark with moisture seeping from the hollows of the eyes. It was a sign that the god accepted the offering. The voices chanted.

> Take your fish
> O great god.
> Your fish is weeping.

Matopahu fell on his side. He grabbed desperately at the earth, winding the wild grass around his fingers, driving his nails into the soil, fighting to feel the warmth and green life of the sunlit patch of hillside.

He lay there, ribs heaving, one hand clenched, clawing the earth, as if he would defy the spirits of the *aha-tu* curse. And at last, by his own will, he felt the moist clay loam beneath his fingertips and the sun's warmth stroking his back, renewing his strength.

The terror was past. Yet the memory remained so vivid that when he touched his face, he nearly felt the long deep welts made by cord pulled tightly across skin. Gradually his breathing slowed and he sat up. He stretched, running his hands down his arms and his shoulders as if to be sure that his flesh was unmarred by the marks of binding. His skin felt smooth and warm, shaped by strong muscle beneath.

The sennit-curse might haunt his mind, but it had not yet ruined his body. Matopahu let his palms slide down his flanks as he got to his knees, feeling the sinewy power of his legs.

Suddenly he was disgusted with himself, for he was caressing his own skin the way he might touch a woman. Part of him knew why he was doing it and accepted the reason. His body, once taken for granted, was now something precious to him; he stroked it to soothe away the sense of violation that still lingered.

Despite the day's heat, he shivered, wanting someone warm and close who could take him in her arms. Thoughts of Tepua welled up. Yes, she could hold him, soothe him, drive away the torment. . . .

Only to replace it with one even worse. Matopahu groaned aloud. It would not be Tepua's fault, but her presence would torture him more than comfort him. He could enjoy her company, but not respond to her caresses.

It did not matter if she understood and sympathized; unmanned as he was, her womanly allure would taunt him, making unspoken demands he could not meet.

No, he refused to think of her. He had to stake his hopes on the *tahu'a*. The healer would lift this curse from him, but first he had to complete the task of restoring the ancient *marae*. And he had barely begun to clear the path!

The bamboo still stood before him. Wearily he staggered to his feet and swung the adze again.

By early afternoon, Tepua was following the priest up one of Eimeo's winding forest trails. The air was moist, filled with rich scents of earth and flowering trees. Branches overhung the path, letting only a few streaks of sunlight through.

After her long time away from high islands, she was still not used to climbing. The priest kept up a swift pace.

Underfoot, tangles of roots crossed the red clay, making every step difficult.

She heard running water, a sound that grew louder. Following Eye-to-heaven down a muddy bank, she splashed across a stream and up the other side. Nowhere did she see any signs of habitation. Only the presence of an occasional ancient breadfruit tree suggested that people had lived here long ago.

She was far inland now, ascending higher, constantly trying to catch her breath in the humid air beneath the trees. From time to time the canopy of branches opened to show a jagged spire of dark stone, a sacred mountain. Suddenly the priest halted, allowing her to rest. She sat down in a clump of giant ferns and closed her eyes.

"My friend is just past that grove of chestnut trees. It is not far," whispered Eye-to-heaven. "I will wait here."

At last Tepua was ready. Giant *rata* trees loomed overhead, their rounded seed cases littering the ground. These trees, she knew, often surrounded sacred courtyards. Gooseflesh rose on her arms as she eyed the fluted buttresses that grew from each trunk and gave the trees a nightmarish look.

Ahead she heard the rhythmic sound of a stone adze chopping. The rhythm faltered. She came out from the shade to an open area that was brightened by the afternoon sunlight.

Matopahu! His broad back was bathed in sweat, his copper skin streaked with grime. She fought her impulse to rush forward and embrace him.

As he turned to her, a strange mixture of emotions shone in his eyes. There was longing mingled with delight and desperation. In the brief instant before his face became stony and his gaze distant, she saw intense fear cross his features. No, not fear, but something stronger. Dread. Why?

He tossed aside the short-handled adze and wiped a sweaty hand across his face. As she advanced a step, he put up a hand and spoke in a hard rasp. "No closer. For your sake as well as mine." He lowered his head, staring at her through a begrimed tangle of curls.

"I am not afraid," she shouted defiantly, taking another step. Eye-to-heaven had explained about the curse. She knew that some harm might come to her if she touched him.

"Keep back!" Matopahu insisted. He stood there breathing hard and watching her.

Dressed as he was in nothing but a *maro*, she could readily see the toll that his exile had taken. He was markedly thinner than when she had seen him last. Bruised hollows showed under his eyes and beneath his cheekbones. The eel tattoos that had once twined so elegantly around his calves were smeared with mud and marred with scratches. There was a strained tightness in his face, and his eyes were haunted.

Compassion overwhelmed both her caution and the uncertainty of her feelings for him. The warnings no longer mattered. Impulsively, she crossed the distance between them. . . .

For an instant she imagined herself caught up in Matopahu's crushing embrace. Then his roar deafened her. With a long cane of bamboo he blocked her path, thrust her away from him. Staggering back, she collided with the fluted buttress of a *rata* tree and recoiled in fright. She slipped on a worn root and landed heavily on her back, tears of astonishment and rage stinging her eyes.

"Must I be tainted twice over?" Matopahu cried. He loomed over her, his fists knotted, his eyes wild. "This is no place for a woman," he shouted. "Go to your dancing. Go to your painted lovers!"

"There are none," Tepua spat back from the ground. "The only one I want is painted with mud."

His face twisted. "Would you rut with a dead man? The priests recited the *aha-tu* over my brother."

"The priests can recite the color of the droppings they leave on the beach! It will not change me."

"You do not understand. . . ."

"You are right," she said bitterly, "I am an ignorant coral islander, not fit to wash your noble feet." She picked herself up, shook leaves and grass from her wrap. Then she turned her back to him and started to walk away, flinging her long hair over her shoulder.

"Wait." The rawness in his voice halted her, despite her rage.

She turned to face him again. "I wanted to comfort you. You flung me away as if I were something poisonous."

He swallowed. "I—I was trying to protect you."

"And yourself as well?"

In a low voice he answered, "When a man is engaged in work for the gods, he must not touch a woman."

She clenched her fists in outrage. Why did men insist that women were profane, that their touch contaminated sacred things? Having seen priests make exceptions whenever it suited them, she no longer believed this.

She thought there was another reason Matopahu had pushed her away, with a violence beyond what was needed. But he refused to confide in her. She stared at his tortured face. "We have been apart for so long. Is that all you can say to me?"

He sighed, his body slumping. In a quiet voice he admitted, "I did not want you to leave Tahiti. You remember how I argued against it. When you were gone, I watched the sea every day, hoping to see your returning sails."

Her hopes rose at his words. "Then we can be as we were. When these troubles are over."

"Land-crab has destroyed that chance." He spread his grimy hands and thrust them toward her. "Do you wish to suffer my fate?"

She held her ground. "I will share it with you."

"No! I must suffer alone as the last of my line."

"That is the arrogant Matopahu talking. That is the Matopahu who takes no help from anyone."

"I am a dead man. Everyone believes it."

"Eye-to-heaven does not. Nor do you."

He only glared at her and straightened up. "I have work, and you are keeping me from it. Perhaps my friends are right. Perhaps I do have a chance to save myself. But I must do it alone." He picked up the adze. "Go! Return to your Arioi and forget that you have been here. If I survive this . . ."

"Yes?"

"Then we will have something to talk about." He turned away from her and picked up his adze. She watched him for a moment as he began hacking at another stand of bamboo. Then, eyes stinging, she found her way back to the trail.

: **FIVE**
:
. . . .

A day later, as dappled sunlight penetrated the trees,
Matopahu descended a mud-slick bank to take his morning
bath. The hillside stream, swollen from recent rains, foamed
over the rocks with a comforting roar. In this place he could
forget the harsh words he had said to Tepua. He could forget
the task that lay ahead of him.

He plunged naked into a deep pool where the stream
curled around boulders. The chilly water enveloped him,
stealing all thoughts. He came up, gasping and shivering,
only to fling himself back in again.

At last he came out on the bank and shook off some of the
water. Standing in a patch of sunlight, he picked up the
small garment he had draped over a bush. First he passed
one end of the *tapa* band between his legs, carrying it
around his right hip and across his flat belly to catch and
secure the front. Drawing the *maro* around his left hip, he
threaded it through itself in back, reversed the direction of
winding, wrapped it several times about his hips, and
knotted it at his side.

He sighed as he forced himself to think about the work
that lay ahead of him. Yesterday he had finished clearing a
path to the old *marae*, finally crouching within reach of the
tumbled ridge of black stones that once formed its boundary. Yet he had put off actually touching the ancient wall
until he felt stronger.

In his memory he saw clearly the abandoned sacred court,

the moss-covered stones of the wall, the overgrown paving within. The site lay deep in shadow beneath the old trees, its aura of dread hanging in the humid air. With a shudder he thrust aside his fears. Yet he could not help wishing for a distraction this morning. It would not hurt to wait until the sun rose a bit higher.

In the distance he heard a faint cry, a human voice, though it came from an unexpected direction. When Eye-to-heaven and the *tahu'a* came to visit, they always used the path on the opposite side of the hill. Matopahu could not imagine who else might be climbing this isolated hillside.

Grateful for a diversion, however brief, he set off through the trees, soon emerging at a broad swath of cleared land that he had never seen before. He heard another shout and then the hiss of an arrow's flight. A moment later he heard a soft impact as the arrow struck the ground. This was a *te'a* court, he realized, a place where the game of the gods was played.

Then a boy charged by, a small white flag in his hand. He stopped where the arrow had come to rest and marked the place. When the youngster turned and saw Matopahu, he jumped back in surprise.

"Who is shooting?" asked Matopahu.

"The noble Fat-moon," the boy answered nervously.

Matopahu's eyebrows rose at the name of the high chief who ruled a large section of Eimeo. "Is there to be a match?"

"In ten days," the boy answered. Then he ducked as another arrow hissed overhead.

Matopahu peered down the long *te'a* court. Far in the distance he saw the shooting platform of piled stones and the figure of the kneeling archer. "Your chief shoots well," he said as a third arrow came sailing in his direction. This one fell short of the others, and the boy didn't mark it.

"Everyone knows that Fat-moon's team is the best on the island," said the boy, frowning. "It beats Putu-nui's every time. But you shouldn't be here. I'm the only one allowed to watch the chief practice."

Matopahu had heard much of this team's victories. "Then I will go," he said with a laugh. "I must not disturb the great chief." He turned to retrace his steps, knowing he must return to the old *marae*. He had found a brief respite; he could no longer put off his task.

At last Matopahu stood before the ruins of the ancient wall and tried to compose himself. These stones had been placed by men long dead. Bones of ancient priests and chiefs lay buried in the courtyard beyond. Their spirits still protected the *marae*. He could sense their presence in the shadows, in the rustling of old leaves, in the scent of decay.

His mouth went dry as he began to speak. In a hoarse voice, he intoned a prayer, asking permission to carry out the work he had planned. Sweat cooled on his back as he spoke, giving him a lingering chill.

The sensation, the priests said, was one that pleased the gods. Matopahu remembered it from nights he had spent in prayer upon the *marae* of his brother. He also recalled the great ceremony of weeding the courtyard. Stripped to the waist, he and a few privileged others had worked slowly down the *marae* from west to east, scraping the moss from the sacred paving stones. The priests, dressed in white loin-girdles, had sat aside while urging on the weeders with their chants.

It is *marae* weeding!
The pulling up of grass
And for the host of gods
The moss shall be scraped.

Matopahu sighed deeply. Those days were gone. The only *marae* he could enter now was this long-abandoned one. Cursed as he was, he did not know how the *mana* in the stones of this place would affect him. Even a momentary touch might kill a man who was out of favor with the gods.

He fell silent, listening, his muscles tensed against the impulse to reach for the stones. Overhead, wind rustled the branches. A voice seemed to whisper. Perhaps the spirits were answering his plea.

"Why?"

He strained to hear more, but the wind dropped and the leaves fell silent. Once again he chanted his prayer. . . .

"Why do you disturb us, living man?" came the response. *"We have been quiet for so long."*

His lips moved, trembling. "I intend no harm—"

"So much time without prayers, without sacrifices," moaned the voice. *"Why start again now? Why trouble the dead?"*

With an effort, Matopahu gathered his wits and spoke. "I wish to restore this place so that the gods will return again." He wiped sweat from his upper lip as he listened to the reply.

"So much toil and thought, so much weariness." The voice made Matopahu drowsy. *"Lie down among these stones,"* it urged. *"Be one of us. We welcome you."*

A sudden gust swept the ground, blowing aside dead leaves that lay on the old paving stones of the courtyard. Matopahu drew in his breath when he saw a long trench exposed, white bones showing in a burial crypt.

"Join us now," said the voice, and its tone became soothing. *"Forget your hopeless plans. Give up a struggle that is already lost. Enjoy the peace that you deserve."*

"Yes." Matopahu felt a heaviness of limb, a weariness of spirit. Since the death of his brother he had forced himself to go on, pretending that the curse was taking no toll. Yet every morning he had found it more difficult to rise and face daylight.

"We are waiting," said the voice. *"Your bed is ready. Lie down with us. Lie down."*

What the voice asked would be easy, he thought. He imagined the comforting dark earth, the warm covering of leaves. But he sensed that he must not touch the paving stones if he wished to find repose among the ancient dead. The stones were charged with *mana,* sacred power, that might destroy him before he reached the crypt.

As he gazed over the wall into the sacred courtyard, he saw how he could get to the grave-site. Cautiously, he swung his legs over the tumbled wall. Keeping to places where soil, branches, or debris covered the ancient pavement, he made his way into the center of the *marae.* Here and there an upright slab of stone rose starkly. He skirted these uprights with caution. They marked the places where great chiefs had come to pray. Only men who had inherited the right from their forebears dared approach them.

Ribs and a few long legbones lay waiting for him. As he stooped, the opening of the trench seemed to widen, as if inviting him in. *"Welcome,"* said the voice. *"At last you are ready to join us,"* whispered another. Invisible hands seemed to tug at him, pulling him down. . . .

"Matopahu!"

Another voice, louder, came from a different direction. A woman's voice. *Tepua's.* What was she doing here? No women were allowed in this sacred place.

"Matopahu. Stop."

He had warned Tepua to keep away! Now her voice seemed to come from every direction. Why could she not leave him alone?

"Go back to your Arioi!" he shouted to the forest, though he could see no one. "Go back to your frenzied dancing!" He looked down at the bones and felt the comforting pull once more. Ghostly fingers tugged at him and he yielded, leaning over the crypt, wanting only to fall into the sleeping place that was prepared for him.

"Land-crab has beaten you!" Tepua's voice taunted him.

He bellowed his fury at the interruption. Losing his balance, he tumbled, arms flailing, into the crypt. His bare foot brushed something hard and charged with power. He shouted with dismay, for he had touched one of the sacred uprights. And now he felt the *mana,* more than he could bear. . . .

A great light poured into Matopahu, flowing up his leg and into his body. He thrashed amid the loose bones, striving to break free. So many voices were demanding his attention that he could not tell what they were saying. He only knew that he was caught in the center of a struggle, the spirits of his ancestors and his living friends on one side, the dead of this place on the other.

With a shock he realized that the touch of the sacred *marae* stones was not the devastating force he had feared; instead, its power renewed his strength. His hands scrabbled in the dirt as he tried to pull himself up to the safety of the courtyard. But he had lost his contact with the upright, and his feeling of renewal faded. The earth seemed to be closing over him, cutting off his breath. He rolled, reached up, tried to find a purchase.

His fingers found something—a sapling, sprouting amid the stones. He recognized it as a young *rata* tree, sacred to the gods of this place. He fought the terrible pressure that was holding him down, struggled to free his legs until, at last, they moved. . . .

And then, gasping, he hauled himself out from the crypt and onto the exposed pavement of the courtyard. The voices kept screaming at him while he struggled to push them aside. To protect himself, he pressed his palms and his cheek against the paving stones. Though not as powerful as the upright, these smaller stones also held *mana,* and radiated warmth as if they were living flesh. He took a deep breath. The gods had not abandoned him after all!

At last he got shakily to his feet and looked down at himself. He was filthy, coated with dirt and bits of decayed leaf. He must wash again, he knew, but first he had to seal the abode of the dead. Hastily he pushed whatever debris he could find—leaves, soil, loose rocks—to cover the bones. Gradually the voices grew quieter until he was hearing nothing but distant birdcalls from the forest.

After another bath, Matopahu returned to the task that he had almost abandoned. Repeating his pleas to the gods, he crouched by the low, tumbled wall. Now he had no more fears of touching the ancient stones. He felt only a tingle when he handled those that bordered the sacred courtyard.

Slowly moving along the boundary of the *marae,* he plucked ferns from crevices, pulled away vines, uprooted small bushes. Then he began replacing the rocks that had fallen.

The repeated acts of kneeling, bending, and lifting grew painful. It was not possible, he knew, to rebuild the wall exactly as it had been. Craftsmen had labored for months, carefully choosing smooth surfaces for the facing, and neatly fitting stone against stone. Yet he felt pride as he looked back at how much he had done.

At last, when only a few rays of sunlight were slanting through the branches, Matopahu heard the welcome voice of Eye-to-heaven. He left his labor, heading for his campsite outside the *rata* grove. The priest had set down his basket of provisions and sat waiting.

"Is there news from Tahiti?" Matopahu asked, as he did every time his friend appeared.

"None," said the priest sadly.

"And . . . Tepua." Matopahu grimaced as he remembered her fleeing down the trail.

"You frightened and angered her. If that was your purpose, you succeeded well."

"I was trying to protect her," he answered moodily. Suddenly remembering something, he turned with puzzlement to his friend. "It is strange. I thought I heard her voice this morning, calling me."

"I assure you that she was not here. I visited the Arioi this morning. She was busy practicing her dancing."

Matopahu felt a surge of envy. "Which you enjoyed watching!"

"My friend, if you insist on driving her away, there will be plenty of others pursuing her." The priest sighed. "I will not be one of them."

"And I can do nothing but talk to her from a distance . . . as if she were my sister. She wants everything to be as before. If she had been sensible long ago, we would now have a son!"

"And he would be afflicted, as you are." The priest's expression darkened. "You are strong, my *taio*. You can fight this curse of Land-crab's priests. But a young child?"

Matopahu stared at Eye-to-heaven. As much as he loathed admitting it, his *taio* was right. No one would want to see this affliction touch a child. The boy would quickly grow pale and weak as death crept near.

"Let us argue no more," said Matopahu. "If you wish to help me, try to soothe Tepua. But make sure she doesn't come here again until I finish my work."

"I will try," said the priest, who turned to eye the food

basket. "And now, after a day of work, I think you must be hungry."

The men headed for the stream, washing off the day's accumulated perspiration and dirt. Returning to the camp-site, the priest emptied his basket, laying out the meal on banana leaves. Matopahu opened a coconut for his friend and another for himself. In congenial silence, they ate and drank.

Later, as the shadows deepened, they built a fire to keep off the chill. "Tomorrow is a crucial day," said the priest. "A day of grave risk. I must be with you."

"Why? I will be doing nothing more than what I did today."

Eye-to-heaven raised his eyebrows. "Still clearing the path? I thought you would be done by now."

"Clearing the path? I finished that yesterday."

The priest gasped and clutched his friend's arm. "I do not understand. I thought I made it clear—"

"I stepped into the *marae* this morning. And see—I am alive. Did you want me to waste a whole day waiting for you?"

The priest slumped back against a tree. "*Aue!* I will not ask you what happened. If you are safe, that is enough."

Remembering his struggle among the bones of the *marae,* Matopahu was glad that Eye-to-heaven did not ask more questions. He still shivered at the memory, and quickly he turned his thoughts elsewhere. "I came across something interesting this morning," Matopahu remarked. "Our friend Fat-moon was practicing archery."

"That is nothing new."

"But a match is planned. Soon."

"That is also no surprise."

"You do not see this opportunity as I do," said Matopahu, patiently. "Let's wait a few days, and then I will explain it."

Those days passed. Matopahu found that his progress was slower than he had expected. He finished restoring one short wall and one long wall of the enclosure, so that he was halfway around the courtyard. His muscles grew accustomed to the work. Every morning he rose before dawn, and did not stop until night had almost fallen.

At last the entire wall was complete. The *ari'i* stepped over it and entered the courtyard, studying what remained to be done. At one narrow end of the rectangle stood the *ahu,* a low stone platform. This was the most sacred part of the *marae,* the place where gods descended to witness the ceremonies.

Matopahu was grateful that this *ahu* was small and simple. When a *marae* was built in a prominent place, visible to all who passed by, the chief who owned it might raise a great stepped pyramid. Such a monument could never be restored by a man working alone.

Making a close inspection, Matopahu saw to his delight that the *ahu* here was almost intact. He had only to remove the ferns that sprouted between the cracks, and pull away the vines. The courtyard itself required more work. Many pavement stones had tilted or lifted and needed to be reset. The uprights, the standing slabs, he resolved not to touch again. Perhaps they leaned a bit, but they were deeply rooted. Their *mana,* he thought, would keep them firmly in place for ages to come.

He drew in his breath. Smoothing the pavement would be his biggest job, requiring him to dig holes so that each stone would lie level with the others. Eye-to-heaven had brought him simple tools—clamshells and digging sticks. With a new determination, he went to get them.

When that day ended, Matopahu looked at the small corner of finished work and wiped the sweat from his face. If this was as much as he could do . . . No, he told himself. Tomorrow he would go faster, better. The archery contest was coming soon. . . .

And late one afternoon, when Eye-to-heaven arrived, Matopahu proudly showed him his work. The *marae* was restored.

"You astonish me, *taio,*" said the priest.

"Tonight you will teach me the prayer of reconsecration," the *ari'i* insisted. "And tomorrow I will gather the offerings."

*   *   *

The night of his vigil had finally come. Wearing only a *maro,* Matopahu sat alone on the chilly pavement and listened to the wind. The moon was up, but only a glimmer of light penetrated the branches overhead. The upright stone before him was no more than a shadow, slightly darker than the rest.

He tried not to think about ghosts. He had sealed up the bones of the dead, but spirits were not always bound to them. In one hand he carried a protective tuft of red feathers. In the other he held a palm leaf that had been folded and knotted in a special way by Eye-to-heaven. Matopahu was depending on these talismans, and prayer, to shield him from harm.

Once again he began the droning chant, focusing all his attention on the words. He had no room for error. Everything must be done perfectly, or the plea would fail.

He addressed the principal god of this *marae,* the ancestor of the people who had lived here long ago. Those people had foolishly neglected their protector; perhaps they had all died. Now Matopahu would set matters right.

> Spirits and messengers
> Arise and run
> To the god who once dwelled here.
>
> Say to him
> Your home is renewed
> Your *marae* is weeded and handsome.
>
> Bid him to come again.
> To these kneeling stones.

When the chant was done, Matopahu rested, but he dared not close his eyes, what would the god say if his supplicant fell asleep in the middle of a vigil? The air grew cooler, but he did not mind the discomfort. It would keep him alert, help him avoid a mistake when his chanting began anew.

Yet he could not stop his thoughts from wandering, especially to memories of Tepua. He remembered when he had first seen her—a mere servant in the house of an underchief, an atoll girl whose claims of high birth were scorned in Tahiti. He could recall every word she had spoken to him that night, of her longing for home, of her hopes for joining the Arioi. He remembered, too, how the scent of her had made his head swim, and how the look in her eyes had haunted him for days afterward.

Not until months later had he learned the full story of her mishap, of the wave that had swept her from a voyaging canoe and left her to drown, of the gods who had helped her survive. Those gods had sent her to Tahiti for Matopahu's sake, he believed. Though he did not know their names, he called on them now as well.

> Arise and run
> O messengers.
>
> Summon the god of this *marae*
> And through him the thousands of gods,
>
> The gods of the atolls
> The gods of the heights.

Something stirred. He drew in his breath and tried to control his shivering. A glimmer showed on the pavement ahead and he did not think this was moonlight. A faint noise came, like the whisper of wind through high grass. He felt as if hands were passing over him.

Something more powerful than anything in the *marae* had arrived. The air around him thickened, pressing close, like moist air before a storm. The noise became a drone. The glimmer grew brighter.

Matopahu clutched his talismans. He tried to recite an incantation, but his lips were numb. An invisible touch passed over his body, probing, stroking. . . . He wanted to cry out.

And then it was gone. The light became only moonlight again. The only sound was the wind.

Yet he felt changed, renewed, strengthened. His mouth fell open in wonder as he realized that a god had come to him. Perhaps the curse was not completely lifted. Perhaps he could not free himself by a single task. What he had been granted was enough strength to continue his struggle, and the hope that someday he would succeed.

Matopahu raised his voice once more, praising the high one who had aided him. The night was far from over, but now he did not feel the chill. Determined to keep his vigil until morning, he settled himself on the hard stone.

....
: : SIX
....

Several mornings after her visit to Matopahu, Tepua was
wakened early by cries throughout the encampment. She
had slept fitfully again, and her eyes felt red from weeping.
She tried to shut Matopahu's angry words out of her
memory, but they still echoed. Groggily, unwillingly, she
wrapped her cape around her shoulders and crawled out of
the palm-leaf lean-to.

She blinked, wondering why everyone was up so early.
Overhead, the last stars were fading. A damp, chill wind
came through the forest and ruffled her cape.

"All of us are going to the main island," said Curling-leaf
excitedly.

"Today?" Tepua asked, frowning as she recalled her
painful encounter there with Matopahu.

"Chipped-rock Lodge has finally invited us. We must
prepare."

"So suddenly! I thought they had forgotten us." For many
days no word had been spoken about the Arioi lodge that
had brought her troupe to this islet.

"I thought so, too," said Curling-leaf. "But Head-lifted
has been talking to their chief."

Tepua sighed. She felt so concerned over Matopahu that
she had almost forgotten the problems of the Arioi. She did
not know why Chipped-rock Lodge had offered to move her
troupe from Tahiti. She was curious to learn what arrange-

78

ments had been made. Surely her leaders had not softened their opposition to Land-crab! Or had they?

Before she could wonder more about this, she found herself in a party collecting vines, flowers, and palm fronds in the fringes of the forest. The women brought their gatherings to the assembly ground to make wreaths. By now the early-morning sunlight gleamed on the lagoon, but the clearing remained in shadow. Tepua's bark-cloth cape was thin and worn, doing little to keep off the chill.

"What a poor appearance we will make," Curling-leaf complained as she plaited a headband by wrapping one coconut leaflet with another. Carefully she worked the stems of scarlet-and-yellow hibiscus blooms into the band until she had a circlet of flowers. "Our hosts will have fresh wraps and capes, and we will have only these." She ran her hand over her frayed and stained *tapa* skirt, which she had worn every day since leaving Tahiti.

"I hear we will be getting new clothing. Our hosts have already sent us face paint," said another novice, who was plaiting a garland of violet beach morning glory.

"Why is the lodge of Chipped-rock suddenly being so generous?" someone else wanted to know. Tepua asked herself the same question. None of the troupes in Tahiti had offered help. Were these Arioi of Eimeo the only ones who did not fear Land-crab?

As soon as she finished her decorations, Tepua joined the rehearsal of a dancing group. When the dancing master arranged the women in rows, he sent Tepua to the rear. She deserved a better place, she thought, but admitted to herself that she was out of practice. Long ago, she had astonished the Arioi with her dancing. . . .

Drummers beat on makeshift instruments as the women slowly swayed their hips. Everyone seemed stiff and awkward this morning. Tepua wondered why the lodge leaders insisted on performing at such short notice. Everything about this new development puzzled her.

Before noon, a fleet of two-hulled canoes arrived to pick up the Arioi, now costumed and painted as well as they could manage, faces decorated with red and black. Tepua saw Maukiri at the rear of the crowd, talking excitedly to one of her new friends. Even attendants had been invited to this gathering.

As Tepua stared at the far shore, she wished she could slip away from the group and search for Eye-to-heaven. The priest would have news of Matopahu's progress.

She found her thoughts drifting as canoes took the party along the coast to a beach where their hosts stood waiting. Tepua's companions, cheered by the prospect of relief from their spartan existence, pranced and chanted as they stood on the decks. The Arioi ashore were splendidly dressed, arrayed in new capes of bleached *tapa* that were printed with rosettes and embellished with black-eyed daisies. Brilliant feather necklaces shone around their necks; pearl and shell ear ornaments glistened in the sunlight.

Drums beat loudly, and flutes sang a high-pitched melody as the visitors waded ashore. Tepua hung back, watching, curious to see how her companions would be treated. She saw the lodge leaders embracing each other, and great merriment as the hosts escorted the visitors toward the Chipped-rock Arioi performance house.

Tepua found her cousin beside her as she approached the high-roofed building, which resembled the one that had belonged to her own lodge. "Now you have some idea what we lost in the fire," she whispered to Maukiri as they gazed at the polished pillars made from whole coconut trees that supported the high thatched roof.

The sides of the wooden structure lay open, mat walls rolled up to let in light and air. Tepua breathed the scent of freshly cut *aretu* grass that had been strewn about the floor. "That is where the chiefs and lodge leaders sit to watch the performance," she said, pointing to a raised wooden platform.

Cooking aromas made Tepua's head turn. From the pit-ovens wafted hints of the coming feast. But before the meal there would be introductions, rituals, performances. Tepua sent Maukiri to join the attendants outside, then scurried to sit under the roof with the other Arioi women of her rank.

The Chipped-rock Arioi welcomed the Tahitian troupe with garlands of black-centered daisies and sun-yellow hibiscus. Suspended on cords tied to the performance-house rafters were many presents for the visitors: capes, necklaces, and ornaments similar to the ones their hosts wore.

On the platform, four-legged wooden stools had been arranged for the highest-ranking Arioi. Lower stools on the ground were for the intermediate members. Tepua seated herself beside Curling-leaf on a mat.

Soon the chief comedians of the host lodge strutted out and introduced themselves, naming the special peak, river, and point of land for which their district was renowned. A traditional chant began, calling on Oro in his peaceful aspect—Oro-of-the–laid-down-spear, setting a tone of good fellowship between the host troupe and their guests. Even if their respective tribal chiefs had been actively at war, the two Arioi factions would now be pledged to a amicable meeting.

So far as Tepua knew, Land-crab had no enemies here on Eimeo. It was not a good place to seek allies against him. If any ill will did exist, it was directed against her own Wind-driving Lodge for defying the man who claimed to be its tribal chief.

The hosts began the entertainment, offering a rousing dance that made the onlookers slap their thighs in approval. The dancers ran off and players arrived. They wore typical garb for satire—outlandish headdresses and baggy loin-cloths. However, Tepua saw several costumes that seemed to mock the tattoos and dress of her own troupe. She stared in puzzlement. Arioi did not usually make fun of them-selves.

The skit began by depicting the start of an Arioi perfor-mance. Several richly dressed players, representing a Tahi-tian chief and his retinue, filed in, took their places, and waited for the show to begin. Other Chipped-rock Arioi depicted members of the Tahitian lodge, who strutted and chanted their opening introduction. But instead of starting to entertain, the Tahitian players began to complain about their "tribal chief." The most vociferous critic was a woman whose hairstyle, voice, and manner resembled Aitofa's.

"We will not perform for this chief." She sneered. "Look how thin he is. A chief must have a big belly to be taken seriously."

The mock chief got up, along with his retinue, and humbly withdrew. Another replaced him, but got no further with the arrogant "Tahitian" Arioi woman and her troupe. He would not do either—he was not tall enough to be chief. This man, too, withdrew and was replaced by yet another.

Each mock chief who arrived was criticized and sent back until at last a disguised messenger from the god Oro appeared onstage and went before the Arioi, requesting a performance. This man, too, was refused. But instead of humbly retreating, as the others had done, he stripped off his disguise, announced his true nature, and said that Oro would punish these arrogant players who insulted tribal chiefs in his name. Instantly the "Tahitian" Arioi lodge house went up in "flames" of waving red cloth, and the lodge leaders fell to their knees, begging forgiveness and promising to mend their wayward behavior.

Then the players all ran off, accompanied by thigh-pounding applause from the Chipped-rock Arioi. The visitors joined in, out of politeness, but many looked chagrined. Tepua could not help a surge of indignant anger. This performance made light of the near destruction of Wind-driving Lodge. Even worse, it suggested that Land-crab had been justified in his attack. How could these people of Eimeo be so hospitable and then turn around and embarrass their guests with this one-sided satire?

She watched the expressions on the lodge leaders' faces. First Head-lifted smiled, and then Aitofa. Tepua knew that neither would openly object to this performance. It must not be said that Arioi could not bear being made the butt of their own humor.

Tepua clenched his fists. The usurper was the one who should be mercilessly ridiculed—until public opinion forced him to change his ways. She saw the same protest in Curling-leaf's eyes and the faces of the other women around her, but none of them dared speak.

Her own lodge leaders had clearly been taken by surprise—or had they? Head-lifted was looking more relaxed now, but Aitofa's smile appeared strained. Was it possible that Head-lifted had been told in advance what the hosts planned to perform for his troupe? Perhaps he had even helped plan it!

Fortunately, the face paint helped to cover her companions' embarrassment. Now it was time for the Tahitians to entertain. Tepua hurried to take her place among the dancers.

The drumming began. Despite her reaction to her host's satire, Tepua tried to do her best. As the dancers turned to face the platform, she saw that the chiefs of the host lodge had taken their high seats. They seemed to be watching her, though she stood in the last row.

She noticed that the Chipped-rock Lodge contained several members of the order's highest rank—Blacklegs, tattooed solidly from ankle to loins. Only two, the male and female chiefs, wore the red *maro* about their hips. The other Blacklegs had the rank but not the authority. And they also seemed to be staring at her. Did her tall and slender figure make her so different from the other dancers?

Tepua still chafed over the unfairness of the skit; the critical gaze of the Blacklegs challenged her even more. If these people were going to stare at her, then she would give them something to look at. As determination took hold, her awkwardness and stiffness began to ease.

She had been struggling to keep pace with the drumbeat. Now she heard the music anew.

Her rebellious spirit became a fire within her breast, flowing out along her limbs, infusing them with suppleness and strength. Her abilities of long ago returned. Her hips rocked smoothly, her arms glided through the air, her fingers moved through delicate patterns.

The drumbeat quickened and her dance grew wilder, her hips moving faster, her hands taking on a life of their own. Now all eyes were fixed on her and she knew that she had left the other dancers behind. The drummers seemed to be playing only for Tepua. She could not stop, could not even think of stopping, for the fever of the dance had seized her. She was no longer the dancer, but the dance itself.

The faces of the Chipped-rock players, the hard stare of the Blacklegs, the awed expressions of her own troupe, all began to vanish in a growing red-orange haze. As if from a distance, she heard the cries of *"Nevaneva!"* from the people watching. "Divine frenzy! The god has seized her." Dimly she grew aware that the other dancers had halted their performance, leaving the stage to her alone.

It was as if Tepua danced within the heart of a flame, whose heat and color grew more intense with every drumbeat. She no longer knew where her body ended and the fire began. She flowed, and the light flowed with her, blossoming with a power she thought she could not stand.

Then, into the flames surrounding her, came a sight that made her gasp. She was dancing alone no longer. *He* had come to her. Oro! Oro-of-the-laid-down-spear!

The god danced before her, a strong golden youth, clapping his knees together and apart at a speed far greater than any mortal partner. He flung his head back, giving great god-laughs of joy. "If I could choose a mortal woman now," Oro said, "it would be you. But you are promised to a mortal man, and not even a god can change that. I will be there when he comes to you."

The next instant he was gone, dissolving into his sacred fire, surrounding Tepua, infusing her, transmuting his power into her dance. She gave the last of her strength to Oro. In one final burst, she tried to free herself from human limitations. Then the light faded and she felt her driven body, exhausted, sinking to the ground.

Hands were on her, not divine hands, but mortal ones, holding her up, steadying her, helping her off the dance area. Voices babbled in her ears. Something cool and soothing was put to her lips, easing her parched throat.

A wave of sound broke around her, as if the echoes of Oro's rich laughter still rang. No. She was hearing the cries and thigh-slapping of applause resounding through the performance house. Applause for her, the dancer seized and honored by the god.

Staggering, leaning heavily on Curling-leaf and several other women, she managed to return to her place. Her friends eased her down, mopped the sweat from her body with their garments, rubbed her with scented oil, and garlanded her with more flowers. She tried to recall the voice that had spoken, but the words would not come back to her.

Gradually the aftereffect of the frenzy wore off. Her breathing slowed, her pulse eased, until she was able to reply to the exclamations and words of praise. She noticed another group continuing the performance. At last the entertainment ended.

Still exhausted from her effort, Tepua tried to listen to the speeches that followed, first by Head-lifted, and then by First-to-crow, the male chief of the Chipped-rock Lodge. She heard talk that puzzled her—of a special pact of friendship between the two lodges, of ceremonies to formalize this agreement. These words roused her from her dreamy state and made her look up in bewilderment. She had never heard of such arrangements between Arioi troupes.

First-to-crow announced that there would be an exchange of members. Tepua's companions were wide-eyed as they gazed at each other in astonishment. First-to-crow ignored the stir and began calling names of men and women of his lodge, Chipped-rock Arioi who would now be inducted into the exiled Tahitian troupe.

"How can this be?" the voices whispered. "Head-lifted would not allow it. And Aitofa—"

But Tepua saw Head-lifted standing by proudly, apparently pleased at all that was happening. Aitofa showed a very different face, her brows knit, her lips pressed tightly together. She wore the look of one who had been forced into consenting to something she did not want.

The first to come forward was one of the Blacklegs, a sturdy woman whose ample belly almost matched that of First-to-crow. Her face was completely covered with scarlet dye, and her skin glistened with coconut oil. Arrayed in a plumed headband of black and red feathers and an elaborately printed *tapa* cape, she held herself proudly as she faced the audience.

Around Tepua, people were whispering. "We are being tricked," someone said. "Our lodge already has a female Blackleg."

"This new one will cause trouble," replied another. "She will be Aitofa's rival."

Tepua studied the interloper, whose short name was Pehu-pehu. She looked strongly built, a woman capable of getting what she wanted through her physical strength alone. That she was connected to the highest families of Eimeo only added to her aura of power. Her gaze slowly swept the crowd, already challenging the members of her new troupe.

Was Pehu-pehu coming as a spy? Tepua wondered. Or was her purpose to give Chipped-rock Lodge an influence over the affairs of Tepua's troupe? She could not understand why her leaders had approved this unless it was the only way to prevent the troupe's destruction. First-to-crow called a few other members forward, but these were from the lowest ranks and seemed unhappy to be changing lodges.

It was true, Tepua thought ruefully, that without the many goods the troupe needed, it would be unable to keep performing. Lack of cloth was an immediate problem. With no breadfruit or taro, and coconut running low, merely feeding the group was becoming difficult. If the other troupes continued to scorn Wind-driving Lodge, it soon would be destroyed.

"And now," First-to-crow continued, "I call those chosen for the honor of joining the esteemed Chipped-rock Lodge." Tepua scowled as she wondered where the "honors" would fall. Her lodge had no spare Blackleg, but there were others of high rank sitting on the platform who might go to the host troupe. She watched with annoyance as a man of the Light-print order, tattooed with short horizontal lines on both sides of his body, was summoned. Tepua had seen this man quarreling with Head-lifted; now he seemed pleased to be leaving. Next, a woman of the same rank, Aitofa's principal advisor and supporter, was called to stand beside him.

Tepua began to feel a nervous chill. *It is a plot to weaken Aitofa and give Head-lifted more power!* The women around Tepua seemed to sense what was happening. Aitofa was a staunch foe of Land-crab. The skit performed today had implied that she was the one to blame for her troupe's exile and misfortune. Evidently Head-lifted agreed, for now he was taking steps to push Aitofa aside. What could this be but laying groundwork for getting back into favor with the usurper?

Tepua sat numbly as a few more names were called. A hand shook her. Suddenly she realized that she had once again become the center of attention. "Tepua-mua," the lodge chief repeated.

She stood up shakily but did not go to join the others. Head-lifted was glaring at her, and Aitofa wore a strained expression. First-to-crow called her name once again.

Tepua turned to glance first at Maukiri and then at Curling-leaf; their looks of dismay cut her deeply. Abandon her cousin and her most loyal friend? How could anyone ask that? She clenched her fist, stood up straight, raised her chin.

"Forgive me, noble chief, but I cannot accept this honor," Tepua declared, trying to clear the hoarseness from her voice. First-to-crow looked back at her with astonishment as she said, "I am not worthy to wear your fine clothes and sleep under your high roof. Not while my companions wear tatters and sleep under palm-leaf shelters." She saw Aitofa give her a penetrating glance, but the chiefess looked more surprised and relieved than angry. Tepua continued, "I can accept this honor only when my troupe is home again, our performance house rebuilt, and my leaders accorded their proper respect by the high chief."

A hush fell over the assembly. Tepua sat down and stared at the ground. They could not expel her for this. Not unless her *own* leaders ordered her to come forward and accept the authority of the Chipped-rock Lodge. She wondered if Head-lifted would risk further antagonizing Aitofa and the other Arioi women.

She heard a hasty, whispered conference among the lodge leaders. Snatches of arguments drifted to her.

"This dancer is headstrong, disobedient, a bad example—"

"But the god did seize her. How can we punish—"

I do not know what they will do to me, Tepua thought

glumly. *Whatever happens, it will be better than leaving Curling-leaf and Maukiri.*

First-to-crow grew impatient and waved the other chiefs aside. "We must get on with this," he hissed. He turned to the assembly and announced that the induction ceremonies would begin. Drums pounded. Voices rose in song. Then came the ritual questions and answers as the chosen ones pledged anew their dedication to the order.

As the ceremony neared its end, Tepua studied the grim expression on Aitofa's face. What had happened here? she asked herself again. Had the Blackleg been deceived about whose names would be called?

Tepua felt a surge of loyalty toward her chiefess. Aitofa had been a severe mistress, but she had brought Tepua into the lodge—against Head-lifted's wishes. Later she had fought hard to keep Tepua with the troupe, and to promote her to her present rank. Now Aitofa risked losing her position to this outsider—the new Blackleg, Pehu-pehu.

It will not happen, Tepua vowed silently. As she exchanged glances with Curling-leaf and the other women, she knew that they felt the same.

SEVEN

When Matopahu woke, he was astonished to see that the day was almost gone. After his ordeal in the *marae,* he had fallen asleep at dawn. Now the sun was close to setting.

He rubbed his eyes and sat up. Eye-to-heaven stood watching him, the *tahu'a* close behind. "We didn't wish to wake you," the priest said. "You look well. Tell us—"

"The god came!" Matopahu wondered what else he could say. Perhaps a vestige of the curse still lingered, but he felt no ill effects.

"You have done well," said the *tahu'a.* "I have never heard of a man with your strength of will."

"And I intend to do more."

"Not for a while," Imo cautioned. "You must rest first. And then there is one more task—"

"I need no rest," Matopahu argued. "And what is this new task?"

Imo gave him a stern look. "The sennit-wrapped corpse of your brother must be found. Only then can we completely free you of the curse. But you are not ready for the task, nor is it one you can do alone."

Matopahu felt a chill at these words. Land-crab's priests had undoubtedly hidden the body at a secret burial site. To search for it and hold off Land-crab's warriors at the same time would require a strong band of men. "To return to Tahiti," Matopahu said, "I must have canoes and warriors and weapons."

"You will have them eventually. But I urge you to wait."

"Why wait? I am restored to what I was. . . ." He hesitated as he realized what this meant. The curse had taken his manhood, making him lose all desire for women. That much had surely changed. If Tepua was here now, Matopahu knew he would not disappoint her. The thought of her was enough to stir his loincloth.

He paused, recalling the cold welcome he had given her. Remorse made gooseflesh run down his back. "My *taio,* do me a favor. Take word to Tepua. Tell her that I cannot see her yet . . . but soon."

"I'll try to make her listen," said the priest, eyeing him cautiously. "But I beg you to hear Imo's advice. Do not rush into anything—not even a woman's embrace—until you have recovered from this night's work."

Matopahu laughed sourly. "I have no time for rest. Fat-moon's archery contest is coming."

"Contest?" The priest appeared startled.

"I must prove myself somehow. If I am to gain support from the chiefs, I must show that the curse no longer weakens me. What better way than to enter the game of the gods?"

The face of the *tahu'a* darkened. "The sacred trials will soon take place," he admitted. "But what are you thinking? You cannot enter the contest now. You are far from ready."

"Besides," added Eye-to-heaven, trying to calm the *tahu'a,* "there is no room for outsiders in the game."

"They will find room for me," said Matopahu defiantly. "The challengers need someone new on their team."

The *tahu'a* scowled. "Even if there is a way for you to join, you cannot just walk into the game. You need equipment and a place to practice. When was the last time you tried shooting?"

"Do not worry about my skills," said Matopahu. "Just find me some good arrows and a bow, even if it is old. I will twist a bowstring. And I'll start to do again all the other things that used to exhaust me. I'll prove to you that my strength is renewed!"

Feeling full of energy, Matopahu jumped up and gazed at the gathering shadows. "Enough of this gloomy place. I want to be back at the shore, where a man can breathe fresh air and see the sun. Are you coming?" Without waiting for an answer, he headed for the steep trail down to the coastal plain.

The day after the exchange of members between lodges, Tepua and her companions returned to the *motu,* bringing back many gifts—articles essential to maintaining the troupe. She knew that her act of defiance had cast a shadow over the induction ceremony and the celebration that followed, but she had no regrets. If there was to be punishment, then she would endure it. She saw her duty clearly now. Aitofa must be protected from those who wished to displace her.

Late in the morning, Tepua joined a group of women who were printing designs onto new bark-cloth that the troupe had just received. Once these rolls of *tapa* were decorated and cut to proper lengths, the women would have fresh clothing. Tepua picked up a paint-covered leaf and pressed it against the *tapa,* but her mind kept straying—first to Matopahu, and then to the woes of her troupe.

With a heavy sigh, she made herself pay attention to her work. It would not do to ruin good cloth through carelessness. She glanced about and saw several women preparing dyes in coconut-shell cups—scarlet color from *mati* leaves and yellow from turmeric root. She tried to cheer herself with the notion that these new garments would be as fine as those that had been left in Tahiti.

The long roll of *tapa* was laid out on palm leaves. Squatting beside her companions, Tepua worked slowly, using a bundle of grass fibers as a brush. She applied dye to a small hibiscus leaf, then used the leaf to print an impression on the cloth. Repeating it, she began to create a design.

There was little conversation. Tepua sensed a tension around her, a feeling that she was being shunned. Perhaps some of these women resented what she had done—defying First-to-crow. But others had whispered their approval.

How would she feel when she danced before an audience again? Tepua wondered. Everyone would be staring at her, remembering what she had said, wondering also if the god might seize her again. No. She did not want such an honor, not for a long while. The dancing had exhausted her, leaving her sore in every muscle and joint. Yet the moment, while it lasted, had been sublime.

"A fine morning for work!"

The unfamiliar voice came from behind and made every head turn. "I see you are making progress," said the new Blackleg, Pehu-pehu, coming closer. The heavyset woman wore a white blossom behind her ear, and a plaited eyeshade of palm leaf atop her close-cropped hair. She seemed relaxed and cheerful, yet Tepua could not feel easy in her presence.

"That is a pretty pattern," said Pehu-pehu, kneeling beside the long length of cloth. As she praised the work of one woman after another, they began to warm to her. "And you—Tepua-mua," she asked finally. "Where is yours?"

"I . . . I am just getting started."

"Ah. Still a bit tired after yesterday. I understand. That was quite a performance. Many people were impressed."

"It was not just a performance," Tepua answered sharply.

The Blackleg gave her a slow scornful smile. "*Nevaneva?* I have seen the frenzy imitated more than once."

Imitated? Tepua stared into the chilling gaze of the Blackleg. "Say what you like," she answered in a level voice. "Oro was with me."

"If that is so, then we will know in other ways," Pehu-pehu answered. "A woman favored by the gods excels in many things. I intend to pay special attention to everything you do."

"And I will try to please you," Tepua answered.

"Good. Then let me watch how your decorate your bark-cloth wrap."

Suddenly Tepua remembered her days as a novice, when she had been forced to stand before Aitofa and recite the chants she had memorized. Her temper flared as she realized that Pehu-pehu was treating her as if she were still a novice. She felt the eyes of everyone on her as she stared at her section of cloth. On the ground beside her lay many twigs and leaves that might be used to mark the cloth.

It would not do to defy Pehu-pehu. Tepua knew that she had already caused trouble enough. She closed her eyes and willed a design to come to her. Then she prayed to her guardian spirit. . . .

Matopahu raced down the beach, snatching up arrows as he went. He had started practicing this morning, shooting from a makeshift log platform. Now, as he sent scavenging gulls flapping from his path, he realized how poorly he was doing. The objective was to aim for maximum distance, and he was far from achieving the shots made by previous champions.

The arrows were slender bamboo shafts tipped with ironwood points. The bow, almost as tall as a man, was a flexible length of hibiscus wood, tapered at each end. The quiver, an archer's most prized possession, was made of polished and decorated bamboo. Matopahu's borrowed quiver was old and weathered, its design nearly worn away.

Some men believed that the power of the archer came from his quiver. Matopahu put his trust elsewhere. After collecting the last of his arrows, he returned to his starting point and picked up the bow again. The string he had made from twisted *romaha* bark was not as springy or as strong as some he had seen. With the help of the gods, perhaps he could do better.

"You are starting early," said Eye-to-heaven, arriving while Matopahu was testing the pull of his bow.

"Fat-moon has had many days to practice," the *ari'i* answered.

"Then perhaps you will reconsider your plan. Later in the season—"

"No, my *taio*. I am strong now. When I find the right bow, you will see how well I shoot."

The priest had with him another bow, of slightly darker wood. Decorations of finely plaited hair were wound in spirals about each tapered end. It was unstrung, the bow-string dangling. "Try this one," he said. "A kinsman lent it to me."

Matopahu closed his fingers around the bow. He saw that it had been well made and cared for. The wood was carefully oiled, silky to the touch. He passed the bowstring loop about the bottom end, seeing how neatly it fitted into the carved groove. He pulled the string, feeling how it slid smoothly and evenly through his fingers.

As he strung the bow, it bent against his thigh with a suppleness and resilience he had never felt before. Sliding the top loop of the bowstring into its groove and moving his hand down to the center grip, he felt his spirits rise. Here was a bow worthy of the contest!

Matopahu picked up an arrow and pressed the flat, slightly sticky end of the shaft against the cord. The breadfruit gum used to keep the end from slipping had almost worn away, however, so he put aside the arrow and took another. He knelt, drawing back the string. The lightness of the piece belied its strength. Matopahu rejoiced as his muscles answered the weapon's challenge.

Where had Eye-to-heaven found this bow? Matopahu wondered. He aimed high, bow-hand thumb against his jaw, and then released. The cord sang, the shaft hissed and disappeared.

"Ah, that is better," he said as he stood up, shading his eyes, trying to see where the arrow had gone.

"You will have to beat that by half," observed the priest. "You only reached the big pandanus."

The *ari'i* handed the bow back to his companion. "Look again. I am well past that tree. You shoot, and then we'll see who is right."

"Wind from your mouth will not make your arrow fly farther," said his *taio* good-naturedly. "But perhaps the sun did blind me for a moment. . . ."

A day later, when Tepua and the others of her rank assembled for dancing practice, Pehu-pehu joined them, replacing the usual leader. The Blackleg was gaily adorned with a crown of hibiscus flowers and ferns, and a wreath of vines over the *tapa* skirt about her hips. "A new invitation has come," she announced. "We'll be performing again."

"How soon?" everyone wanted to know.

"We have only a few days to get ready. And since I know Eimeo well, I want to help you learn what the local people like to see. Surely you've noticed some differences between the styles of dancing here and in Tahiti."

The other women moved closer, curious about what Pehu-pehu had to offer. Tepua was content to remain in the rear. The Blackleg had been giving her far more attention than she wanted.

"My old dance master used to say," Pehu-pehu began, "that when you watch an Arioi move her hands, you should not see her. Instead, you should see the picture she is making. This is true not only for the hands, but the whole body. The dancer should vanish, leaving only the opening flower, the rising sun, the palm swaying in the wind."

"But how is it possible?" came questions from every side.

Pehu-pehu smiled. "Watch. I will give you an example."

The Blackleg strode out onto the hard-packed earth of the practice area. She went into a crouch, with one knee raised and the other lowered. Throwing back her head and extending her arms, she signaled for drums.

This beginning took Tepua by surprise. The Blackleg had chosen a difficult starting position, one that made Tepua's legs ache every time she practiced it. She watched skeptically, doubting whether Pehu-pehu had the required strength or hip control.

She's too heavy. She'll lose her balance.

Tepua expected that Pehu-pehu would start with a slow beat. Instead, the drumming began with a fast clatter from the slit-log *toere,* followed by frenzied pounding from the deep-voiced drums. Suddenly Pehu-pehu's knees were pumping, her big hips moving in a fluid rotation. Her shoulders held rock steady, as if her upper half had no connection to the rest. Slowly and smoothly she rose from the crouch.

The young dancers gasped. Tepua knew that her own thigh muscles would be screaming in protest, yet Pehu-pehu came up with no seeming effort. Tepua watched with mixed admiration and scorn.

She tells us not to draw attention to ourselves, but she is showing off.

Yet, as she watched, Tepua began to see what Pehu-pehu meant. Gradually she lost her awareness of the dancer's body. What rose before was the gathering ocean swell with foam trembling on its crest.

What magic was this? Other women evidently saw the transformation for they rubbed their eyes and stared again. The Blackleg reversed her motion, going slowly down into the crouch again, the vibration of her hips tight and fast. She came up once more, and signaled for the drums to stop.

"This is not something you can learn in a day," Pehu-pehu said, slightly out of breath. "It takes discipline and effort. But we can start. Here. You two. Let me see you try."

Tepua was relieved when Pehu-pehu focused on two of the older members of the group. It was not long, however, before the Blackleg took notice of Tepua.

"Yes, you can do it, too," she said, "despite your atoll background. I want to see you blend in better with the rest of the group. This is a good place to start."

"I will try."

"I hope you'll do more than try. I said about this nothing before, but your flamboyant style draws too much notice. This kind of training can help you control yourself."

Tepua winced. Perhaps the Blackleg was right, but she could not help thinking that Pehu-pehu was criticizing her for other reasons. Perhaps the Blackleg already knew of Tepua's loyalty to Aitofa. By separating Tepua from her group, Pehu-pehu could begin to strengthen herself at Aitofa's—and Tepua's—expense.

"Show me what you can do," Pehu-pehu demanded, signaling for the drums again. "Let me see you put some effort into it."

Tepua held back her sigh of resignation as she lowered herself into the crouch. She began to move her hips, but the movement was far from smooth. Angrily, she watched Pehu-pehu strutting about, joking with the other women. A few were laughing.

The day of Fat-moon's gathering arrived, none too quickly to suit Matopahu. He and his two companions rose early and brought their canoe to a cove not far from the center of activity. They had not been invited, of course, and Matopahu wished to keep out of sight until the appropriate moment. The three men brought their equipment ashore, found a comfortable place in the forest, and settled down to wait.

But Matopahu could not sit for long. He crept down to the water and watched the canoes of the arriving guests and Arioi. This was to be a grand celebration, involving all the important people of Eimeo. He had learned from his *taio* that even Tepua's exiled troupe would be here.

When he had first planned this surprise appearance, he had not realized that Tepua might be present. Of course, the gathering was large. There would be other contests that might draw her attention. But he could not shake off the idea that she would be in the crowd when he came forward to shoot.

More double canoes arrived as he watched, their high pennants waving in the breeze. More brightly clad Arioi strode up onto the shore. Somehow he had not reckoned on the size of the crowd. So many eyes on him. So many to witness his victory or defeat.

Yet he knew no other way to show that he could defy Land-crab's curse. If everyone saw that he was alive and strong and had the favor of the gods, then they would know that he could win back his brother's land and people. Warriors would flock to support him. Chiefs would pledge their aid.

If he lost, everyone would know that the curse still bound him.

As Tepua walked up from the beach where the Arioi canoes had landed, she saw people scrambling in all directions. She guessed that they were members of Fat-moon's household or belonged to other performing troupes. Behind her, she heard shouts as more canoes arrived.

Ahead lay Fat-moon's assembly ground, a broad open area surrounded by breadfruit trees. Tepua felt little interest in being here.

"This is exciting!" said Maukiri, catching up to her. "I've never seen such a gathering. Why did you never tell me about these events?"

Tepua glanced at Maukiri's flushed face and dancing

eyes. She was glad that her cousin was adapting so quickly to local ways. For Tepua herself, everything had turned sour. She had begun to wish she had remained with her own people and never come back to Tahiti.

The only cheering news was of Matopahu's recovery. Eye-to-heaven had told her that his *taio* was eager to see her—but not until he proved to everyone that he was renewed. This last part infuriated her all over again. Why must the man continue to put on his pretenses? She had seen him weak and sick, and had not turned away from him.

Trying to shake off her mood, she studied the crowd. She saw Arioi from several lodges greeting each other, noses pressed to cheeks. Other players strutted about displaying their finery, feathers and shell necklaces gleaming. Drums boomed as a few dancers held a final practice session.

Maukiri gestured eagerly toward a knot of people who were watching an impromptu performance. She raced off. Tepua watched her go.

The morning sun still cast long shadows, but Tepua felt the growing heat of the day. She gazed toward sharp, black peaks that rose behind the assembly ground and wondered if the air would be any cooler on the heights. The garland about her neck felt heavy; her new bark-cloth wrap chafed her skin.

Soon the dancing would begin. Though she would be standing in the final row of performers, she knew that Pehu-pehu would be watching her carefully. The interloper's opinion did not matter, she tried to tell herself. So long as Aitofa was satisfied, Tepua could feel that she was doing her best to serve the troupe. Yet she remembered Pehu-pehu's cold, measuring eyes and harsh criticism during the practice sessions. Tepua wished she could slip away into the forest and avoid the performance entirely. . . .

The brilliant and outlandish costumes of the milling Arioi became a blur before her eyes. Something caught her attention and her gaze followed it before she even knew why. The object of her interest was a sunshade, worn by a tall man in the crowd. She did not see his face, only the peculiar headgear perched atop his bushy hair. There was something utterly strange, yet familiar about it.

The brim was not an open weave, like the sunshades she often wore, but a solid, flat piece of cloth. Instead of shading only the eyes and face, it encircled the whole head. It was closed at the top, like an overturned bowl that fit over the crown.

She could not help staring, trying to recall where she had seen such a sunshade. This was unlike anything the local people made. She gasped as she remembered. In her vision she had seen similar things on the heads of the foreign sailors. And before that, two visitors to her atoll had worn them. But how could a foreigner's headdress be here?

The tall Arioi wearing the curiosity noticed her stare and strutted toward her, displaying all his finery. "Why are you staring, pretty one?" he asked, giving her a casual inspection. "You are from Tahiti, I see, by the style of your garlands. Let me be the first to welcome you."

She pursed her lips, unsure whether he had heard about the misfortunes of her Arioi lodge. She certainly did not wish to tell him that her troupe was in exile. "I am curious about that thing on your head."

He looked startled, and the anticipatory gleam in his eyes faded. Obviously he had thought her interest was of a more intimate nature.

Well . . . perhaps it could be. Lately she had become far too serious. Here she was at a celebration, and no one had forbidden her to enjoy herself. She studied the stranger more carefully. His cheekbones and nose were highlighted with red, making his long face appear even longer. Yet she found something sensuous about the shape of his mouth, the generous lower lip. . . .

But where had he obtained that sunshade? Aitofa had assured her that no foreigners had been seen anywhere near Tahiti. And the events of her vision, Tepua thought, would not come for many seasons. "Have you been traveling?" she asked cautiously.

He touched the brim of the sunshade. "This came from far away," he said. "An atoll trader brought it to my father, who is chief of Hitiaa. But don't take such an interest in the thing. I cannot give it up."

"I don't want your sunshade. I am only curious about

foreign sailors—where they were seen—how long before
they find these islands."

"Ah. Your questions can be answered," he said with a
smile. He pulled her to him, affectionately pressing his nose
against hers. For a moment, she found the embrace comforting. "My name is Uhi," he whispered. "We can meet
later."

"Yes," she said, finding no reason to refuse. Matopahu
did not want her yet, and she was tired of waiting for him.
The excitement of the day was finally starting to reach her.
Why not permit herself some enjoyment?

"Good," Uhi said, releasing her. "I will look for you. Do
not forget." Suddenly he saw a friend, far off in the crowd,
and shouted a greeting. In a moment he was gone.

Then the conch-trumpet sounded to announce the arrival
of Fat-moon, the host of the gathering. Everyone turned
toward the herald. Tepua spotted the leaders of her lodge,
their pennant fluttering from a raised staff. She hurried over
to stand with her troupe for the high chief's entrance.

Matopahu returned to Eye-to-heaven and the healer, Imo.
He sat with them, listening to the preliminary ceremonies,
the chanting and the drums. At last, when he thought that
everyone had headed up to the archery course, he led his
friends on a shortcut by a steeper trail. He knew this
territory. Long ago, as a boy, he had accompanied his father
on visits to the former chief of the district.

The site of the contest lay atop a small plateau. As he
threaded his way through the crowd, Matopahu caught sight
of the triangular shooting platform, assembled from stones
neatly fitted together and made level on top.

Nearby, almost entirely screened from view by *rata* trees,
stood the archers' *marae* beside a brook that was dedicated
to their use. Here the contestants cleansed themselves in the
water before offering prayers and donning sanctified garments. Evidently Fat-moon had completed the ritual. He
was seated on a stool atop the archery platform, watching
the arrival of the other contestants.

Two attendants stood below, holding up large palm
fronds to shade him. The chief wore a simple bleached

maro, and a turban of bark-cloth decorated with a single red feather. Matopahu examined his sturdy figure, noting the well-fleshed arms and wondering about the muscles beneath the skin. Fat-moon's jutting chin and square face made him think of a canoe's prow.

Near the platform stood important people of Eimeo, *ari'i* garbed in their finery. They were spectators, here to watch how their favorite archers did against Fat-moon's. Matopahu knew many of these people. During his exile he had visited them to ask for help, but they had refused to support him against Land-crab or even to share a meal. Now, when the Eimeo *ari'i* saw him confidently striding before them, their eyes seemed to bulge in amazement.

"I am alive," he called gaily to the crowd. "And strong. Look at me!" He raised his arms, holding up the bow. The closest onlookers moved nervously from his path as he approached Fat-moon's seat.

The high chief curled his lips in distaste. "What is this?" he asked. "I did not invite you."

"I am here to offer you a *true* challenge."

"We have players enough." Fat-moon gestured impatiently. "Go challenge the women archers. They will enjoy your company."

Matopahu ignored the laughter behind him. To the chief he said, "It is easy to win if you always take the best archers of the island for yourself. That explains why no team from Eimeo can beat you." He paused, drawing himself up, thrusting out his chest. "Of course, you have not extended the challenge to anyone from Tahiti."

He saw that his words had stung the chief. Fat-moon stood up angrily. "Do you think we are afraid of Tahitians? They are weaklings. They are children still sucking their mother's teats."

"Then you need not fear my bow. Let me shoot for your opponents."

"Hah. You are full of empty words. Putu-nui does not want you on his team."

Matopahu knew the history of the long rivalry between these two chiefs, Fat-moon and Putu-nui. "He has never beaten you," said Matopahu. "I cannot do his team any harm."

"What is all this talk about?" From the direction of the archers' *marae* strode a bull-necked man who was heavily tattooed over his chest and shoulders. This was Putu-nui, a lesser chief of the island, whose exploits were well-known in Tahiti. His father and Fat-moon's had often been at war. Sometimes they had declared peace solely to permit the archery competition.

Putu-nui scowled as he eyed Matopahu. "I have heard of your troubles," the lesser chief said. "You look strong enough. But you must be sanctified with the others. Are you fit to enter the archers' *marae*?"

The *tahu'a,* Imo, came up beside him. "Noble chief," he said firmly. "The gods have touched this man. Look at him. He not only lives—he thrives."

"I have nothing but your word for that," answered Putu-nui. He narrowed his eyes and glanced up at the high chief.

"The priest who purifies the archers will agree with me," said Imo, addressing one chief and then the other. "And he will explain his reasons."

Matopahu felt a tingle of anticipation as Putu-nui glanced at him again. He noticed a gleam of eagerness in the lesser chief's eyes, a hope for the victory that had long eluded him.

Fat-moon saw it, too. Matopahu read the other man's thoughts from the way his face hardened.

I have put a scorpion in his food basket, Matopahu thought mischievously. *If he forbids Putu-nui to choose me, he will assure his victory once again, but it will bring him no pleasure.*

Fat-moon turned his head slowly, assessing the mood of the crowd. Until now it had been casual, as if everyone already knew the outcome. Now a ripple of uncertainty and excitement ran through the gathering, sharpening everyone's attention.

Matopahu tightened his fist on his bow grip. *Thank the gods for the rivalries between chiefs. Fat-moon cannot deny me now or the people will sneer at him behind his back.*

"Call the priest of archers," Fat-moon barked. Then he

and Putu-nui listened intently while the man spoke in a low voice that Matopahu could not hear. Imo had taken this priest to see the results of Matopahu's labor in the ruined *marae*. The other man had come away awed.

Yet it was Fat-moon who would have to make the decision.

"Enough!" said the high chief, waving his priest away. He turned to address the onlookers and spoke loudly. "It is settled," he announced. "Matopahu will shoot with Putu-nui's team."

The crowd responded with roars of approval. Matopahu grinned, already imagining his victory. But then, as the other archers paraded out from the *marae,* his feeling of triumph faded; his fist tightened about his bow. The men of Fat-moon's team were as strongly built as any he had seen. Their oiled biceps glistened. Their faces beamed with confidence.

Putu-nui's archers seemed a different breed, some wiry, some plump, but none with the look of a champion. Every face appeared grim as the challengers sized up their opponents. Matopahu drew in his breath. His chances did not look good, but it was too late to back out now. He hurried toward the *marae* to prepare himself.

After their performances on Fat-moon's assembly ground, the Arioi mingled with the crowds that climbed through forest trails to the archery range. Maukiri caught up with Tepua, and together they ascended the shady path. "There will be games for women," said Maukiri. "I would like to see you shooting again."

Tepua's eyebrows rose. She had almost forgotten the rare but celebrated archery matches on her atoll. Teams of women from every islet shot for distance across a sandy clearing. One time the contest had continued for three days as team after team approached victory and then faltered. Finally, late on the third day, Tepua's arrow sailed past all the others. When the points were counted, her team had won. She remembered now how her companions had carried her home, then paraded with her up and down the beach.

"Tepua, will you try?" asked Maukiri.

"At home, archery is a game like many others," Tepua replied. "Here, the people make more of it, especially the men. They say it is a sacred contest, and that the spirits of their ancestors attend the matches."

"Then I—will stay away—from the men," Maukiri replied nervously. "But we need someone strong. . . ."

"You have a team?"

"One of the novices invited me."

Tepua let out a long breath. "No. You play. I'll watch and cheer you on."

Maukiri grimaced with disappointment, then quickened her pace. Ahead, the forest opened onto a grassy plateau. The crowds were even thicker here than they had been at the assembly ground, and the humidity was worse. Tepua wondered if she could find a quiet stream, relax in cool water awhile before the match began.

As she and Maukiri were making their way toward the women's archery course, she heard a voice behind her. "Tepua! You must come." Curling-leaf broke through the crowd and caught Tepua's elbow. "Matopahu is here. He has challenged Fat-moon."

"Challenged?" She felt her pulse beating. Eye-to-heaven had said that the *ari'i* intended to prove himself. Now she understood his risky plan.

"Come," said Curling-leaf. "I know a place where we can watch him."

"He won't want me there," Tepua answered sharply.

"I cannot believe that."

"You watch for me," Tepua urged her friend. As Curling-leaf hurried back toward the thickest cluster of people, Tepua fought an impulse to follow her. If she could hide somewhere and observe without being seen . . .

Maukiri tugged at her, and Tepua tried to forget Curling-leaf's news. Teams were assembling around the smaller stone platform used by women. Aitofa, Pehu-pehu, and others of high Arioi rank stood together, peering along the uphill course, pointing out features to each other and speaking in low voices.

Suddenly Tepua pulled away from her cousin. "You'll do fine without me," she said, then darted after Curling-leaf.

"It is you again!" A tall figure stepped in front of her. She looked up and saw Uhi, the long-faced Arioi, with his foreign sunshade.

"I want . . . to watch . . . the men's match," Tepua said, catching her breath. "But I must not be seen."

"That is easily done, my pretty," he answered, taking her hand. "I'll show you where to hide." He led her away from the crowd and into a wooded area by the side of the course. They were not the first here. Other spectators, many in pairs, had found places, but some seemed more interested in each other than in watching the contest. Tepua's thoughts were far from *hanihani,* but she knew she could not say the same about Uhi's.

"You promised to tell me about that sunshade you are wearing," she reminded him.

"It belonged to a stranger, a sailor from a distant land. That is all I can say."

"You said you knew more," she protested.

"Why are you so interested?" He turned and stared at her intently.

Tepua's tongue felt dry and she wondered how to answer him without revealing too much. She certainly did not intend to talk about her troubling vision; so far, only Aitofa knew about that. Tepua thought about her recent visit home.

"When I was traveling in the atolls," she said awkwardly, "a small foreign boat nearly smashed on the reef."

"That is all?"

She stiffened, trying to hold the painful memories at bay. "I have seen foreign sailors. I know what their weapons can do," she whispered.

"Then the atoll people must be weak and their gods helpless," he answered with a laugh. "Foreigners avoid our waters. They would not dare approach Tahiti or Eimeo, where so many war canoes are ready to defend the land."

Tepua gritted her teeth at his insult to her people. "Someday it will happen," she retorted. "A foreign vessel will reach our shores—"

"*Aue!* That old prophecy! I have heard it too many times."

A sudden blast of the conch-trumpet made Uhi spin

around. "They are already starting the match," he said
ruefully. "We have wasted time arguing when we could
have been . . ." His voice trailed off as the first archer,
Fat-moon himself, mounted the platform. The chief knelt,
faced uphill, muttered a prayer, and sent his arrow skyward.
A cry of excitement went up from the crowd. Tepua shaded
her eyes, peering up along the rising stretch of the course. In
the distance, a man carrying a white flag ran to plant it
where the arrow had landed.

The archers stood in line, one after the other, each taking
a single shot. By waving their flags, attendants told the
spectators when someone had beaten the current distance
mark. After Fat-moon's team finished, Tepua drew in her
breath as Putu-nui's first archer approached the platform.

When she had last seen Matopahu, his shoulders sagged
and he was covered with dust. Now he looked freshly
washed and oiled. His chest gleamed; his white *tapa*
garments were dazzling even in the hazy sunlight.

"This fool will not last long," Uhi jeered.

"Wait until he has shot," she retorted.

"You know this Matopahu?" Her companion came up
behind her, his arms twining about her midriff, his *maro*
pressing against her lower back. "Yes, if you are from
Wind-driving Lodge, I am sure you do. All the women of
that troupe have spread their legs for him. But he's no use to
you now."

She suppressed an urge to stamp on Uhi's foot. Matopahu
was kneeling, drawing back his bow. She dared not make a
sound.

In the still air she heard the twang of the bowstring and
the arrow's hiss. The crowd remained silent as the attendants marked how far the arrow had flown.

"What is this?" shouted Uhi, suddenly pushing her aside.
He rushed from cover and peered along the course. "The
Tahitian has beaten Fat-moon's mark!"

Tepua felt jubilant. Perhaps Matopahu's shooting would
prove something today. If he could lead his team to victory,
the chiefs would see him with new eyes.

"It is only one point," she admitted. She understood the
difficulties of the game. On this first round, Fat-moon had

set the distance mark for his team. Now his opponents would score one point for each arrow that passed it. But if they failed to score again on the next round, they would lose all their accumulated points.

"You are right," said Uhi. "It will not happen again."

Tepua watched tensely as the game went on. For two or three rounds, Fat-moon's arrow would fly ahead and Matopahu's would land just behind. For another two, the reverse would happen. Even when Matopahu scored, his teammates rarely were able to do the same. Several times Fat-moon's team neared victory, but was held back by the requirement that the winning points be made on successive rounds.

Meanwhile, the sky grew cloudier, and Tepua heard a stirring of wind in the trees. The first raindrops pattered onto leaves, sending a few onlookers to seek cover. The heavy scent of moist vegetation filled the air. "Now we will all have a bath," Uhi muttered, taking shelter under the broad leaves of a *hotu* tree. Tepua did not follow him. Matopahu was approaching the platform.

A sudden torrent of rain fell just as he raised his bow. Matopahu shot, but the arrow, caught by the downpour, plummeted, falling only a few paces ahead of him. Water streamed down his grim face as he gave way to the next member of his team.

Tepua watched as the archers resolutely tried to continue despite the downpour. She knew that nothing short of a hurricane would stop them. This match had been repeated for generations, team positions passing from father to son. Someone must have given up his precious place to allow Matopahu to shoot.

Yet for all their determination, the others on Putu-nui's team turned in a dismal round, easily outdistanced by their opponents. Each time that Fat-moon's archers planted an arrow beyond the best shot made by Putu-nui's team, his team scored. How many points, she wondered, could he gain in this single round? Perhaps enough to end the game.

"It is over," said Uhi, gesturing toward the scorekeeper.

"Nine!" came the shout from down the course.

"Count again," Fat-moon demanded. But he was still a point short of victory.

The weather proved fickle. Or perhaps, Tepua thought, the gods were having sport. In the next round, a gust of wind blew Fat-moon's arrow far off course. Matopahu's team scored three, and the other team's points were wiped out again. She began to shiver from the rain on her wet skin.

"I know a comfortable place nearby," suggested Uhi, coming up behind her. "These games go on and on, sometimes for days. Why suffer when we can learn the outcome later?"

The rain grew heavier. The archers' garments were soaked, plastered to their bodies. All the onlookers had moved under the trees. Tepua saw paint running in bizarre patterns on the faces and bodies of other Arioi, but somehow Uhi had kept dry. "I will stay here," she said firmly, not caring that water streamed down her cheeks or that her garland hung in ruins about her neck.

Matopahu felt a burden of weariness as he approached the shooting platform once more. The game had gone on far too long. On this stormy afternoon darkness was closing in early. He could barely make out the distant flags behind the veil of rain.

In the recent rounds he had lost track of the score. He was convinced that there could be no victor before dark. The contest would have to continue in the morning, and perhaps last another full day.

All he could do now was hold off Fat-moon for one more round. Then the contest would certainly be postponed. He knelt, put his arrow to the bow, but the shaft slipped from his fingers and fell at his feet. Behind him he heard groans of despair. This was not a good way to begin.

He felt numbness in his hands and recalled, with dread, the *aha-tu* curse that had bound him. But all that was gone. Nothing mystical was at work here, he told himself. Cold and rain had caused his fumbling. He flexed his fingers until the feeling returned. Even then he did not shoot. A premonition of defeat made him pause and collect his thoughts.

What is the true purpose of this *te'a* game? he asked

himself. It was not intended for the glory of men, though many made it so. This was the game of the gods, governed by rules they had set down long ago. It was to please the mighty ones that men played it.

Matopahu thought of his own ancestors, whose spirits had long watched over his family. His brother had turned away from those protective spirits, Matopahu believed, putting his trust in gods who had no special interest in his affairs. That was the reason for Knotted-cord's downfall.

"It is for you that I make this shot," Matopahu whispered, invoking the name of his great ancestor. "It is your name that I will teach to my sons—if I survive to have any." He felt a stiffening of tension in his arms and a rush of heat to his fingers. He took a deep breath.

Then he drew back the string and released. In the gloom he could not see where the arrow went, but he heard a cry from behind him. To his astonishment, men left their places and began charging up the course. In the distance he saw the attendants vigorously waving their flags.

"It is over," people shouted. Matopahu remained on the platform. He saw Fat-moon far up the course, pointing and arguing, then examining the arrow that stuck from the ground.

Matopahu felt an odd shock go through him as he stepped down from the platform. Had he really won? As the cries rang down the course, the tense muscles in his face gave way to a grin.

Still not quite believing that he had made the winning shot, he noticed that his companions were already carrying the traditional peace offering from the victors to the losers. As a token of consolation, each man must present a drinking coconut to a member of Fat-moon's team.

Putu-nui whooped and gave Matopahu such a hearty slap on the back that it nearly knocked him over.

"Come," said the lesser chief, who could barely contain his glee. "You must make the offering to Fat-moon since yours was the winning arrow." He handed a coconut to Matopahu, who approached the leader of the losing team. Fat-moon glared at him, took the nut from his hands, and threw it in the mud.

Matopahu stared in disbelief as rain mixed with the spilled coconut juice. Putu-nui gave an angry cry, clenching his fist about his bow. Players and spectators alike turned fearfully, eyeing the scene. Wars had started over such insults.

Would Fat-moon and Putu-nui dare break the peace of the gods? Quickly Matopahu interposed himself between the two chiefs before they could confront each other. He turned to Fat-moon and tried to put an ingratiating expression on his face. "I regret," Matopahu said, "that the gift I offered you was not good enough. When you come to visit me in Tahiti, I will give you something far better."

From the corner of his eye, he saw Putu-nui back off, as if the other chief were having second thoughts.

Fat-moon sneered. "In Tahiti, you have nothing. Not a pig. Not even the dung of a pig."

Matopahu refused to be baited. The stakes were too great. "I will have all that was taken from my brother," he answered quietly.

"You have won an archery contest, not a war," Fat-moon retorted. "Do not talk of victories that are not yours."

"Then I will say only that the gods are watching us. This is no time for ill will." He felt someone nudge his arm. It was one of Putu-nui's men. A coconut, among the largest he had ever seen, and already cut open for drinking, was thrust into his hands. He sent a silent prayer to the gods. To Fat-moon he said, "This one is suited for a great chief, is it not? Will you share it with a man who has nothing, only the strength in his arms and the spirit in his body?"

Fat-moon gave no answer. Petulantly he let his gaze scan the crowd, as if he expected to find support for his bad temper. After all, no one alive had ever seen his team beaten. Matopahu sensed the tense feeling of everyone around him. It was unthinkable to break the peace of the gods.

"You are the man who returned from the dead," said Fat-moon grudgingly. "Do not imagine that you will have another day like this one." He extended his hands, and Matopahu delivered the coconut. A chorus of cheers erupted.

"*Maeva ari'i rahi!* Hail the high chief!" came relieved cries from every side.

Matopahu repeated the shout. But as he looked at the faces around him he realized that his victory might be less than it seemed. He had proved his worth before the gods. What if Fat-moon kept him from enjoying the rewards?

EIGHT

As the cheers for the high chief died down, Tepua felt the rain stop. The cloud cover thinned, revealing a glow of sunset in the western sky. In the distance, she saw Matopahu being lifted to the shoulders of his teammates amid new cries of admiration from the crowd.

For an instant she wanted to join the tumultuous throng and add her voice to theirs. How much like a young god he looked, raised up above the eyes of men. She watched the procession as it moved along the course, closer to where she was standing.

With a proud toss of his head Matopahu flung back his hair, sending out a shower of raindrops. The people around him received these droplets with upturned faces, as if basking in his strength and good fortune. Tepua felt a flutter in her throat. The anguished man she had seen on the hillside was gone. This was the true Matopahu.

At his moment of triumph she could not stay away from him. She dashed from cover and lost her footing on the rain-slick ground. Someone caught her, helped her up, and then she was off again, trying to make her way through the people swarming about Matopahu.

One of Fat-moon's guards gave her an ugly look. Another put out his arm to block her way. "No closer, woman!" he ordered.

"Aue!" In frustration and anger, Tepua retreated. What was she thinking? Matopahu and his winning teammates

112

were still wearing their sanctified garments. No women were allowed near them!

She clenched her hands as the procession continued toward the archers' *marae*. She watched the new champion scanning the crowd, turning to admire one beauty after another, never once glancing at her. Later, when he bathed and changed his clothing, he could have all the women he wanted. Being Matopahu, he would probably want them all!

Her joy at his victory drained away. She turned back, no longer caring to watch the tumultuous celebration. Thoughts of Uhi returned to her. The brash young Arioi was undoubtedly looking for her. If she wanted *his* attentions, she would not have to compete with every woman on the island.

But she was not ready for Uhi. Hoping to find how her cousin had fared, she made her way toward the women's archery range. The people she passed asked for news, and she had to proclaim Matopahu's victory again and again.

At last she found Maukiri and embraced her as if they had been separated for weeks. "What is the trouble now?" her cousin asked, peering at her in surprise. "Your man is a hero. You should be happy!"

"He has overcome his curse. Of course, I am glad for him."

"Then why . . ."

Tepua bit her lip and could not answer. It was not reasonable, she knew, to begrudge a man his pleasure. If he wanted other women, why shouldn't he have them?

"Tepua, what are you thinking? He will celebrate his victory, as a man must, but he will not forget you."

"Perhaps . . ."

Maukiri rolled her eyes in mock dismay. "What does it matter if he has a few others? A man is like the plank of a canoe, the more seasoned the better!"

"And you have seasoned enough planks to build the whole canoe!" Tepua glared at her cousin, but admitted to herself that she envied her light and easy affections. Whatever joy she had had from Matopahu inevitably turned to suffering. For too long she had given him all her thoughts and feelings. If she could break free, take an interest in someone else, even Uhi . . .

Maukiri took her hand. "Do not fret about Matopahu. Just enjoy yourself here. I am." She gave a deep, appreciative sniff. "Oooh! I smell the feast cooking. It makes me hungry."

Feeling the rumbles in her own stomach, she let Maukiri lead her, following the crowds, descending the slippery path to the assembly ground. Tepua looked up to see the first star shining in a patch of rose-and-gray sky between the clouds. Below, fires were blazing, welcoming the guests to their repast. She wondered if she could follow Maukiri's advice. At least she could try to enjoy the meal.

Shortly, after a few incantations, the cooks opened the ovens and distributed steaming bundles of fowl, fish, breadfruit, and bananas. Carrying her portions in a simple coconut-frond basket, Tepua passed the high, thatched roofs where the foremost guests dined on pork, albacore, and other delicacies. She happened to catch sight of Pehu-pehu, whose stool sat at the extreme edge of the sheltered area, almost outside. This was not the first time that she had noticed how the Blackleg isolated herself during mealtime. Eating apart from others was considered good manners, as well as protection against sorcery, but this woman carried it to extremes.

Tepua was too hungry now to wonder about the Black-leg's behavior. She joined the Arioi of lower rank who had places outside the shelters. Squatting on her heels, she saw firelight glimmer on coconut cups filled with sauces, on white chunks of fish, on glistening banana leaves.

Fat-moon was certainly not stingy, Tepua admitted to herself as she ate. At last the well-fed guests yawned, patted their stomachs, and looked for places to sleep. Temporary palm-leaf huts had been put up for the lesser visitors. These accommodations were no better than those on the *motu,* but she was too weary to complain. She stretched out on a mat and quickly fell asleep. . . .

Boom-boom-boom. Tepua's eyes opened, but she was not really awake. She rolled over on her side, pillowing her cheek on her hand. *Boom.* Moonlight lit the sand outside the shelter. Faint shadows flitted across the ground. Feet ran by. *Boom-boom-boom.* She poked her head out and saw people hurrying toward the assembly ground.

In the clear sky hung a moon just past fullness, a moon that always brought men and women together. Half the night was over. She knew that no one who could stagger, walk, or crawl would be sleeping through the rest.

Tepua refused to stay here alone while everyone else was dancing. She wound her new bark-cloth wrap around her, repaired the garland she had worn earlier, and found a flower to put behind her ear.

When had she last danced under such a moon? No, that was too long ago, and far off; she refused to think about it. Now her feet suddenly felt light as she hastened toward the beat of the drum. She breathed in the rich night air, full of scents from blossoms and sweet ferns. Around her she heard snatches of conversation in excited, high-pitched voices.

Fires of coconut shells and dry palm fronds were blazing, but the moon cast as much light as anyone needed. All over the assembly ground, people had gathered in clusters to dance. Above the drumming sounded the sweet, high tones of the nose flute. Tepua stopped in a small clearing and looked around, wondering if she would find Maukiri or Curling-leaf. . . .

"There you are, my elusive beauty." She frowned as she heard Uhi's voice behind her. "Landing you will take the patience of a fisherman!"

She turned, and her frown began to vanish. In the moonlight the young Arioi looked taller, more impressive than she remembered. His chest gleamed with coconut oil. When he approached, she saw that he had woven shiny crimson seeds into his hair and topped it all with a fine display of feathers.

Pleased and flattered by his appearance, Tepua did not resist when his warm hand closed on hers and he began to lead her toward a group of local Arioi. She had seen some of these men and women perform; they were among the best dancers of Eimeo.

The performers were in couples, face-to-face, dancing brilliantly. The men clapped their knees together with blurring speed. They lunged and stamped, the firelight glowing on their tattooed calves and thighs. They moved with inhuman grace and energy, springing from the ground in impossibly high leaps.

The women glided back and forth so lightly that they did not seem to move on legs, but floated like ghosts or goddesses. Their hips rotated smoothly; their hands wove entrancing patterns against the moonlight.

Tepua watched, torn between a longing to join in and a feeling that, good as she was, she had not reached their level. Even if Oro seized her . . .

No. She had no intention of losing herself to divine frenzy now. She wondered if she could pray that the god *not* take her.

Uhi pulled insistently at her hand.

"We need not get so close to those people," she protested.

"Do not be modest," he answered. "I have heard a few things about you, Tepua-mua."

She was startled to hear her name, for she certainly had not given it to him.

"Everyone knows how you danced for Chipped-rock Lodge," he added. "My friends are eager to welcome you."

For my inspired dancing? Or because I defied First-to-crow? Tepua had no chance to ask. The powerful drumming and the haunting trill of the flute were getting into her.

Uhi lifted his arms and began to dance, his feet treading the rhythm against the sandy ground. His arms swayed, his fingers stroked the air, his hands clenched, swelling the muscles in his arms and shoulders. A shudder of excitement went through Tepua. She found herself swaying with the rhythm of the drum.

Willing, now, to display herself for his friends, she turned from Uhi, rolling her hips and keeping time with her fingers. But she refused to get close to him, gliding away whenever he tried to approach her.

"You are a sly, twisting eel of a woman," he shouted at her. "But I will have you anyway."

Uhi redoubled the energy of his dance. His eyes, hot with desire, were fixed on her. She felt her own response, a pulse of warm excitement shooting down her belly into the nest between her legs.

A deep voice called from the crowd, "Uhi! You brag that you can spear any fish on the reef. How about that one?"

Matopahu became a distant flutter on the edge of Tepua's thoughts as she watched the young Arioi flaunt his strength and agility. She let her eyes rove down his body, marveling at the way his stomach muscles rippled above the low-slung band of his loincloth.

If anyone seized her tonight, he would not be Oro. Unless the god was hiding within the body of this handsome young Arioi. . . .

She laughed invitingly, threw back her head, and extended her arms to Uhi. From half-closed eyes, she watched delight break over his face.

"Now I have you, wild little fish," he crowed, dancing closer. The intoxicating aroma of his scent wafted around her.

While the other guests slept off the huge meal, Matopahu went out alone for a walk along the shoreline. He listened to the restless rumble of waves washing over the reef and felt the cool, wet sand between his toes. A sense of triumph still clung to him. The victory was his, despite the ugly scene afterward.

But Fat-moon's words still echoed. "You have won an archery contest, not a war." Now Matopahu knew he would be a welcome guest at the houses of many chiefs. Whether anyone would agree to help him, he could not say.

And what of Tepua? He stared into the clear, moonlit water, barely noticing the tiny fish in the shallows. He pictured Tepua's face at the moment he had flung her away from him—her look of bewilderment and hurt. She had not understood that he was only protecting her. What would his victory mean if she was lost to him now?

For a long time he brooded. Eye-to-heaven had spoken with her recently, but had come away with no insight into her feelings. Perhaps it had been wrong to send his *taio* to speak with her. He should have gone himself. Ah, but then he might have lost the power that the gods had granted him—the power that he had shown in the *te'a* match.

At last, sitting in the lee of a pandanus grove, he dozed off. When he awoke, the faint sound of drumming from afar told him that the night's festivities were far from over. *And I am a man again,* he thought with satisfaction.

He retraced his steps slowly, pausing now and then to toss a bit of coral into the water and watch the ripples spread. He still did not know what he would say to Tepua. With other women, he had never had to say anything—it was enough to beckon.

At last he reached Fat-moon's assembly ground, which stood a short distance from the shore. Against the firelight he saw silhouettes of dancers, men and women, moving with graceful rhythm. Not only Arioi were here. Many local people had come to join the fun. Children were dancing, too, imitating the steps of their elders.

Matopahu watched with amusement as two young girls showed how rapidly they could wiggle their hips. Then a pair of boys even younger joined them, flapping knees and elbows until tears of mirth rolled down the onlookers' faces. Still laughing, Matopahu moved on, trying to keep to the shadows. He did not care to be recognized now, drawing crowds of admirers that would keep him from Tepua.

Then he saw her, dancing with a young Arioi called Uhi. Despite her simple costume, she looked as lithe and beautiful as when he had first seen her. Every movement was perfect. He stood for a moment enjoying the sight of her graceful arms and supple waist. Her gaze seemed focused on her Arioi partner; she did not seem to notice Matopahu.

Matopahu had the unaccustomed feeling of not knowing what to do next. If she were an ordinary woman, he might simply charge in, lift her from the ground, and bear her away to a secluded refuge. He felt perspiration gathering beneath the crown of aromatic ferns on his brow. He was the hero of the day, a man who could have whatever he wanted, yet here was a prize he could not carry off.

Matopahu's skills at dancing were no match for those of

the best Arioi. It did not matter. Soon all eyes would turn to him, including those of the one he sought. Remaining in the shadows, he slowly limbered up.

As soon as he stepped out into the light, a cry went up from the other dancers. Women abandoned their partners to cluster about him. Their eyes shone as they put on their best displays. He danced easily, facing each in turn, trying his best to favor no one.

The scents of their flowers and their warm bodies filled his nostrils. Lovely shapes enticed him. Each young woman seemed to beckon subtly with a nod or a movement of her eyes. Each one, he knew, would be glad to have whatever he offered—a quick embrace beneath the trees or a longer encounter in some private place. The possibilities, after his long forced abstinence, made his head swim.

Tepua leaned forward, expecting to be caught up in Uhi's embrace, but instead the young Arioi seemed to want to savor his impending conquest.

He stepped back and kept dancing. "Let everyone see us together," he crowed. "Let my friends know what a fine one I have caught!"

"You do not have me yet," she answered back.

"You are hooked," he countered, laughing scornfully. "I need only pull in my line." Around him, his companions had gathered to cheer him on.

"She dances well," they shouted. "Imagine how she will wriggle on the end of your spear."

Tepua wondered if Uhi was right after all. Desire was weighting her breasts, sending heat low, beneath her belly, and streaking fiery traces down her thighs.

Once more, she thought. Once more and then . . .

With an effort of will she broke away from him and fled across the dancing ground. He gave a cry, a mixture of a triumphant shout and an angry roar, and dashed after her.

Matopahu danced within a circle of lovely young women, yet each time one caught his eye and he started to move toward her, something held him back, and he turned to another.

None of these women would do, he realized. Not tonight, when he was filled with triumph and the blessing of the gods. There was only one woman who could share this with him. If only he could get away and search for her.

If he found her now, she would surely forgive him the harsh words he had spoken. . . .

As Tepua ran across the dancing ground, keeping just ahead of Uhi, she saw a cluster of excited young women. And in their midst, bathing in their admiration, was the champion of the day. She froze in midstep, almost losing her balance.

Matopahu had been here all along! She tried to tell herself that it did not matter.

The Arioi youth caught up with her, but she evaded his clutch. Instead she started dancing more wildly than ever, forcing her gaze away from Matopahu.

She had seen enough. The young beauties surrounding Matopahu filled her with contempt. These women had cared nothing about him when he fell into disgrace. Now they came to him like flying fish leaping at torchlight.

Trying to turn her attention back to Uhi, she danced on, yet she sensed Matopahu watching her. I will not look at him, she told herself. When, at last, she did glance toward him, she could not read the expression in his eyes. *Is he taunting me? I need no proof of his manhood.*

She spun around. When she turned back again, she saw that he had broken out of the circle of young women and was coming toward her. She heard the disbelieving cries of the abandoned lovelies.

"Is he leaving us for that coral-island girl?"

"What can he see in her? She hasn't even been fattened!"

In a last, exasperated effort to make him notice them, several girls pelted him with flowered garlands. The garlands fell, unheeded.

Tepua saw Uhi move to block Matopahu's approach. Uhi changed his step to an Arioi prance, mimicking the proud strutting of a Blackleg before an audience, or a cock fowl before its rival.

Dismay fought with excitement in Tepua's stomach. Uhi was not going to yield easily, even to the winner of the sacred game. Tepua saw Matopahu's brows rise in astonishment. For an agonizing instant, she feared he would turn away. Instead he folded his arms with exaggerated patience.

"You are wanted over there," he said to Uhi, gesturing with his head toward the knot of beauties he had left.

"I prefer the company of this woman," Uhi replied. "Because you were lucky with an arrow, do not think you can win every contest."

The two men now stood facing each other, nostrils flared, crouching slightly as if preparing to do battle. Eyes were starting to turn, whispers to run among the gathering.

Tepua got between Uhi and Matopahu. "There can be no fighting here," she said fiercely. "We are under the sanction of Oro-of-the-laid-down-spear. If you fight, I will have neither of you."

"Then choose between us," said Uhi, snarling a grimace at Matopahu.

The contest was starting to become the center of attention. People stopped dancing to watch.

"It is that coral-island girl," she heard them mutter. "She makes men crazy. Why get angry over a woman?"

Exactly, Tepua thought, with a snap of irritation. "We are here to enjoy ourselves, not to quarrel," she said to the two rivals. "Both of you, dance with me."

Before either man could object, she launched once again into the flurry of motion driven by the drumbeat. Uhi was the first to react. Cupping his right elbow in his left hand, he struck his chest defiantly with his open palm. She whirled to face him as the booming slap of his challenge rang out.

Her tension gave her new energy as she stamped on the hard-packed earth and rolled her hips. Uhi matched her pace, adding repeated chest-slaps as taunts to Matopahu. He kick-stepped, throwing out his arms and legs to display his Arioi tattoos.

She watched through narrowed eyes. The same attraction that had drawn her to him was working again, warming her. . . .

Matopahu was suddenly dancing behind Tepua. She did not need to look to sense his presence. Now she was between the two men, as each strove to outdo the other. Uhi, without question, was the more spectacular dancer. But Tepua could not help turning to face his rival.

Matopahu was answering Uhi's chest-slaps with a lunge and stamp of his own. The cords of his neck stood out and his face was grimly determined. The fierce blaze in his eyes startled Tepua. The sheen of his copper skin was sweat, not scented oil, but it made him look harder, tighter, more controlled.

The tickles of anticipation that had been running up and down her thighs became burning tracks as her gaze traveled across Matopahu's shoulders and chest. She remembered the heat of that skin, how it felt beneath her fingers. She remembered pressing herself against the full length of his body.

Tepua speeded up her dance, turned to Uhi, forced him to match it, turned back to Matopahu, and did the same. Sweat was pouring from the bodies of the two men. Now the drums were following her pace, but she asked for a faster beat.

She could hear each man's harsh panting as she challenged him in turn. Uhi's friends were clapping, urging him on. Her ribs were heaving, her breath burning, but the fire of the dance consumed all else.

Would she lose them both at once? Uhi was staying with her, but she heard a sharp whistling note in his breathing. Matopahu also looked drained, yet he wouldn't give up. She suddenly knew that he would burst his heart before he faltered. This was no mere love game to him.

Abruptly Uhi stumbled, caught himself, grimaced in disgust, and staggered aside. *"Aue!"* he gasped at Matopahu while gesturing at Tepua. "Send this one back to the atolls before she dances us to death!" Then, surrounded by his friends, he disappeared into the crowd.

Matopahu looked at her, barely able to register the triumph over his rival. "Have you not had enough, woman," he rasped, "or are you really trying to kill me?"

She lowered her lashes. "The moon is still high."

With a bellow, Matopahu seized her by the waist and flung her over his shoulder. She beat her fists against his back.

Once.

NINE

Tepua squirmed impatiently against Matopahu's grip, yet she did not try to break free. The excitement rising from the dance remained with her, growing stronger. Her breasts were pressed against him, her nipples tingling with every step he took.

"Here!" she cried out as he strode through a moonlit glade. "We have gone far enough. Put me down."

"I know a better place." He laughed and carried her on, reaching a steep slope, brushing through foliage as he began to climb. Cool, moist leaves stroked her arms and back as he ascended.

Where had he found the strength to haul her off like this? She thought the dancing had exhausted him, but here he was, bounding up a hillside in the moonlight.

"How much farther?" she asked.

"You will see," he said gaily. "The game began on your ground, Arioi dancer, and now we are on mine. We are going where no one will interrupt us."

The smell and feel of him was all around her, filling her, intoxicating her. Every part of her body was prickling with desire. She had been separated from Matopahu for more than ten moons. She had almost forgotten the effect he had on her.

"Let me down, you cliff-climber!" The words caught in her throat as she glimpsed where he was heading. Now the way was so steep that he needed his free hand to pull himself up. The terrain had grown rough, with scrubby trees growing from outcrops and boulders. High above she saw moonlight shimmering on a mossy face of rock. Was he really taking her up there?

"Hang on," he called out, and she felt the lurches as he hoisted himself from one handhold to the next. She might have been a roll of *tapa* flung across his shoulder; her weight did not seem to impede him at all.

"I can climb on my own," she protested, but he took no heed. One look at the drop below made her decide not to struggle. The sense of danger added another thrill to those already coursing through her. Wrapping her arms more tightly around his neck, she prayed to Tapahi-roro-ariki that he did not lose his grip.

At last, with a grunt, Matopahu heaved her off his shoulder and set her on a ledge of stone. "You do not have to climb," he said. "Only walk a short way. We are nearly there."

She looked out and saw how moonlight painted the plain below in haunting shades of silver and shadowed green. The celebration fires still burned, seeming no larger or brighter than candlenut lamps.

"Hina's road is open tonight," Matopahu said softly, extending his hand toward the moon. The abode of the night goddess hung above the distant horizon, at the end of a shimmering path of light. He brought his hand around, caressed the angle of Tepua's jaw, then tipped her face up to his.

"If I shot an arrow up there," he whispered, lifting a hand to the sky, "I think the gods would catch it."

She closed her eyes and leaned into his embrace, feeling her nose meet and press against his. A warm, wide streak of longing grew as she felt his nose sliding back and forth against hers, their upper lips just brushing.

How rich the perfume of his maleness was, dominating even the strongest floral scents that suffused the night. How silky his skin felt. Her fingers glided over it, feeling the unique molding of muscle and limb.

Deep in her loins she felt something heavy, warm, yet empty and demanding to be filled. She moved closer to him, wishing she could stay this way, wanting never to open her eyes.

"Come," he said softly. "We are almost there. Just a short way more."

The pleasant sound of a waterfall splashing rose above the chirp and trill of night insects. Tepua followed Matopahu through the languid night, her hand warmed by his. Another turn and twist of the trail brought her the sight of a silvery cascade soaring from above the trees. As they drew nearer, Tepua saw the shape of the moon rippling against the falling water.

The cascade's song grew muted as Matopahu led her around a bend. At last they reached his destination, a grotto whose mouth was cupped by a rough balcony of rock and whose cleft lay open to the sky. Here was a fine shelter from the cool night air.

"This is my little niche," Matopahu said, the grotto making his voice resonant and sending a shiver down Tepua's back. "When I was young, my father used to take me on visits to this island. While he conferred with chiefs, I went out climbing. One day I found this hideaway."

Tepua peered into the opening. "It reminds me of someplace else."

"In the highlands of Tahiti? Yes," he said thoughtfully. "I remember that, too. Now, come, help me find soft leaves for a bed."

Tepua enjoyed the warm recollections. How long ago that other time seemed. As she joined Matopahu in gathering ferns from the sides of the rocks, she recalled how she had spent a night with him in that other cave—the first night they had been together.

The memories lingered as she finished covering the grotto floor with fragrant, springy ferns. Then she watched Matopahu stretch out in the rock-sheltered nest, his eyes inviting. Moonlight filtering into the grotto gleamed on the planes of his chest, sculpted the muscles of his belly, and played down his long sinewy thighs.

"So many moons have passed," he said with a sigh. "Every time I saw Hina's beauty, I thought of yours. I prayed to my ancestors to keep you safe and bring you back to me."

"Perhaps they did hear you," she answered dreamily. Her fingers touched him gently, moving down the firmness of his belly, coming to rest where his *maro* was tied. He raised his hips, allowing her to unwind the loincloth and toss it aside. Her breasts felt aglow as she removed her own wrap and laid herself on top of him.

"Tepua," he said softly, as his arms circled her, rocking her gently. "Today, after my victory, I could think about no other woman. I only wanted to find you. Is this some trick of the gods?"

"To make us desire only each other?"

"Yes."

"Perhaps it is your punishment. For wanting too many different women before you found me."

He laughed. "And are you being punished for the same reason? You came to me knowing nothing of love!"

"Nothing?"

"Very little," he conceded.

"Aue!" She felt dizzy from desiring him. Her heartbeat seemed as loud to her as a mallet pounding bark-cloth against a board. He reached up and stroked her softly, making her feel as warm and full of light as Hina herself. The longing inside was more than she could bear.

Slowly he caressed her, sliding his warm hands up behind her knees and along the insides of her thighs. His fingers played over the mounds of her buttocks, moving higher, igniting whatever they touched. She heard him breathing deeply as his palms pressed warmly against her back. Then his fingers slipped around, working gently, massaging the sides of her breasts. She lifted herself, allowing his thumbs to slip under and caress the hardness of her nipples.

Tepua gasped with pleasure and wriggled against him. Once more she felt his hands behind her knees again, slowly moving higher. His hardness pushed against her, and she thought she could not endure any more delay. But Matopahu only sighed in his joy of holding her close to him.

"You are my only *vahine*," he said. "I am glad that I want no other." She felt him touch her breasts again, revolving his thumbs around each nipple, and now she felt mad with longing. She sensed his own excitement matching hers. How could he stand any more of this teasing?

As if in answer to her question, she felt his silky spear begin to slide into her. Crying with relief, she pushed herself up on his chest, arching her back until her legs lifted from his, and the only meeting point of their bodies was the glowing center of pleasure. She started to rock herself on that upthrust spear, letting it enter her more deeply. She felt the pulsations within the hardness of his flesh, heard him groan with delight. A new fire began to spread, coursing outward to her belly, her thighs, her breasts. The searing crests came faster, each more intense than the last.

A brightness surrounded her until she could see nothing else. Then she heard the great laugh of joy that she had heard only once before. *Oro!* He had spoken to her when she danced, but he had made her forget his words. Now she heard his voice again. "You are promised to a mortal man. I will be there when he comes to you."

Then she understood that she had both Oro and Matopahu inside her, joining her in ecstasy. She heard a voice that must have been her own, a cry of triumph or joy or pain, she could not say which. The light exploded, sending her into spasms, wave upon wave, lifting her to the sky. Then she was truly the goddess of the moon, sailing across the stars.

"Muriroa ana hoki, te matangi . . ."

Matopahu roused slowly from the deepest sleep he had ever known. Nearby a woman was singing softly, in a sweet haunting voice that blended against the music of the waterfall.

The flutter of an eyelash touched his cheek. His hands, groping in the dark, met smooth, warm skin. They traveled up, feeling the form of slender ribs, then the soft underside of a breast that felt firm as a ripe fruit. . . .

She met his hand with her own, then sang again.

"E ho ake taku aro, e he to au e!"

He blinked with wonder at how her voice brought beauty to words that were so foreign to his ears. With a sigh that was half amazement, half annoyance, he said, "You know I cannot understand that atoll language of yours."

He heard a quiet laugh. Her fingers played about his chest as she repeated the lines in his own tongue.

> A pleasant breeze was stirring
> When I lay beside him, overcome. . . .

Matopahu drew her to him, buried his face in the sweet warmth of her belly. His voice muffled, he said, "You were not the only one overcome."

"Then something remarkable did happen," she replied mysteriously. "I remember, long ago, how you used to fall into a trance."

He hesitated, wondering what she was hinting at. Before the curse fell on him, Matopahu had been known as a favorite of the gods. Sometimes a spirit seized him, spoke through his lips, even took control of his body, leaving him afterward with no memory of what had occurred. But nothing of the kind had happened since his brother's death. "Last night, I was myself," he declared happily. "I am happy to say that I recall every moment."

She began to sing again.

> "Like a scented fern,
> Bending over me,
> He whispered sweetly. . . ."

"I was more than a fern," Matopahu said with a laugh, clasping his hands behind his back.

Light fingers descended on his lips, pressing them gently together. She sang,

> "Like a coconut palm,
> Bending over me . . ."

"That is better," he answered. "Where did you get that song?"

"It was sung long ago by a woman of my islands to a

chief of Tahiti. The words were in my head when I woke
up."

He let his hand stray to her thigh and then ran his fingers
gently along it.

"My scented fern . . . My coconut palm . . ." Her
voice was soft in the darkness.

"Mmm?"

"Will you bend over me?"

From the coolness and crispness of the air wafting over
his skin, Matopahu knew that dawn had arrived. There
seemed to be a fresh new note in the sound of the falls and
the birds that called through the trees.

He lay with his arms about Tepua, his eyes closed, feeling
sated and blissful. Yes, there was a certain newness in the air
today. Perhaps the gods were telling him in another way that
his strength had returned—by hinting that now he might
have a son.

Tepua had always insisted that her dedication to the Arioi
was more important than having children. Yet perhaps, now,
she might relent. The thought made him shiver. He cradled
the woman beside him as if she were the newborn babe he
so wished to hold. Should he tell her what he felt? No. If it
was true, she would find out for herself.

What was it to be a woman? he wondered, feeling an odd
twinge of envy. What was it like to have a new life growing
inside? To have a belly as great as a chief's, yet holding
something far more precious than taro or breadfruit?

He was starting to drift into sleep again when he felt her
stirring. He let his arms go lax, but kept his eyes closed,
curious about what she would do now. Sing him another
song again? Caress him in an exotic way? She was Tepua,
but she was not the same girl who had left him. Everything
she did now seemed new and exciting.

Yes, she was up to something, he thought as he felt her
rise up to look at him. He was tempted to peek, but kept his
eyes closed. He wanted to feel, not see, what she would do.

Her face was coming near his. Ah, the warmth, the
fragrant moist breath. His limp member stirred, anticipating
the next sweet encounter.

Her nose brushed across his cheek, but it was her lips that came actively seeking his. *Lips?* And her tongue, wiggling like a little eel, was playing about the side of this mouth.

He jerked his head back, away from the unfamiliar touch, but not before the velvety tip of her tongue sent a strange warm shock running down his belly, making his manhood twitch.

No, this was not right! The mouth was where food went, a pathway for *mana.* He hitched himself up on his elbows, guarding his face with the back of his hand. "What . . . what did you do?"

She was sitting on her heels before him in the faint dawn light, her head cocked to one side, her hair draped over her breast, her lips slightly parted. "You did not like that?" she asked, glancing down. "Your eel likes it."

Matopahu stared at her, the echo of that strange sensation still running through his body. Something in him wanted her to do it again, but something else remained wary. Perhaps the act was not *tapu,* but it was certainly new to him. "Why this strange caress?" he asked. "Is it some trick from your savage island?"

He felt uneasy, although he could not say why. It was almost as if something different, foreign, was trying to intrude on his happiness. His muscles tightened as if to spring to the defense . . . against what?

"Tepua . . ." He reached out and caught her hand, his thoughts turning to disturbing possibilities. "What happened when you went home? What kind of men did you find there?"

"I wanted to tell you," she answered quietly. "But there was no chance."

He waited, not sure if he cared to hear. Her voice carried a dreamy quality as she continued. "It seems so long ago now. Outsiders came to our atoll, men with sun-darkened faces and pale bodies beneath their peculiar clothing. They learned some of our ways and taught us a few of their own."

"Yes?" He gripped her arm, waiting uneasily for the rest. The dawn light was growing stronger, and Matopahu thought he saw her color slightly.

"The first time I felt the mouth kiss, I pulled away," she

said, "just as you did. But I began to like it. I thought you would, too."

He felt a disturbing mixture of emotions. His delight in her was still strong, and the thought that she had meant to please him added to his affection. Yet her confession made him wonder. Had Tepua lain with one of these strangers? No. He had no right to question her or to be angry if she had. Everyone understood that men and women separated from each other took new partners.

The past must be forgotten, he told himself. Irritably, he tried to put aside his objections to her new form of *hanihani*.

"Matopahu, I did not mean for this to trouble you. You looked so happy only a short while ago."

"If you lie down beside me, you will bring the happiness back again." Obediently she curled up next to him. They rested in silence, listening to the sounds of the world waking to a new day.

"How long did the strangers stay on your island?" Matopahu asked.

Tepua gave a restless sigh, as if she wished to end the discussion. "You do not have to outdance another rival. I told you the men are gone."

"I am curious, that is all. I've heard tales about strangers from afar, and the impossible vessels that carry them. You are the only person I know who has actually seen such people."

"If they had stayed with us only one day, it would have been too long," she began. "I admit that I had affection for one of the men. He was kind, and even beautiful in a foreign way. He could not help the harm that he and his friend did to my people. In the end, we had to send them both away, back to their home island."

Matopahu lay quietly, his arms about her. Something in her voice told him of the pain she had endured, an experience that had steadied and matured her. He sensed that she would not tell him the full story yet, but perhaps in time . . .

The stranger, whoever he was, might be gone now, but he had left his trace. Tepua had departed Tahiti still a girl in spirit and had come back fully a woman. Matopahu wondered whether he should praise or curse this unknown, unnamed rival. Perhaps both.

He stirred, growing restless as the air in the grotto warmed. His affection for her was not damped, but now he felt a certain ambivalence. The blissful contentment was gone, the spell of the grotto vanishing in the brightening daylight.

He sighed at the loss. The night had been so sweet. Who knew when there would be another like it?

His thoughts turned to the troubles in his home district. He wondered whether he would ever be able to drive out the usurper. If not, would Tepua join him in perpetual exile? He could not ask her that yet.

He held her a brief while longer, until she reminded him that she would be missed by the leaders of her troupe. She arranged her wrap and tidied her hair. "This time you won't carry me," she insisted. "Show me the handholds and I will *climb* all the way down."

TEN

Tepua returned to the Arioi encampment, her skin still tingling from Matopahu's touch. The grass was wet with dew and soothing under her feet. She approached her shelter quietly, expecting her companions to be asleep after the previous night's late dancing.

To her surprise she saw yawning women crawling from under the coconut palm lean-tos. The stout figure of Pehu-pehu passed by, her voice calling cheerfully as she roused the ones still drowsing. "Canoes are waiting," the Blackleg kept announcing. "Everyone out!"

Canoes? Tepua did not understand. Then the Blackleg noticed her. "You look wide-awake," Pehu-pehu said, grabbing her arm firmly, almost painfully. "Good. You can make sure the others don't dawdle. Get them down to the beach. Hurry!"

Tepua blinked and watched the Blackleg hustle off to the next cluster of shelters. "Is someone eager to get rid of us?" she asked of no one in particular. "I thought we were to stay a few days."

"We are off to Tahiti," answered one of the younger Arioi.

"Tahiti!" Tepua's mouth fell open in surprise and dismay. "We just left not long ago."

"We have an invitation to go back," someone else explained. "To entertain another chief. Someone friendlier than Tutaha."

"But . . . Land-crab . . ."

134

"We will stay away from our old district," said the first girl. She lowered her voice to a whisper. "No one knows what Head-lifted is planning. Do not be surprised if he sends a banana shoot to Land-crab."

A token of peace. Tepua groaned at the thought that her troupe might reconcile its differences with the usurper. But there was a chance that the new chief they were visiting might take her side, and help drive Land-crab out. . . .

The sudden change in plans made her thoughts swim. Matopahu was expecting to see her later in the day. What would he think when he discovered that she had vanished without a parting word?

The other women were heading for the beach. Tepua glanced about wildly, hoping she might somehow delay the departure or find a way to send Matopahu a message. At last, she saw Curling-leaf.

"Tepua," said her friend, "I watched you dance with Uhi last night. Did you and Matopahu quarrel? I was not sure."

Tepua answered happily. "I think that all is well between us. But now . . ." She took a deep breath. "I need your help."

Curling-leaf's smile lit up her plain features as she walked beside her friend. "Yes. Anything."

"We thought we would have a few days together. When he looks for me, I'll be gone." She sighed regretfully, seeing that the pebbled shore lay just ahead. Other members of the troupe were already wading out to the large double hulls, their *tapa* garments tucked up above their knees.

Why such haste? Tepua asked herself again. If only she could stay a short while longer.

"I know what to do," Curling-leaf said with a sly smile. She halted suddenly, clutching her stomach. Then she doubled up in apparent agony. "*Aue!* The fish I ate last night is trying to jump out of my belly."

The ruse had its effect. People clustered around Curling-leaf. In a moment, Tepua knew, Pehu-pehu would arrive and begin to shout orders.

"Go find him!" Curling-leaf whispered to Tepua, pushing her away before they were both surrounded by curious onlookers. "I will be here awhile, until this pain leaves me. One canoe will have to wait."

As Tepua neared Fat-moon's fenced compound she saw servants coming and going through the gate. She caught up with a young woman who was carrying a section of giant bamboo filled with water. "Will you take a message to Matopahu?" Tepua pleaded.

The serving woman eyed her with curiosity. "The archery champion is not inside," she said with a toss of her head. "You will find him at the stream."

Tepua rushed off, caring nothing now about who might see her. Why should she care if people took her for the champion's plaything? The gods had given her a single night with Matopahu, and now they were sending her away.

She found him sitting on the streambank, his feet trailing in the slow-moving water. Droplets beaded on the sunlit copper of his skin. He looked as fresh and new as the young grass sprouting above the bank. Damp black curls tumbled down the back of his neck, inviting playful fingers to twine in them.

As Matopahu caught sight of her, the dark brown of his eyes lit up, revealing flecks of amber and gold. The remembered glow of *hanihani* filled Tepua again.

"I thought you would sleep late," he said amiably. His words were casual, but the resonant undertone in his voice and the look in his eyes were definitely not. "I was not planning to search for you until the *tiare* blossoms opened."

He pulled her close to him, wrapped her in strong, warm arms. His skin was moist and silky from his bath. She shivered with delight as he pressed his nose to her cheek, and wished she could slip away with him again to the secluded nest beside the waterfall.

"I will be gone long before that," she said, her voice thick with misery. "My troupe is going back to Tahiti."

He stiffened. "To which district?"

"I haven't heard. But Pehu-pehu seems happy about it."

Matopahu raised his eyebrows, showing his suspicions.

"I think I know what's coming," she told him hotly.

"Head-lifted will take us on tour. Meanwhile he'll be sending gifts and flattering words to Land-crab."

She broke off as growing bitterness sharpened her voice. This was not the right time for such anger. She paused, looking up into Matopahu's face. "What will happen to you?"

"If I have any hope of reclaiming what my brother lost, I must stay here in Eimeo. Putu-nui now owes me a lot. If I can get help anywhere, it will be here."

"Is there no one in Tahiti who might support you?"

Matopahu sighed. "So far, I have been turned away by everyone I approached. Putu-nui is my best hope."

Tepua felt her spirits sink. She laid her head against Matopahu's chest as his fingers gently stroked her shoulder and back.

"Then that is all. . . ."

"Do not be angry," he chided.

"I am not angry at you. The Arioi pull me one way and my feelings for you another."

His arms tightened about her. "Would you leave the troupe?" he asked incredulously.

She took a deep breath. "You know I cannot. My influence counts for something. If I can keep us from returning to Land-crab, his position will weaken. But if the troupe returns to him, who will doubt that he is the rightful chief?"

"Is that your only reason for staying with the Arioi?" He looked at her sharply.

She knew what he wanted her to say—that if Matopahu destroyed the usurper, she would give up the Arioi to become his wife and bear his children. "I serve Oro-of-the-laid-down-spear," she whispered.

"Do not forget that there are Arioi *fanaunau*."

Tepua looked away and did not reply. Of course there were members who left the troupe and had families— suffering ever afterward the scorn of the others. Never again could they take part in Arioi rites. Never again could they serve Oro-of-the-laid-down-spear.

He touched her gently. "Let us not talk about this now. There are too many other troubles ahead of us."

She closed her eyes and pressed her face to the moist, fragrant warmth of his chest, not wanting to leave his embrace. She did not want to pull away. "The canoe is waiting," she said. "You stay here. I must go."

His arms loosened. "We will find each other again, soon. Then we will not be torn apart so easily."

"Yes," Tepua whispered, letting her fingers trail down his chest as she drew away. She heard doubt in his voice that all his charm could not hide.

Then she was hurrying down the trail, seeing everything through a blur. When she was safely away, she paused and wiped her eyes. Now was no time for weeping. Hurriedly she glanced around, studying the small vines and saplings sprouting at the edge of a sunny clearing. Curling-leaf's charade would be more convincing if someone had gone to gather curing herbs. Trying not to think about Matopahu, Tepua snatched up a handful of leaves.

When she arrived at the shore, Pehu-pehu was standing over Curling-leaf, who had managed to sustain her grimaces and groans. Tepua's friend sat on a log with her hands still pressed to her stomach. "I brought a remedy," shouted Tepua, holding up her leaves.

Pehu-pehu tore Tepua's collection from her hands and threw it to the ground. "There you are again, never where you're supposed to be," she said harshly. "What do you know of cures? I have a healer coming. Get into the canoe and wait."

Curling-leaf let out a gut-rending moan that sounded more than convincing. Tepua knew that her friend would have to go through with the performance. She could not stage a sudden recovery now, or Pehu-pehu would catch on to the trick. Curling-leaf would have to swallow whatever foul potion the healer brought her.

I know why she is groaning so loudly, Tepua thought. *The healer's dose will probably really make her sick. I could not have a better friend.*

By late afternoon the players had settled into new quarters, in a Tahitian district that lay south of their own. From the shore, Eimeo was visible on the horizon, a brooding mass of dark peaks topped by clouds. Gazing at the sight did not help Tepua's sense of loss. She wondered how long Matopahu would have to remain there. When he did return to Tahiti, he might not be able find her.

"Walk with me," came a voice from behind.

Tepua turned and saw Aitofa standing deep within a grove of breadfruit trees. The Arioi chiefess beckoned. Tepua tried to bring her thoughts back to the problems at hand.

"You are my eyes and ears," Aitofa said in a low voice as they continued through the grove.

"Yes." With a sigh, Tepua recalled her earlier discussions with Aitofa. The Blackleg had explained her difficulties in preserving the troupe. Only Chipped-rock Lodge had offered assistance. Aitofa had accepted the plan to exchange members as a way to establish the needed bond of friendship, but she had not been told in advance that a rival female Blackleg would be sent to her own troupe.

"I see the worst side of Pehu-pehu," Tepua said. "She always singles me out for criticism. With everyone else, she is patient and good-natured."

"Then she is gathering her strength," said Aitofa grimly. "She cannot take your position."

"In time, maybe she can. I think that is what Head-lifted wants. Then he can say he has rid himself of the troublemaker, the one who tried to shame Land-crab."

"It was not just you!" Tepua answered indignantly.

"The others may give up their opposition to Land-crab. Life in exile wears us all down."

"And Pehu-pehu is always working against us, undermining our resolve. She cares nothing about the people of our district."

"Do not speak too quickly, Tepua. Neither of us understands her yet."

"I know why she was glad to leave her own troupe. Too many Blacklegs. She had no chance of becoming a lodge chief. Now she wants what is yours."

"Perhaps ambition is not all that drives her."

"Not all?" Tepua stared at the Arioi chiefess.

"The other lodges think that we are harming the good

name of the Arioi. I have heard this opinion from several people."

"Pehu-pehu is doing nothing about that."

Aitofa frowned. "You may not think she is helping. I know that she wants to preserve the reputation of Arioi as loyal supporters of the tribal chiefs. She will try to push us back to Land-crab even if she gains nothing for herself."

"Then we are both in her way," Tepua replied hotly, "and there are others." She walked on, clenching her fist in anger, as she named Arioi whose sentiments against the usurper had not softened. Yet she had seen too many of these women clustered eagerly about Pehu-pehu, courting her friendship. . . .

That night, Tepua had difficulty falling asleep. The guest house was warm and dry, a pleasant improvement from what she had known on Eimeo, yet too many worries kept her awake. She kept tossing, feeling every lump in the cushion of grass between her mat and the dirt floor.

She tried to soothe herself by remembering the night with Matopahu. How odd, she thought, that images of Uhi kept pushing the pleasant ones aside. In truth, she had cared nothing for that arrogant dancer. She had been drawn to him for one reason alone—curiosity about his unusual sunshade.

Matopahu . . . Uhi . . . Aitofa. The night on Taharaa Hill. Images swirled, bringing foreign faces and the ship with wings. She remembered the weapons that spat stones and spoke thunder. She saw again the wreckage of canoes that had been struck.

Now she felt herself carried on a great dark tide, to a place she did not want to see, to a time distant from her own. She tried to resist, to bring herself back to wakefulness, but the current would not relent. Darkness turned to brilliant blue as she came to the surface and looked out across Matavai Bay.

The vision had carried her off again, and this time it was even more vivid than before. All her senses came alive. She breathed the salty tang of the air and felt its refreshing chill. Long, heavy hair brushed against her neck as the wind stirred. Her body felt firm and strong as she shifted, her weight balancing the buck and roll of a seagoing canoe. But this was not her own body!

She felt the swell of breasts against a bark-cloth robe and looked down at arms that were heavier and older than her own. As she gazed at the blue water frothing by, and listened to the beating of wind against the woven sail, Tepua discovered something new. Not only was she sharing a stranger's body and sensations—she was sharing her thoughts as well.

And what thoughts! The mind burned with pride, defiance, and an arrogant confidence that could only belong to a woman of the highest rank. A grand name came to her, though she had never heard it before—Te Vahine Airoreatua i Ahurai i Farepua. Fortunately, there was a shorter name— Purea. But who was this woman? What connection did she have with Tepua and her struggles?

As she looked out through Purea's eyes, Tepua began to sense Purea's importance to the people of this time. She sat regally on the raised deck of a double-hulled voyaging canoe and kept her gaze forward, paying little attention to the men who crewed her vessel. Eyes were lowered in respect when people turned toward her. Yet Tepua sensed more admiration than fear in their expressions.

Tepua wished she could catch a reflection of this new body. She could tell by feel that Purea was well fleshed, but also tall and majestic. And today something alarming flamed in her mind. A catastrophe threatened the shores of Tahiti. Purea had learned about the visit of the terrifying foreign vessel and had come to see it.

But what of Tepua herself? What part had she in this? As she struggled to maintain her own identity, she felt herself slipping deeper into Purea's mind until they were one. . . .

Fine black sand clung to Purea's feet as she walked from the beach to the council house near the shores of Matavai Bay. Some of the men in her party had to hurry to keep up with her, for she was an energetic woman, scarcely hampered by the voluminous *tapa* robes she wore.

She had already scrutinized, from a distance, the monstrous invading ship as it lay at anchor. For a time she had watched the foreign sailors—the so-called demons—until she believed some of the tales she had heard. Now she wanted to hear how the great men of this district planned to respond.

Beside Purea strode an impressive male figure. As she glanced sideways, her gaze took in a strong-featured face and sweeping robes that covered a lithe, powerful body. Tupaia of Urietea served her not only as a high priest of Oro, but as her primary political advisor. He had tried for days to discourage her from making this journey to Matavai.

"You are brave, my lady, to turn your back on that foreign vessel." The priest's voice was deep and resonant as he glanced toward the distant ship. "I have heard that it can slay anyone within sight."

"It did us no harm when we sailed into the bay," Purea answered. "Why should it attack us now?"

"Demons are fickle. I wish you would take the simplest precautions," Tupaia said, flourishing a tuft of sacred red feathers.

"You are the priest. You hold the talisman." Purea had little hope that the gods could protect her from attack, or do anything to drive the foreigners from Tahiti. Days of prayer and sacrifice had brought no result. She heard drumming from the nearby *marae* and knew that the priests were trying yet again. If the priests failed, she asked herself, what hope remained? Yet she refused to give in to despair.

With an experienced eye, Purea measured the size and temper of the welcoming throng that lined up along her path. The crowd was decidedly thin, and the people's mood somber. She lifted her chin, putting on a courageous yet gracious expression. *For the sake of the people, who have seen too much fear in their leader . . .*

Though she had no direct power in this district, she was well-known here, and always received a good reception. Now eyes widened in a few faces as she approached. Then a cheer went up, traveling ahead of her. She saw, with satisfaction, that her presence was beginning to hearten these people.

The rumors said that even the chiefs had hidden in the *marae* for fear of the enemy. She tried to imagine the mighty and ferocious Chief Tutaha cowering behind his little wall of stone. Purea snorted to herself as she trod the path to the council house. Extending the power of his father, the venerable Tutaha i Tarahoi, the present Tutaha controlled not only the districts of Pare and Arue, but had influence over this entire corner of the island.

Perhaps the rumor was a lie, she thought. She had yet to see an enemy that could make Tutaha cower in hiding.

Purea quickened her stride. She had sent word that she was coming, so that the chiefs could meet her, and she had no doubt they would be waiting. She might be outside her home district, but she commanded great respect, both through her family connections and those of her husband. Moreover, her five-year-old son was the most important young man in all of Tahiti. By means of the honors and titles he inherited, Teri'irere would someday stand above all other chiefs of the island.

The crowd grew thicker as Purea neared the meeting place, but it opened, clearing a lane for her party into the great open-walled house that served as a performance hall and meeting place. The hugeness and grandeur of the polished pillars impressed Purea, though her own district boasted a building almost as fine. She paused regally on the threshold and waited for the crier to announce her.

With her full title still echoing beneath the high thatched roof, Purea entered the longhouse. Within, she saw a crowd of lesser chiefs seated on low four-legged stools. Of the high stools set out for the more distinguished guests, only one was occupied. She recognized the aged, yet still majestic figure of Tutaha. He towered over most men; the mere sight of his huge arms and broad chest was enough to frighten his enemies.

Close by him sat a lesser chief called Hau. Hau's straggly white beard and dry, parchment skin proclaimed his age as greater than Tutaha's, but his eyes were still bright and his body vigorous. Purea knew that Hau had been trading with the foreigners, and might have some insight into their nature.

When the welcoming formalities were finished, Purea and her advisor took their seats. "And the others?" she asked, waving a hand at the empty stools.

Tutaha gave a sharp bark of a laugh. "Did you really think those great cowards would come? No, Purea. Dealing with the troubles at hand is left to men in their dotage."

Despite the chief's gentle deprecation of his age, Purea saw the strength in Tutaha's sturdy shoulders. There was something new in him as well, a tightness of face and body that was at odds with his usual stately manner. The patience and warmth in his brown eyes had been replaced with an icy rage, born of fear.

This change in Tutaha shook Purea more than anything else. Throughout her life he had been an overshadowing presence, the true man of power in this part of Tahiti. It was said that he feared nothing, not even death.

One thing had changed that. . . .

"Tutaha," she began. "Help me understand. I have seen the invading vessel and the men who sail it, yet—"

"Those who sail it are *not* men," Tutaha interrupted.

"My chief," objected old Hau, but Tutaha silenced him with an impatient roar.

"They are not! Yes, Hau. I know that you carried on the trade with them across the river. But after seeing how they made war on us in the lagoon, can you still argue that they are human?"

Purea leaned forward. "Your fleet was defeated and your people fled," she said bluntly. "That may be bitter, but not new. We have seen raiders from other districts, even from other islands. They are cruel but they are still men."

"Did you hear that they destroyed canoes on the beach?" Tutaha asked harshly. "Eighty craft hacked and broken apart. Not only those of fishermen, but the exalted sacred canoes as well."

She pursed her lips. "Harsh as these acts seem, the same tactics have been used in our own wars."

"Only after making proper petition to the gods," Tutaha answered. "Were these demons not afraid of the *mana* in the great canoes? Or of Oro's anger? The foreigners do not seem to fear our gods."

Purea saw the priest glancing at her, his eyes wide at the thought of invaders who obeyed no gods at all.

"Perhaps there is one piece of news that will convince you," Tutaha said wearily. "Hau. Show the skin from the shark that the foreigners killed."

The old man picked up a wrapped *tapa* bundle and undid it carefully, drawing out a long strip of belly skin. "From a *blue* shark, as you can see," Hau announced.

Purea stared at what he held and felt deeply stricken. The blue was the most revered of all sharks. At the initiation of a chief, these great fish were sent by the gods to bless the new ruler. They were divine messengers, sometimes gods themselves. "How was the shark killed?" Purea asked, her voice husky with emotion.

Hau took a deep breath and answered. "In the same mysterious way that our warriors were struck down at a distance. After it was hooked, a foreigner pointed a stick at the poor creature. The weapon spoke twice, and then the shark lay writhing and bleeding in the water."

"Even worse," added Tutaha angrily. "They towed the body ashore and put it beneath the pennant they had set up on the beach. As a 'gift' for us."

"I put my fingers in the wounds, to discover how the noble fish had died," said Hau, "but I found nothing. I could not leave it to rot on the beach, so I had my priests pray over the remains and then take them for burial. I saved only this." Purea studied the place he showed her, where two holes pierced the skin.

"So you still think these strangers are men?" Tutaha said to Hau with grim satisfaction.

Hau looked back at him, an infinite sadness in his old, watery eyes. "If they are not, my chief, then your plans have no chance at all."

"Plans?" Purea looked intently at the grizzled chief.

Tutaha sat upright in his seat and his eyes took on a hard glitter. "I am sending messengers to all the districts to gather men and war canoes. There will be such a force as Tahiti has never seen."

"But the powerful weapons . . . the thunder . . ."

"May protect the invaders for a while, but we will

overwhelm them by sheer numbers. If it takes the weight of thousands of dead men to sink that ship, then I will give those lives."

Purea found herself staring at Tutaha with horrified fascination. She wondered if a malevolent spirit had taken possession of him, or whether frustration and fear had driven him mad.

He brought a closed fist down on his thigh. "If these invaders can die, then we will repay them for what they did to us. If not, then we will be the ones destroyed." He paused, struggling to keep his dignity, and then said in a more controlled voice, "Perhaps the old prophecy will prove true. The canoe with no outrigger has come, just as we were warned. Now it will mean the end of our people and our ways."

No! Purea cried out silently in protest as she looked into Tutaha's fear-ravaged face. In his eyes she could see the horror of the slaughter that had taken place, and the even greater one that threatened to follow. If such things happened, her ambitions for her son would be meaningless. What good would it do Teri'irere to wear the sacred *maro* if his people were destroyed? "Chief of Pare and Arue," she said respectfully to Tutaha, "the prophecy may be true, but you need not make yourself an instrument of it."

Tutaha's eyes blazed. "What would you have me do?"

Purea turned to Hau. "You carried on trade with the invaders. What did you learn?"

"They have the desires of human beings," Hau answered. "They eat. They take pleasure with women."

"Even demons have been known to take food and women," retorted Tutaha. "I hear the skins of these foreigners are as pale as shades from the Great Darkness. . . ."

"Have you offered them hospitality?" Purea asked.

"We have given gifts," Hau said cautiously. "The strangers have taken them, and more."

"But you have not invited them ashore to feast and be entertained."

"Had they behaved like guests, they would have been treated so," Tutaha retorted. "It is not possible now."

"It is possible," Purea said insistently. "And it is our only hope."

"You would invite such murderers ashore? To make it easier for them to kill and plunder. *Aue!*"

Purea felt annoyed with him. "If only a few of their people come ashore, they will not make trouble. They will know they are outnumbered. Suppose we invite their leaders and honor them as visiting chiefs."

Tutaha's eyes narrowed, then his eyebrows lifted. "Now I see where this is going. . . . Tell me who would give the feast and where."

Purea was startled by his sudden change in attitude. Was he plotting some deceit? For the moment she focused on setting forth her plan. "The feast could take place here."

"No. My throat is too thick with hate to speak to such people without spitting. I will not receive them."

Purea took a deep breath. "Then I will." The two men looked at each other.

Tutaha's face showed a mixture of distaste and awe. "You are willing to sit . . . with these ghosts from the Darkness?"

"I am."

Tutaha thought awhile and seemed to brighten. "I accept the idea," he announced. "I will give you all the pigs you need to feed the guests well. I will also provide the warriors."

Purea stared at him, understanding at last the reason for his capitulation. He would wait for her to lure the visitors to a feast, and then . . .

"What is the matter, my dear lady? This was your idea, was it not? Cut off the head of the lizard before it can bite."

"No!" Her retort was sharp. "Such an act would give grave offense to the gods."

"Only if these enemies are men like us," Tutaha tried to argue, but Purea remained adamant. She was surprised to hear Hau adding his voice to support her.

"Honored chief, I agree with Purea. Not only would such an act be a blow to our own honor, but it might well prove useless. The newcomers are too cautious to send all their principal people ashore. They will leave behind some who are resourceful enough to take over leadership. Then they will punish us for our folly."

At last Tutaha seemed to back down. "So you think you can save us from these strangers—without using force?" he asked Purea gruffly. "Try it, then. Use the great house in Ha'apape. I will provide whatever else you need. But I want nothing to do with these 'guests.' Whatever the outcome, send me word—if you survive." The Pare-Arue chief rose from his seat, indicating that the meeting was over.

When he was gone, Hau remained. The old man sat quietly while Purea turned the sharkskin over in her hands and put her fingers through the wound holes. She held the skin for a long time before returning it to Hau. . . .

Tepua woke from her vision before dawn, trembling, and found no comfort in the thin cape that covered her. Resigned to wakefulness, she drew up her knees and reflected on the moments she had just experienced.

After living awhile as Purea, her own body seemed frail and slender by comparison. Tepua felt admiration for the physical presence of Te Vahine Airoreatua i Ahurai i Farepua. And something else about Purea inspired Tepua—a willingness to stand up to the most influential men of her day. Perhaps only a woman of Purea's eminence in Tahiti could dare such a feat.

Tepua's thoughts filled with the people she had seen. Through Purea she understood that the aging Tutaha of her vision was the *son* of the current Tutaha i Tarahoi, who had been such a poor host to her troupe. Now the son was barely a youth! These puzzling events would not take place for at least fifty years.

Yet Tepua felt an urgency about the visions, a need to learn why the gods had brought her them. Somehow they were tied to her own life, maybe even to the troubles that Land-crab had started. She lay back and tried to remember every detail of Purea's encounter. Perhaps the gods would help her understand.

ELEVEN

From the deck of an arriving canoe, Matopahu saw hundreds of people standing on the shore, all waiting to welcome Putu-nui's victorious archers. Young women carrying crimson hibiscus garlands waded into the shallows, almost swamping the vessels in their eagerness to greet the heroes. The girls draped wreath upon wreath around Matopahu's neck, embraced him passionately, whispered invitations. The young *ari'i* laughed with pleasure but offered no promises. The rich scent of flowers made him light-headed as he waded ashore.

These were the people of Putu-nui's district, in another part of Eimeo. The captain of the winning team had invited Matopahu and Eye-to-heaven to join his celebration at home. Now children leaped high for a better look at the new champion, or crawled onto their parents' shoulders. Boys waved their own small bows and arrows in the air. Even dogs were caught up in the excitement, one slipping through the crowd to beat its tail against his leg.

Matopahu bore this attention with good grace. He understood how long these people had been waiting for such a victory. Fat-moon was far too powerful to be challenged in war. Only in the archery contest had they ever had a chance to beat him.

At last, Matopahu's party reached Putu-nui's compound. Though the surrounding bamboo fence was only waist-high, it belonged to the chief, and no one would dare step over it.

The crowd of onlookers remained outside as Putu-nui's guests filed through the narrow opening.

Inside the compound, the scene was almost as hectic as outside. The servants gawked at Matopahu while the women of the chief's household rushed forward to greet him. Every one of them made clear that she would welcome the hero's attentions. Most vigorous in flirtation was Putu-nui's prodigious wife, Feather-of-the-tropic-bird's-tail. Matopahu pressed noses with her, felt the grip of her huge hands, but gave her no encouragement. After light refreshment, the customary dance performance began, to be followed by sporting competitions.

Later Matopahu found himself standing in a large circle of onlookers surrounding a pair of sweating wrestlers. He knew that the two combatants had prepared for this match with the same reverence as archers, each making offerings to their tutelary god. Now they stood belly to belly, fiercely gripping each other, neck cords standing out as each strained for a throw.

The crowd remained totally silent as the struggle continued. The wrestlers broke their hold, then came at each other again with a flurry of tattooed legs. Dust and grass flew as feet scuffled for purchase. The larger man hissed through clenched teeth, his face turning red. He leaned slightly. His opponent's foot made a sudden move, knocking his leg out from under him. With a cry the larger man fell onto his rump.

Then a din rose on all sides, the kin and friends of the victor dancing and shouting while the loser's supporters raised their voices to drown out the others. After each side had finished praising their man, a fresh pair strode to the center of the ring. Matopahu had witnessed many such matches. Only when he saw an unusual hold or a subtle trick did these contests pique his interest.

At last the women had their turn. Matopahu was not surprised to see the chief's wife, Feather, step forward to issue her challenge. It was customary for people of high rank to attempt to excel at many sports—and often they succeeded.

Strutting about the ring, Feather struck her right hand

against her left arm to make a hollow slap. She was not as tall as a man, but Matopahu imagined that her solid build would make her a formidable opponent. She had her black hair tied back and slicked with oil, to discourage the hair-pulling tricks that wrestlers often used. She wore a simple white bark-cloth wrap about her enormous girth. Each pale thigh was as thick as the base of a palm tree.

"I hear that she has beaten many men," whispered Eye-to-heaven.

Matopahu drew in a breath when he saw Feather approaching. She stopped right in front of him and issued the challenge again.

"*Taio*, you must accept," said Eye-to-heaven. All around Matopahu, voices urged him on.

Trying to make light of the situation, the *ari'i* laughed, put aside his feathered cape and his wrap of painted bark-cloth. Clad only in his *maro*, he stepped forward, urged on by cheers from the crowd. He glanced at Putu-nui's eager face and then at the pugnacious features of his wife. *I cannot harm my host's wife,* he thought. Yet to lose to a woman . . . How would that affect his prestige?

This is Putu-nui's trap, he thought glumly. *He enjoys the victory I brought him, but not the glory I brought myself.* Matopahu was tempted to refuse, but insulting Putu-nui would not aid his cause.

The crowd hushed as the *ari'i* prepared to meet his opponent. What kind of woman was this, he wondered, who could whisper of passion one moment and ask for combat the next? She had greeted him warmly. Now her deep-set eyes glittered like the sea beneath a thunderstorm.

Extending his arm, he touched her fingertips in the customary opening gesture. Then he moved nearer, looking for a way to grab her. She took the initiative, seizing him at the arm and shoulder.

He felt sweaty rolls of fat as she pressed close to him, the great gourd mounds of her breasts squashed against his ribs. Her grip was as tight and unrelenting as the sennit that bound his brother's corpse. He leaned his weight against her hold, trying to drag her off balance, but to no avail.

Then he tried pressure from his leg, but she pushed back

just as fiercely. He managed to wrench one hand free, and tried to get a grip across her back. Her oiled flesh oozed from his grasp. Her sheer bulk threatened to bear him down.

Now her arm was firmly about his neck, and he could not pry himself loose. Sweat prickled on his forehead at the prospect of defeat. The usual wrestlers' tricks would not serve him now, but perhaps he could try another. He sensed a mood of excitement in her that went beyond the thrill of combat.

Subtly he began to move his body, rubbing his bare chest against the thin cloth of the garment that covered her breasts. He felt her fleshy chin turn against his neck, and then he heard her speak, far too loudly. "That feels nice, my taro pudding." Matopahu's face burned as she began to undulate, complementing his motion.

Laughter broke out as Feather's coquetry reached the ears of the spectators. Putu-nui seemed to be laughing loudest of all. With a shock, Matopahu realized that Feather's meaty hand was now clamped over one of his buttocks, kneading fiercely. The match was in danger of turning into an exhibition of *hanihani*.

"I want to feel your yam in my *umu*," she offered throatily, and the onlookers roared. "But not now." Suddenly she released her hold and slipped away from him. He came at her again, crouching low, but she grabbed him about the middle, squeezing so tightly that she drove the breath from his body.

He was only partially relieved when he felt the voluminous torturess laughing as hard as the audience. "Have no fear, my tall archer," she said sweetly. "You are too good-looking to be maimed."

Matopahu did not see what she did next. Somehow his feet came off the ground and his body went flying. He landed with a hard thud and heard the cries of triumph all around him. While Feather's raucous friends beat drums and loudly proclaimed her accomplishments, only Eye-to-heaven raised his voice for Matopahu.

The *ari'i* rose stiffly and dusted himself off. Casting a wary glance at Feather, he strutted once around the circle, bringing cheers for himself and a few more voices to sing his praises.

Eye-to-heaven gave his friend a measured look when Matopahu rejoined him.

"I trust you enjoyed that," the defeated wrestler whispered in exasperation.

"Do not look so unhappy," said the priest. "You did well. The people will think more of you now."

Matopahu wrinkled his brow. Perhaps his *taio* was right. The victory against Fat-moon had come through the aid of an outsider—himself. Putu-nui and his tribe needed to equalize things a bit, and this ridiculous match with Feather had served their purpose. Sighing in resignation, Matopahu accepted a servant's offer to pour cool water over his head, then tried to enjoy the rest of the matches.

The wrestling gave way to footraces along the beach. Matopahu was relieved when his host invited him to retire to the shady comfort of the compound. "This is a day that no one will forget," said Putu-nui as they sipped cool coconut milk.

Certainly I will never forget Feather, Matopahu thought ruefully.

Putu-nui went on. "It is a day of celebration. Let us continue to put all serious things aside. But do not think I have forgotten how much I owe you. I know what is uppermost in your thoughts. Be satisfied that I have already spoken to my priests."

Matopahu accepted the chief's words, but with a sense of foreboding. Putu-nui understood Matopahu's desire for an ally to help him regain the land and *marae* of his forebears. Of course the chief would not make any such alliance without first consulting his diviners. The priests would have to declare that the signs were auspicious for such a risky adventure.

Alas, there would be no disputing the findings of the priests.

When the days of celebration had drawn to a close, Matopahu and Eye-to-heaven sat alone with Putu-nui on a shady knoll above the beach. Despite the genial manner of his host, Matopahu felt uneasy. He knew that Putu-nui's priests had gone out at night, some searching the forest, others gazing into the lagoon, all seeking omens. But with what result?

"I have heaped you with gifts, Matopahu," said the chief, "yet I know that rolls of bark-cloth and feathered head-dresses are not what you want. I would like to give you a far greater gift, the birthright that has been taken by Land-crab."

Matopahu leaned forward eagerly. "Then you will call a council?"

"To debate this issue of war? Yes. My underchiefs are entitled to have a say. I am sure it is no different in Tahiti."

Matopahu raised his eyebrows in agreement. "Of course, the question must be discussed," he told his host. "But it is *your* influence that will sway everyone."

"That is so, my friend. And I have a good argument. If you are restored to your land and your people, then we will have an ally in return, someone to check Fat-moon's ambitions to rule all of Eimeo."

"Certainly." Matopahu studied Putu-nui's expression, wondering why the chief was being so evasive.

"And yet, my friend Matopahu, I ask myself if I really want to call this council. Everyone will enjoy hearing the fine speeches. In my district, some men think debating is a better sport than wrestling." Matopahu smiled, still faintly embarrassed over his match. "Yes"—the chief waved a hand—"the arguments will be loud and sharp."

"That should not discourage you," Matopahu tried. "You will have the last word."

Putu-nui sighed mournfully. "No, in the end it is the gods who always decide."

At this, Matopahu stiffened, and glanced toward Eye-to-heaven. He had hoped that the local priests might confide in their fellow, but they had not. "The signs. I have heard nothing."

Putu-nui raised his fly-flap and idly flicked at the air. At last he shrugged. "Ah, my good friend. Now you will understand my sadness. The priests are done with their night walking, and now I have their report. Here is the grim news—the gods will not stand with us. I dare not risk my warriors and canoes to help you."

"The diviners are wrong," Matopahu replied angrily. "The gods favor me. The outcome of the archery contest can leave no doubt."

"My strong young friend, I understand what a hard blow this is, after your magnificent triumph, but there is nothing I can do about it. If I refuse the advice of the priests, the people will turn against me. You would not have me thrown down, would you? Let us be reasonable. Take my gifts. Depart in peace. Wait for a more auspicious time."

Matopahu felt as if the wind had been knocked out of him. For a moment he relived the end of the wrestling match with Feather. He was sprawled on his back again, blinking at the sky while the crowd cheered his defeat. He tried to speak but couldn't. He was relieved when Eye-to-heaven answered for him.

"You have treated us well, Putu-nui. We will ask nothing more."

For a time, Matopahu wandered forest trails, unaware of where he was going. The hills that he had scorned became his home again. He ate wild plants, tasting nothing. He drank from chilly streams, throwing himself down and guzzling like an animal.

When darkness came, he slept where he fell. The sounds of the night meant nothing to him. Ghosts? Wild boars? What could they do to him that was worse than what he had suffered?

One afternoon he came down to the sea at a familiar cove. He stood in the shallows feeling the waves lapping at his knees. His fury was almost spent. He walked farther out, dove, swam until he felt exhausted. Then he drifted back, caring only dimly if he managed to regain the shore.

"Matopahu, it is enough," said Eye-to-heaven, who was waiting for him on the pebbled beach. The priest had been somewhere nearby all along, the *ari'i* suspected. The *ari'i* wiped salt water from his eyes and staggered ashore. "Come with me to see the *tahu'a,* Imo," the priest insisted. "Better that than wandering the hills again. I am tired of chasing after you."

Looking at the pained expression on his friend's face, Matopahu began to feel foolish. "I am ready," he said, turning toward the path. "But you will not find me good company."

Imo lived in a small thatched hut not far from the larger dwelling of his brother's family. When Matopahu arrived, he saw a pile of gifts—cloth, necklaces, feathered garments, laid out on a mat. They looked familiar. He realized, suddenly, that these were his presents from Putu-nui.

Nearby, two men were erecting another house like Imo's. "For storing your riches," Eye-to-heaven explained, "until you can take these things home."

Matopahu gazed at his friend. Not only had Eye-to-heaven patiently trailed after him while he roamed the woods, but the priest had arranged to safeguard the valuable gifts he had abandoned. Had Eye-to-heaven not taken charge, they would have disappeared.

The two house-builders turned to stare at Matopahu.

"Yes, I am the one Feather threw," he told them angrily. "Look at me all you want."

"You're the champion archer," said the darker of the two men. "And now you have the riches of a chief." He turned to the brightly painted cloth and the glittering shells.

They will not bring me what I want, Matopahu thought. Then he picked up two of the best rolls of *tapa* and laid them before the workmen. "Take these. I give them to you."

The men's mouths fell open at his generosity. "It's too much," said one.

Matopahu tossed his head and walked away.

"Do not be bitter, my friend," said Imo, offering Matopahu what appeared to be his best seat—a battered four-legged stool with the usual bowed seat. He and Eye-to-heaven had acknowledged Matopahu's superior birth by sitting cross-legged on pandanus-leaf mats. The *ari'i* pushed the stool aside and joined them on the mats.

"You are not defeated yet," Imo continued in a patient tone.

"What more can I do?" Matopahu asked despondently. "Even Putu-nui has found an excuse to turn me away."

"His priests found true omens," Imo said. "And I can tell you why. You have your strength back, but a cloud still lingers over you. Have you forgotten your brother's corpse?"

"You bring that up again!" Matopahu said in an exasperated voice. "You know that I need an army to recover the body. So long as Land-crab rules, my dead brother will stay where no one can find him. *Aue!* I am trapped. No chief will help me, because I am tied to my brother's corpse. And without help, I cannot get free!"

"That is a dilemma," admitted Eye-to-heaven. "And now that you are restored to health, we will have a while to solve it."

TWELVE

"So you are still with us, cousin," Maukiri called gaily one morning when Tepua was returning from her bath.

Chagrined, Tepua paused on the trail. It was true that lately she had been neglecting Maukiri. But her cousin seemed to need no looking after. The good food of Tahiti had filled her out, and every other aspect of the Arioi life seemed to satisfy her. Tepua replied, "I am happy to see you so cheerful, cousin."

A month had passed since the return to Tahiti. The chief of another district, one a bit closer to home, had invited the troupe to settle in for an extended stay—so long as their performances steered clear of politics.

"But what about you, Tepua? Are you still thinking about your archery champion? There are so many men here who would gladly help you forget him."

"I have seen them—"

"Yes. But I know you, cousin. You did nothing but look!"

"Matopahu will return to Tahiti," she said firmly.

"By then you'll be shriveled up like a crone." Maukiri stepped closer and felt Tepua's arm. "You do not eat enough, because you are unhappy. If Matopahu comes, he'll want to see you at your best. He will not complain if another man has been keeping you warm for him."

Tepua smiled and embraced her cousin, not wanting to argue. How could she explain that she had no interest in other men?

*   *   *

That night, Tepua once again felt sleepless as she lay on her mat in an Arioi house. Unaccountably her breasts tingled, as if Matopahu were caressing them. She noticed a feeling of fullness, and her nipples seemed unbearably sensitive. She had to turn on her side to keep the *tapa* cover from touching them.

She tried to blame Maukiri's words for her discomfort. She did not want to think about the absent *ari'i* now. She did not want to think about men at all.

As often happened of late, Tepua's thoughts drifted toward Matavai Bay and the experiences she had shared with Purea. Her interest had been piqued, yet she felt unsatisfied. She wished she could find a connection between this chiefess and the people of her own time. It might even turn out that she and Purea were distant kin!

As for foreign sailors, Tepua had already encountered a few of her own. Others were out there somewhere in the vast ocean. Though they were not demons, she understood how careless and deadly these foreigners could be. Someday they would make their impact on Tahiti.

Tepua sighed and turned over. Suddenly she did feel weary, though it was not the usual sensation. Her limbs felt heavy, yet her mind remained fully awake. In the darkness of the guest house she saw distant glimmerings. Then the light grew. . . .

Standing atop Taharaa Hill, Purea thought that Matavai Bay looked unusually tranquil, its azure waters shimmering in sunlight. The foreign ship, anchored off the cape at the northern end, appeared tiny and innocuous, but this was only the illusion of distance.

The old chief, Hau, knelt beside a strip of raw earth that had been gashed open, a wound on the grassy turf of the hill. "The stone cannot be seen," Hau was saying, "but here is where it struck among the crowd. Remarkably, it missed the people and buried itself."

"The stone was flung all the way from the foreign vessel?" Purea found it hard to contain her disbelief.

"The ship was farther away then than it is now," Hau said solemnly.

"Why are you showing me this?" Purea asked, feeling a surge of anger. Was Hau trying to dissuade her from her plan, perhaps at Tutaha's instigation?

"To make you aware of what you face," the old man answered. "The knowledge may cause you to draw back, or may increase your resolution. Either way, you will act with open eyes."

Hau rose and strode toward the path. Purea turned from the patch of exposed red-orange soil and walked after him. "Hau, give me your wisdom. Is this a foolish thing I am attempting?"

Gently he answered, "Only the gods can tell you. Perhaps Tupaia will bring the question to them. I know only this. If you fail to make peace, Tutaha will carry through his plan to make war."

And perhaps he will not wait to see if I fail. "Will the other chiefs support him in such a show of force? They already grumble that he has too much power."

Hau sighed. "If the threat of the enemy is great enough, the chiefs will gather behind Tutaha. What threat could be greater than this?"

Purea fell silent. In her imagination, threads of crimson spread slowly through Matavai's aquamarine waters and bodies lay in heaps along the beach. Saying little more, she followed Hau down the hill.

As Purea approached the foreign vessel, there was a long interval of silence on board her double-hulled canoe. For a time she heard only the dipping paddles and creaks of sennit bindings. Mist curled around the great hull ahead, making it appear ghostly and unreal.

Standing next to her on the platform were Tupaia, her priest and advisor, and also old Hau. She felt the deck rock beneath her feet as the *pahi* breasted a few low waves. Two large pigs grunted in their lashed-pole cages. She was taking them as presents to the strangers.

Tupaia still looked stern and disapproving, his bleached *tapa* cape drawn tightly about his shoulders. He had argued with her this morning before the craft set out. Was it not sufficient to send a messenger to invite the strangers ashore? Even if she had no fear for herself, what of her family? What if she were somehow contaminated by foreign evil?

To placate the priest she had accepted his tuft of protective red feathers. She had also spent a long time petitioning her ancestral spirits to watch over her. Now she uttered one last prayer.

Perhaps Tupaia was overly cautious. Certainly Hau understood why she was here. It was essential to learn all she could about these strangers. What better way to start than by visiting the vessel that brought them?

As Purea drew closer to the ship, the onshore breeze brought her unfamiliar sounds. No Tahitian craft made such drawn-out creaks and groans, or had anchor lines of stone loops that clanked and rattled. Her gaze lifted to the masts, standing like great trees above the deck. Sections of exposed sail thumped against the spars, making sounds that resembled a beating drum.

As her double-hull came alongside the ship, Purea shivered in the shadow cast by the huge vessel. She looked up, startled to see that some faces were as brown as hers, but others were red or as pale as bleached *tapa*. Some men had the temerity to grin at her, showing missing or rotting teeth.

"Tell them I wish to visit," she asked Hau. By means of gestures and several short words that the old man had picked up while trading with the strangers, he conveyed her message. He did not have to add that she had brought gifts, for the foreigners were pointing excitedly at the two pigs, making sounds of hunger and rubbing their bellies.

A rope was let down from what looked like a very stout fishing pole fixed to the side; Hau tied it to the cages. One at a time, the startled hogs were swung aboard. The rope was let down again and Hau told Purea that she might be lifted aboard in the same manner, if she desired.

"I will not be hauled up like an animal," she replied haughtily.

A man who wore a tight blue garment about his arms and chest shouted an order. Someone unrolled a contrivance of tied ropes down the side. Hau seemed familiar with this; he put his foot on the first horizontal section and commenced to climb, amid a chorus of enthusiastic whistles and cheers. Purea was glad then that she had brought the old man—the strangers seemed to like him. Now it was her turn.

As she came forward, however, her feet momentarily refused to leave the deck of her canoe. In her youth, she had scaled many a high rock, yet she hesitated at the strangeness of the great wooden side looming over her. How could such a tall hull stay upright without an outrigger? she wondered. The addition of her weight on the ladder might overwhelm the precarious balance and bring the monstrosity crashing down on its side.

But Hau had gone up safely. She realized that the fear was a foolish thing. Drawing in her breath, she reached up and began to climb. Yet the sights, sounds, and smells of the ship battered at her resolve.

Purea knew from experience that voyaging canoes took on unpleasant smells after days at sea. Without fresh water for bathing, crew and passengers began to stink. Bilge water in the hulls turned sour. Odors lingered from fish that had been gutted on deck. But this . . .

Aue! Not even sacred feathers could ward off the unpleasantness. From the men, though some looked freshly scrubbed, came a cloying, rotten-pork odor. From others came a daunting reek of feces, urine, and old sweat. The briny, wet-wood smell of the ship's timbers was combined with harsh odors that stung her nose and made her eyes threaten to water.

Purea was sorely tempted to retreat to her *pahi,* or even to dive into the lagoon. She had to exert great willpower to keep her expression pleasant and her manner gracious as a ghost-pale hand extended to help her aboard.

At last she stood directly facing these strangers from afar. Now she could see that they were no taller than men of her own kind, and, if she ignored their bizarre clothing, similar in most ways. Only their features—eyes and noses and lips—seemed odd.

A curly-haired man who seemed to be a leader swept off his blue headpiece and bowed low before her, speaking hard-edged words that Hau said were a greeting. The foreigner was well muscled and hearty, with crisp brown hair and a cheerful disposition. As soon as Tupaia joined the group, this man took charge, escorting Purea to what looked like a square pit in the deck, surrounded on three sides by a kind of fence. Wooden planks, stepped like terraces on a hillside, led into the depths of the ship.

As Purea stared into the unfamiliar opening she once more fought her revulsion. Why would the strangers want to show her their bilges? She stood fast for some time until Hau convinced her that living space lay below.

The ship's interior, she discovered, was like an enormous house partitioned by numerous walls. The passageways were narrow, and the ceilings too low. Some portions were lit by holes overhead, others by lanterns that shone far more brightly than any candlenut lamp.

Her party was ushered into a long whitewashed chamber whose inward-curving wall had small, square openings for light, spaced at intervals. Here the visitors were invited to sit, not on low stools or mats, but on high seats with wooden backrests. Food was brought to a platform with legs that reminded Purea of a sacrificial altar in a *marae*. The food was not placed on banana leaves or served in wooden troughs, but laid on shallow round platters.

Purea picked up an empty platter, turned it over, tapped it with a fingernail. This was stone of some kind, but stone carved to such fineness that it rang sweetly when struck. There were no coconut shells to drink from. Instead liquids were poured into cups made from the same thin, fine stone. The cups had loops on the sides for fingers so that they were easier to hold. How clever these strangers were!

When she was invited to partake, Purea regretted that she had to refuse. "Tell them I am under *tapu*," she said to Hau.

"They do not understand our ways," the old man replied, "but I will try."

The dismayed looks on the faces of the strangers told Purea that they, like her own people, wished to have their hospitality accepted. For a moment the welcoming atmosphere turned uncertain, then tense. Purea did not want to insult her hosts, but neither would she risk the gods' wrath.

The restrictions placed on her, first as a woman, second as mother of the noble Teri'irere, could not be ignored.

It was Hau who broke the strained mood, accepting a small round cake offered to him by one of the blue-coated men. He uttered the customary prayer and flicked a crumb to the spirits. This act made the foreigners frown, as if they did not comprehend. Then Tupaia threw off his priestly caution and accepted a slice of a loaf that smelled faintly like cooked breadfruit. He, too, made the offering, took a bite, chewed slowly but with evident appreciation. At last, the foreigners showed signs of approval.

Purea relaxed. Hau and the priest had spared her from insulting her hosts, and for that she felt deeply grateful. "I wish to visit the chief of all these men," she said to Hau. "Can you arrange it?"

"They say their commander has been ill. He is recovering but is still weak."

Purea shuddered inwardly at the thought of a sick man having to lie in these dark wooden caverns with their dank smells. "It would be better for their chief to lie in the shade and enjoy the breeze. Say that I wish to meet him and invite him ashore."

She waited while Hau conveyed her reply to the man in authority. At first he shook his head at the request, a gesture that Hau had told her meant refusal. But as the old man continued to speak with the foreigner, and Purea added one of her coaxing looks, the sailor finally laughed tolerantly and agreed.

"He will take us both to his chief," said Hau. "Tupaia will stay here."

Purea wondered if their escort was a subchief in the foreign hierarchy. He seemed to have an air about him that commanded obedience and respect from the others. After leading her and her companion along a narrow passageway, he paused at the threshold of a room and swung aside the slab of wood that closed it off. Purea heard him speaking briefly with someone; then he motioned his visitors inside.

A weak, high-pitched male voice spoke Hau's name and then words of greeting. Purea peered past Hau at the sick man, the master of this great vessel. She half expected to see him lying on a mat on the floor, but of course these people did things very differently than did her own. Instead the invalid reclined, propped up on pillows, on a raised bed that was built into the wall.

He was a short, middle-aged man, gaunt with illness. Purea imagined that he had once been stout. His hair, sparse and thinning, was plastered to his head with fever sweat. His skin was pale with a tinge of yellow, except for a flush over his cheekbones.

The skin crinkled at the corners of his watery blue-gray eyes as he beamed in welcome at Hau and then gazed curiously at Purea. His appraisal evidently gave him pleasure, for his eyebrows rose, and the careworn lines that illness had etched in his forehead momentarily vanished.

She waited while Hau introduced her, giving her titles and then the shorter name by which she was known. The old man then tried to speak the commander's name. It had odd sounds in it that Hau could not pronounce. To Purea's ears it sounded like "Tapani Vari."

"*Ia ora na.* Life to you, Tapani Vari," she said.

Reaching out with a tremulous hand, the invalid patted the cushion of another backrest seat, near the bed. He spoke briefly with Hau, and she could hear the astonished pleasure in his voice. His eyes never left Purea as she took the seat and extended her hand to him. Weak as he was, the commander struggled up from his pillows, raised the back of her hand to his face, and touched it briefly to his lips. Though she was not acquainted with the gesture, Tapani Vari's demeanor made his intent clear. He was greeting her with the honor and respect due a noblewoman.

The commander spoke briefly to Hau, but his gaze remained on Purea.

"He says that he is greatly pleased to have such an important *ari'i* visit him. He wishes that he were in better health so that he could extend a fitting welcome to you," said Hau.

"Tell him that his hospitality is most gracious. Say also that I invite him to visit me ashore. There he will get well."

Tapani Vari replied through Hau. "He cannot come now. He must rest and gain strength. Tomorrow morning he may feel better. Perhaps then." Hau listened as Tapani Vari added some more remarks. "He speaks of you with great respect," Hau said. "As if you were high chiefess over all of Tahiti."

Purea felt a glow of pleasure. It would do no harm to let the foreigner have an exaggerated sense of her importance.

"Tapani Vari is a wise chief," she said mischievously. "All he lacks is the belly of a great man. If he comes to my house to eat, he will grow one." She patted her own stomach, then made a circle with her arms and puffed out her cheeks to emphasize her meaning.

Tapani Vari laughed heartily before Hau had finished the translation.

"He says you are a fine lady, and that he is eager for tomorrow to arrive."

Then he brought out gifts. Sitting up in bed, he draped her shoulders with a pretty blue cloak made from cloth much finer and stronger than *tapa*. The garment tied loosely at the throat with ribbons. He also gave her something that resembled a short-handled paddle. Its center was clear like shallow water. When she lifted her gift by the silvery handle, she cried out and nearly dropped it. A face appeared, as if she were looking at another woman who stared with equal amazement back at her.

It was a reflection, of course, but far clearer than any she had seen in any pool. The water in it was perfectly smooth and flat and did not run out. What a wonder to show to the ladies who attended her!

When the visit was over, their curly-haired escort accompanied them to the gap in the rail, where the rope ladder hung down to Purea's canoe.

"Tell them that we enjoyed seeing the ship. . . ." Purea began, turning to Hau. She did not complete her request. A raucous yowl erupted as she hastily withdrew her heel from something ropelike and furry that whipped away from beneath her foot. An animal's tail?

Tupaia gave a shrill battle cry and lunged to protect his chiefess from the small but ferocious beast that crouched, hunched and hissing, in front of her. Its eyes were orange coals aglow in its black face. In an instant he snatched it up in his two big hands. Holding the writhing black-and-white animal above his head, he turned to throw it into the water.

Shouts of protest rang out from the foreign sailors. A pale-haired youth ran at Tupaia, tried to seize his arm. The priest's eyes flashed and he shifted his squalling captive quickly to one hand. The other went to his shell dagger.

Purea knew that everything she had accomplished could be undone in an instant. She grabbed Tupaia's weapon hand. The priest's face turned to hers, his eyes bulging, his features contorted with battle frenzy and bewilderment. For a moment he froze.

Then with a disgusted grunt he thrust the struggling animal into the hands of the red-faced boy. The youth clutched it tightly and shrank against the tall, curly-haired man, who lifted both hands to calm the other men down.

"Have we broken some *tapu*?" Purea asked Hau as her priest stood stiffly beside her with an air of affronted dignity. She could not guess what this creature meant to the foreigners. Her people kept only dogs and pigs—animals raised for meat—yet sometimes coddled and fondled young ones.

Purea turned to the curly-haired sailor and tried to make him understand, with words and gestures, that her priest had intended no harm. He seemed to grasp her meaning, for as he took the little beast from the flustered youth and stroked it, he smiled with his eyes. The creature also seemed soothed by his touch. Its lashing tail stilled and its flattened ears came up. As it turned its head to fix a baleful gaze on Purea, the intense copper of its eyes startled her.

"Oh," she cried as the curly-haired man began to hand the little beast to another sailor, "do not take it away!"

The foreigners exchanged puzzled looks, but the curly-haired man turned back with the animal in his arms. Her interest seemed to please the others.

Intensely curious, Purea peered at the creature. At first she had taken it for a strange kind of short-muzzled dog, but as it opened its mouth in a yawn and blinked at her, she saw many differences. The large lustrous eyes fascinated her. They shifted and shimmied like the light on the lagoon at sundown. The unwavering gaze seemed to reach deeply into her and touch something there.

A god would have such eyes, she thought, looking into the leaf-shaped black pupils that narrowed to slits in full sun.

"What is this animal called?" she asked, reaching out to feel the shiny black fur. The curly-haired man caught her hand, but instead of thrusting it away, he guided her fingers over the fur in a stroking motion while speaking softly.

"Nai puhi," she imitated, struggling with the hissing sound that these people put in their words. The fur of the *"puhi"* was not like a dog's—it felt soft and silky beneath her fingers.

She was amazed when the curly-haired man eased the creature into her arms. The only animals she had ever held were puppies and piglets, which felt rigid in her hands. The *puhi* melted warmly into the crook of her elbow and reclined there with a certain regal grace that enchanted her.

"The foreigners do not permit anyone to harm these animals," Hau explained. "It is *tapu* to cast one into the sea. Their gods will send punishment."

"Then they *do* have gods." Purea cradled the *puhi* thoughtfully. What would Tutaha say about this? she wondered. Would he still insist that the foreigners were ghosts from the Darkness?

When the curly-haired man extended his hands for the *puhi,* she returned it with a reluctant sigh. He evidently noted her reaction, but did not, as she had hoped, offer the creature to her as a present. Perhaps Tapani Vari would be more generous. . . .

She followed Tupaia down the rope ladder and boarded her own craft. Looking back, she saw the foreign sailors cheering and waving their headdresses. Purea called a final greeting.

Then she turned away, her head filled with what she had seen. She had hoped to learn more about the strangers. But what puzzles they offered!

These people worked wonders in wood and stone, yet did not take proper care of their bodies. They claimed to fear their gods, yet she had seen them make no offerings. They showed great fondness for women, yet had brought none of their own.

Perhaps, in time, she would understand these things. But her first task was to make a peace agreement. So long as Tutaha did not interfere, she thought she could have that agreement.

THIRTEEN

"You have heard my opinion," said Eye-to-heaven, "but I see you are still determined to go." Matopahu finished heaving a net filled with green drinking coconuts into his single-hull outrigger canoe, then glanced up at the priest's frowning face. The two men were not often at odds, but in this case Matopahu refused to be swayed. He was leaving Eimeo.

Eye-to-heaven stood on the beach, watching his friend's preparations but offering no assistance. Matopahu turned toward the lagoon and studied the ripples on the water. He felt a steady wind against his face, a wind from Tane, the sea father.

He gazed past the breakers, though he could not see his destination from this low beach. Yesterday, from a high lookout, he had glimpsed the coral ring of Tetiaroa glittering far off in the sun. This atoll lay less than a day's sail from Eimeo. If the gods did not turn against him, he would arrive before dark.

For now, it was not the opinion of the gods but that of his *taio* that troubled Matopahu. "I don't understand your objections. What harm can it do me to speak with Otaha?" he asked.

"You will waste many days in Tetiaroa," said the priest. "Once you reach that place of idleness, you won't want to leave. I know what will happen there. Otaha will entertain and flatter you, but give you nothing."

170

They were arguing about a prominent chief of Tahiti, who had taken up temporary residence on the nearby atoll. Matopahu knew that in Tetiaroa a great man like Otaha might be approached informally. It was a place where chiefs went to relax, cure their ills, fatten and beautify their daughters. The *ari'i* was counting on a long tradition of amity between his family and that of this chief. Otaha might be willing to support a raid on Land-crab.

"Listen," said Eye-to-heaven, "I have another plan."

Matopahu carried a mat-wrapped bundle of clothing and gifts into the canoe. "Come with me to Tetiaroa," he said. "I'll hear your idea along the way."

"My *taio,* I do not need to go to the atoll," the priest said gravely. "The place that draws me lies in Tahiti. I think there is a way to retrieve the corpse of your brother."

"You can't find the body by yourself." The thought of digging up old burial crypts made Matopahu's neck hairs rise.

"*Taio*, I have new hope. Three men, *opu-nui* who once served under me, have gone back to work in the high chief's *marae*. By now they may have learned something useful."

"But *opu-nui* are mere underlings. Why should the priests share their secrets with such men? I do not think your friends will learn where the body is hidden."

"It is certainly worth trying."

"And if Land-crab catches you, you'll be meat for the sharks."

"My *taio,* I recall that I used the same argument when *you* went to spy on our enemy."

"In those days, one could masquerade as an Arioi, and I went only during celebrations. How will you disguise yourself, now that Land-crab has chased away his performers? Even if you could hide your face, it would not be enough. Everyone knows your walk. I'm certain that Land-crab has his men watching for you."

"Then what can we do?" asked Eye-to-heaven. "Keep wandering from one chief to another until we are known as vagabonds?"

"Otaha will be the last," said Matopahu firmly.

"And if he refuses?"

"Then I will live as I deserve. I'll become a fisherman and forget that my family is descended from the great gods."

"That will not do," the priest answered.

With a sigh, Matopahu sat down on a fallen palm tree that lay on the beach. He stared at the loaded canoe before him, the single-hulled *va'a motu*. "Then I'll find another island, far from here," Matopahu suggested. He reached over and stroked the solid wood of the bowboard that extended from the front of his outrigger craft. "In this canoe, I can sail all the way to Porapora."

His gaze fell on the small but well-crafted vessel. Its high, rounded stern kept breaking waves from swamping the hull. The nearly vertical cutwater beneath the flat bowboard sliced cleanly through the sea. In a moment he would put up the sturdy mast, and the sail, made in the shape of a crab's claw. Yes, he could even reach more distant islands. . . .

"Let me see what answer Otaha gives," the *ari'i* offered. "I'll resist the charms of Tetiaroa. I will not let him keep me long. Then you and I can talk again." Matopahu looked up at the face of his friend, whose expression seemed to be softening. "I ask for one thing more. Help me pray for a safe journey."

"I will do that much. I will even lay the 'sleeping sennit' under a stone for you."

Matopahu knew this trick of divination. By placing a straight length of sennit beneath a *marae* stone, Eye-to-heaven could learn if the voyage had succeeded. If he later found the cord twisted over, then the canoe had come to grief.

"When two days have passed, I'll lift the slab and learn your fate," Eye-to-heaven said.

"I know a better way," Matopahu replied, "and a more reliable one. Come along with me!"

The priest's mouth twitched. Matopahu sensed victory near. "Let us pray first," said Eye-to-heaven. "Then I'll decide."

Midafternoon found Matopahu and the priest on the way to Tetiaroa, blue water rolling beneath the outrigger's hull. Tane's wind had held steady all day. Matopahu sat astern, steering with a sweep oar while the priest perched out on the balance board to counter the canoe's heel.

Squinting through the salt spray that dashed in his face, Matopahu cut open the end of a drinking nut and lobbed it to his friend. He threw wide, and thought he had missed, but the priest, hanging on to the stay lines, lunged and caught it in one big hand.

"Nothing that is good to eat or drink can get past you," Matopahu shouted, grinning. "When you finish that one, I'll toss you another. The wind is picking up, and I need more weight on the board."

He shifted the steering oar beneath his arm, pointing the outrigger's bow slightly east. Tane's wind, while providing swift sailing to Tetiaroa, could make a canoe drift too far westward, causing it to miss the tiny atoll.

The feather pennant at the top of the sail streamed over the outrigger float. The wind was coming directly across the side into the crab-claw sail, an angle that gave the greatest speed. If this kept up, they would reach Tetiaroa even sooner than he had hoped.

Not long afterward, a shout from Eye-to-heaven made Matopahu squint past the sail at the horizon. Yes, those were the feathery tops of palm trees appearing over the blue backs of the swells. First he saw two, then three, then seven. Overhead, a flock of gulls wheeled about his fluttering pennant, as if celebrating his arrival.

As his craft sped closer, the shape of the atoll became more apparent, coral islets spaced irregularly around a ring. He caught glimpses of the turquoise water in the center—the marvelous lagoon—and flashes of brilliant white sand.

"I'll try the pass," he said, turning toward his *taio,* whose disapproving mood had lifted a bit during the voyage.

"It will be tricky," the priest warned.

"Yes, it will." The entrance to the lagoon was shallow and treacherous, Matopahu knew, with barely enough water to keep his vessel afloat. Many sailors preferred to carry their canoes over the reef. Yet he thought the tide favored him, making the pass the quickest way in.

The pass lay at the northwest corner of the atoll. Staying well clear of the surf line that marked the barrier reef, he skirted the atoll's western coast. With the wind now coming from astern, Eye-to-heaven was no longer needed on the balance board; he climbed in to handle the sail.

Matopahu brought his canoe around and pointed it toward the shallow channel, little more than a cleft in the rock. With the sail luffing in the direct wind over the bow, he left the steering oar and helped Eye-to-heaven loosen the stays that braced the mast. Together they brought down both mast and sail, then unlashed the paddles. The channel was far too narrow to be approached under sail, against the wind.

Stroking hard and deep, the two brought the craft through a gap in the surf. Matopahu aimed the bow toward a rippling patch of blue-green water that marked the inrushing tidal current. To the side he saw breakers, foam shooting high as waves struck underwater coral. But ahead, the water was relatively smooth. He felt the hull surge forward as the current caught it, pulling him toward the inviting lagoon.

Eye-to-heaven moved to the bowboard and called out warnings, using his paddle blade to fend away coral heads looming up from the bottom. The hull slid past jagged rocks that rose almost close enough to touch. Matopahu's paddle kept scraping bottom, and he braced himself for the sound of splintering wood. Then came a cry of relief from Eye-to-heaven. "We are over the reef, my *taio*. The gods helped us through."

The water of the lagoon was faintly rippled, almost perfectly calm. The deep turquoise color paled in the shallows, shading to tints of aquamarine, yellow green, and finally light yellow. Among the forests of branching coral on the bottom, Matopahu saw an eel feeding. The black loops and swirls on its green back showed as it darted from one spot to the next.

Schools of brilliantly striped lagoon fish fled the canoe's shadow as it glided over the bottom. In the depths, giant clams opened the wavy edges of their shells and extended their mantles of intense orange or yellow or violet, marbled with black. Matopahu drew in his breath, startled by the beauty of the scene. Here was a place that Tepua would enjoy, but he wondered sadly if she would ever see it.

Many canoes were afloat on the glittering lagoon, some

for fishing, some for sport. Numerous islets lay at the periphery, their beaches backed by dense stands of coconut palms. Matopahu steered toward one of the largest of these *motus*.

As he drew closer, he saw even more canoes pulled up above the beach. Thatched-roof houses stood everywhere in the dense shade beneath the trees. A small crowd of servants came to watch his arrival and to help him drag his canoe up onto shore.

First the travelers made offerings at a small *marae* situated near the end of the islet. Then they unwrapped one of Matopahu's bundles, donning fine wraps and cloaks from Putu-nui's wealth of gifts.

It did not take much time to find Otaha. The chief emerged from his lattice-walled dwelling and gave a warm greeting to Matopahu and Eye-to-heaven. "It is good to see you again," Otaha said. "Do you know why I like this atoll? It is because I can meet all my old friends, the ones who never visit me at home!"

Otaha was a sturdy man with graying hair and a friendly gleam in his eyes. He was not looking as hale as Matopahu remembered, however. It was rumored that Otaha had come here to regain his health, after overindulgence in the peppery drink made from *ava* roots. Matopahu noticed scaly patches on the man's skin and a slight watering of his eyes, but sensed that the chief was recovering.

"Yes, it is unfortunate," Matopahu said, "that at home we rarely leave our own districts."

"But now that you are here, you will stay with me," Otaha insisted. "And you will meet Fleeting-star. We are feeding her well, and she grows more lovely every day."

Fleeting-star? The name seemed familiar. Perhaps she was the daughter whose charms had been praised in a song he'd recently heard. His curiosity was piqued, but he knew that the daughter would not appear for a while.

After light refreshments, Matopahu took a stroll along the white sand beach. A party of fishermen had just come in, and he admired the iridescent blues and golds of the reef fish they had netted. He watched briefly while the men parceled these out into baskets, then carried the fish inland to the ovens of their patrons.

A couple of supply canoes arrived from Tahiti, bringing loads of breadfruit and taro. Matopahu overheard crewmen joking about the highborn people their canoes served. One sailor held aloft a ripe breadfruit as big as his head. "Feed this one to his daughter and she'll get just as plump," he said with a laugh.

"You don't want a girl that big," said another. "What happens if she rolls over at night? She'll flatten your clams!"

Matopahu smiled and walked on, passing low houses that were set back from shore. Occasionally someone called a greeting, but no one stirred from his seat in the shade. Overhead, coconut fronds rattled in the breeze and the trees swayed gently.

He quickly reached the end of the islet, where tough, woody bushes grew almost to the water's edge. Nearby he found several sprouting coconuts and picked one up. Inside, he knew he would find the coconut germ, a light, spongy delicacy.

He levered off the dry, brown husk on a stake that someone had set into the ground, then broke the inner shell against a slab of coral. He bit into the germ, which had a milder flavor than fresh coconut meat. This piece had an airy crispness, yet melted deliciously against his tongue. He found a place to sit while he savored his find. His only wish was that Tepua could share it with him.

As he gazed out over the tranquil scene, watching the last outrigger canoes sailing in for the night, he began to understand the lure of Tetiaroa. Here one could easily forget Tahiti. The woes of home seemed so distant and unimportant. It was enough for a man to lie beneath the trees, eat good food, doze with only the quiet sounds of surf and birdcalls to wake him. . . .

When Matopahu returned to Otaha's house, he found Eye-to-heaven in animated conversation with their host. Clearly the priest had cast his earlier reservations aside; now he seemed to be enjoying his visit. "People here have heard about your victory in the sacred game," he told Matopahu. "You will be welcome wherever you go."

"But you came to me first," Otaha pointed out. "You are my guest now, and I will take it poorly if you leave me. Sit. I have a surprise waiting." He gestured toward the stool next to his.

Matopahu complied. Two musicians appeared, one playing a nose flute, the other a small drum. Three girls did a provocative dance, but they were so heavily wrapped in bark-cloth that he could not even tell if they were attractive. After several other dances, the music's rhythm changed to a slow and dignified beat.

Then, from the shadows, a figure advanced slowly toward the three men. Matopahu stirred, leaning forward. "My daughter, Fleeting-star," the chief announced with satisfaction. Matopahu could see only a huge bundle of cloth with two eyes peering out the top and a pair of pale feet below.

Two servants came forward to assist the girl. Fleeting-star stood before Matopahu and slowly began to turn around. As she did, the servants grasped one end of the cloth, which was bleached *tapa* of quality suited to a chief's daughter, painted with intricate designs. The cloth began to unwind, revealing first the smooth, broad face and fine shoulders of Fleeting-star.

Matopahu knew that the cloth, once fully unwound, would be a gift to himself from Otaha. He was far more interested in the girl wrapped inside. Seclusion under the dense shade had left her complexion fair and delicate.

She revolved slowly so that he could savor every detail. Her nose was delicately shaped, her teeth even and white, her eyes expressive, surrounded by black lashes. And the rich diet here, as Otaha had suggested, had filled her out to classically beautiful proportions. Now her well-rounded arms were exposed and she still kept turning.

The flute and drum reached a crescendo as the last layer of cloth peeled away. The girl did not hesitate. When her plump glory was fully visible, she continued to revolve, making sure that Matopahu missed nothing. Then she gave a shriek of delight and ran off into the arms of her attendants, who quickly covered her.

"She will make someone a fine wife," said Otaha, eyeing Matopahu sharply. "Few men are worthy of Fleeting-star. I have already turned down several *ari'i* of good standing."

"I understand your problem," the guest agreed, feeling his voice catch in his throat. "Your other daughters all made good matches. I am sure you want to do as well for this one."

"Until you came to visit me, I was not so certain I could manage it," Otaha replied. "To my thinking, birth is everything. It does not matter what happens to a man. If he has the proper ancestry behind him, little can keep him from triumphing in the end."

The guest could only raise his eyebrows in response to Otaha's words. Matopahu was the firstborn son of a firstborn son, going back to great men of legend. If birth alone were the only requirement, then Fleeting-star could not find a better husband than himself. And yet . . .

Otaha seemed to sense Matopahu's indecisiveness. "Now is no time to discuss these things," the chief added heartily. "Food is waiting for us, and I hope you are hungry. You cannot get fish like this in Tahiti."

Long after dark, Matopahu lay awake on his bed of mats in the guest house. At last he rose, wrapped himself in his cloak, and crept out into the cool air. He heard a stirring behind him—Eye-to-heaven. A moment later, his *taio* joined him on the beach.

The moon had not risen, and the inky sky overhead was sprinkled with stars. Across the calm lagoon came faint sounds, distant voices. Lights moved, the torches of spear fishermen who stalked their prey in the shallows.

"I'm not sleepy," said Matopahu quietly. "Walk with me."

The beach ahead was only faintly visible, the border between land and lagoon blurred by darkness. As Matopahu led the way, he felt hollows in the sand, smooth bits of shell, and sometimes the coolness of water beneath his toes. The men soon reached Matopahu's quiet spot and made themselves comfortable, resting against a pair of palm trees.

"*Taio,* we both know what Otaha wants from you," the

priest said softly. "The girl is very beautiful and as wellborn as any in these islands."

"Are you urging me to take her for my wife?"

"It is a tempting offer."

"But—"

"Do you hesitate because of Tepua? I have talked with her many times. I know her dedication to the Arioi. I feel certain that she will not leave her troupe."

"Even so, there have been signs. You saw one of them. I think that she will come to realize . . ."

The priest sighed. Matopahu's thoughts took him back to another shore, to the place in Tahiti where Eye-to-heaven had performed a cleansing rite long ago. While Tepua and Matopahu stood in the water, a pair of blue sharks, sent by the gods, had paid them homage as if they were great chiefs.

"Yes, my *taio*," said the priest. "I did see a sign. But its meaning has never been as clear to me as it is to you. Perhaps someday Tepua will be your wife, but not now. Meanwhile, Otaha is offering something we did not anticipate."

"So that is your advice? Take the woman. You surprise me tonight. You are the one who keeps insisting that the curse still lingers."

"It does, but its influence is limited now. If you mount an attack against Land-crab, the curse will bring you down. That is what the omens predict. But I see no reason why you cannot take a wife and live happily in another district of Tahiti. Otaha will give you a fine tract of land—"

"Abandon my brother's people?"

"You must be patient. Land-crab eventually will over-reach himself. Meanwhile, by marrying Fleeting-star, you can become a man of influence once again."

Matopahu fell silent. His friend's advice was sensible, but he couldn't forsake Tepua. "I will not sleep tonight," he told the priest. "Go back to the guest house. Take this with you." He handed his cloak to his friend, leaving himself garbed only in a loincloth.

"Another vigil?" Eye-to-heaven asked.

"I think not," said Matopahu with a laugh. He strode out into the water, heading for the nearest moving light.

*   *   *

Matopahu waded slowly across a coral shelf that lay just below the surface. The kelp covering the rock felt refreshingly cool beneath his feet. A short way ahead of him stood a fisherman with a long spear, accompanied by a boy. A torch of bundled palm-leaf ribs gave off a yellow light, illuminating pools where fish moved sluggishly. When the torch burned down, the boy lit another.

With a smooth, quick motion, the fisherman struck. *"Aue!"* the man cried in dismay when his spear missed. "They are slippery tonight." Then he turned toward Matopahu. "Are you catching them in your hands, my friend? Maybe that works better."

"I am just watching," said the *ari'i.* "If you lend me your spear, I'll see what I can do."

"Maybe your hand is swifter than mine," said the fisherman, "or your eyes keener." He offered the spear to Matopahu, who ran a finger along the carved tip, pleased at its sharpness. The whalebone point was mounted to a short section of hard *tamanu* wood, which was fitted and lashed to the spear shaft. Matopahu stepped past the fisherman, hefting the spear to judge its balance. The wrapped sennit handgrip felt good against his palm.

Matopahu grinned in anticipation as the boy held up the torch. He had not been spearfishing since he was little older than the boy. Of course, he remembered the tricks that water played, making fish appear in a different place from where they really were.

He peered down, waiting until he saw a long, dark shadow. Making a quicker thrust, he felt the point strike, pierce something solid, and slide in. The struggle began at once, the spear jerking in his hand. He brought up the fish, which flipped madly, spraying him with salt. Somehow he got it into the boy's basket before it could free itself.

"Ah, I think you have the right touch," said the fisherman. "Let me see you do that again."

The fisherman gave his name as Long-oar. When his basket was filled, he invited Matopahu to accompany him to his home on a small islet across the lagoon. The *ari'i,* calling himself simply "Mato," asked his new friend to wait.

Then he crept back into the guest house and gently woke Eye-to-heaven.

"So you have decided," the priest said sleepily.

Matopahu squatted beside his friend. "We both know," he said quietly, "that the first son of an *ari'i* is special, a child of the gods as well as the man."

"That is so," agreed the priest. "And Fleeting-star will make a fine mother for that son."

"No, my *taio*. You are trying to help me, but I feel no conviction behind your words. We both know this. Tepua will be the mother of my son, or I will die childless."

The priest sighed gently. "You may be right, but it would not hurt to try with Fleeting-star."

"I must leave you," Matopahu said regretfully. "My *taio*, you have been more than loyal to me. My canoe is yours now, with everything in it. Stay here as long as you wish, Give gifts. Enjoy the hospitality. Find a chief who needs a priest."

"But you—"

"When Otaha wakes, I will be gone. Tell him I had a message from one of the supply canoes. Let him think I went back to Tahiti."

"Matopahu—" Eye-to-heaven put his hand against his friend's arm.

"I'll try fishing for a while. That is what I promised I would do. When Tepua is finished with her Arioi, I'll take her far from here. That is the only choice the gods have left me."

"You may change your mind," the priest said hoarsely.

"Don't give Otaha any hopes." Clad only in his loincloth, taking nothing with him, Matopahu turned away before his *taio* could offer any more arguments. Dawn was at hand. He hurried to the water and waded out toward Long-oar's canoe.

FOURTEEN

"Move yourself. Wake up!" Tepua groaned at the sound of Pehu-pehu's grating voice. She struggled to open her eyes.

A hand clamped on her arm and shook her roughly. "What is wrong with you, girl?" the Blackleg asked. "Every morning I have to send someone to drag you from your mat."

Tepua pulled free and stood up on her own before Pehu-pehu could yank her to her feet. "You should be setting a good example for the others," the Blackleg scolded. "They look up to you as an experienced player. Soon they will all think they can sleep late."

Pehu-pehu was right. Tepua glanced unhappily at the empty mats around her in the guest house. The other novices had already left, somehow without waking her. Streaks of bright sunlight filtering through the mat walls announced that morning had long since arrived. Why did she still feel so groggy?

"Go and wash. Quickly. Catch up with the others," snapped Pehu-pehu. Tepua felt only a moment's relief when the Blackleg stormed out of the guest house.

Resisting an overwhelming urge to return to her sleeping place, Tepua tied on her wrap. This drowsiness had lingered for days, and she wondered if some sorcerer was working against her. Other feelings had been troubling her—gnawing sensations in her stomach that turned to queasiness when she moved. *Especially in the morning . . .*

The obvious explanation was wrong, Tepua thought. Her monthly flow had come twice since her night with Matopahu, and she had been with no other man.

It must be the visions, she concluded. Though many days had passed since her encounter with Purea and "Tapani Vari," she still saw remnants in her dreams. She woke often in the night. That was why she felt sleepy all day.

I have had enough! she wanted to cry to the gods. *Let me have rest.* Only Aitofa understood her suffering; Tepua had confided in no one else. But Aitofa could not allow her to evade her responsibilities to the troupe.

Wiping away a tear, Tepua left the guest house and hurried down the path to the stream. A cold bath would wake her, she thought, and then she would take her place in practice with the others.

Dust swirled in the dancing area, raised by the feet of the novices and the women of the lower grades—Pointed-thorn and Seasoned-bamboo. The morning sun shone on backs and bare legs. Sweat gathered and trickled down faces.

Ordinarily Tepua enjoyed the practice. Today, however, she kept wishing for the session to end. The bath had helped, but her body had not exhausted its repertoire of tricks to play on her.

He breasts strained and chafed against her wrap as she danced. As she swayed her hips, the feeling of her inner thighs rubbing against each other sent little trickles up into the nest between her legs. The sensation created a moist, expanding heat that quickly grew insistent, then demanding.

She glanced at the other women. Everyone knew that dance movements caused excitement; such feelings gave fire and spirit to the performance. She had seen the signs in other dancers and felt neither shame nor embarrassment. But the surges of raw lust she felt now could only cause distraction.

Aue! It was fortunate that she was not a man; then her condition would be unmistakable. To make matters worse, she needed urgently to urinate.

At last, the dancing master's voice rang out, ending the session. Tepua tried to make herself walk, not run, to the bushes, but halfway there she was overcome by the urgency. She crouched behind some low foliage and, with a groan of relief, released the water she had kept dammed up in her body. She let her head fall forward as her stream gushed softly into the soil, and the maddening sensation eased.

Standing up, she was glad to see that the dancers had dispersed. Right now she did not want to talk to anyone, not even Maukiri or Curling-leaf. She walked into a shady breadfruit grove, then leaned her back against a tree and sat down.

Beside being hot, the day was humid. Her breasts chafed against her wrap. As she loosened the cloth, her hands brushed against her nipples. She gasped at the warm rush of pleasure that went through her body.

Her breasts had often been sensitive lately, and they were not the only part of her that had changed. Her whole body felt warm, languid, earthy. She thought of Matopahu and the last time he had been with her. She remembered the touch of his hands and the look in his eyes.

How she had desired him then and how she wanted him now. She found herself trailing her fingers up the inside of her thigh, toward the place that was already damp and swollen, lips opening as if to receive the length of a man. . . .

She rolled her hips, amazed at how aroused she felt. She was expanding inside as if she could take in *anything*. If she could only understand what was happening to her.

Thoughts of her atoll childhood crept back, scenes of her foster mother, Ehi, and the large family that crowded around her. Young Maukiri and her sisters were there, along with a few older girls. Tepua remembered how one was constantly going off to find her lover. The others would joke, saying that she was already filled with a growing child, so how could she want more?

Filled. Tepua lifted her hand, placed it on her belly. Could that be the answer? There was something strange about her body, a sense of deepening, a sense of change. Could there be a child growing, after all?

So stunned was she by the thought that she surrendered to it and lay back against the tree, her mind whirling. She needed to talk to a woman who knew more about these things. Perhaps Curling-leaf could help her.

She sighed and stood up. There was no denying that something was wrong. And as she retraced her steps back through the forest, she found that she had to stop once again in the bushes.

"You can be carrying and still have a moon flow," Curling-leaf explained, sitting back on her heels in the guest house. "At least it can happen for a while. Do you remember how much there was or how long it lasted?"

"Barely two days," Tepua answered, looking up from the mat where she lay. "And the flow was light."

Beside Curling-leaf, Maukiri sat cross-legged, her face solemn, her eyes round.

"Two of my mother's sisters grew big bellies when I still lived at home," Curling-leaf added. "I learned a lot from them."

"So you think—" Tepua broke off.

"If I touch you, I may be able to tell." With a feeling of trepidation, Tepua lay back and drew aside her wrap. Curling-leaf's palm, warm and dry, pressed deeply into Tepua's belly just above the curls of her nest.

"My mother showed me how to check for the beginning of a child. She pressed my fingers in, like this. Once you have felt it, you never forget." Curling-leaf's face showed a frown of concentration. "Here. I have your answer."

Trembling, Tepua let Curling-leaf guide her hand to the place and press her fingers into the flesh. Low in her belly she felt a small round firmness, like the pod of the *rata* tree. Now all doubts fled. She let out a groan of despair.

The rules of the order. No child of an Arioi may live.

Yet she pushed that knowledge aside as a feeling of wild joy burst upon her. How could she explain it? She felt as if she contained a ball of golden light. If left alone, this ball would expand. She would grow round and ripe, sweet and strong, like the breadfruit at harvest.

Tepua had often envied women with their outthrust bellies, proudly standing where they could be admired by all who passed. When they came to term, she had heard their

cries and knew that these were far more than protests of pain
or grunts of effort. Perhaps the act of pushing out the life
within ignited something more intense than even sexual
release, something that spilled from between their legs in
the form of a living, open-eyed child.

"It is true," Tepua cried, but her voice sounded too thin
and faint to her ears to express the immensity of what she
felt. Curling-leaf seemed to understand. Maukiri, staring
solemnly, did not.

"I am sorry, Tepua," Curling-leaf said. "I can tell that you
are hoping, somehow, to hold on to this child."

"I cannot help it." Tepua wished she could make Maukiri
understand. How could she explain to her cousin what it felt
like? A vast gulf had suddenly been crossed. Tepua had left
her girlhood behind.

She was seized by an unexpected rush of energy. Leaping
up, she pulled her friend with one hand and Maukiri with the
other. "Come with me, down to the lagoon. I want to run
into the waves and sing and splash."

Though their expressions showed puzzlement, the other
two came with her to a place where breakers rolled in on a
black-sand beach. Usually the waves inside the reef were
gentle, but today the wind had whipped up their strength.
When Tepua saw that this section of beach was empty, she
threw aside her wrap. Maukiri and Curling-leaf shed theirs
and they all plunged in. Slowly her companions caught
Tepua's mood, and all three began to frolic like children.

The waves caught Tepua and tumbled her over, but she
fought free and popped up again, leaping high in celebration
and throwing spray around her.

Matopahu's child.

She slapped the waves out of sheer exuberance, dunked
and splashed Curling-leaf and frolicked like a dolphin in the
surf.

Oro's child.

Curling-leaf surfaced beside her, her expression grown
solemn again, but her eyes still sparkling. She cupped her
hands, filled them with foaming seawater, lifted them over
Tepua's head to let the water drain out and flow down over
her hair.

"I am a fool to be happy for you," she said. "But I am."

Tepua reached out, hugged her friend and received a briny hug in return. Over the crash of the waves and Maukiri's delighted shrieks, she shouted, "Yes, it makes no sense. This will only bring me pain. But somehow, I want to shout and sing."

Her friend's voice was steady. "It is not something you *can* make sense out of."

Curling-leaf groped beneath the water and came up with a handful of seaweed and a starfish of midnight blue, all of which she arranged on top of Tepua's head. "There is your new headdress." She giggled.

Tepua took down the slowly curling starfish and held it to the place low on her belly where Curling-leaf had pressed her fingers. She looked out over the reef, at the heaving back of the sea. A voice out of the past sounded in her mind. The priest, Eye-to-heaven, speaking in ritual.

"There is prayer in the moving ocean. The ocean is the great *marae* of the world."

My . . . child.

With a sudden mischievous laugh, Maukiri surfaced like a prowling shark, grabbed the starfish away from Tepua, and threw it at Curling-leaf.

"You daughter of an octopus!" Curling-leaf shouted, and dragged Maukiri backward into an oncoming roller. Tepua joined the noisy, splashing fray. At last the three staggered ashore, weak with laughter.

"She made me swallow so much water that there is a new ocean—inside me!" Maukiri complained to Tepua, pushing Curling-leaf.

"You won't have it long," the accused retorted. "You and your cousin can crouch side by side in the bushes."

Tepua wrung the brine out of her hair. The ocean had reclaimed her crown of seaweed, but she felt as if she still wore it. Curling-leaf's little ritual had been purely impulsive, yet Tepua felt the depth of feeling in it.

All three sat down on a log beneath the shade of a huge ironwood, their wraps plastered against their wet bodies, their feet crusted with fine black sand.

For a long time they talked, then fell silent. Maukiri finally wandered off.

"She will understand, someday," Curling-leaf said. "For this to come and then go away without some celebration—that would be sad. Our dance in the sea was not much, but at least it was something." She sighed. "What will you do now?"

"I have no choice. I must tell Aitofa."

"She cannot punish you," said Curling-leaf.

"I was careless," Tepua confessed. A priest had taught her chants to prevent pregnancy, and had urged her to bathe in the sea after lying with a man. On that night with Matopahu she had been so caught up in her feelings that she had done neither. . . .

"Even so, she will not blame you. Look at how often this happens in our troupe!"

As soon as Tepua stepped across the threshold of Aitofa's quarters, she wished she had not come. The lodge chiefess looked tired, and there were new lines under her eyes. Tepua sensed a deep weariness of the spirit that made her wonder if Aitofa had already lost the struggle with her rival. Tepua wished she did not have to add her woes to Aitofa's burden.

The chiefess greeted her, but her voice lacked warmth. "You look pale. Not more trouble with Pehu-pehu, I hope."

"Only if she finds out. That is why I have come." Tepua tried to keep her voice steady as she explained her predicament.

"You know then what you must do. What you swore to do."

"Noble chiefess, I cannot bear the thought of growing large with this child and then killing it when it is born."

Aitofa was silent.

Tepua's lips and tongue went dry. "Are there ever reasons . . . for sparing a child?"

"Only when the woman is of the highest Arioi rank. You are far from that. And you understand that your atoll ancestry gives you few privileges here."

"The father is Matopahu."

"The father's rank alone cannot help you," Aitofa answered solemnly. "And look how precarious Matopahu's position is now. Even if you were foolish enough to leave the order and keep the child, it would be constantly in danger. Land-crab wants no rivals to his chiefhood."

Tepua clenched her teeth, not wishing to be reminded of Matopahu's struggles. "There is another reason I ask for an exception."

Aitofa cocked her head, indicating that she would listen.

"The great gods do not usually bother with our affairs, but you know that Oro has seized me more than once. And when I joined with Matopahu, Oro was there as well. I carry the seed of the god as well as that of my lover."

Aitofa folded her arms. "So you ask me to make an exception because the child was sired by Oro. Do you know how many girls with growing bellies have told me the same tale? I thought you, at least, would come up with something more original."

"The god did come," Tepua cried, stung.

Aitofa began to tap one finger on her knee, a sign that she was losing patience. "Even if I believed this wild tale of yours, what would I say to the priests? Where is the sign? they would ask. What can I show them?"

Defiantly Tepua laid her hand on her belly. "It is here."

Aitofa took a deep breath. "Have you not understood what I struggled to teach you? It was Oro who commanded the Arioi to be childless. How can the god make such an edict, then plant his seed in a woman of his order? It makes no sense, unless he is trying to test your obedience."

Tepua's mouth fell open. "Test? No. It is too cruel."

"Be careful, Tepua. Only the priests can tell us what the gods expect of us. And the priests have made themselves clear."

"Yet I know you have doubts about some of their pronouncements."

"Doubts, yes. But I cannot overturn such a basic rule as this. I have already learned how much trouble even a small rebellion can bring."

Is that why you are weak and Pehu-pehu grows stronger? Tepua wanted to ask the question, but kept silent, knowing the answer would not change anything. She could see that in Aitofa's face.

"Be reasonable, Tepua. Let us take care of this ourselves, before anyone else finds out. I will get you a potion made from herbs and the roots of wild yam. It will bring on your moon flow."

Tepua sighed. "I have felt the tiny fruit. It is starting to grow."

"Better to cast out an unripened fruit than to strangle a newborn baby," Aitofa said, her face hard. "Would you like to discuss this with Pehu-pehu?"

I should not have let myself feel any joy. I should not have danced in the sea. Then this would not be so difficult.

She tried once more. "What if my claim is true, and Oro has sired this child?"

"That is for the gods to decide. If the drink fails, then your argument will be a little stronger."

Tepua cast her gaze around the room, searching for an escape, but there was none. She remembered when she had begged Aitofa to allow her to join the Arioi. The chiefess had emphasized this harsh rule of the order, and Tepua had sworn to obey. What choice had she now?

If the unborn seed was washed away in the moon flow, it would be as if it had never existed. Matopahu would never know. Everything could go on as before.

"If you wish to serve Oro, this is the right way." Aitofa's voice was gentler now. "If I get you the potion, will you take it?"

Tepua's answer slid from her tongue, as leaden and dull as the grief she felt.

"Yes."

Early the next afternoon, Tepua stood once again in Aitofa's quarters. The Blackleg held out a coconut cup half-filled with a murky liquid. Tepua could not help wrinkling her nose at the unpleasant smell. Reluctantly she took the cup between her hands.

She thought of Matopahu, of all his hopes for a son. Yet she had not misled him into thinking that she might bear his child. Long ago they had agreed that she would abide by the rules of her order.

Matopahu would not be the first nobleman whose entry into fatherhood was postponed because of the Arioi. Some people of high rank were actually glad to delay the appearance of a child, for at birth the infant inherited the titles held by the father and mother. The first son of a chief became chief at birth, taking over his father's high rank, though, in practice, the father continued to rule until the son was of age.

A tear seeped from Tepua's eye, but she refused to give in to sorrow. She steadied herself and brought the cup to her mouth. The odor made her gag. She tried not to breathe as she uttered a short prayer, then tipped up the cup. . . . Why was she tormented by an image of Matopahu's face?

"Drink, and spare yourself an unhappier task," said Aitofa softly.

"*Aue!*" After three long swallows it was done. Tepua looked about wildly for something else to drink, something to wash away the sickening taste. Aitofa offered her another half coconut, but Tepua turned it away. She ran outside to a nearby stream, threw herself down, and gulped water.

When she was done, she looked up and saw Aitofa watching her. Tepua raised a hand to warn the chiefess away. A black bitterness was sweeping through her. It did not matter that Aitofa had done this out of sympathy and friendship.

The chiefess seemed to recognize the signs and kept her distance. "Can I send someone to help you?" she asked.

"Maukiri and Curling-leaf," Tepua gasped as she sat up. She felt as though small stones were jumping around in her stomach. A spell of nausea swept through her, and she feared the brew might come back up.

She did not move until the feeling in her stomach eased. Now she felt perspiration gathering, first on her forehead, then on her back and chest. Craving a breeze, she staggered to her feet and headed seaward, emerging above the beach where a fresh wind blew in her face and finally offered some comfort. For support, she put her arm around a coconut palm that leaned toward the water.

Opposite a break in the reef she watched a youngster playing with the stern of a broken canoe, trying to ride it to shore on the crest of a wave. How cool and refreshing the water looked. She took a few steps and several more, until the water reached her knees. A fierce cramp started in her belly.

She turned back, collapsed on the beach, and lay moaning until the spasm eased. Nearby she heard voices. "Can you find . . . Maukiri . . . ?" she asked a passing group of girls.

"Mau—" The first girl looked at her in puzzlement.

Tepua kept forgetting that Tahitians, knowing only the soft sounds of their own language, could not pronounce her cousin's name. "Mau'iri," Tepua repeated, dragging herself to the foot of the palm tree.

Her head was aching and her vision starting to ripple. She groaned, laying her damp forehead against her arms, until her cousin arrived.

"You must rest," said Maukiri. "I will help you keep cool." She took Tepua's arm and assisted her up the gentle slope that led from the beach. She spread coconut fronds for a bed and plaited a simple fan.

"What will you tell your man?" asked Maukiri as she kept a soft current of air flowing.

"He . . . must not ever know," Tepua answered. "We were together only one night. He should not expect—" She doubled up in a cramp, rolling on her side with her hand clutching her belly. "He . . . should not think . . . a man can sire a child in just one night. . . ."

Staying on the shore with Maukiri beside her, Tepua resigned herself to a long bout of severe cramps and nausea. As the afternoon wore on, her arms and legs shook with weakness, and the throbbing in her head made it difficult to open her eyes. When she was not curled up in pain, she lay in a bath of sweat and misery, waiting for the bleeding to start and the agony to end.

Maukiri, and later Curling-leaf, tended her, fanned her, washed and cooled her with seawater, and tried to get her to drink fresh coconut milk. Between cramps, they massaged her sore belly lightly, to ease the ache. Somehow the night passed.

She woke from a restless, delirious sleep to find that daylight had come. Maukiri and Curling-leaf had built a lean-to over her to shade her from curious eyes. Finally the racking pain subsided. Too weak to move, she could barely raise her head to drink from the coconuts that her friends held to her lips.

"Have I bled?" she asked in a whisper, her vision so blurred that she was unable to make out who sat with her.

"No," came Curling-leaf's reply.

Tepua closed her eyes, feeling drained, empty. The effects of the potion had wrung everything out of her—everything except the child. She felt herself spinning, drifting away. . . .

When she woke again, it was evening. Some of her strength had returned. She looked up to see Aitofa kneeling beside her.

"I am sorry, Tepua," the lodge chiefess said. "To put you through all this, and leave you no better off than before—"

"But what am I to do?"

"The *tahu'a* who provided the potion has gone away. She is a good woman, and I trust her. When she comes back, we will both go see what she can suggest. Meanwhile, stay clear of Pehu-pehu."

Tepua tried to follow Aitofa's orders. After another day of rest she returned to her group, asking the others to make sure that she did not sleep late—even if they had to carry her out of the guest house. She drank little before retiring, hoping to sleep through the night.

Long after dark she woke, feeling a need to urinate. She threw the cloak around her and crept out carefully, trying to avoid disturbing anyone. Fortunately she had moonlight to guide her way to the place where she squatted to relieve herself.

As she stood up, Tepua thought she heard footsteps. She froze, hairs prickling her nape. It could only be someone else coming out for the same reason, she told herself. She peered along the shadowy path. . . .

Someone grabbed her roughly from behind. She managed a single cry before a hand clamped down over her lips. Someone else held her legs. She squirmed and bucked, trying to get a look at her attackers.

Pehu-pehu's bulky figure loomed on the trail ahead. As Tepua fought her captors, she saw the Blackleg signaling them to bring her closer. While the women tried to hold Tepua steady, Pehu-pehu put her hands just above Tepua's pubic bone and kneaded harshly. Tepua tried to scream, but no sound came.

"As I thought," Pehu-pehu whispered to her companions, women of high Arioi rank who had become the Blackleg's allies. "Follow me."

Tepua fought Pehu-pehu's friends as they carried her, but she could not open her mouth for a warning cry. By the time they brought her to their destination—a small hut that smelled of dampness and unpleasant herbs—she had nearly exhausted herself.

The place was lit inside by a few candlenut tapers. "Scream all you like now," the Blackleg told her as the hand covering her mouth was pulled away. "We are far from anyone who will help you."

"You will answer to Aitofa for this," Tepua spat back as the women forcibly stretched her out on a mat. Her terror began to rise as she noticed the strange artifacts hung along the walls—a human jawbone, crude figures carved in wood, necklaces strung with teeth that were impossibly long.

"I am called Nimble," said the occupant of the hut, emerging from the shadows. "You'll suffer less if you don't fight. Let me do my work, and you'll be free."

Tepua could not judge Nimble's age. Her eyes were deep set, her face fleshy. Her arms and wrists were heavily tattooed. In her ears she wore tiny tufts of yellow feathers. Could she be the woman Aitofa had wanted to consult? Surely this must be some other *tahu'a*.

"Do not do this," Tepua whispered, searching for some signs of kindness in the wrinkled face. "I will obey the Arioi rules. I have already made arrangements. My lodge chiefess—"

"Ignore her," the Blackleg ordered. "We have no time to waste."

Nimble knelt beside Tepua and began to probe her belly. "The seed clings tightly," proclaimed the *tahu'a*. Tepua wriggled under the onslaught of pressing fingers. "We must force it to let go." When she spoke, her tongue darted in her mouth like the tongue of a lizard.

Nimble began to chant, calling on the gods of her profession to aid her. As she sang she began to probe more deeply.

Tepua whispered her own prayer—to Tapahi-roro-ariki. *Do not let this woman harm me.*

Meanwhile, Pehu-pehu's companions bore down harder, grinding her legs and arms against the thin mat and the hard ground beneath. These were the same women she often saw clustered around the Blackleg, the ones who were surely scheming with her to displace Aitofa.

The *tahu'a* began a deep massage, causing new agony with every stroke. Tepua squirmed and cried, but she could not budge under the combined weight of her captors. She remembered, as a girl, how she had endured the tattooing of her buttocks. The pain had seemed bearable at first. After a time she began to beg for a rest, but two cousins sat on her until one side could be finished.

Never had time passed more slowly. Yet this was far worse. Nimble's fingers seemed to be reaching inside Tepua's body, squeezing pain from every place she touched. She clutched and kneaded and grabbed until Tepua shrieked from the torment. Sweat poured in rivers from Tepua's face and back. Thrashing like a wounded animal, she lifted her head and tried to bite Nimble's arm.

"Enough!"

Tepua struggled up from a red haze of pain. The voice— surely she was dreaming—Aitofa's?

The grip of the *tahu'a* became harder, as if Nimble sensed her prey would be torn from her hands. The pain flamed, seized Tepua, bent her back in an upward arch, and tore a scream from her throat.

"I said, enough!"

Suddenly the claws were gone from Tepua's belly and the worst of the agony with them. With an effort, she looked up. Nimble was sitting stiffly, her muscular arms raised. Aitofa and a dozen Arioi women had crowded into the hut. Several carried spears.

"Aitofa, why do you interrupt us?" asked Pehu-pehu in an even voice. "I am doing what is best for her . . . and our troupe. We all know that."

"Is that why you snatched her at night, when you hoped I was sleeping?" Aitofa took another step forward, her voice cold and her eyes glittering.

She turned to Nimble. "Your work is done. You will not touch her again."

Tepua tried to sit up and sank back, dizzy. The bleeding had not begun, but she assumed that it would start soon. She wanted to be away from here, with her friends looking after her. Looking up at Aitofa through eyes blurred with tears, she attempted to speak, but could not.

"Someone heard footsteps outside and noticed you were gone," Aitofa explained as the women loyal to her helped Tepua up. "It was not hard to follow Pehu-pehu's tracks."

She took Tepua to the lean-to near the beach, where Maukiri and Curling-leaf came to tend her once again. This time Tepua recovered more quickly. What good had the cruel hands of the *tahu'a* done? she began to ask herself. Night and morning and night passed, but she suffered no cramps or bleeding. All signs convinced her that the seed within still flourished.

A day later, Tepua stood with Aitofa in a quiet place away from the practicing Arioi. Sunlight gleamed on the waters of a brook and on shiny black rocks, but the mood was somber.

Tepua studied Aitofa's tired face. Beneath the eyes of the chiefess lay heavy pouches. How many nights had the poor woman lain awake trying to find a way to defeat the rival Blackleg? Had she gained anything in making that show of force?

"Pehu-pehu has found another *tahu'a*," the lodge chiefess whispered.

Tepua cried out in alarm and moved her hands protectively over her belly. "She will fail like the others."

"There will be more foul drinks," warned Aitofa. "Massage, treatments even harsher. If those fail, she will thrust a strong stalk inside you—"

"No! I have endured enough. Let the child be born, and then I will deal with it. That is what other women do."

"Ah, Tepua. Don't you understand? She wants to make an example of you. So the other girls are more careful. So no one tries to beg for an exception."

"Why single me out? Is this for my refusal to join Chipped-rock Lodge?"

Aitofa stared at her and did not reply at once. "Perhaps," the chiefess said sadly, "it is because of me. Pehu-pehu has spies of her own. She knows that you work against her."

"*Aue!* Then it is *me* she wants to destroy."

"I do not know for sure if it is you or the child. I cannot see what dark thoughts she holds in her bowels. In either case, how can I protect you? There is no one to keep watch day and night. You have to get away from her. Go inland and hide until the child is born."

Tepua tightened her fist. "Who will help you speak up against Land-crab if I am gone?"

"It does not matter now," said Aitofa. "The season is almost over. When the harvest festival is done, the troupe will disperse."

"But our lodge—"

"It will not die. When the next season turns, we will assemble again to prepare for the Ripening Festival. By then your belly will be flat. You will rejoin us, and Pehu-pehu will have no more excuses to harm you."

"My belly . . ." Tepua fell silent. Aitofa's unspoken assumption was clear. She expected Tepua to do away with the child at the moment of birth; that was how Arioi fulfilled their vows. Otherwise she could not return to the troupe.

"Go at once," said Aitofa. "Do not give Pehu-pehu another chance at you. She is occupied now. Take your cousin and slip away quietly."

Tepua's eyes began to sting. She embraced the chiefess.

"Do not disgrace yourself," said Aitofa. "We need you with the troupe. Next season, everything may change for the better. Carry out your duty and come back to us."

Matopahu sat in the cool shade of coconut palms and watched two girls dancing. One was plump and had a pleasantly languid way of moving—she reminded him of Fleeting-star. The other was thinner, an atoll girl, almost pretty. The more he looked at her, the more she made him think of Tepua.

"They both like you," said Stingray, the fisherman beside him. "That one is from my home island." He pointed to the slender girl. "What a nice morsel. Too bad she is my cousin, or I would have her myself."

Matopahu complimented the girl's dancing. He glanced sideways and saw other fishermen eyeing her performance with great interest. *When the dancing is over, she won't lack company,* he thought.

The drummers quickened their beat. From all sides, he heard cries of encouragement as a third dancer joined the pair. This girl he had not seen before. Her skin glistened with oil and her face was radiant. Her small, firm breasts were draped with a garland of tiny white flowers. Matopahu felt an unexpected stirring. . . .

"*Aue!*" said Stingray. "My home atoll is too small. That girl is also my cousin!"

The *motu* where Matopahu sat among his friends was one of Tetiaroa's smallest. Here the fishermen lived in simple palm-leaf shelters, eating coconuts, local bananas, clams, and fish. Many of these people had come from the swarm of atolls to the east. Drawn by the lure of Tahiti, they had left home, but had found no welcome on the high island.

Matopahu understood why Tetiaroa attracted them. Here the surroundings were familiar, and they could continue to live in the manner of their ancestors. But they also had ready access to high-island goods from Tahiti—bark-cloth, sharp stone implements, as well as breadfruit and other desirable foods. Best of all, life was peaceful here, free of the pressures that often erupted into war on the main island. . . .

Cries and shouts broke Matopahu's reverie. He saw the new dancer wildly undulating her hips. Sweat streaked the drummers' chests as they strove to keep up with her. The dancer gave a final flourish. She staggered, paused to catch her breath. Then she shook her hips once more, evoking a final round of cheering.

Later, as the shadows were lengthening, Matopahu found the girl beside him as he walked along the shore. This girl did not remind him of Tepua at all, except in her manner of speaking. Perhaps she even came from the same atoll.

"Everyone can see," the girl said boldly, looking up at him through glistening, dark lashes, "that you were not born to be a fisherman."

"Then what was I born to do?" he asked, smiling with pleasure at the sound of her voice. He paused to gaze out at the water, then once again faced his companion.

"You must be a nobleman in exile," she said. "Where is your *marae*? Where is your family's sacred point of land?"

"You ask too much," he said. Her soft hands rested against her arms. He leaned down and pressed his nose against her cheek. She had a warm scent, fragrant from the tiny blossoms in her wreath.

"How long will you stay here?" she persisted. "When all the fine people go back to Tahiti, will you go with them?"

"I . . . have no home there."

"Then you will stay with us when the weather changes," she said happily. "Don't worry. You will be safe here. If a bad storm comes, I'll show you how to tie yourself into a *tamanu* tree."

"Then I look forward to the storm season—just so I can have my lesson."

She put her arms around him and began gently stroking his back. "There are other things I can show you." Coquettishly, she pressed against him and rolled her hips once. "I can do that even lying down."

Only the thin material of his *maro* and that of her waistcloth separated them. He felt a throbbing of desire. "I heard a song once," he said, "about a lover bending like a fragrant fern. An atoll song. Do you know it?"

She took his hand, and began to lead him deeper into the privacy of the forest. "I do," she said softly.

"Then I will close my eyes and listen."

FIFTEEN

Tepua and Maukiri set out for the Tahitian highlands with no clear sense of where they were headed. Each carried a palm-leaf basket, the first filled with provisions that Aitofa had hastily gathered, the other holding extra clothing as well as a few tools and utensils. In addition, Tepua carried an ironwood spear with a long, serrated tip. If Pehu-pehu came after her, Tepua was ready to defend herself.

But she did not expect the Blackleg to pursue. Getting rid of Tepua had been her purpose and now she had achieved it. Tepua angrily imagined Pehu-pehu's smile of triumph as she bullied Aitofa's remaining supporters. There would be a score to settle when Tepua came back . . . *if* she came back. But, of course, she must do what Aitofa had ordered. She could not abandon her friends and her lodge leader.

Tepua sighed, and trudged on, up a little-used path that wound inland over red clay soil, slowly ascending through grass and low bushes. Here and there a hibiscus tree or a coconut palm shaded the trail. *"Aue!"* said Maukiri, pausing to catch her breath. "I—forgot. I was supposed to meet someone this afternoon."

"Be glad you missed him," said Tepua sourly. "It may save you some pains in your belly."

"Your trouble, cousin, is that you stuck with *one* man." Maukiri wiped her hand against her damp brow and squinted toward the high hills ahead. Resolutely she started

201

walking again. "If you had listened to me and changed partners every night—"

"That old tale again!"

"How do you know that it doesn't work?" Maukiri retorted. "You never tried. And now what will I do for company in this wilderness? Swim in the river and hope for a friendly eel?"

"It will not hurt you to give up men for a few months," Tepua retorted.

"Men, yes," Maukiri grumbled. "And not only men. A dry mat, decent food—"

"Cousin, do you already want to go back?"

"I will stay with you," Maukiri answered in a subdued voice.

"Good. Then stop arguing and help me find a place to live." Aitofa had told her about hidden valleys where people dwelled long ago. One needed only to keep walking to locate them.

The two women continued awhile in silence, climbing ever higher. At last, stopping to catch her breath, Tepua looked back. She was still wary of pursuers, but saw none. The coastal plain lay far below, its dense stands of trees stretching toward the lagoon. Beyond the shore, the azure lagoon ended in a milky band of breakers.

Farther out, waves tossed on the dark surface of the Sea of the Moon. Tepua glimpsed a few distant sails of fishermen and imagined the cool wind at their backs. Here there was no breeze, only hot, humid air.

"I'm hungry already," said Maukiri. "Did you see the piles of food they were preparing for the festival? Because of you, I am missing the biggest feast of the season!"

"You'll eat when we stop."

"And when this basket is empty? I can fend for myself by the sea, but I know nothing of mountains."

"There will be plenty to eat. I'll show you how to live on wild foods."

Maukiri grimaced as she shifted the basket to her other hand. "When this is over, I'll be as thin as a *motu* woman again."

"Then think how much you'll like fattening yourself!"

Tepua glared at her cousin, who had never been slender. Then, tired of arguing, Tepua took the lead at a brisk pace. The trail ran over a crest, began to descend. In the distance she heard running water.

Here the forest canopy was so dense that only a muted green light reached the ground. The air grew dense, humid, and full of heavy fragrance. Ferns and other clinging plants dangled from branches or curled out of crevices in the bark of trees. The welcome sound of water became louder.

Soon the women approached a cataract that leaped and foamed over black boulders in its bed. From downstream, Tepua heard the roar of a waterfall. After pausing to drink at the bank and splash herself with cool water, she led her cousin upstream.

Here wild taro grew, spreading huge, glossy leaves that hung from slender stalks. The trail wound through a grove of *rata,* the Tahitian chestnut. The *rata* trunks looked as though smaller trees had been twisted and melded together, creating strange ridges and hollows where malevolent spirits might hide. The weird forms and the weathered bone-gray color of their bark gave the trees an unsettling skeletal appearance, even in daylight. Both Maukiri and Tepua kept well away from them.

The deep shade under the chestnut trees kept the ground damp. Tangles of surface roots crossed the muddy path, making the footing slippery. A dark red-and-brown carpet of decaying leaves was dotted with the yellow green of fallen chestnut pods. Tepua picked up a kidney-shaped pod. "You can roast and eat these," she said, stripping off the fleshy husk to show the nut inside. Maukiri glanced at it with only mild interest.

The trail continued along the river, skirted a pile of rock. A toppled hibiscus blocked the way; the women had to walk to the edge of the stream to get by it. Others trees had fallen, and each required a special effort to climb over or under it. At last, in disgust, Maukiri put down her basket and sat in a clump of ferns. "This is where I am spending the night," she proclaimed.

Knowing from experience that nothing would move her, Tepua agreed.

*   *   *

By the time the sun was falling toward the valley wall, the two wayfarers had erected a crude shelter of branches covered with pandanus-leaf matting. Tepua speared two fish in a pool of the stream. She asked Maukiri to pick wild plantains while she got out the fire-making tools.

When Maukiri returned, Tepua was working with the fire plow and bed stick she had brought. The bed stick, held under her heel, had a narrow trough down its length. As she rubbed the pointed plow stick down the trough, she recited a traditional atoll chant.

> *Tukakahe, tukakahe!*
> *Tupepere, tupepere!*

Maukiri laughed and began a different version of the chant.

> The big stick rubs
> Vigorously, strenuously
> Back and forth it strokes.

The smell of hot wood dust tingled in Tepua's nostrils. She blew the sparks to a flame that caught on dry coconut husk, then spread to kindling. Finally she got a good blaze going, burning dry branches snapped from the upper sides of fallen trees.

"I'll teach you how people cook in the mountains," she told her cousin, pointing to green lengths of giant bamboo that she had cut with a shell knife. Tepua put pieces of fish into some bamboo sections, chunks of a breadfruit from her basket into others. After sealing the ends of each section with fresh leaves, she dropped it into the open fire. By the time the outside of the moist bamboo blackened, the food was cooked.

As darkness fell, she and Maukiri recalled the life they had abandoned. They sat under the shelter singing old songs of their distant atoll. What a pleasure, Tepua thought, to speak in the familiar way again, sounding the hard "k" and the nasal "ng" that Tahitians omitted. She remembered the people left behind, especially Ehi, Maukiri's mother. Tepua had grown up in Ehi's household, and Ehi's ample arms had always been there to comfort her.

Many nights, after dark, the family had sat together inside their snug house singing just these songs.

> Here I go, riding the waves.
> Here I go, blown by the wind. . . .

In the highlands, the night air quickly grew cool. The women wrapped themselves in the extra bark-cloth cloaks they had brought. After the long walk and the heavy work of setting up camp, Tepua felt pleasantly weary. She barely noticed how hard and lumpy the ground was beneath her bed of ferns. Her eyes closed and she began to drift off. . . .

Until Tepua felt her cousin's hand clutch her arm.

"What was that?" whispered Maukiri.

Tepua sat up, trying to shake off the frantic grip so that she could reach for her spear. From outside the shelter she heard soft rustling. "Ghosts!" Maukiri hissed. "With long teeth!"

Tepua's pulse raced as she listened. A twig snapped and then another. *Pehu-pehu and her nasty friends?* She found the weapon's shaft and held it tightly while she whispered a prayer.

Then came a soft grunt. "Yes, they have teeth," she cried with relief. "And four legs."

"Ghost pigs!"

From outside came more sounds of grunting and pawing. The breeze shifted; a strong swine odor drifted through the shelter. "No," Tepua answered. "These are the meaty kind. Wild ones."

"That is just as bad." Maukiri's arms were about Tepua and her body was trembling.

"They smell the cooked food," said Tepua, trying not to think of long tusks, or of the legendary Man-slaying Pig. "After they root around awhile, they'll leave." She had buried the fish bones and other remains of the meal, but perhaps she had not made the hole deep enough.

Maukiri stirred. "If the pigs are still hungry . . ."

"*Aue!* They will not eat you. But if you let go of me, maybe I can use this spear. How would you like baked pork tomorrow? There are no men around to say it is *tapu.*"

"I can't . . . think of food. Cousin, why did we come to this terrible place? Why don't we go home?"

"Home?" Tepua paused, and was relieved to hear the sound of the pigs departing. "Do you know what you are saying, Maukiri?"

"Yes. My mother would be glad to have us. And to raise your child."

Tepua sighed in dismay. She had entertained such thoughts, and knew where they led. "Ehi would be the only one to welcome me. Have you forgotten all the trouble I caused when I went back the last time? Remember that I am my father's firstborn, even though my brother rules."

Tepua was descended from a long line of chiefs, each the firstborn of his or her family, each inheriting more *mana* from the parents than did later children. Accordingly, the firstborn was always the preferred choice for succession to the chiefhood. If she produced a child, it would have precedence over everyone now alive.

Imagining the strife that a child of hers would cause brought tears to Tepua's eyes. How could she disturb the peaceful reign of her younger brother, who had already shown such promise as a chief? "No. Everything is settled," she said. "I cannot go back in this condition. You know that, Maukiri. We are high islanders now." She put her arms around her cousin and tried to ease Maukiri's trembling.

"Then tomorrow . . . tomorrow we need to find a better place. Where pigs can't get to us."

"Yes. Tomorrow." Tepua lay down again on the mat. Outside now, all remained silent. She closed her eyes and envisioned the delicate blue waters of her home lagoon. She and Maukiri were paddling a small outrigger canoe, heading into shore, approaching a dazzling white beach. . . .

In the morning the pair set out early, following the river upstream as soon as they could see their way. At times, rock walls forced the trail to the bank and then to the stream's other side. At each crossing, the women disrobed, holding their bark-cloth wraps and baskets high as they waded through the chilly flow that sometimes rose above their waists. At last, the trail ran straight for a time.

"This might be a good site," said Maukiri, as they approached a grotto hollowed from the fern-covered stone of the valley wall. Grass and young bushes sprouted near the cave's mouth. "The sides and roof look solid. I think we would be safe in there."

Tepua put down her burdens and studied the small cave. A thick carpet of old banana leaves inside suggested that other people had taken shelter there. What kind of people? she wondered, frowning. She hoped that Maukiri had never heard tales of Lizard People, reputed to still live in remote high valleys of Tahiti.

"If we stay here," said Tepua cautiously, "we will need to put up a fence. That will keep out the pigs." She refrained from mentioning other dangers.

"Good," said Maukiri, opening her basket. "I'll take the knife and go cut bamboo canes."

As the sun rose higher, Tepua squatted on her heels and dug holes in the hard-packed soil before the cave. She had crudely fashioned a digging stick by snapping off a twig and rubbing its end to a point. The valley kept growing warmer. The air was alive with twittering birds and whirring insects.

When Maukiri brought the bamboo canes, she and Tepua pushed them into the ground as deep as they would go, spacing them closely. The women left no opening, but instead made the fence so low in one place that they could step over it.

"I will sleep better tonight," said Maukiri when they were done.

"Not if your belly is empty," Tepua retorted, insisting that they dig a pit-oven and line it with heavy, black stones. She sent Maukiri to dig up wild taro, which required lengthy baking, and went off on her own to look for bananas. There were no coconut trees growing this far inland. Wild tubers, freshwater fish, and crayfish would be the main sources of food during her exile.

Carrying her spear, Tepua continued up the twisting

gorge, rounded a jagged outcrop, and suddenly found
herself in a different setting. The valley was broader here,
the forest open. Several trees bore upland bananas, their
purplish stalks raised high as if to show pride in their crop.
Her mouth watered as she ran to the nearest tree.

Then a sound made her freeze. From nearby came voices.
She felt sweat bead on her brow and trickle down, stinging
her eyes.

The voices were getting closer. She thought she might
pull down some broad leaves and hide underneath. As she
reached for one, she heard a shout and then another. Men's
voices. Footsteps. Before she could run, they surrounded
her.

Lizard People! The six men were darker and shorter than
most Tahitians. Their beards were not neatly shaped and
plucked, but grew in tangles under their chins. Their hair
was long, tied back in the fashion of atoll warriors. They
wore loincloths ornamented with designs of crude human
figures. Each man carried a heavy club, and these too were
carved with human images.

Tepua stifled her cry of fear. She did not want to bring
Maukiri into the trap after her. She clutched her weapon,
wondering if her cousin would sense the danger and flee.
Her initial instinct was to fight, but six men circled her, and
they all looked strong. One began to speak.

At first she could not understand him. Then she realized
that his language was not so different from that of coastal
Tahiti. It was spoken with an odd intonation, and contained
a few words whose meaning she had to guess. "Who are
you? Why do you steal our bananas?" he asked harshly.

"I—" Her mouth felt dry. Suddenly she drew herself to
her full height. "I am Tepua-mua-ariki," she said, "daughter
of Kohekapu," and proceeded to recite part of her lineage.

"Ari'i?" The squat men looked up at her and then at each
other. They pointed at her rudely, discussing her appearance. Then the one who seemed to be their leader took a step
forward and addressed her.

"You have no claim on this land. This is ours, from before
the time of the *ari'i*. Do not think you can come and seize

it. We will defend this land." He raised his club and shook it at her.

She faced him squarely. "I wish only to dwell . . . in that other valley." She gestured toward where she had been.

"There?" The men's scowls vanished. From all sides came high-pitched peals of laughter.

"What is wrong with that place?" Tepua demanded.

Again, the men laughed, and Tepua saw no way to get an answer from them. But now that the tension was broken, she thought that a peace offering might serve her. If only she had a gift . . .

Her hands went to her neck, fingering her necklace of polished shells. "Take this," she said to the leader. "We will be friends."

He grasped the necklace in his stubby fingers and turned it over, his eyes wide with delight. He dangled it before his friends, but when they showed too much interest, he pulled it over his head, glancing down with pleasure at the way it hung across his brown, muscular chest. "All right, *vahine ari'i*," he said cheerfully. "We will be friends. And I will tell you why you do not want to live in that other valley." His companions crowded closer, all seemingly eager to see Tepua's reaction to his news.

"It is because the evil spirits live there," the man with the necklace said. "You will recognize them. They look just like us, but they float this high above the ground." He put his palm at the level of his knee.

"But . . . I do not know where else to live. Last night I heard only wild pigs."

Once more the men dissolved in laughter, turning around and doing little dances of mirth. "Do you think the savage ones make noises? No. They slip up on you quietly. When they finish, there is nothing left but your bones."

Tepua bit her lip. She did not know what to make of this warning. She recalled the old bedding in the cave. Other people had stayed there. She saw no signs that harm had come to them.

"So," said the leader. "You will go? If you change your mind, come ask for me—Pig-bone. I am headman. I will welcome you to my house."

Tepua glanced back longingly at the bananas. "Yes. Take some, " said Pig-bone, reaching up to break off a stalk. "Put a few out as an offering to the evil ones. Maybe they will leave you alone."

When Tepua returned to the cave, she found Maukiri in front, plucking feathers from a brightly covered jungle fowl. "How . . . how did you catch that, cousin?" she asked.

"Have you forgotten how good I am at throwing stones?"

Tepua raised her eyebrows. At home, Maukiri had often been sent out to bring back a few chickens. The birds roosted in trees and seemed to know when anyone was eyeing them for a meal. It took sharp aim to bring one down. "Then we will have a good dinner," Tepua said, adding nothing about her encounter. She hoped that Maukiri's prize did not belong to Pig-bone's people.

After darkness fell, and the women had entered the cave, Tepua tossed three of the remaining bananas outside the fence. She whispered a short prayer to keep out intruders. "What are you doing?" asked Maukiri, but Tepua did not answer. She slipped back inside, wrapped herself in bark-cloth, and placed her spear close at hand.

"I hear something," said Maukiri. "From *inside*."

Tepua sat up and listened, turning her head. "It sounds like water seeping through the rocks."

"That's what it must be." Maukiri pressed herself closer to Tepua. "But what's *that*?"

Tepua had heard it also—a soft rustling just over her head. "Maybe an insect . . . or a gecko." She wished her blood would stop pounding in her ears so that she could listen. The talk of evil spirits was only meant to frighten her, she told herself.

"We are safe in here," said Maukiri. "Geckos don't bother me." She yawned. Shortly, her breathing slowed and deepened.

Tepua lay wide-awake, thinking about the men she had seen today. Lizard People were supposed to be able to scale sheer walls of rock; that was the reason for their name. But perhaps Pig-bone's men were nothing more than they seemed—people left over from the old times, the first *manahune,* whose ancestors had been conquered by the arriving warriors of legend. As for the warning, these men were just having fun with her. Perhaps.

Tepua found herself wishing that she had taken the headman up on his offer. No matter how coarse the hospitality he offered, it would be better than staying in the isolation of this cave. Even if no hungry spirits haunted the place, she did not think that she could sleep here.

SIXTEEN

When the morning shadows were still long, Tepua and Maukiri, carrying all they possessed, entered the valley of the upland *manahune*. Maukiri was still complaining, "After all that work of making the fence—"

"Then live in the cave by yourself," Tepua snapped.

"All right, cousin. I will visit these wild people, but I cannot promise that I will stay with them."

The banana groves were silent, their leaves scarcely astir in the morning breeze. Behind them Tepua saw breadfruit trees, most bare of fruit, a few holding a small crop. The season for breadfruit appeared to be over.

She looked around cautiously, hoping to avoid another surprise. Where were Pig-bone's people? To keep from alarming them, she held her spear low.

Suddenly a chorus of whoops and cries rang out. From all sides, men and women emerged from behind trees. Many carried clubs or short spears.

The men were as fierce looking as those who had surrounded her on the previous day, their ornaments of bone and tusk giving off a menacing sheen. The women looked just as wild. Their black hair was short, frizzy or curly, adorned with tufts of chicken feathers and wreaths of jungle vines.

"Cannibals!" Maukiri shouted in alarm and turned on Tepua. "What have you done to us?" She wrenched the weapon from Tepua's hand and swung it around to defend herself.

"No. They are our friends," Tepua answered. She gazed in dismay at the sea of approaching faces, frantically seeking one she knew. Where was the headman? Where were the others from yesterday?

As she watched the strangers advance, she shouted, "Pig-bone has invited us to stay with him." She plucked a young banana shoot, a symbol of peaceful intentions that everyone should understand. "Maukiri, lower that spear," she hissed as she held the shoot high.

"Pig-bone?" said one man, who strode cockily to the fore. "Pig-bone is your friend?" He turned to confer with a knot of men behind him. Others began gesturing wildly, with their hands or with their weapons.

One who was slightly taller and pudgier than the others approached Tepua. "I will escort you to the headman," he said roughly. With a swift motion, he plucked the spear from Maukiri's grasp. "You will not need this pig-sticker," he added with a harsh laugh.

The *manahune* closed ranks behind the two lowlanders. Tepua glanced back nervously, noting that all the weapons were held ready. With Maukiri pressing close to her, she marched along the path, until they reached a cluster of thatched houses.

Tepua felt goose bumps as she studied the unfamiliar scene. Unlike the houses she knew, these dwellings were raised above the sloping ground, built on platforms faced with stones. For walls, the houses had only dangling mats. Children peered from behind the mats, and a few brave little ones ventured out to stare at her.

The neatly kept yards of the lowlands were not in evidence here. Trees and underbrush grew densely around the houses. As she watched, a few chickens darted from cover, then quickly vanished in the greenery. The sunlight filtering through dense forest overhead bathed the whole scene in an eerie light.

"Here is the headman's house," said the escort, halting before the largest platform.

Tepua glanced up and saw a round-faced woman looking

back at her. The woman, who wore earrings of bone that
resembled fishhooks, emerged from behind her mat curtain.
"My husband is gone," she said loudly. "Who are these
strangers?"

The people all spoke at once. She silenced them with a
gesture. Tepua noticed then how heavily tattooed her hands
were; from a distance they appeared solidly black.

"Ah," said the headman's wife, looking directly at Tepua
with new interest. "You must be the one who gave my
husband that necklace of shells. A fine gift! What have you
brought for *me*?"

After Tepua took from her basket one of her precious
wraps of bleached bark-cloth, the headman's wife became
more amicable. She beckoned the visitors up her rough
stone stairway, accepted the gift, then ushered them into her
house. "I am called Stay-long," she said. "I do not know
your names."

Aside from her intricately woven headpiece of vines and
flowers, the chief's wife was plainly dressed, with only a
rough *tapa* cloth about her middle. She draped Tepua's
garment over this and seemed delighted with the gift.
Certainly it was made of far finer cloth than any Tepua had
seen here. At last Stay-long put the new wrap away.

"My house is big," the headman's wife said proudly. "We
have plenty of room for you both."

"You are kind," said Tepua, ignoring her cousin's disapproving look. The thatched-roof house was not very different within from those of coastal Tahiti. Plaited mats,
cushioned by a layer of cut grass, covered a floor of
hard-packed earth.

The furnishings were sparse, the utensils somewhat
exotic in appearance. The wooden bowls bore tiny carved
figures. A hollowed log with a broad slit along its length
served to hold small belongings.

"Come," said Stay-long, "I will show you all the rest."
Two open-walled cooking sheds lay behind the house, each
merely a thatched canopy that sheltered a pit-oven—one
shed for men, another for women. At the far end of the
platform stood another small house. The chief's wife led

them to it, pulled aside a hanging mat, and invited Tepua to put her head inside.

The strong odor of herbs made her wrinkle her nose and pull back. With a start, she realized that this woman was some kind of practitioner. Tepua's hands went protectively to her stomach as she remembered her earlier ordeal with a *tahu'a*.

"This is your first?" asked Stay-long, who had somehow sensed Tepua's condition. "Do not worry. I will help you when the time comes."

Tepua did not wish to ask what sort of aid the woman would offer. She turned away, but Stay-long took her hand and led her down an irregular ramp from the rear of the platform. Maukiri trailed along with obvious displeasure.

"Now I will show you my little helpers," Stay-long said brightly. In the grove ahead, Tepua glimpsed a low stone wall enclosing a rectangle of stony ground—a simple *marae*. Just outside this sacred site stood a tiny house raised on poles. At Stay-long's insistence, Tepua peered inside.

In the dim light she could barely see anything. She caught a harsh, musty smell that repulsed her. Then she began to make out the shapes of tiny human figures garbed in cloth tied on with cord.

Maukiri grabbed Tepua's arm and dragged her back. "Do you want to die?" her cousin whispered hoarsely. "Stay-long is a witch-woman, a *vahine tahutahu*! Those are her pet imps!"

Uneasily, Tepua glanced from her cousin to Stay-long to the house of images, then again to Stay-long.

"Do not be afraid," said the *tahutahu*, cheerfully. "You are my guests. Nothing here will harm you."

Soon afterward, Pig-bone and his two young brothers showed up at the house. Pig-bone's brothers, bushy-haired twins, were greatly preoccupied with a centipede they had caught. They vanished back into the woods almost at once. The headman lingered, pleased by his new visitors. "You will stay with us until the child is born," he insisted.

Tepua did not need to look at her cousin to know her reaction. Maukiri would already be back in the cave if her cousin had agreed to go with her. But Tepua tried to put aside her concerns about the headman's wife, who seemed to have little in common with the cold-fingered Nimble. In any case, she knew that it was better to have such people as friends than as enemies. Tepua might someday need aid from Stay-long's unpleasant little helpers.

At last, after telling of the wild pigs he had pursued that morning, the headman left to confer with his hunters. The women went out to gather vegetables. Now Tepua saw how these people managed to reap harvests from the difficult mountain terrain. Using stone retaining walls to hold back the soil, they had built broad, level terraces for growing taro and yams. They diverted river water to irrigate the terrace fields, and used layers of thatch as mulch and to discourage weeds.

By early afternoon the women had cut and wrapped tubers, bananas, and a few small river fish in hibiscus leaves. These now lay baking in the heated stones of the covered pit-oven. Six other women, relatives of Stay-long or Pig-bone, had come to join the meal. Two of these, Pig-bone's mother and aunt, were part of the headman's household. The others lived in a smaller house on a nearby platform.

Curiosity about the new guests kept the conversation animated. Tepua did not want to reveal too much about herself, but she found the company pleasant, and soon was answering the questions put to her. *Manahune* women, she discovered, knew little of the sea. Her atoll background seemed to mean nothing to them. When she spoke of the Arioi, they looked bewildered.

It was only when Tepua talked of her dancing that the women grew excited. "We will have a little gathering," Stay-long cried, and the others shouted agreement. "You will teach us the lowland way, and then we will show you ours."

Gradually the two visitors settled in, growing accustomed to a different way of life. In the days that followed, Tepua and her cousin were often called on to entertain, and did so with relish. They also began sharing the work of the women in Stay-long's household.

Days passed and the season changed, bringing cooler, drier weather. Tepua and Maukiri accompanied the highland women on long expeditions through the wilderness, gathering fern roots and other wild foods to supplement the dwindling crops from the terrace gardens.

The many new activities kept Tepua occupied, yet she found Matopahu constantly in her thoughts. As months passed, the changes in her body reminded her that she carried a part of him. Did he know about the coming child? she wondered. If he did, wouldn't he have tried to find her?

Her womb was starting to swell, rounding out her belly. She could feel herself loosening within, preparing to accommodate the growing child. Sometimes she caught herself trying to imagine the baby's face, and its tiny fingers. . . .

As Tepua was gathering herbs one morning with Stay-long, she halted, troubled by an unsettling feeling in her stomach.

"What is it?" asked the *manahune* woman, eyeing her keenly.

"I think I ate too many bananas last night."

Stay-long put down her basket, a knowing expression on her face. "Let me feel," she said. Tepua hesitated. She had already endured too many meddling hands. But Stay-long conveyed a motherly feeling that Tepua needed.

"It must be too early for the child to be moving," Tepua protested as she opened her wrap. Stay-long just smiled and laid her palms against the swelling abdomen. Her touch was warm and comforting.

The *tahutahu* cocked her head and gave a delighted chuckle. "Too many bananas, hah! I have seen many girls with their first baby, and they all blame something they ate. Come back to the house and I will teach you how to feel what is happening inside."

When they were under the roof, Tepua stretched out on a mat while Stay-long crouched beside her, placing the edge of her hand against Tepua's belly just above the curls of her nest. "Do you notice a little tickle right there?"

"You mean—" Tepua broke off, falling silent in order to concentrate on the sensation. There it was, a tiny flutter low down in her abdomen.

"Now you know," said Stay-long solemnly. "The child is stirring."

Tepua kept her fingertips on her stomach to mark the place. She could feel no movement from the outside, but inside . . . yes. She breathed out slowly, trying not to be overwhelmed by the emotions sweeping through her. She almost resented the tiny seed for reminding her that it was still alive, growing and moving. So long as it stayed still, she could almost persuade herself that she wasn't pregnant; she could ignore the problems that lay ahead.

Yet, at the same time, she felt a rush of joy and awe. Suddenly the child within felt real.

"Wait until he is beating around in there like a little typhoon," said Stay-long, cheerily. "Then you will really start to know him."

The headman's wife brought a stoppered gourd and poured a few drops of the contents into her palm. "This is rubbing oil," she explained. "I will show you how to keep your skin soft so that it stretches easily as the baby grows."

Stay-long began firm, yet careful strokes that kneaded Tepua's belly muscles without pressing too deeply. She alternated long strokes with a series of light fingertip circles that made the younger woman feel warm and at ease. Then Stay-long showed Tepua how to do the circling motions herself. "When the baby starts to come, this will feel good."

When the baby starts to come. Tepua grimaced, wishing she did not have to be reminded of that moment. How would she feel when she held the infant in her hands? How would she find the strength to fulfill her Arioi duty?

Stay-long seemed to sense her turmoil. "There is something troubling you. Tell me."

The grief that Tepua had been able to push aside returned, tearing at her. She groped for words. "All this care . . . does not matter. It may comfort me. But the child . . . the child will not live."

"You are wrong," said the headman's wife, gently but firmly. "I'm sure that all is well."

Tepua wished she could keep silent. Why should Stay-long share her agony? But the woman's warm gaze melted her reserve. "The child will not live," Tepua whispered hoarsely, "because I must do away with it. That is the Arioi way. That is the rule of our order."

"Ah." Stay-long's eyes widened. "I thought you were keeping something from me." She fell silent awhile. "Tell me, Tepua. Do the Arioi know where you are?"

The younger woman paused. Aitofa had given her only general directions, and no one had followed her here. But on expeditions with the *manahune* women she had sometimes glimpsed foraging parties from the coast. What if someone had recognized her? That seemed unlikely, since she had always been careful to duck out of sight. "I do not think so."

"Then, perhaps, little mother, the decision is not yet made."

Tepua felt tears coming. Suddenly she was gathered up by Stay-long's small but capable arms. She laid her head against the other woman's breast and let her misery run. As she sobbed, the *manahune* woman cradled her and smoothed her hair.

The stream of tears slowed to drops and her sobs became sniffles. Stay-long still held her, rocking her, crooning over her. "What of the child's father?" she asked. "Do you care for him?"

"Yes. Very much."

"Then let me help lift the weight of this decision from your shoulders. I understand little about the Arioi, but by every custom I know, you must consult with the father and his family. It is up to them to say if the child should survive."

"The father is far off . . . on another island. But I think I know how he would answer."

"Then abide by it."

Faced by an impossible choice, Tepua grew angry. "Not if it forces me to desert my friends and my troupe."

"What about his family? You cannot ignore their opinion."

Tepua hesitated. "His family is gone. He is the only one left."

"I sorrow for him," murmured Stay-long. "Yet, perhaps I still can help you."

"But—"

"Do not forget my skills," she chided, with an odd grin. "The living are not the only ones who can advise. If you wish to consult with the father's ancestors, I can help."

Tepua drew in her breath at this suggestion. She had never asked for favors from a *tahutahu*. One glimpse of Stay-long's spirit images had been enough to make her tremble.

But now that she trusted the woman, Tepua found the offer more appealing. Matopahu's wish for a son was not enough to justify preserving the child. Perhaps the spirits of his ancestors could offer a stronger reason for defying the rules of the Arioi.

"If you want my aid," said the headman's wife, "tell me his genealogy. As much of it as you know . . ."

Later that afternoon, Stay-long went to the raised little house, reaching up to put an offering of fruit inside. Tepua went with her, bearing a skewer strung with dried candle-nuts, the first nut burning. Nervously, she stood by, holding the sputtering flame aloft.

The shadows across the valley were deep now. Tepua heard the *vahine-tahutahu* chanting, imploring a particular spirit to speak to her, flattering it with words that Tepua could not fully understand. Then Stay-long reached up to her house of images, took a large, whorled shell from under the roof, and held it to her ear.

While Tepua shivered in the gathering chill, she watched Stay-long's face. The headman's wife called out questions, and the voice from within the shell seemed to answer. Soon Stay-long grew angry, shaking the shell and hurling foul language at the spirit in the house above her. By now, Tepua's hand was trembling so much that she feared the flame would go out. She watched Stay-long listen again; this time the woman appeared satisfied.

"Bring the light closer," Stay-long ordered. Tepua gritted her teeth and forced herself to obey. She let the smoke from the burning candlenut into the house of spirit figures. Then she recited the words taught to her by Stay-long—sounds of an ancient tongue that had no meaning to Tepua. The light flickered on the little figures, the round, dark faces glaring at her. She saw slitted eyes and protruding lips. One mouth seemed to move. . . .

Tepua gasped and jumped back.

"It is all right," Stay-long said, gesturing her away from the place. "Your part is done. I must stay awhile." With her teeth chattering from fright, Tepua made her way back through the gloom to the house platform. Numbly she climbed up. Fortunately, Maukiri was waiting. Tepua collapsed into her cousin's arms.

From outside, behind the house, Tepua still heard chanting.

On a morning soon afterward, Tepua and Stay-long set off on a trail that was overgrown from disuse. Vines brushed their faces. Huge ferns arched from the forest floor.

The thought of where she was going made Tepua's knees weak. Somehow Stay-long had learned from her ghostly messenger how to find the cave of Matopahu's ancestors. As was common among *ari'i* families, the skulls that housed the ancestral spirits were hidden within a high rock face.

Tepua didn't want to approach these spirits. Yet she owed it to Matopahu to ask them what to do about the child. And she knew, in any case, that she might someday have to face them. If she and Matopahu wed, the skulls would be brought down for the ceremony. She dared not slight the sacred dead who would be called on to sanction the union.

The air was warm and moist as the two women trudged over ridges and across valleys, through rushing water and meandering streams. Tepua had trouble maintaining the pace. She kept stopping to drink, or to take a banana from her basket.

When the sun had passed noon, Stay-long led Tepua to the edge of an overhang. She clutched a sapling tightly as she peered down a steep slope that plunged into a gorge. She saw moisture dripping down the face of black stone below, and tiny ferns sprouting from crevices.

Stay-long pointed to a place about halfway down. Tepua followed her hand and saw a round opening in the wall.

"It cannot be that," Tepua insisted. "Only a lizard could climb down there. . . ." The words died on her lips. Stay-long was looking at her with amusement. Perhaps the *tahutahu* was of the legendary Lizard People after all.

"We do not have to climb," said Stay-long with a laugh. From Tepua's basket she pulled a long rope plaited from strips of hibiscus bark. She ran this around a well-rooted tree, leaving half the length on each side. "Watch," she ordered.

The *tahutahu* threw the free ends of the rope into the gorge, letting them dangle below the cave. Then she stood with her back to the drop. Taking the doubled rope, she ran it under her arms and across her back.

"The rope must be able to slip," she explained, and showed how to let it slide slowly through her right fist while using her left hand as a brake. She could stop her descent by bringing her braking hand across the front of her body, locking the rope.

Tepua gaped as the headman's wife walked backward over the cliff edge, leaning out against the tension of the rope. Stay-long alternately locked and released the rope with her left hand, guiding it through the fingers of her right. After descending a few steps, she looked up and grinned. "You can do it. I will show you."

While Tepua trembled, Stay-long climbed hand over hand back to the top. She let Tepua try the slip-and-brake technique while still standing on level ground.

"As you move back, turn slightly sideways to the tree," Stay-long instructed. "Then the rope can slip around you more easily. When you bring your hand across your body to stop, turn *toward* the tree. That will help lock the rope."

Tepua was not at all convinced that the rope would support her. She was still on level ground—a relatively safe place for testing. Leaning backward, she was surprised to find that she could hold herself.

"Keep going," Stay-long told her. "Over the edge and down."

Tepua's mouth was dry. She wondered if there might be

an easier way to do this. "Tapahi-roro-ariki," she called softly, imploring her ancestress for aid. She kept stepping slowly backward until at last she planted one foot on the steeply sloping face. Resting a moment, feeling the rope supporting her, she gathered her courage.

"Keep looking up," Stay-long told her. "Do not worry about the bottom."

Not even a lizard would try it this way. Tepua knew that she was hanging in midair, but was determined to follow Stay-long's advice. A puff of wind chilled the sweat that ran down her face and back. She was breathing quickly. "Don't stop!" urged the *tahutahu*.

Unlocking the rope a bit, Tepua took another step down and then froze. Looking at the steep wall rising in front of her, she realized suddenly that there was no going back. The longer she took, the longer she would be out here! She forced herself to go on.

After a time, she fell into a rhythm. Slip the rope and step. Again and again. Stay-long, gazing down at her, kept growing smaller. Tepua kept checking the *tahutahu*'s hand signals, depending on them to guide her to the cave's mouth.

Then Tepua saw frantic waving and hastily looked at her feet. Had she arrived? To one side she saw only bare ledges. To the other . . .

Aue! She clenched the rope in sweaty hands and moved sideways. Her feet reached the lip of the opening, but her body was still leaning away. *What now?* Stay-long was shouting instructions, but the wind whistling past Tepua's ears drowned out the words.

Once more she prayed to her guardian spirit, and this time she thought she heard a reply. Taking a deep breath, she kicked herself away from the cliff, then lifted her feet. The rope swung her out and then into the cave. She let go, fell onto her backside, her head still dangling over the gorge.

For an instant she panicked, thinking she would slide out, go plunging headfirst down the cliff face. Somehow her scrabbling hands found holds and her belly muscles contracted so hard that they cramped, curling her up and into the cave. She scuttled deeper inside like a crab, away from that sheer drop.

For a while she could only close her eyes and shudder, wrapping her arms around herself. The rock beneath her seemed to sway, as if threatening to tilt and dump her back out of the entrance. She did not open her eyes until the swaying stopped.

SEVENTEEN

The stone floor beneath Tepua was chilly and damp. She could see nothing in the depths behind her but shadows. The air in the cave was musty, difficult to breathe. Anxiously she edged closer to the brightness near the entrance, though she refused to stick her head out. The sunlit area about the grotto's mouth seemed her only refuge.

In that cramped place she sat with her knees drawn up, watching for Stay-long's descent as the rope swung past, vanished, then appeared again. Birds sailed by, squawking angrily. Tepua heard small cascades of pebbles rattle down the face of the cliff. At last, the *tahutahu* swung herself to the opening. Tepua scrambled back to make room for her.

Stay-long had tied the basket to her waist. She quickly brought out a mat and two cloaks, laying one about Tepua's shoulders. Feeling a bit warmer now, Tepua forced herself to peer into the darkness. At first she saw nothing.

Stay-long began praying softly, calling on her gods to protect her. Tepua added her own shaky voice. As her eyes adjusted to the gloom, she felt herself stiffen with dread.

The grotto was quite shallow, the rear wall almost within reach. There, on a shelf of stone, stood a dozen skulls, their vacant eye sockets watching her.

The *tahutahu* uttered a protective chant. "Look on this woman," Stay-long declared, addressing the skulls. "See what she carries. It is the seed of Matopahu, growing ripe.

Is she to be the mother of his line? That is what we come to ask. That is the question you must answer."

Tepua wrapped the cloak tighter about her shoulders as the chanting continued. The *tahutahu* pressed against her, providing additional warmth. Even so, she trembled from chill, and from fear of these ancient spirits. How long would she have to remain in this place? And how would she get back up to the cliff top? Even thinking about that made her dizzy.

The repetitious droning of the chant made Tepua's eyelids begin to close. She had walked far today and had missed her usual midday nap. Her head slumped forward.

She tried to fight the drowsiness. Of all places, she did not want to fall sleep here. But she was not actually falling asleep, she realized. Something was drawing her into the darkness where the skulls rested, as if the ancient bones held an answer.

Tapahi-roro-ariki, be my guide, she prayed silently. To Stay-long, she wanted to whisper, "Keep chanting. The gods may open a path to the answer I seek." But Tepua could no longer speak; she could only watch, listen, and feel.

Then she was drifting beyond herself, to a place far from the cave. She glimpsed sunlight and sharp shadows. Scents of coastal flowers wafted to her on a breeze from the bay. She sensed again the presence of that woman of another time—Te Vahine Airoreatua i Ahurai i Farepua.

At last, Purea's guest had arrived. The foreign chief, Tapani Vari, had finally accepted her invitation. In the cooling shade of the longhouse, she watched her bearers lower him onto a finely plaited pandanus mat. Because of his infirmity, he had been carried here from the beach, with his armed men walking ahead.

These guards, outfitted in brilliant scarlet from shoulder to knee, stood just outside the open-walled building. Purea did not like the tight expressions on their faces as they turned from the crowd of onlookers to see what was happening within. Yet she understood the need for caution. Tutaha had agreed to keep his distance, but she did not completely trust him.

"Tupaia," she said, beckoning the priest to her with a downward sweep of her hand. "There must be no disturbance."

"Your own guards will maintain order," Tupaia answered smoothly.

"Keep checking on them," she told him. "The crowds out there will cause no problem. The people who worry me are the ones I *cannot* see."

"I will go and look myself," he promised, leaving her to attend to the guest of honor.

Purea put aside her concerns, and approached Tapani Vari with pleasant words on her lips. He had raised himself to his elbows and was gazing at the grand sweep of beams that held up the palm-thatched roof of the longhouse. She could tell from the awed look on his face that he had not expected such an impressive structure. But surely his own people — who could build such a grand vessel — had even larger meeting houses. What a pity that they were so foolish in the ways they cared for their bodies.

It was Purea's hope that she could restore Tapani Vari to good health. With an imperious gesture she summoned four young women, attendants skilled in the art of massage. All had been chosen for attractiveness as well as their ability to heal through the suppleness of their fingers. Heads turned as the four paraded in, dressed in fine *tapa* with garlands about their necks and flower-crowns on their shining black hair. Purea directed two of the young women to Tapani Vari's mat.

Eyes wide, they took their places on each side of the visitor. Bowls of scented oil lay beside them. The women knew what they must do, but neither ventured to touch him.

Purea opened her mouth to scold, then realized that it would do no good. They were frightened of the strange-looking man, and not just because of his appearance. Her priest had offered them protection — chants and feather amulets — against any evil that might come from touching the foreigner. Yet they still were reluctant. It was up to Purea to smooth over the threat of an insult to her guest.

When she knelt beside Tapani Vari, Purea felt her own reluctance to begin. The outlandish garments, with their

tight coverings, strange flaps, pouches, and slits, baffled and
dismayed her. Though her visitor's blue eyes were gentle,
the pallid coloring of his skin and sharpness of his features
screamed at her to draw back. She prayed to her ancestress
for the strength and vision to see the visitor as he was and
not be turned away by his outward appearance.

She found enough resolve to keep her hands from trembling
as she reached toward him. Gently she pulled at the heavy blue
cloth that covered his arms and chest. He did something with
the flaps and disks that made the front of the garment open up.
Then he drew out his arms and put the garment aside.

Following her example, the two female attendants began
tugging at the unfamiliar covers that encased Tapani Vari's
feet. Purea noticed that these casings were very thick on the
underside. Why, she wondered, did the visitors need such
protection? Had they no soles on their feet?

Her question remained unanswered even when the casings pulled free. Each foot and calf was still covered in a
tight sleeve of fine white material, closed over the toes and
extending upward toward the knee. At Purea's request,
Tapani Vari seized these inner garments from the top and
peeled each one off like a second skin.

Purea drew in a sharp breath as she gazed at her guest's
feet, pale, bony, narrow, and blue-veined. The toes, instead
of spreading, were all crushed together. How could a person
stand such discomfort? She summoned her courage once
more, dipped her hand into a bowl of oil, began the
massage.

Seeing Purea at work, the two young women overcame
their own fears. They knelt to the mat and began rubbing the
visitor's forearms, which were covered with coarse hair and
dotted with odd little brown spots. He lay back, gazing at
them with a dreamy pleasure in his eyes and an odd smile on
his lips.

But Tapani Vari was possibly the only one relaxing now.
Purea heard frenzied whispers of servants behind her. "My
women will take care of you," she assured her visitor. "I will
be back soon." Trying to keep her worries from her guest,
she rose without haste.

She went to Tupaia, who was standing with Hau and a

group of her own men. "My lady . . ." The urgency in the priest's voice startled her. Outside the longhouse, the meeting ground lay inexplicably empty. When had the crowd of onlookers vanished? She noticed Tapani Vari's guards watching for signs of movement in the distant bushes.

"What is this?" she demanded of the priest. "Has Tutaha betrayed me?"

"I do not know," he said unhappily. "But men with slings and stones are crouching just out of sight."

"The foreigners must not see them!"

"The warriors may attack," Tupaia said. "I advise you to send your guests back to the safety of their vessel."

"And let them learn that I have no control over these people? The visitors believe I rule all of Tahiti!"

The priest stared at her in astonishment and dismay. Hau spoke first. "Must you continue this pretense, Purea?" he asked bluntly. "Tell the foreigners the truth."

"That they have ventured among quarreling chiefs? No. If they discover that, they will forget about making peace and think only of conquering us. It is far better to let them believe that I command the entire island."

"Then we must do something about these hidden warriors," Tupaia said.

"You, Hau," she replied quickly. "Can you learn if Tutaha has sent these sling-men?"

"I will try." She saw the conflict of loyalties in the old man's expression as he turned away and headed across the clearing. He owed allegiance to Tutaha, yet he seemed to understand the larger stakes.

"I have no wish for a battle with Tutaha over this," she said to the priest. "He is a great chief, and I respect the way he rules. But on the matter of the visitors he is blind."

To assure her guests that all remained well, Purea called for refreshments to be set out on the ground adjacent to the house. Servants scurried to lay down banana leaves and coconut cups in a great ring. Others went to fetch baskets of fruit.

While these preparations were under way, a messenger arrived. Tupaia spoke with him briefly. "Chief Tutaha wishes to speak with you," the priest told Purea gravely. "He is waiting at a house nearby."

"At this moment?" A warning prickle lifted hairs on the back of her neck, making her shiver. At the same time, she felt the corners of her mouth draw back in a scornful grimace. Did Tutaha believe that she was a fool or a coward? Did he think she would abandon her guests to his ambush? "If the esteemed chief wishes to see me, he can come here," she answered firmly.

The messenger argued with Tupaia, but to no avail. At last the envoy's face hardened. He turned on his heel and strode off.

Chief of Pare-Arue, you will not drive me as the stone fishermen drive their prey by striking the water.

Hau arrived next and his expression was grim. "If an attack comes, you can be sure that Tutaha is behind it."

"And what will that gain him? Hau, you have watched these visitors closely. Do you think that the loss of their commander will frighten them away from Tahiti?"

The old man's face paled. "I don't believe we have seen the full power of their weapons. These strangers will not run. They will destroy us first and then take our land."

"Do you support your chief in this folly?"

Hau looked away. "He is at the *marae,* waiting for a sign from the priests. The gods will tell him what to do."

"I have already heard from *my* gods," Purea answered. She glanced out from the shade of the longhouse into the foliage beyond the clearing and felt cold streaks down her arms. She had seen the remains of men who had been killed by sling stones—chests smashed, foreheads cratered. This was no fate she could wish on her guests.

"Tell me this, Hau," she continued. "If I send my own warriors out, will Tutaha's men attack them?"

"My lady, perhaps you should ask him."

Purea followed Hau's gaze. A small party was approaching on the path from shore. Flanked by his advisors and orators, the formidable Tutaha came closer. Then he stopped, keeping his distance from the foreign guests. Purea let him wait, turning first to escort Tapani Vari to his dining place. Her guest now seemed happy and relaxed. With signs she told him that she would shortly return.

Summoning her strength, Purea advanced with a slow and regal tread to where Tutaha awaited her. "I regret that you have chosen to deceive me," she said coldly.

Tutaha's expression darkened. "And I regret that we disagree so strongly on what must be done."

"You will not harm my guests."

"Finish your entertainment," he offered.

"And afterward? Do you plan to attack them on the shore?"

"Once the strangers depart from this house, they will not be your concern."

Purea turned and gestured toward the distant trees. "Withdraw your men. That is the only answer I can accept from you."

"I will," he replied. "For now. But you must agree to something in return. You will stay behind when the foreigners depart. You will not leave this place."

Purea felt his sharp gaze. "I agree to nothing. Remember this, mighty chief. I am *your* guest." She watched the expressions of the men around Tutaha, several of whom were her kin by marriage. She wondered if they would permit any harm to come to her.

"You are, indeed, my guest, noble lady," Tutaha conceded. "And you are a sensible woman. At the proper moment, I know you will take care for your own safety . . . and remain behind." With these words he turned away and departed.

Purea was trembling with rage. She tried to calm herself as she went back to join the foreigners. To her relief she saw that her guests remained at ease.

When the feasting and entertainment were done, Tapani Vari stood up to address Purea. "We are saddened that we must take our leave," he said through Hau. "Your hospitality has refreshed us and renewed our spirits."

"I, too, am sad," Purea replied. "You must come see me again. Soon you will be fully well again." The words seemed to die on her lips, however. She did not even know if these men would survive until evening.

Laden with rolls of *tapa,* fruit, hogs, fowls, and other gifts, the foreigners prepared to return to their landing place. Tutaha's warning echoed in Purea's ear. She imagined the sling-men posted somewhere down the path . . . and the destruction that would follow.

Tapani Vari signed that he felt well enough to walk now. His guardsmen, in their red garments and tall headgear, strode on ahead. They had become lax in their vigilance, Purea thought. Now they had eyes only for the young lovelies of Purea's court who accompanied them. Must these girls, too, fall victim to Tutaha's attack?

Purea suddenly strode forward. "I will come with you," she announced to her guest, trying to put gaiety into her voice. Tupaia called her back, but she refused to listen. She caught up with Tapani Vari, strode beside him, keeping as close as possible.

As they went, she spoke merrily to her guest, aware that not a drop of perspiration could make its way down her face, nor a doubt show in her eyes. Ahead, breadfruit trees grew close on each side of the path. She had never thought of these trees with anything but appreciation for the crop they gave. Now they only provided hiding places for Tutaha's warriors.

Her voice grew louder. *Let Tutaha know I am defying him.* She glanced behind and was gratified to see that Tupaia had joined the party, marching with the lesser masters of the vessel.

Tapani Vari laughed, his eyes twinkling and a pleasant ruddiness showing in his cheeks. His mood had improved greatly by this visit ashore, yet he remained infirm. She offered him her arm. She helped him cross streams, aston-ishing him with her strength when she lifted him over a narrow creek. "You must regain your lost weight," she said jokingly. "A woman should not be able to lift a man."

And all along the way she kept alert for any signs of movement, for leaves shaking, for the whispers of hidden warriors. Were they behind her now, creeping up, readying their slings? Or were they just ahead, where the path turned? The walk went on and on, as long a walk as she had ever taken. She prayed to her guardian spirit that Tutaha would not be so foolish as to kill Te Vahine Airoreatua i Ahurai i Farepua. . . .

EIGHTEEN

The vision faded. Groggily, Tepua opened her eyes to see the gloom of the cave and Stay-long bending over her. "What—"

"You have been with the spirits," the *tahutahu* said quietly.

"But . . ." Vivid memories flooded over her. "They gave me no answer about the child," she wailed.

"Perhaps it is there, and you do not grasp it."

Tepua's thoughts were a jumble. What had she gained by coming here at all? she asked herself bitterly. She had visited Purea twice before simply by falling asleep on her mat.

Yet she had felt something extraordinary when she gazed at the skulls. Perhaps Matopahu's ancestors *did* have a special interest in Purea and the days to come. If Matopahu managed to produce an heir, then Purea might be one of his descendants!

"We must leave," Stay-long said, helping Tepua up. "This is no place to remain after dark."

"Yes, we must go." But Tepua's head was still filled with questions. The gods had frustrated her again, holding back what she needed to know.

She watched uneasily as the *tahutahu* tugged at one end of the doubled rope, letting the other end up to slide free of its pivot high atop the cliff. When Stay-long had retrieved the whole length, she found an eyehole near the mouth of

234

the cave, threaded the rope through, and dropped the ends into the gorge. "We will go all the way down," the headman's wife explained. "Tomorrow we will have a long walk back to the settlement. But after this, no more dangling from ropes!"

The promise encouraged Tepua as she started the tedious journey down. Knowing that there would be solid ground below, and a stream for drinking and bathing, also helped. Her lips and throat felt parched. She had been without liquid for half a day.

Step-by-step she descended. All the while her thoughts churned. The idea that Purea might be of Matopahu's line opened a wealth of possibilities. *Purea, who are you? Do I carry your seed or, perhaps, that of your mother? If I destroy this child, will I protect Tahiti or assure the end of our people?*

Not even Stay-long could supply an answer. Tepua's problem remained unresolved as she returned to her life with the highland *manahune*.

The season progressed and rain became scarcer. In the woods, many kinds of leaves turned yellow. Wild ginger and turmeric died out. In the tended groves, bananas were less abundant.

The *manahune* frequently went in search of wild foods. Though Tepua's belly was growing large, she joined the less strenuous expeditions, gathering chestnuts, fern roots, and wild taro. Maukiri, meanwhile, became renowned for her ability to recover straying chickens.

As the days passed, Tepua noticed the child growing more active within her. Sometimes it pushed out with its feet, creating a bump she could feel with her hands. Often, especially at night, it grew restless, seeming to spin around inside her like a small tempest.

Her body changed in other ways. A dark line developed from her navel down over the arch of her stomach. The light brown skin around her nipples grew darker, and the nipples began to leak a thin milky fluid. Eventually, her walk changed to the wide-footed strut she had seen in other heavily pregnant women. With her stomach thrust out, she balanced on her heels, leaning back to counteract the weight in front.

The first time Tepua felt the tightening feeling at the top of her belly, she thought she might be going into early labor. Stay-long reassured her that this wasn't so. Soon this became familiar—a pulling sensation just beneath her rib cage, spreading slowly and evenly around the sides of her bulging middle until the whole felt hard and tight. Then, just as slowly, her belly would relax.

Tepua frequently visited Round-pebble, a cousin of Stay-long's, who was nursing a child she had borne shortly after Tepua's arrival. Round-pebble was a devotee of dancing. When Tepua had been slimmer, she and Round-pebble had spent much time practicing together. Now Tepua could only sit and give instructions while Stay-long's cousin improved her technique.

Sometimes Tepua watched Round-pebble suckling her child while the women sat in a circle and talked. She had seen this countless times before, and it had never seemed extraordinary. Now, with her own breasts swelling, she could not help imagining herself in Round-pebble's place.

So many days had passed that her last conversation with Aitofa seemed like a distant dream. The Arioi rarely entered her thoughts anymore. Even her memories of Matopahu came less frequently. Her attention was constantly on the child within her. Before the next full moon, her time would come. . . .

One afternoon Maukiri went off with a foraging party. Tepua was shuffling back from the stream alone when she heard distant shouts. Men raced by on the path that crossed hers. She saw their clubs and spears and suddenly felt alarm. *Invaders?* This was the time of year when food was scarcest. Desperate people might have come to see what they could steal.

Tepua had no weapon with her, nor was she in any condition to put up a fight. She put her hands to her great belly, wondering how to protect what lay within. Hurrying as well as she could, she took refuge near the headman's *marae,* under Stay-long's house of spirit figures. This was a place that most people dreaded approaching.

She squatted, clutching a wooden talisman that Stay-long kept suspended from a thong. Could Pig-bone's people defend themselves? she wondered. She had never seen them fight.

Tepua did not know how to call on the aid of the spirits who lingered in the house above her, nor would she dare attempt such a dangerous feat. Where was the *tahutahu*? she wondered furiously. Tepua could only pray to her own gods, and she did not know if they would help Stay-long's people.

After a short while she was startled to hear voices calling her. "You have a visitor, Tepua," came several cries. "Where are you hiding?"

Was the danger past? These did not seem the voices of people who were under attack. She pulled herself to her feet and brushed off a few clinging leaves. *Visitor?* A hope struggled within. Perhaps Matopahu had managed to find her. She imagined his look of astonishment when he saw her huge belly. . . .

No. That was not what she wanted. He would only make her problem worse. But what other visitor could she have? Aitofa? Curling-leaf? Eye-to-heaven? Or someone she would not welcome at all?

She made her way cautiously around the house platform. Peering from behind the cover of a bush, she saw a crowd gathered in front of Pig-bone's house. The weapons had been put aside and everyone seemed at ease. She saw small gifts—wristlets, earrings, implements made of seashells— passing from hand to hand. Men and women chattered in excited, high-pitched voices.

Then Tepua caught sight of the newcomer and almost fainted in surprise and dismay. She sank to her knees and gave a soft moan. *Pehu-pehu!*

Her thoughts raced back to the times when she had seen parties of Arioi foraging for food in the hills. Despite all her caution, she knew now that someone had spotted her. The news had reached the Blackleg.

In panic, Tepua clutched at her stomach, and wondered if she could escape. She recalled the cave that she and Maukiri had discovered long ago. If Maukiri helped her . . . Tepua tried to remember where her cousin had gone. *Gathering arrowroot.* She might be away all afternoon.

Her mind whirling, Tepua wondered what else she could do. Without someone to scout the way, she could not slip out of the settlement. And if she showed herself, there would be no escaping the Blackleg. Pehu-pehu already had ingratiated herself with the important people of the settlement. Now they were obliged to make her their guest.

But what was the Blackleg's purpose in coming here? Tepua and Aitofa had argued about Pehu-pehu's motives, never reaching a conclusion. The interloper had always claimed to be acting in the best interests of the troupe. Perhaps Pehu-pehu had no intention of harming Tepua. Perhaps she only wanted to make an end to Matopahu's heir. . . .

Hoping that Maukiri might appear, Tepua remained in hiding. But voices kept calling for her; children kept poking about in the undergrowth. At last someone found her and told the others.

Feeling both foolish and angry, Tepua emerged, to be ushered by a boisterous crowd into Stay-long's house. "Your good friend is here," people kept telling her. "You will be so happy when you see her."

When Tepua stepped inside, she saw the Blackleg seated in a circle of admiring women. She bit her lip in anger and held back her words. Until now, these women had been Tepua's friends! Had they deserted her for bits of glossy shell?

Pchu-pehu greeted Tepua as if they had the warmest feelings for each other. Tepua tried not to flinch from the visitor's embrace. "You have filled out," the Blackleg said with a laugh. "No one can call you a skinny atoll *vahine* anymore."

"Your friend has agreed to stay with us," the headman's wife said excitedly. Tepua managed to mumble a few words of acknowledgment. What would Maukiri think? It did not matter. Pehu-pehu had arrived, and there was no easy way to get rid of her. If Tepua could only have a private word with Stay-long, perhaps she could explain.

But the headman's wife seemed entranced by the new

guest, as did her many relatives and friends. The women pooled their resources and began preparing a huge meal. Tepua was astonished to see the Blackleg pitch in, gutting brook fish as if she were a common *manahune*. Never before had Tepua seen this woman at domestic labor. Pehu-pehu had always been surrounded by servants and novices who hurried to carry out her wishes.

While the food baked in the *umu,* the new visitor demonstrated the dances of the Arioi. Tepua recalled wistfully how she had done the same in her early days here. Now she had to watch, holding back her resentment, while the Blackleg captured the attention of everyone present. Her hand movements were perfect; her heavy legs moved with precision. And when she did rapid hip rolls, everyone shouted with glee.

Just as the dancing ended, Maukiri returned from her foraging trip along with several young relatives of the headman. Her face was damp with sweat, her hands and arms grimy from digging up roots. When she saw what was going on, she rushed to Tepua. "This is a nightmare, cousin," Maukiri said. "I am asleep and dreaming."

"Go wash yourself in the stream," Tepua answered. "The cold water will wake you up."

Two days later, the cousins were sitting beside the headman's house, watching the other women practice their dancing. A young drummer was striking vigorously at his slit-log drum. Pehu-pehu stood at the center of attention, a place she had commanded since her arrival.

"This has gone on long enough," Maukiri told Tepua in a quiet voice. "When are you going to talk to Stay-long?"

"What will I say?" Tepua answered glumly. "How can I convince her that Pehu-pehu is my enemy?"

"But she tried to—"

"All she did was take me to a practitioner. Stay-long and that claw-handed Nimble follow similar arts. Stay-long will not believe that Nimble intended to harm me."

Maukiri stared at the rows of dancing women and did not answer for a time. "Tepua, you must decide what you want to do about the child. If you carry out your oath, then I think the Blackleg will be satisfied. We can return to the Arioi."

"Is that what you want?"

"What will happen otherwise? If you leave the troupe, then how will you live? I don't want to stay up here. Every night I dream of the sea."

"Yes," Tepua agreed. "You are right about one thing. We two are not mountain people. At night I imagine that I hear the breakers on the reef and the old songs—" She broke off, wiping away a tear.

Maukiri slid closer and spoke into Tepua's ear. "I heard plenty of tales while I lived with the troupe. You must have heard them, too—about women who hid their children and returned to the Arioi. If others can—"

"Of course I have thought about it," Tepua snapped. "And Pehu-pehu knows that. Why do you think she is here?"

Maukiri's voice faltered. "Then you must do what she expects. There is no reason to keep this child."

"No reason," Tepua muttered. Her arms went protectively about herself and her head slumped. She had begged the spirits for a sign, and they had offered only another cryptic vision. Perhaps Aitofa had been right—that this would be a test of Tepua's obedience to Oro. How could anyone know if the great god wanted this child to live?

"It will be over soon," said Maukiri. "We will forget all this. Think of the new crop of breadfruit coming in. Think of reef fish dipped in coconut sauce and salt water."

"Yes," Tepua agreed, though the prospect gave her no cheer. She tried to interest herself in the dancing. Stay-long and two friends were showing off one of their favorite routines. . . .

Suddenly a new thought chilled Tepua. If Pehu-pehu was willing to take her back in the troupe, then she no longer viewed her as a threat. Had Aitofa already fallen?

Coming back from the stream on a bright morning, Tepua managed to catch Stay-long alone. "I must talk to you about Pehu-pehu," she tried to explain hastily. "She is not what she seems."

Stay-long frowned. "She is now my guest and my friend. I see no reason to distrust her."

"She is an Arioi," Tepua protested, "a skilled performer playing a role. You have not seen the true face of this woman."

"And you are also an Arioi," Stay-long replied thoughtfully. "Do you think I am fooled by appearances? I welcomed you into my house and have not regretted it. I welcomed Pehu-pehu, and she has delighted us all."

"Watch her," Tepua persisted. "She does not trust *you*. Have you seen how far from you she sits while she is eating? And every morning she picks the stray hairs from her sleeping mat and takes them out to be buried." Tepua knew well that food leavings or hairs or fingernail parings could be used in sorcery, though she did not understand exactly what was done with them.

Stay-long's eyes narrowed. "That is just ordinary caution."

Tepua sighed. "Then keep watching her, if you care for me."

Stay-long raised her eyebrows. "Tell me this, Tepua. Have you made your decision about the child? I know what Pehu-pehu expects of you."

Tepua opened her mouth but gave no answer.

"Then I will not interfere. This great god Oro you Arioi follow is not one I wish to anger."

That night Tepua woke in darkness and could not find sleep again. She lay listening to the wind in the high branches and the rustling of geckos under the roof. She felt huge and awkward. When would the child come? she wondered. It seemed she had been pregnant forever, and that the end would never arrive.

The flesh surrounding the entrance to her birthway had softened and slackened. Stay-long had told her that no matter how large the baby was, the birth passage would stretch enough to ease the child out. She had tried to believe this, but now began to doubt again. Her stomach felt as if she were carrying a baby whale.

And a lively one at that, she thought, feeling the latest round of wriggles and kicks. The child no longer tumbled around inside her; it had grown too large for that.

Suddenly a new contraction started, similar to those she

had felt many times before. She expected her belly to relax afterward, but instead it stayed tight. Another contraction began in the same place, but this one was harsher, peaking into a cramp. Soon they were coming at rhythmic intervals, like breakers washing over the reef.

She knew that her time had come. Stay-long had promised to help with the birth. But if she woke the headman's wife, Tepua would wake Pehu-pehu as well. Whatever happened, she was determined that the Blackleg would play no part in it.

She reached over to Maukiri, who lay beside her, and gently prodded her cousin awake. Tepua whispered a plea. "Come with me now. The Blackleg is sleeping soundly."

Feeling their way in the darkness, the two found their way out of the house. Then they had moonlight to show them the path. Maukiri had managed to bring the basket that held their belongings. Tepua hoped it contained everything they would need.

The next contraction caught her only a short way from the house. Tepua had to stop and brace herself against her cousin while she struggled to keep from crying out. "I must go on," she whispered fiercely. Bent over, clutching her distended stomach, she started to walk again.

She did not go far before another spasm struck. They were coming too quickly now. If she could only reach a hiding place where no one would hear her . . .

"Help me," Tepua begged. Leaning on her cousin, she staggered forward again. The houses were behind her now. Ahead she saw the supple shapes of banana trees. Perhaps she could get past the grove. . . .

A gush of water cascaded down Tepua's inner thighs. "Go!" she cried to Maukiri. "Gather leaves. Prepare a bed." While her cousin ran ahead, Tepua used a makeshift staff to support herself as she made her own slow way along the path.

The walk went on and on. Each time a contraction struck, she closed her eyes and gripped the staff. Sometimes her lips moved and she whispered a prayer to her guardian spirit.

"I am back, Tepua." Dazedly, she felt Maukiri take her

arm again. "Just over there," her cousin said. "Away from the path, out of sight."

Somehow they reached the bed of banana leaves. Tepua lay down and tried, in vain, to find a comfortable position. Maukiri began a long, droning chant.

It was a song that Tepua had heard many times as the women of her family gave birth. A new spasm came, but the chanting helped her through it. Repeated again and again, the words began to lull her into a daze.

This is not what I want! Tepua needed to be fully awake. She tried to tell Maukiri to stop droning, but she could not find the strength.

Then she realized what was happening. From far off, something seemed to be calling her. Not now! This was no time for the gods to be bringing a vision.

Yet Purea's presence summoned her. Tepua prayed that the moment would be brief.

On the wooded path along a riverbank, Tapani Vari strode beside Purea, seeming stronger with each step he took. His face showed no worry. His confidence in her appeared complete.

What a betrayal if Tutaha should attack now! What would Tapani Vari think, in his dying moment, of the woman he had dubbed chiefess over all of Tahiti? Trembling with concern over what lay around the bend in the trail, Purea edged even closer so that her arm brushed against that of her guest.

Everything seemed to be happening more slowly. She felt each motion as she lifted one foot, then the other. She dared a glance to the side, expecting to catch sight of warriors crouching behind the trees. Had Tutaha abandoned his plan? She saw the river flowing quietly beside the path, its smooth surface reflecting the overhanging branches. Were men hiding among the clumps of fern?

Then she saw the high ironwood trees beside the beach and the glistening water beyond. No sling-men or warriors stood anywhere in sight. A crowd had gathered to see off the foreigners. She called to them gaily, beckoned them closer.

With onlookers on every side, she advanced toward the shore.

Purea felt dizzy with relief as Tapani Vari raised her hand to his lips in his strange salutation. He made a brief speech. Watching his party leave shore in their small planked vessel, long-shafted paddles propelling them backward, she could barely grasp that she had kept her guests from harm.

But nothing had been settled! Tutaha had withdrawn this time, but the conflict had merely been postponed. She turned, knowing that she must end his foolish notion of destroying the foreigners.

She saw Tupaia close behind her. "Tell Tutaha that I will meet him at his house. I have something important to say to him."

Then Purea closed her eyes, moved her lips in silent prayer. Her feeling of relief was gone now. She retained only a steadfast determination. "Stand with me, mother of my father, brought on waves from the sunrise. Support me, Grandmother, you who have helped me for so long. It is your strength and wisdom that must guide me now, Tepua-mua-ari'i. . . ."

NINETEEN

Tepua felt the vision fading while the words still echoed in her mind. *Tepua-mua-ari'i*. Her own name, as a Tahitian would say it. At last she knew her connection with the noble chiefess who had not yet been born, the woman who spoke of Tepua as "grandmother."

She still did not know, in those days yet to come, whether the *ari'i vahine* would achieve her goal of peace. But she understood how important that attempt would be. *If my child does not live, there will be no grandchild, no Purea to confront Tutaha.*

With those words ringing in her thoughts, Tepua emerged fully out of her trance. She felt a new contraction coming, but she had a moment of respite to look around her. How much time had passed? she wondered. Though the vision had not seemed long, dawn was already spreading gray light across the leaf-strewn ground. And Maukiri . . .

Then Tepua gasped as she turned her head and saw a crowd of women around her. Stay-long stood closest, chanting loudly to the spirits that aided childbirth. And Pehu-pehu stood just behind.

How had they found her? Had she betrayed herself with cries of pain? Tepua felt her heart beating faster in panic. The women here all understood what the Arioi required her to do now. Stay-long had said firmly that she would not interfere.

A heavy contraction hardened Tepua's belly. She felt it

245

begin at the top of her womb, just beneath her rib cage and her breasts. As it rippled down, she felt as if powerful bands were tightening slowly, but inexorably, about the greatness of her pregnancy. Then other bands squeezed her lower down, through her loins and into her back.

The Blackleg sat watching, seemingly indifferent to Tepua's labor. Pehu-pehu toyed with a thick piece of soaked *tapa,* winding the wet cloth around her fingers. *The suffocation cloth.* Tepua knew its purpose. *To stifle a newborn's life before it takes a first breath.*

The sight of this sent a stab of fear through her, a stab that seemed to go right through her stomach and into the laboring womb. She could feel her muscles clamping down on the baby. The flower of her birthway, which had been opening, shrank and closed. Her body knew. It would not let this infant be born into murderous hands.

Yet the contractions continued, and because the infant was no longer progressing, they became frightening and painful. Tepua wanted to get up and run away, but her body was too heavy, her strength devoured by the spasms of her womb. She could only lie with her head back, sweat streaming, while her belly heaved with the struggle.

The baby would die now, Tepua thought in despair. And she would die as well, still distended by the child inside her. Pehu-pehu would be rid of both problems.

She ground her teeth against the racking pain. "Gods curse you, Pehu-pehu. Take that cloth away!"

She saw Stay-long's eyes narrow, first at Pehu-pehu, then at her. Pehu-pehu ignored the outburst.

A rage filled Tepua. *You think I will make it easy? I will not give you my baby's life or my own. You can sit there playing with that cloth for as long as you like. I am going to produce this child alive!*

She shut her eyes, blanking Pehu-pehu and the others from her vision. "Help me," she said to Maukiri, who was standing protectively over her. "You know what to do."

Wearily, Tepua pulled herself up into a crouch. She felt Maukiri take up a cross-legged sitting position behind her. Tepua leaned back into Maukiri's comforting embrace, feeling her cousin's arms wrap around her. She controlled her urge to bear down. It would do no good. Fear had closed the birthway tightly like a bud. She had to open it again.

She made herself think of slow yet powerful things. A wave, far out to sea, rolling toward the reef, building, arching over, spilling and then ebbing away. She imagined fruit, full and ripe and ready to fall.

Then she formed the image of a white *tiare* bud, glistening with dew. The morning sun bathed it and the flower, warmed, began to open. Spaces appeared between the petals as they unfolded and spread back, exposing the flower's heart to the sun.

She let herself open like the sun-warmed bud and felt the baby sink deep into her pelvis. The hard ball of the head pushed down insistently, stretching her, but now the birthway was loose and ready and she could expand at each outward shove. Now nothing existed for her but the feeling of the infant tunneling down through her body. The intensely sexual sensation made her vaginal lips grow warm and engorged. She was opening for the outward thrust of the new life as she might open for the inward thrust of a man.

"It is coming," she gasped. Maukiri helped support her as another contraction drove the infant deeper into her pelvis. Now she felt the baby's head like a coconut between her legs, making the skin there bulge outward. She squatted, spreading her feet as far apart as she could. From behind, Maukiri laid her palms on the top of the womb and pressed down firmly.

This time, when the contraction came, Tepua felt her abdomen being relentlessly squeezed by a huge fist, slowly, but harder and harder, until something must burst. The loosened flesh of her birthway stretched and spread over the crowning head. Suddenly she feared the baby had grown to giant dimensions, that however much she opened, she would never be wide enough.

"Maukiri . . . I can't. . . ." she panted. "It's too big!"

Her cousin continued to croon the birthing song in her ear and hugged Tepua against her, her grip firm, but gentle.

Tepua was seized by an impulse to push. Not only did she have to, she wanted to. Her despair evaporated as excitement took its place. Now it felt good, very good. With each push, a grunting cry welled up from deep in her belly. It was coming; yes, it was coming and the flower was open wide.

Her womb heaved with the powerful force gripping her body as Maukiri held on to her. The flesh of her birthway, stretched tight about the infant, pulsed in waves, as though in orgasm. Pain was there, too, but was so flooded with ecstasy that it became all one sensation.

Stay-long crouched in front of her. "You must let me help you now," she said softly.

"Do not let Pehu . . ." Tepua could no longer speak. Another powerful surge made her open just a little more. Suddenly she felt the baby's head sliding through. Tepua put her own fingers down, cradling the tiny head that was slippery with the coating of birth. One last long push and the infant's body slithered out into Stay-long's hands.

"A son," Maukiri said in a trembling voice. Stay-long held the child carefully to avoid pulling on the umbilical cord. Tepua curled forward to see the tiny figure of an infant boy, resting in the hands of the *tahutahu*. His hair was darkened from the birth fluids, and his pale brown skin was smeared with birth blood and the white, waxy womb coating. His blue-gray eyes were open, and his tiny hands and feet flailed silently as Stay-long held him low between Tepua's legs. He had not yet taken a breath.

Maukiri reached out with a bamboo blade and cut the glistening cord. Suddenly another hand appeared within the sacrosanct arena of the birth. It held the damp suffocation cloth. Maukiri gave a startled cry. Tepua looked up into the harsh features of Pehu-pehu.

"Take it, Tepua, and do what you must," hissed the Blackleg. "This is what Aitofa demands, what all the Arioi demand. Hurry, before it is too late."

For an instant Tepua wavered, her conviction weakened by exhaustion and the threat of Pehu-pehu looming over her. The dance, the companionship, the protection. All these the Arioi had given her. Most important was her duty to serve Oro. He had come to her more than once. She remembered the words he had spoken.

Tepua plucked the cloth from the Blackleg's hand. . . .

And tossed it in Pehu-pehu's face. "This is Oro's child,"

she shouted. "I will not destroy it." Taking the baby from Stay-long, she clutched it to her breast.

With a scream of anger, Pehu-pehu was on her. Sharp-nailed hands pulled apart her arms, dragging the newborn from her frantic embrace. She cried out in horror as Pehu-pehu locked an arm about the infant and, with her free hand, raised a stone-blade knife.

Tepua was caught up in a frenzy unlike anything she had known before. It was as if she had become a female shark, driving swiftly at her prey. Grabbing Pehu-pehu's weapon hand, she wrenched the stout arm back so hard that the woman hissed in pain. The knife fell, but the Blackleg reached with her fingers for the baby's delicate throat.

Tepua rammed her knee into Pehu-pehu's stomach, but this did not stop her attempt to strangle the child. With the heel of her palm, Tepua aimed a hard blow to the Blackleg's nose. She missed, but only slightly, and Pehu-pehu staggered, her upper lip split and oozing blood.

With a final outflame of strength, Tepua snatched the infant away. At the same instant, the baby gave a huge gasp and began to wail. Tepua cradled her son to her in exultation. The child had taken its first breath! Now the baby was truly alive, filled with its vital essence. To harm it after this would be a grave offense against the gods.

She stood back, her son in her arms, staring defiantly at Pehu-pehu. In the growing light of the morning, the Black-leg wiped the blood from her upper lip and returned the stare. Cold anger spread across Pehu-pehu's features. "Have you forgotten the curse on Matopahu?" she asked harshly. "His line must end. Everyone accepts that. Everyone but you."

"Not everyone," Tepua answered, taking another step backward.

"If this child survives, your people will be plunged into war again. Wind-driving Lodge will be destroyed in the battle. Is that what you want?"

"Why should you care about the lodge or my people?" Tepua flung back. "You belong in Eimeo. Go back to your own troupe and leave me to deal with this."

"I am not through with you, Tepua. The child has no right

to live." Suddenly the Blackleg snatched her weapon and lunged forward again. Maukiri gave a sharp cry and tried to block her. Hugging the infant, Tepua dodged the clutching hands, but that was all she could do. The birth and the struggle had drained her.

Pehu-pehu slapped Maukiri aside, but the younger woman attacked again, leaping onto the Blackleg's back. Even while Tepua's cousin clawed at the Blackleg's face, Pehu-pehu struck again with her knife, trying to wound the child. Tepua had no strength left, and Maukiri could not hold off Pehu-pehu by herself.

Suddenly someone grabbed the Blackleg's elbow. With a shock, Tepua realized that it was Stay-long. Other *manahune* women joined in, dragging Pehu-pehu off.

"How dare you interfere?" the Blackleg bellowed as a female hand wrested the blade from her and lobbed it into the bushes. "You do not understand!"

Tepua saw Stay-long's face harden. "You had your proper chance," she answered sternly. "I did nothing then. But the child has drawn breath. To kill it now would be a sacrilege."

As Pehu-pehu continued to struggle in the grip of the others, Stay-long spoke to Tepua. "I thought she was my friend, but now I know why you did not trust her. She makes herself out to be an instrument of the gods. If the child is to die after this, then the high ones will see to it without her help."

Stay-long turned to Pehu-pehu sternly. "You are no longer welcome here. Go now—at once—and we will not harm you. Remain, and I promise nothing." At Stay-long's signal the women released their captive. "*Manahune* pig," said Pehu-pehu. "Your meddling will change nothing." She angrily strode off in the direction of the nearest stream. There, Tepua knew, she would chant a prayer for purification and wash off the birth blood that the struggle had left on her.

Trying to ignore the Blackleg's threatening words, Tepua accepted a drink of cool water while she held the baby to her breast. He was not ready to try sucking yet, but seemed content just to stare in wonder at the strange world around him. She gazed down, almost unable to believe that her body had brought forth this amazing little creature. He had Matopahu's ears and crisp curly hair, but the sculpting of his cheeks, the line of his jaw, and the large eyes beneath arched eyebrows all seemed her own.

I will call him Ruro-iti, she thought, *because he fluttered like a little bird the first time I felt him.* Someday, of course, he would take a formal name from his ancestors. But for now, Ruro would do.

Finally Tepua felt exhaustion claim her. She lay down and closed her eyes, the baby in her arms a warm and satisfying weight. Now she could sleep. . . .

But no. Suddenly she grasped what Pehu-pehu had meant. Her eyelids flew open and she sat up, gazing at Maukiri. She had saved the child, but its life was still in danger. Land-crab must never learn of this birth.

"We must stop Pehu-pehu," she said weakly. "If she tells what has happened, my son is doomed."

"Stop her?" asked Maukiri. "Is it possible?"

Stay-long frowned. "I will do anything I can to help my friends. But that woman is high in the ranks of the Arioi. To take her life would be too dangerous."

"Is there no other way?" asked Maukiri. "Those demons of yours—"

Stay-long's eyebrows raised. "She was always so careful. If only I had a lock of her hair . . ."

Maukiri began searching the ground where she and Pehu-pehu had scuffled. Suddenly she snatched up something. "Look at this!" She thrust out her hand, showing a crumpled piece of bark-cloth. "It tore from the Blackleg's robe when I was fighting with her. Can you use it?"

A cold smile lit Stay-long's face. "Let me see what I can do."

Tepua woke with Ruro-iti in her arms when she felt a shadow fall over her. She looked up and saw that the women were building a shelter over her where she lay, tying sheets of pandanus thatch onto roof poles. With surprise and gratitude, she realized that they were erecting the traditional *fare-hua,* where a new mother and her infant could be secluded from the rest of the world. But the moment was ruined by the sight of Pehu-pehu standing close by, washed, garbed in a fresh robe, looking fully recovered from her struggle. The Blackleg had seemingly forgotten her defeat. Now a glow of triumph stretched across her face.

"She is leaving," said Stay-long, who sat outside the shelter, directing the women who were building it. "Pay no heed to her, Tepua."

"There is one last thing," the Blackleg said, taking a single step closer. "Someday you will come back to see your friends, and I will be there to watch them greet you with jeers. Let me tell you the one piece of news that I have been saving all these days. The players are back home. Wind-driving Lodge has already made peace with Land-crab."

"A lie!" Tepua shouted. And yet, she knew it was possible. Pehu-pehu had been willing to take her back in the troupe, so long as she remained childless. Why, unless Tepua no longer posed a threat to her?

"It is so," the Blackleg explained cheerfully. "While you were gone during the dry season, I worked hard for the reconciliation. Soon I will have my reward. I will replace Aitofa in title as well as in power."

"No." In her fury, Tepua almost forgot the child. What had she done—abandoning the people who needed her? Her son—Matopahu's son—had been saved, but at what cost?

"I know little of these squabbles," said Stay-long, interrupting. "But let me warn you of one thing, Pehu-pehu. You must tell no one that the child is alive. Otherwise, I promise you such pain that you will cast yourself from a cliff to end it."

The Blackleg's face paled, but she quickly recovered. "I sneer at *manahune* sorcery," she answered. "There is no way you can harm me."

Stay-long smiled calmly and replied, "Surely, in the lowlands, they speak of 'setting the hook.'"

"Yes. And I know what is needed for that. You do not have it. Not a hair. Not a scrap of anything that touched my lips."

"I trust that you buried your bloodied robe carefully."

"No one will find it."

"Except for the piece that you left behind."

The Blackleg's eyes widened. Stay-long suddenly began to chant, using words that made Tepua shiver. She knew what had happened to the crucial piece of *tapa,* which had been in intimate contact with the Blackleg's skin. Stay-long had taken it, with elaborate ceremony, to the strange-eyed figures in her little house. She had made promises and threats, until the demons agreed to serve her. Now they possessed a means to invade Pehu-pehu's body. . . .

"I have heard enough nonsense," the Blackleg said, but her voice was nervous. "I am leaving you now. I have no doubt that my guardian spirit will keep me safe." She turned, lifted her basket of belongings, strode off. Tepua half rose to her feet with a hopeless notion of trying to stop her. Stay-long's chants grew louder, calling on her minions to attack. The Blackleg strode quickly toward the path.

Then came a scream as Pehu-pehu clutched her belly, stumbled, and sprawled in the dust. "Stop this," she cried between gasps. "Call off your fiends."

"Not until the hook is well set," answered the *tahutahu.*

The Blackleg screamed again. "I am high Arioi. I am *avae parai* of Wind-driving Lodge!"

"Good. Then people will believe it when you say the child is dead."

Writhing in her agony, Pehu-pehu pleaded again.

"I am waiting to hear your oath," answered Stay-long unhurriedly. "Swear by all the gods—by Oro himself."

Pehu-pehu's wail split the air.

Tepua held Ruro-iti close and looked away.

TWENTY

The days that followed were filled with rituals—to protect the child and mother and keep spiritual harm from coming to everyone involved in the birth. Not all the ceremonies that Ruro-iti required could be performed here, with his father absent and his ancestral *marae* far away. Stay-long's husband, who was the local priest as well as the headman, did his best for Tepua and her new son. The rest would have to come later, perhaps when Ruro was much older.

For some time, mother and child lived in the temporary nursing shelter, the *fare-hua* that the women had built for her. Tepua wore special clothes, given to her by Stay-long, and had to change out of them whenever she went outside. She was also forbidden to feed herself, because the sacred essence that was so concentrated and powerful in the newborn *ari'i* might enter her food and prove too powerful for her stomach.

Her cousin cheerfully served as her assistant, placing food in the new mother's mouth. Maukiri was not above teasing Tepua, however, and the eating ritual became a game that both women enjoyed. But this could not go on much longer, Tepua knew. She would have to be freed of the restrictions far sooner than was customary for a woman of her class.

At the proper time, Pig-bone placed the child's detached navel cord in a length of bamboo and buried it secretly, after

254

many prayers, in his *marae*. This was the first step in permitting Ruro to come forth safely into the world.

Tepua kept the child at her breast until an entire moon had passed. Every clear night she glanced anxiously at the sky, watching the progression of the stars. Soon the Ripening Festival would come, marking the beginning of the season of plenty, the period for feasts and celebration. Her Arioi troupe would be active again, a vital force in the life of the people, even though they now served Land-crab.

She knew that Aitofa needed her now more than ever before. Perhaps Pehu-pehu hadn't won her victory yet; Tepua might help turn the tide. But if Tepua did *not* return soon, suspicions would arise about the outcome of her pregnancy. She saw no choice but to leave her son behind in the care of the *manahune*.

Gradually, and with great unhappiness, Tepua began bringing "the little bird" to Stay-long's cousin, Round-pebble, for feedings. Round-pebble had nearly finished weaning her own son, and had readily agreed to nurse Ruro for as long as Tepua needed.

Another moon passed. Tepua could delay no longer. She knew there was a risk. Pehu-pehu might not honor the oath that Stay-long had forced on her. But the Blackleg understood what swift and harsh punishment the spirits would bring.

At last, with her breasts still aching, Tepua, along with Maukiri, took her leave of the highland settlement. The *manahune* women groaned and wailed at their departure. Tepua promised she would soon return with many gifts, but her promise only made the wailing louder.

Tepua thought her own grief was the greatest, for she was leaving her son behind. Ruro-iti had become such a part of her life that she could no longer imagine being without him. "I will be back for you," she promised on the morning of departure, pressing her nose for one last time to the smooth and fragrant skin of his cheek. "It will not be long."

As Tepua journeyed downhill toward familiar territory, she began to feel the exhilaration of going home. After descending the steep mountain trails, she and Maukiri reached the first signs of a coastal settlement. Emerging into a valley, she saw breadfruit trees in neat rows, and thatched houses surrounded by low bamboo fencing. Dogs with upright ears lolled in the shade. Children played quietly in the well-swept yards.

The perfumes from flowering trees filled the air— hibiscus, jasmine, and many others. Birdsong that she had not heard in months cheered Tepua as she walked. Now and again she caught sight of a swooping gull, a sign that the sea could not be far off.

The women followed a riverbank as the valley widened. All this lush and green land belonged to the district of Tahiti that Tepua loved best—the realm of Matopahu's ancestors. This was the domain that now belonged to her son. How Ruro would claim it she did not know, but she was determined to gain him his birthright.

The thought that someone here might have news of Matopahu sped Tepua's steps, making Maukiri hurry to keep up. Soon she was passing houses that she recognized, calling greetings to women who sat at their work in the shade. These women looked unexpectedly thin, and decidedly glum. They barely acknowledged her cries of "Life to you!"

Tepua paused to wait for her cousin to catch up. "Did you see those women? The dry season must have been harsh. But soon—" Tepua swept her hand toward high branches where the yellow-green globes of breadfruit hung. The time for first harvest was fast approaching.

Maukiri licked her lips at the mention of food. She, too, looked thin. Months had passed since either woman had tasted breadfruit, coconuts, or reef fish. "For your sake, I missed one great festival," said Tepua's cousin. "I do not want to miss another."

Yet Tepua knew that she would not enjoy herself in the coming season. She would have to face her old Arioi companions and act as though she deserved to be among them. She would have to perform in front of Land-crab and treat him with respect he did not merit. Perhaps, worst of all, she would have to deal with Pehu-pehu.

Tepua was willing to endure all this for Ruro's sake. To

protect her son, she would pretend that he had never drawn a breath. Everyone must see her dancing again, an active member of the Arioi troupe. And perhaps she could do more than just dance—she could work to bring the usurper down.

"I smell the sea air!" Maukiri proclaimed, suddenly sprinting ahead of her cousin. Indeed, Tepua was now catching glimpses of the lagoon through the trees. After so many moons! She forgot her gloomy thoughts and hurried after Maukiri. Ahead, beside the river's mouth, lay a gravel beach where waves rolled to shore through a break in the reef.

Maukiri flung her wrap aside and plunged in, with Tepua at her heels. How wonderful to taste salt again! And to hear the roar of distant breakers! As Tepua frolicked in the surf, she remembered the last time she had played in the sea—and felt a twinge of pain at the memory. How excited and foolish she had been then. How much she had endured since that time to keep her child.

At last the two women came out and stood, still dripping, on the shore. The sun was setting, and the sea breeze had started to come in. "We could spend the night right here," Tepua suggested. She did not want to face the Arioi until morning.

She turned her head at the sound of familiar voices, and realized that she no longer had a choice. Led by Curling-leaf, a small crowd of Arioi women was converging on the beach. Tepua's special friend broke from the rest, ran up, and embraced her while the others looked on with curiosity. "I was afraid for you," Curling-leaf said, hugging Tepua tightly. "But you look well."

Tepua was glad that her friend asked no further questions. She was unwilling now to tell anyone here, no matter how trustworthy, about Ruro. "Yes, I am well. But I have heard only rumors about our lodge—"

"You must be careful," answered Curling-leaf, lowering her voice. "Everything has changed. We are back home, but we are not the same troupe that left. No one dares speak against Land-crab."

Tepua stiffened. "That is what I expected. Tell me about Aitofa."

Curling-leaf spoke in a whisper. "She tried to stop it. Now she can only whisper of rebellion."

"Against—"

"No more now," Curling-leaf cautioned.

Tepua stamped her foot in frustration. *What news of Matopahu?* If only she could ask. "We will talk later," Tepua said, and straightened up, remembering the impression she must make on the others. Her hopes depended on bringing off this deception. Everyone must think that she had carried out her duty and was now returning to her proper place.

"So you are back," came the booming voice of Pehu-pehu as Tepua approached the first cluster of thatched huts near the beach.

She turned to face the Blackleg, but stood her ground. Tepua remembered how this woman had writhed in agony and begged for relief from Stay-long's friends. Perhaps the experience had made her just a bit more humble.

"You have been gone a long while," said Pehu-pehu. "I trust you have not forgotten your recitations and your dance movements."

"I have not," she answered staunchly.

"Good. I will watch you carefully to make certain."

And I will watch you also, you treacherous eel. Tepua knew that she was playing a difficult part now. She and Pehu-pehu were both part of a performance that neither wanted. They must go on as they had before—the demanding Blackleg and the troublesome young dancer. She wondered how long they could keep up the pretense.

Early the next morning, a party of women went to gather fronds for plaiting mats. Tepua had already seen that a new performance house stood almost ready on a fresh site near the shore. Polished timbers made from entire palm trees supported the high, thatched roof. A viewing platform, of planks lashed together, was nearing completion by a large gang of men. Floor mats remained in short supply, so she joined the women assigned to make them.

Tepua went with her companions to gather coconut fronds that had been spread to dry in the sun. Far better work could be done with the scarcer and tougher leaves of pandanus, but time was running short. Soon the performance house must be ready for the opening events of the season.

On her third collecting trip she saw Curling-leaf. "Slip away with me," Tepua begged. She longed for a few words alone.

They went deep into the palm grove, out of sight of the others. "Matopahu is back in Eimeo," Curling-leaf whispered, in response to Tepua's first question. "Eye-to-heaven is now an underpriest at Putu-nui's *marae,* and your *ari'i* has become his humble attendant. That is all I have heard."

Tepua halted, and whispered praise to all the gods who had helped her. At least Matopahu was safe. So long as he remained on sacred ground, no man would harm him. And one day she would show him his son. . . .

Still daydreaming, she didn't watch where she was walking until she felt Curling-leaf's warning touch on her arm. She glanced up with a start to see a tall wooden figure scowling at her from beneath the trees. *The boundary of the high chief's land.*

"Too many people have been careless lately," whispered Curling-leaf. "Almost every day we hear that someone was caught trespassing against Land-crab. Then a warrior appears with his club, and another body is sent off to the *marae.* Or thrown to the sharks."

Tepua was filled with outrage. "But none of it is *his* land!"

"Do not say such things." Curling-leaf's expression was darkened by pain. "While you were gone, a priest here was possessed by the gods. He pronounced Land-crab to be the true ruler of the district. If anyone opposes him, the priest says, a great wave will sweep from the sea to punish us."

Tepua clapped her hand across her mouth to keep from shouting in anger. "Who would believe such a lie?"

"Of course, not everyone accepts this oracle," Curling-leaf admitted. "But we know what happens to those who speak against it."

Tepua wrapped her arms about the nearest coconut tree and tried to expend her fury by shaking it. Suddenly she heard voices.

"Shhh." Curling-leaf pulled her down. Both women lay on their bellies and whispered hasty prayers. The voices came from within the high chief's boundaries, and Tepua realized that she was hearing a pair of Land-crab's servants.

She poked her head up just high enough to see. Within the protected land, palms gave way to breadfruit. Tepua watched with astonishment as one servant lifted a forked pole and used it to pull a barely ripened fruit from the tree. When the breadfruit dropped, the second man caught it deftly and lowered it into his basket.

Tepua's mouth fell open. The time for harvesting had not yet come! The trees were still under *tapu*. The first fruits must be dedicated to the gods after elaborate ceremonies at the *marae*, and these ceremonies were still days away.

The fools will die for this, she thought. But as she watched, she realized that the two servants seemed unafraid, talking and laughing as they worked. They were evidently following Land-crab's orders. She lowered her head and waited for the pair to finish and move on.

As soon as the footsteps died away, Curling-leaf grabbed Tepua's hand and tugged her back in the direction of the performance house. "We saw nothing," Curling-leaf insisted. "Land-crab cannot be eating breadfruit yet."

"Is he collecting them for sport?" Tepua asked, disgusted. *What kind of man is this Land-crab, who thinks himself more worthy than the gods?*

Tepua left her friend and returned to her task of plaiting mats. Sitting with the other Arioi women near the new performance house, she felt none of the gaiety that had marked preparation for previous festivals. And she was not the only one affected by growing apprehension. Everyone worked in silence, their expressions glum, their shoulders bowed.

The situation with the Arioi men was hardly different. Tepua glimpsed no sign of enthusiasm as they lashed planks to the viewing platform. Everyone seemed driven by the fear of Land-crab's priests and warriors rather than by a joyful desire to please the gods.

She saw now that her hopes for sparking a new rebellion against Land-crab were in vain. He was as firmly in control of his Arioi as he was of everyone else. No one here would dare risk rousing his ire.

Had her visions before Ruro's birth misled her after all? What future was left for her son? She wanted to speak with Aitofa, but how could she face the chiefess when she must lie about her child?

Tepua tried to fight a rising sense of despair. Land-crab had the upper hand now, but he could not keep it forever. He was already so arrogant that he defied the gods' *tapu*. In time he would answer for his sins.

The start of the Ripening Festival finally arrived. When she went out at first light, Tepua saw people from the closest precincts already coming with their offerings. The men carried poles across their shoulders, a basket holding bread-fruits and bananas hanging from one end, a piglet dangling by its feet from the other. These first fruits were to be laid before the gods. After a share was dedicated to the divine ones, the rest could be eaten by mortals.

The excitement of the day seemed to make people forget the tyranny that oppressed them. Even Tepua tried to put her grievances aside. There would, of course, be no satire directed against Land-crab at this time. But the entire Season of Plenty lay ahead. Perhaps a chance would arise.

In the bathing pool the splashing of the Arioi women grew boisterous. When Pehu-pehu came to intervene, Tepua thought she saw a twinkle of merriment in the Blackleg's eyes. This was a day of rejoicing, after all. The gods should be pleased to see everyone happy.

Only when the Blackleg's gaze turned toward Tepua did her expression harden. She barked a few words of rebuke. *As everyone expects her to do.* Tepua gritted her teeth and climbed out of the pool.

Soon all the Arioi had donned their costumes and paint. They stood on the beach, helping to greet the arriving visitors, whose canoes were laden with gifts. *These offerings are for the gods, not for Land-crab,* Tepua kept telling herself. Yet she knew that the chief would have his pick.

At last, with great pomp, the usurper came, riding his bearer. Criers ran before him, proclaiming his greatness in flowery words. Men and women along the route lowered their eyes and bared their shoulders in humble acknowledgment of his authority. Tepua hid behind a palm tree so that the chief's attendants would not see her lack of deference.

She could not help peering out as Land-crab was carried past. She had hoped that, like other chiefs, he might grow fat and soft with overindulgence. To her chagrin, she saw that he had not changed much. His gaze remained sharp and his body still appeared powerful. He held himself in regal fashion, seemingly paying no heed to the masses who lined the way. Yet Tepua sensed that nothing missed his gaze. In a single glance he had taken in the wealth of offerings displayed, but he kept his reaction to himself.

Following Land-crab's appearance, priests garbed in feathered breastplates and fine mat skirts began the grand procession. Their conch-trumpets made such a din that Tepua knew the distant gods must take notice. She watched in silent fury as the priests headed toward the *marae*, followed by an army of attendants who carried the offerings. *He is the false chief. Matopahu and his son deserve these honors.*

Tepua and most of the others had to view the ceremonies from a distance. Only noblemen of the highest rank were permitted onto the sacred paving stones of the *marae*. Common people stood beneath the surrounding high trees and chanted their own prayers, bringing out small images of the personal gods who protected them. Tepua possessed no image of Tapahi-roro-ariki, but she required none. If she closed her eyes, she could see the strong features of her ancestress, the great chiefess of long ago.

Tapahi-roro-ariki. Was she not much like the Purea of Tepua's vision? Though Purea's life lay yet ahead, though she had not even been born, Tepua saw a similarity between the two women. Each had a quiet strength, a determination to fight when necessary, and a willingness to try peaceful means for gaining her ends.

Tepua herself lay in the middle, the cord of sennit that joined these extraordinary figures. If the cord frayed and the joining failed . . . No. Tepua prayed softly, gathering her courage. She thought of Ruro, growing rapidly in Round-pebble's care. Someday he would return to his family's lands. He would be the next length of the sacred line. . . .

Cries of rejoicing rose as the first great ceremony ended. A procession of attendants began carrying away the portions of food that would be eaten by the chiefs and by the Arioi. Tepua lingered awhile, watching the common people wait impatiently for their own shares. When the temple attendants finally did bring forth what was left of piles of fruit, coconuts, fowls, and pigs, she heard a low rumble of disappointment from all sides. How little had been left to the people!

"Come. You are wanted." Tepua heard Maukiri's voice behind her. She tried to put aside her indignation over the greed of Land-crab and his friends. She hurried back to the performance house, where the members of the troupe were assembling. *Some will go hungry today,* she thought. *Others, who do not deserve it, will be too stuffed to move.*

Late that evening, after the day's formalities had ended, the drummers started up again. Moonlight flooded the assembly ground as the Arioi and their many admirers gathered for dancing. Tepua needed no partner. The exhilaration of the earlier performance by her troupe remained with her. She felt the music guiding her feet, making her hips roll. She laughed as she watched a group of children trying to imitate her.

From the shadows, a tall figure stood watching. Tepua felt a momentary shudder. Until now, she had tried to remain inconspicuous. During the performance she had been glad to stay in the back of the group, keeping her dancing subdued. Evidently this one man had noticed her. He took a step forward and she caught a glimpse of red and black paint smeared over most of his face and body.

The strange Arioi was adorned in comical fashion. Strings of mismatched shells hung across his chest. Short feathers stuck out in odd directions from his headdress of beach vines. His cloak was absurdly short, barely reaching his knees. She was sure she had never seen him in the troupe, but something about him seemed hauntingly familiar.

He took another step forward. Tepua gaped. No Arioi she knew moved in such a smooth and powerful manner. As soon as she recognized his stride, she saw through the absurd costume. She controlled her urge to leap out of the dance and run to Matopahu's side. Instead she lifted her hand in recognition, blending her signal into the movement of her dance. She saw him retreat into the deeper shadows beyond the clearing.

Somehow she kept herself from running to him. She frolicked with the children, giving the girls a short lesson, all the while imagining what lay ahead. Then, her pulse pounding with the drumbeat, she slipped away in search of Matopahu.

What a risk he had taken, walking right into Land-crab's camp. She knew he had done this before, but now the danger seemed far worse. Her thoughts returned to her own plight. Had he heard about her exile in the highlands? She dared tell him nothing about the outcome. For now, little Ruro's existence must be kept secret even from his father.

Tepua found Matopahu leaning against a palm tree. "Who is this Arioi dancer?" he asked quietly. "With so much paint on her face, I do not recognize her."

She flung herself into his embrace and whispered fiercely, "Land-crab's men—"

"Mean nothing to me," he answered, pressing his warm hands against her back and his nose against her cheek.

She could scarcely catch her breath. How long it had been since she last saw him! She feared he had become just a beloved image in her memory. Yet he was here now, surrounding her with the aroma and warmth of his presence. She wanted to sing out her affection for him, but other words had to come first, words on which his life and future might depend. "The people who were your friends are afraid now," she tried to warn. "This false oracle—"

Matopahu drew her close, wrapping her so deeply in his arms that she felt she might melt into him.

"Do not worry for me, atoll flower," he murmured, stroking her hair. "Only fools believe that babble."

Tepua nestled her head beneath his chin. She could feel the powerful throb of his pulse at the base of his neck. She wished she could cast all interfering thoughts aside and just enjoy the moment. Yet her doubts spoke. "Land-crab has become so strong. What can we do?"

"I have allies. On Eimeo. Putu-nui cannot support me openly, but some of his warriors have promised to fight with me."

She stiffened and pulled back, looking into his eyes. The thought of his going into battle dismayed her, yet she had long known that this must come. "Then you plan an attack? Soon?"

"Not yet. We will choose our time. We would not do our cause any good by defiling the ceremony of the gods."

"Then I will be your spy," she whispered. "I will make it my business to know everything that Land-crab does."

"Yes." His hands drew her to him again, caressing her shoulders, the hollows of her neck. She snuggled closer to him, basking in his warmth.

A new hope grew. The return of the Arioi to their home might indeed be a sign of the gods' favor. Now she would be able to help Matopahu as she could not have done otherwise. In time Land-crab would get careless, drink too much *ava*, allow his guards to grow lax.

"Come," said Matopahu. "We cannot stay here. I have my canoe nearby. It may be a bit uncomfortable, but—"

Tepua laughed, and followed him to the beach.

Together the couple paddled from shore until the rush and sigh of waves breaking on the outer reef swallowed the distant drumming. Looking back, Tepua saw fires on the beach and tiny figures moving. Soon the figures grew too distant to see and the fires showed as flickering orange stars far across the water.

This part of the lagoon was open and deep, with no sandy islets or coral heads; the canoe could drift safely. Matopahu took the paddles and laid them aside. He whispered her name as she turned to face him.

The hull seemed too narrow and deep for *hanihani,* but he was undaunted by the challenge. Moonlight gleamed on the strong curves of his arms as he placed a bundle of mats in the bottom of the canoe.

"You are well prepared," she chided playfully. "You have done this before."

"Before I found you, I did many strange and foolish things." The craft rocked slightly as Matopahu took off his absurd necklaces, then beckoned her to him. His *maro* fell away; she saw that he was ready for her.

She came close, kneeling on the mats, and leaned into his arms. The heat of his body pressed against her.

The dancing had started little tickles of pleasure running up through her breasts and down past her belly. The firmness of his embrace heightened the feelings that the dance had begun. He pulled her closer, wrapping a cloak around them both to keep off the sea breeze.

The canoe rocked gently, but the outrigger kept it from tipping. Floating in the middle of the lagoon, surrounded by night, she put aside the troubles that had followed her for so long. Here was Hina the moon goddess again, as bright and radiant as on the evening of Matopahu's triumph. Here was the fresh smell of the sea. . . .

When he lifted her onto him, she cried out with delight, not caring if she startled every fish in the lagoon. He moved slowly at first, whispering, and then starting to sing softly. For an instant Tepua was startled to hear the words that she so often sang to herself—in the language of her own people.

"Here I go, parting the waves," he chanted. "Here I sail, cleaving the sea." His voice was low and teasing as he moved with the same rhythm as the rocking canoe.

Her sighs were soon overwhelmed by a much stronger pleasure as he thrust himself deeper. Abandoning herself to sensation, she braced herself against his shoulders and did her part. *You are the canoe and I am the vast deep,* she thought.

Beyond her, over the water, she imagined torches burning, flying fish leaping toward the light. Everything around her was filled with brightness and color. She pictured the glowing mantles of giant clams on the sandy bottom, and luminous jellyfish rising. The images grew brighter. The moon rivaled the sun.

*   *   *

After they had clung together awhile, Tepua gently pulled away from Matopahu. He heard her whisper a women's chant, then plunge into the water. She splashed a short while before urging him to follow.

With a cry of delight, Matopahu dove after her, plummeting toward the depths in a cloud of bubbles. What a fine night for swimming, he thought. He would catch her, and then they would go back to the canoe.

But a sudden and unexpected fright gripped him. Why was the water so cold? And why did he feel such a desperate need for air? Fighting panic, he stroked with broad sweeps of his arms and began to come back up.

The surface seemed too far away. He lost his sense of direction and could not tell if he was actually rising. Water pressed in on his ears and mouth and nose, and he thought that he could not hold it back.

Then his head broke the surface and he took large, gasping breaths. Where was Tepua? He hoped she did not hear his labored wheezing.

At last Matopahu found strength to swim slowly toward his canoe. He still did not know what had happened, but certain incidents came back to him. In the last round of the archery contest his fingers had briefly gone numb. He had blamed that on the cold, but he wondered if the lingering effect of Land-crab's curse was to blame. Now that he was in Tahiti, close to the corpse of his brother, perhaps he was even more vulnerable.

Clinging to the outrigger, Matopahu tried to will away his fears. The god of the *marae* had touched him, but he was not free of the binding. So said Imo and Eye-to-heaven. Tonight he was almost willing to believe them.

"Tepua," he called in a voice that sounded hoarse and weak to his ears.

"I am here," she answered. "Come after me."

Matopahu frowned. He had no strength left for games. "Not now. I have to take you back."

When he was in the canoe again, he began to feel better. They paddled in silence toward a dark stretch of beach. In the distance, drums still beat for the throngs of dancers.

"Where will you sleep?" she asked him as the canoe grounded softly in the shallows.

"I have a hideaway up the coast, but there is only room for one. Otherwise I would take you with me." He dragged the canoe up the beach a short way, then stood with her on the shore.

"Tomorrow—"

"I will find you." He clasped her to him for one parting embrace. But he could not leave yet. "Atoll flower, there is something I must ask."

He felt her stiffen. Perhaps there was a secret she had kept from him. He freed her from his arms, but held her gaze, looking deep into her eyes. "You left the troupe," he said. "I heard rumors that you were carrying a child. I did not want to ask you about it, but now my thoughts are on nothing else."

"I left for my safety," she answered in a strained voice.

"To protect the child." His excitement grew.

Her words came out in a whisper. "There could be . . . no child. I have taken an oath." With a sinking feeling in his stomach, he watched her look away from him.

He shook her harshly. "No, Tepua. If you carried my child, you would not destroy it."

"I—had no choice."

"Tell me it is a lie. Woman, look at me."

Instead she pulled back.

"Aue!" Matopahu shouted. Here was the final proof that the curse still held him. The child of his loins was dead. He wailed again, a cry of anguish that carried far down the beach. He did not care who heard it.

"Matopahu, listen. You begged me to leave the Arioi. I will do that."

His voice caught and he stared at her, openmouthed.

"Yes. But not now. I must stay here so long as Land-crab rules. I must watch and plot against him."

His brows lowered, and at first he could not reply. What good was her offer now? It was too late for him to father another child. His moment of glory had passed, and the curse was claiming him again. "What does it matter?" he hissed, turning away. With an angry heave, he slid his canoe down the sand and waded after it.

He heard her behind him. "I am sure of one thing," she called. "When the time is right, we will have a son."

"We will have nothing," he threw back as he began to paddle. She shouted other words, but he would not listen or even turn around.

Her hands hanging helplessly at her side, Tepua watched Matopahu disappear into the night. She sighed, wishing that she could have given in to him. But all the while he spoke to her she had imagined the priests of Land-crab carrying her son to the *marae* as an offering.

She had wanted desperately to blurt out the truth, but her protective instinct held her back. *Even if Matopahu dies, I will still have the child.* But why had he scorned her offer? She had only asked for a little more time. . . .

At last, filled with grief, Tepua waded ashore. She glanced about nervously, fearing that someone had heard Matopahu, recognized his voice. Seeing no warriors, she began to walk, paying no heed to where she was going.

After a time, she felt a friendly touch on her arm. "What is wrong?" asked Curling-leaf. "I heard shouts."

"It is . . . nothing." Tepua slumped to her knees.

Curling-leaf lowered her voice. "It was Matopahu. I know how he feels. But he will recover."

"He will do something foolish."

"Why? He could not have expected—"

Tepua stared at her and did not answer.

"Of course, there is no child," Curling-leaf went on. "Everyone sees that you are still an Arioi."

Everything became a blur. Suddenly Tepua sank forward, collapsing into the sand.

"What is wrong? What are you hiding?" Curling-leaf tried to comfort her, yet Tepua sensed her stiffness, her confusion.

"Do not ask me any more," Tepua whispered.

Curling-leaf drew in her breath. Tepua wiped her eyes and saw the expression on her friend's face, first astonishment and then a glimmer of delight. "Then you are bolder than I thought."

"There is no child," Tepua said in a toneless voice.

"Of course not," Curling-leaf agreed.

"I must do—something. I cannot let Matopahu be so angry." Thoughts whirling, Tepua clung to her friend. There was one man she could trust with her story; she should have gone to him sooner. "If I can reach Eye-to-heaven . . ."

"Listen, Tepua. Tomorrow we will have only games and feasting. If you disappear, nobody will notice."

She turned toward the water. The night was almost gone. At daybreak she could find a canoe that was heading for Eimeo, go to Putu-nui's *marae,* locate the priest. Surely Matopahu's *taio* would help her. "Tell Maukiri where I went," she said softly. "Tell no one else. I will be back before dark tomorrow."

After a brief morning downpour on Eimeo, the sun grew bright and the air steamy. Tepua left the canoe that had brought her, hurried through palm groves, following the shore that bordered Putu-nui's district. Soon she approached the chief's *marae.* Past the hardwood trees ahead she saw low walls built of black stones surrounding a rectangular courtyard. The area outside the courtyard, where sacred god-houses stood, was alive with priests and attendants.

As a woman, Tepua was allowed no closer. She called to a young attendant, requesting him to find Eye-to-heaven. Oppressed by the moist air and the heat, she waited in the shade of a sturdy *tamanu* tree.

Soon she heard footsteps and saw the stocky figure of the priest coming toward her. He had left his ceremonial garments behind and wore only a *maro* of white bark-cloth. His round face was filled with concern. "Tepua, what has happened? I tried to keep Matopahu here—"

"I saw him last night," she answered hoarsely. "He was angry—"

"He has been plotting something. I hope he does not rush into it."

"Will Matopahu attack Land-crab? He said he has warriors."

Eye-to-heaven snorted. "Two or three men."

"But he needs hundreds!" Her eyes brimmed with tears. "He will not listen to reason. Maybe you can talk to him."

She could scarcely find breath to answer. "He wants nothing to do with me."

The priest took a step closer. "Tepua, I don't understand. Matopahu came back from Tetiaroa to look for you. He tried to find you several times. He even searched the hills—"

"*Aue!* He said nothing to me about that. And now I must tell you what happened."

When she began to explain, the priest's eyes widened. "This is a great surprise," he said. "I do not blame you for preserving the child, but now we must tell Matopahu. It will change everything. He will put aside his hopeless plans and wait for a better time."

"Yes. I want to tell him," she agreed sadly. "But my son needs protection. He is not safe in Tahiti."

"Bring the child here," said the priest. "Putu-nui will guard him. We need not reveal his true parentage. We can tell everyone that the child is . . . mine."

Tepua felt a moment of shock. "Yours!" It was not uncommon, she reminded herself, for a man to share his lover with his *taio*. Of course Eye-to-heaven had always seemed more like a brother to her, but outsiders would not know that. "Yes. That is what people must believe. Everyone but Matopahu."

"Then bring the child here. I will arrange everything." The priest glanced back over his shoulder. An attendant was coming, presumably to call him to his duties. "The ceremonies . . . you understand. I cannot linger now. But in a few days I will be free." Hastily he explained how he would bring a canoe to a cove in Tahiti that they both knew. He would take her and Ruro-iti to safety in Eimeo.

Then he was gone, hurrying off where she could not follow. He glanced back once, and she made a sign of agreement. The prospect of facing Matopahu again made her knees weak, but soon he would see his son.

TWENTY-ONE

Te Vahine Airoreatua i Ahurai i Farepua marched grandly into the high-roofed house where Tutaha held his court. Tutaha glowered at her from his high seat. "What do you wish to tell me?" he asked her hotly. "That these strangers suffer illness? That they fear their gods? I know these things now. They only strengthen my resolve."

"Then you think you can destroy my visitors?"

"If you stand aside and do not interfere."

"*Aue!*" she shouted. "Tutaha, you understand nothing about these people. Their land has as many huge vessels as we have canoes. Even if you burn their ship and kill every man, others of their kind will come here."

"We will destroy those as well," he growled.

"No. If you make war again, you will only die like the first wretches who attacked them. You and all your fine family will end. But I have a better plan."

Tutaha snorted, turning to exchange glances with his advisors.

"Go out and look at this fine harbor of yours," she persisted. "Where else on our shores can such a huge ship anchor safely? It is here, in your district, that the foreigners will stop whenever they visit us. Each time they arrive, they will bring gifts—wonders that we have never seen before. If you step forward and present yourself as the chief of the district, all honors will go to you."

Tutaha's attention returned to Purea, his eyes narrowed,

his expression showing a hint of greed as well as distaste. "I need no gifts. When I destroy these invaders, I will take whatever I want."

"*Aue!* You are hopelessly stubborn, Tutaha." In frustration, Purea tightened her fist. "Listen, you mighty leader of Pare and Arue. There is only one way that I can stop your foolishness. My people will keep watch on the shore. Whenever the foreign chiefs land, I or one of my principal women will be there to accompany them. Any attack on the visitors will be an attack on my family. Are you ready for the consequences of such a battle?"

Enraged, Tutaha stood up. At his full height he dwarfed the men around him. "Go from here, you meddlesome woman," he shouted. "I am tired of listening to your words."

Purea turned, satisfied that she had made herself clear. She had issued the challenge, but she did not think that Tutaha was ready to test her. In time he might make her suffer for thwarting his plans. And perhaps he would learn someday that she had been right. . . .

Tepua stirred, emerging slowly from her dream. The vision still held her thoughts as she looked around the riverbank where she had fallen asleep. Purea's courage seemed to fill her own body, just as Tutaha's angry voice still echoed in her ears. Perhaps the vision carried a lesson. Or had it merely been a reminder of Ruro's importance?

Thoughts of Ruro made Tepua sit up abruptly, pushing the remnants of the dream aside. Maukiri had helped bring the baby down from the hills. Now she was bathing him in cool river water. Tepua wanted the weight of him in her arms, the warmth and silkiness of his skin against hers.

Giggles mixed with the sound of splashing drew her to the river where Maukiri was playing with Ruro. Tepua waded in, reaching for her son. She had wasted time in sleep while she could have been with him. Soon she would have to leave the child again. . . .

She hugged him to her, then held him up as he smiled and chortled at the sight of his mother. She wanted to feast on him with all her senses. She delighted at his warm weight in her arms, the strength in his little limbs, the way he wriggled and crowed when she tickled his tummy. She laid her face against him, smelling and tasting the clean milky sweetness of his skin.

How fast he was growing! His eyes were losing the blue of the newborn and darkening to a rich brown. His skin would soon be the luminous bronze of his father's; his hair was starting to curl.

"You are as plump as a little breadfruit and as lively as an eel," she said, pressing her nose to his as he squealed in delight.

Cradling the baby in her arms, she put him to her breast. She felt a tightening and tingling in her nipple as the child began to suck, and then, to her delight, the release as the warm milk flowed from her breast. She had feared that her milk would not come back after so many days away, but Stay-long had helped her with an herbal drink.

"We have been here too long," said her cousin, climbing out of the water. "The priest will be looking for us soon."

Tepua looked at the shadows, handed the baby up to Maukiri, and followed. With a sigh of regret, she picked up the basket of food and supplies, then headed back onto the path.

Soon she and Maukiri emerged at the beach, coming out under the shade of a spreading ironwood tree. Overhead, the dangling needles whispered softly in the breeze. Tepua shaded her eyes and stared in the direction of Eimeo. From here she could see the neighboring island as a shadow looming up on the horizon, the setting sun hanging just above its peaks.

She noticed several double canoes crossing the Sea of the Moon. Inside the lagoon, she saw smaller vessels moving about on the calm water close to shore. One might be the craft carrying Eye-to-heaven, but she could not tell yet if any were coming toward her.

From behind came a hissing sound that made her jump. "Maukiri?" she called.

"I am here," said her cousin from another direction.

Then the familiar figure of Eye-to-heaven emerged from

the shadows. "There is no time to talk," he said, sounding worried. He motioned for her to follow him.

A man she did not know was standing beside an outrigger canoe that floated in the shallows, its bow grounded on the beach. He pushed the boat farther out. After Tepua and Maukiri climbed in, there was barely room in the hull for the men.

Hastily they got under way. With its sail catching the wind, the canoe skimmed over the lagoon, bouncing in a slight chop. "What is the trouble?" Tepua asked, trying to shield her infant from spray.

"Matopahu," the priest answered with a sigh. "I did as you asked. I told him about his son. But I do not think he believed me."

"He was so eager to have a child. . . ." Her words trailed off mournfully.

"He acted as if I were trying to deceive him—to make him change his foolish plans. And he was determined to go through with them. He and his friends have already gone to confront Land-crab."

"He hasn't enough men!"

"I'll catch up with him and do what I can. There may be others in this district willing to fight."

What could a handful of men do against Land-crab's warriors? A sick feeling grew in her stomach as she tried to keep her fears at bay.

Dusk fell. The other canoes headed in, but Eye-to-heaven continued along the coast, keeping far from shore. When the sky was almost completely black, he steered into the shallows.

Grimly she stared at the shadowy beach. How could anyone know what was happening in the darkness? An entire army might be waiting just a few paces back. She spoke a prayer as the canoe glided in.

"You must not return to the Arioi," the priest whispered. "You must go to Eimeo with my companion. No matter what happens here, Putu-nui will take care of you and the child."

"Leave *now*?" He was telling her to stay with her son, yet how could she desert Matopahu? Her thoughts returned to

Purea, whose courage would never falter. "Am I to hide
while others fight?" Tepua asked angrily as Eye-to-heaven
climbed from the canoe, taking a club and a short spear.
"The child is important. I am not," she protested.

"Tepua—"

"I will come with you." Hastily, trying not to feel the
pang of separation, she handed her son to Maukiri. "You and
little Ruro stay with the canoe," she told her cousin. "Wait
out there." She pointed to deeper water. "If you hear
fighting nearby, get away quickly."

"But I cannot feed him," Maukiri wailed softly.

"I'll come back and call to you. If I don't, then one of
Putu-nui's women will be his feeding mother."

"What are you saying?" Maukiri clutched at her. "You
must come back."

Tepua did not answer. Nor did she remind Maukiri that
she had fought in more than one battle. Before the priest
could talk her out of it, she waded ashore.

Matopahu peered from behind the breadfruit tree that
shielded him and once again studied the nearby cluster of
thatched houses. Within the compound glowed a few lights,
strings of candlenuts. There was no movement in the
enclosed yard. The large house that the usurper occupied
remained dark.

Matopahu and his warrior companions had been watching
the house since dusk. He knew that Land-crab was inside,
either asleep or engaged in *hanihani*. He smiled grimly,
hoping for the latter, and that the chief's attention was still
on his *vahine*.

The time to act had come. The effects of Land-crab's
curse, evaded for so long, now seemed to be growing
stronger. Matopahu thought he still had a chance to destroy
the man responsible for all his woes. And if he failed, he
could not be worse off than he was now.

Land-crab was a man, Matopahu reminded himself, and
could be destroyed by a man. The usurper had gods to
protect him, but so did Matopahu. The *ari'i* knelt behind the
trees to make a final plea to his guardian spirit.

Then he turned and whispered a word to his companions.

One warrior had brought hot embers, covered with sand, sealed within a coconut shell. In the darkness, Matopahu heard the rustling of coconut fronds. Someone blew on the coals while another man fed the small fire. In a moment, smoky light flared up from palm-rib torches.

Matopahu took two in one hand, a spear in the other, then gave the order to begin. The fires would have to be set quickly, before the drowsy guards spotted the flames. The four men spread out along the fence.

At Matopahu's signal, he and his warriors tossed the blazing bundles in high arcs, over the fence and onto the dry roofs within the compound. Flames leaped up and spread. A ferocious crackling sounded as the coconut thatch began to burn.

From within the houses came shrieks of alarm and shouts of enemy attack. Matopahu's men seized their war clubs and hefted their spears.

A moment later, confusion reigned, servants screaming, guards rushing to protect their chief. Holding a spear in one hand, his war club slung by a cord from his wrist, Matopahu vaulted the waist-high fence into the compound. Smoke pouring off the blazing thatch filled his nostrils and made his eyes burn.

Now, in these first moments of surprise, he had his best advantage. A sleepy guard staggered toward him. With two blows from his club he felled the man, then went after another.

This one put up a fight. He feinted, swung, then recovered quickly enough to parry Matopahu's swing. Land-crab's warrior lunged with his foot, trying a wrestler's trick to topple the *ari'i*. Matopahu caught him with a glancing blow to the chin, and the second guard went down.

By this time, the *ari'i* had lost all contact with his companions. Noise and smoke surrounded and isolated him. He saw dim figures fleeing, carrying off rolls of *tapa* or other valuables from the fire. Matopahu headed to the burning house of the usurper. He could not let Land-crab get away.

Even through the rolling billows of smoke, the chief on his bearer should be easy to spot. Or had Land-crab given up his pretensions of grand nobility and fled on his own feet? As the *ari'i* ran, he saw only a few straggling servants hurrying from his path. Ahead, the entire roof of the chief's house was ablaze.

Matopahu rushed up to the cane-walled dwelling and peered inside. The flames in the rafters lit the smoky interior with a flickering orange light. *Empty!*

The *ari'i* turned and saw two warriors closing in on him. The first was broad-shouldered and heavy, the second wiry and fast. The *ari'i* parried the wiry man's blow and ducked the other's; he heard the club crash above him into the wall of the burning house. In the moment it took for the burly guard to yank his weapon free, Matopahu swung at the other man, but this one was too quick for him. He parried with a blow that knocked the club from Matopahu's grip.

With a growl of defiance, the *ari'i* lunged, headfirst, ramming his head into the slimmer man's gut, knocking the wind out of him. Matopahu just had time to snatch up his weapon before the second man attacked again. This fellow was huge. Nothing short of a solid strike to the head would bring him down.

Matopahu blocked a massive blow that set his whole arm tingling. His fingers felt numb. He danced forward and back, waiting to recover sensation in his hand. The other man closed in.

The fighters were so near the burning house now that the heat burned Matopahu's skin. He ducked and feinted, trying to bait his opponent into making an awkward swing. The other man grinned and raised his weapon for the killing blow.

This time Matopahu was a bit quicker. He swung low, striking at the knee, setting the warrior off balance. Land-crab's man toppled against the broken wall just as the rest of the house began to collapse. He screamed as he tried to free himself from the splintered bamboo and the falling sheets of burning thatch.

The *ari'i* had no more interest in these two. Their chief was gone, probably heading for the sanctuary of a *marae*.

But which *marae*? He knew that the usurper had ordered a grand construction on a new site, but it had not yet been dedicated to the gods. Perhaps there was still time to catch him.

Tepua and Eye-to-heaven had been cautiously making their way toward the high chief's compound when they heard the first sounds of fighting. Led by the glimmer of distant firelight, they quickened their pace, following the shoreline and then heading inland through breadfruit groves. By the time they reached the scene, nearly everyone had fled.

Groaning men lay sprawled on the ground. Some did not move at all. Tepua's mouth went dry as she saw someone who resembled Matopahu. No, it was not him. Her pulse hammered as she rushed from one fallen warrior to the next.

"My *taio* is gone," said the priest, after making his own search of the ruined compound. "And so is Land-crab."

"We must find Matopahu." She glanced around, seeing a flash of white near the remains of the compound fence. A four-legged figure was moving. . . . *Te Kurevareva.* Tepua had almost forgotten the dog that she had been forced to give Land-crab. It had survived the fire, she was glad to see, but when she called its name, the dog turned and fled.

Then Tepua noticed a crowd gathering, people staring in astonishment at the smoldering remains. Everyone hung back, unwilling to trespass on the high chief's land. "Look what has happened," Tepua called to them. "The usurper gave up and ran away. Is there not a warrior among you? Take arms! Reclaim what is yours."

The onlookers shrank from her exhortation, creeping back so that the glow of dying fires did not shine on their frightened faces. "Who will lead us now?" they muttered. Other men arrived, some carrying weapons. They stared at each other in bewilderment.

"Matopahu will lead you," Tepua declared.

Eye-to-heaven strode forward and addressed the crowd. "It is true. Matopahu has returned to drive the usurper out."

Voices rose. Several onlookers recognized their former high priest and muttered his name. A small group surged forward. Tepua knew some of these men, who had been respected leaders under Matopahu's brother. Now they looked gaunt and disheveled; they stood, shoulders slumping, and stared at the ground. "Why do you taunt us with lies?" asked one. "Matopahu is dead."

"Is that what Land-crab told you?" Tepua asked indignantly.

"He showed us Matopahu's skull," the first elder answered.

"My *taio* will be amused to see it," answered the priest.

"Even if the *ari'i* lives," another man pointed out, "the curse is still on him. We saw what happened to Knotted-cord. There was no deception then."

"And what about this?" asked Eye-to-heaven, sweeping his hand across the scene of destruction. "If my *taio* was cursed, how did he manage to launch the attack? Where are Land-crab's renowned guards?"

A shout from the rear seemed to answer his question. "Away from the high chief's compound!" a sharp voice declared. "The fire was an accident. Land-crab is in control. Go back to sleep, all of you, unless you want to feed the gods."

As the warriors drew nearer, the crowd broke up in haste. Some people were so confused that they first raced *toward* the oncoming warriors before realizing their mistake and turning aside. Cries of anguish ran through the smoky air.

Tepua felt Eye-to-heaven's hand grasp her arm and pull her in another direction. "We cannot fight by ourselves," he said. "But there is something else we can do that is more important than finding Matopahu."

"No, we can't desert him! He needs our help."

"Be patient, Tepua. He is not far away and he knows how to take care of himself."

By now the moon had risen over the island's central peaks, but little light filtered through the leaves overhead. The priest led her by a circuitous route; at last she saw where he was heading. Breadfruit trees gave way to plantings of the sacred *miro*. The venerable *marae* where the priest had once served lay just ahead.

"We must watch," the priest whispered, pointing to the row of thatched houses at the edge of sacred ground.

"Attendants may be awake. I am sure they heard the fight, but most of them are probably cowering on their mats."

Tepua saw no illumination in the houses. She eyed any shadows that might be men. Nothing moved.

"Good," pronounced the priest after waiting awhile. "Now I'll go to work while you stand guard." He beckoned her to follow him.

"Into the . . . *marae*?"

He paused. "I will show you where to wait." A small storehouse stood nearby. He went inside and emerged wearing a priestly loincloth of bleached *tapa* that gleamed faintly when moonlight struck it. Carrying a digging stick, he went to the wall of the courtyard, prayed briefly, and entered.

Tepua could not see exactly what Eye-to-heaven was doing as he knelt, but she heard grunts and the scraping of stone against stone. *Searching for the corpse of Matopahu's brother!* What would be left of Knotted-cord now, she wondered, except a sennit-wrapped collection of bones?

Uneasily she moved closer, trying to glimpse what the priest was doing. She saw him leaning over something, peering into a crypt. Then he rose and she caught the look of disappointment on his face.

He turned to dig in another place. From somewhere behind her, Tepua heard cries and blows, men shouting challenges. Her blood pulsed as she tightened her grip on the spear.

The sounds of battle changed, but she was not sure if they were approaching. In the shadows beyond the *marae* she could see nothing. Glancing toward the priest, she noticed that he had moved again.

Then he leaped the courtyard wall and she heard his footsteps pounding. "The corpse must be somewhere else," he called. "I'll have to search the smaller shrines." He seemed to take only a moment to change from the sacred garment to his own and rush out to pick up his weapons.

"You go back to the canoe," he ordered as the sounds of fighting grew louder. "Get the child to safety. The rest will be over soon."

"Over? Yes," she retorted. "A few men cannot last against hundreds. That is why you want me way."

"Go!" the priest insisted. "I will look after my *taio*."

What can a lone priest do for him? Tepua felt prickles of fear and then a fierce determination. She recalled the discouraged expressions of the men she had seen at the compound. They needed hope. They needed a reason to fight. And without their help, Matopahu was doomed.

Leaving Eye-to-heaven, she rushed off toward the canoe where Maukiri was waiting. *This is where Matopahu's son belongs,* Tepua thought. *Not in hiding. Not in exile. This is his land.*

In the shadows, the *ari'i* could not tell how many men were chasing him. Land-crab's warriors had painted special markings on their faces and bodies, enabling them to recognize each other in the dim light. They would have little trouble now rounding up the intruders.

He stood perfectly still and wondered if he could find a way past them. His enemies, too, had halted, waiting for him to show himself. Glancing from one tree to the next, he saw dark figures standing erect. If there were only some way to distract them.

He did not know what had happened to all his companions. One had accompanied him to this grove, and was crouching not far away. If Matopahu took off in one direction and his friend in the other, that would split the enemy force. . . .

A shout interrupted his planning. Suddenly fighting broke out in another part of the grove. Land-crab's men came alive, plunging toward the battle.

Matopahu did not know which of his comrades had touched off the commotion, but he could not leave the man to struggle alone. Whatever plans of strategy he might have evolved were gone. He broke into a run, dodging warriors that turned out to be shadows.

Then suddenly, the solid bodies of men stood before him. Matopahu made quick work of two. His friends were shouting encouragement to each other. Land-crab's defenders backed off.

Only five remained standing. Five against Matopahu's three. Yet a warning nagged at him. There were not enough down to account for the rest. Had some fled, or merely circled behind?

He smashed back the blows of the painted man before him as he wondered frantically how to protect his back. He shouted a question to his friends, but they had no time to reply.

With a desperate parry, he knocked the club from his opponent's grip. While the man scrambled to retrieve the weapon, Matopahu turned completely around. He just had time to see what was coming. Then the night exploded and the heavens went dark.

As Tepua carried the child up the beach and through the groves of coconut palms, she wondered what had come over her. Eye-to-heaven had given her the only sensible advice—to take the infant to safety.

Yet a stronger voice drove her. She remembered the people of this district as they once had been—proud and self-sufficient, fearing no enemy. They had always been ruled by Matopahu's line. The first canoe to reach these shores from the ancient homeland had brought his noble ancestor, a descendant of the gods. In her arms, Tepua carried proof that his line was not ended.

Now that the moon had emerged, she found her way easily along the familiar paths. She tried not to think what would happen if Land-crab's men discovered her. Getting rid of both father and son would end all possible challenge to the usurper's rule.

Yet, despite the danger, she could not turn back. If Matopahu were killed, what life would there be for Ruro? As an exile in Putu-nui's court he would never see the home of his ancestors. There would be no honors for him, no illustrious marriage, no daughter Purea of the many titles. . . . Gritting her teeth, Tepua walked on.

Something darted from the bushes. For a moment, she clutched the child to her in fright. Then she saw Te Kurevareva dancing about her, leaping with excitement. "So you do remember me," she called softly. The dog lifted her muzzle, sniffing at the child. The long tail wagged and the dog rose briefly on her hind legs.

"Stay with us," Tepua whispered. "Warn us of danger." She continued up the path and was glad that the dog followed.

As she passed open-walled houses, Tepua saw that people were still awake. They sat huddled under *tapa* cloaks staring out, listening to the distant sounds of battle. She knew this part of the district. Ahead lay the large dwelling of a man who had once possessed much influence.

Hanging mats kept her from seeing inside his house. Tepua nervously approached the doorway. She could not be certain how anyone would react to her news. They might even scorn her. Yet she knew no other way to help Matopahu.

"Ia ora na," she called in a nervous voice. "Come out and meet your new chief. Come see the son of Matopahu."

From within she heard mutters of disbelief. "He is here," she continued. "The firstborn of the firstborn." The child gave a soft cry and shifted in her arms.

Then the old man who had been Knotted-cord's advisor came shuffling out. "Is this possible?" he asked. "I prayed to the gods that his line would survive. Now I cannot believe it is true."

She stood in a pool of moonlight. The elder stepped forward and bent over her for a better look. "It is so!" he cried suddenly. "Anyone can see his father in him. But why endanger the infant on this night of battle? Take him to safety. When he is fully grown, bring him back to us."

"By then there will be no one left to fight for him," she answered. "What happened to all the brave men? Even now I cannot find them."

Others emerged from the house, younger men, then women, finally a few boys. "What do you want?" asked a scowling man who carried a short spear.

"Stand with Matopahu!" she demanded.

He looked at the ground, then at the weapon in his hand. "I used to be one of the high chief's warriors," he replied in a weary voice. "Now I tend a yam garden."

"And your crops feed the usurper!" whispered a woman behind him.

"Watch what you say," cautioned another. "Do you want to bring the great wave?"

"If there is a punishing wave, it will wash away Land-crab as well," Tepua retorted. "Then the gods will have no one to look after the land. Can anyone believe that will happen?"

"Perhaps the prophecy is false," the old man admitted. "But there is danger on every side. Land-crab's men may be listening—"

"They are too busy trying to kill Matopahu," she answered. "But there are ten of us for each of his warriors. If we all rise together . . ."

"My people have lost the will to fight," the elder said with a sigh. He turned slowly to look at his sons and grandsons.

"Even this animal has more courage than you men!" Tepua answered. "Look. This is the high chief's dog. Now it follows my son." She held out the child. Te Kurevareva trotted closer and wagged her long, bushy tail.

"I am not afraid," replied one young man, going back inside. He emerged carrying a *paeho,* a wooden sword whose edge was set with gleaming shark's teeth.

"Then come with me while I find others like you," Tepua shouted. Several more fighters came forward, and she saw that she had attracted a small crowd from the surrounding houses.

"Spread the word," she told them. "We are defending Matopahu's son. We are driving the usurper from the land." She plunged on up the path, wondering how much time she had, unsure if her child's father still lived.

Matopahu's first awareness was of pain. Somehow the *ari'i* had returned from death. He was alive, yes. He knew little more than that.

The world around him remained black. He sensed that he was lying on something rough and gritty, with sharp pebbles that pressed into his back. Try as he might to shift his position, he could not move. All his efforts only intensified the throbbing at the back of his head.

The leaden feeling in his limbs frightened him. If the head blow had cost him the use of his arms and legs, then he was finished. The thought alarmed him so much that he retreated back into nothingness.

Yet his sense of pain returned and with it came another awareness—of sounds, voices, low, controlled, and sonorous. These were not the rough voices of warriors, but the trained ones of priests.

"Even if this man appears dead, be cautious," said the deeper of the two. "He evaded the curse placed on his brother. Who knows what else he can manage?"

"He may be full of tricks, but none will help him now," said the second voice scornfully. A hard finger poked into Matopahu's side. He felt himself rock limply, like a corpse.

"He managed to father a child," the first priest replied. "And a healthy one, too, from what I hear. Somehow we failed to set the curse deeply enough."

Child? Matopahu felt a shock go through him, though not a muscle moved.

"The news may be false," the second priest argued. "I haven't heard the report."

"A messenger was just here. He saw crowds gathering for a fight. The mother had the child in the center, surrounded by guards, and people were cheering."

"*Aue!* Then you are right. The *aha-tu* ceremony must have had a flaw. This time, we will make no mistakes. Neither the cliff climber nor his squalling brat will survive."

The priest is lying. I have no son! He tried to put the possibility from his mind.

But why would a messenger bring such false news? Maybe there was something to it. He recalled Eye-to-heaven's talk about a son, words he had dismissed in anger. Perhaps Tepua *had* chosen her child's life over her dedication to the Arioi!

Matopahu tried to keep listening, but throbbing in his skull and the buzzing in his ears would not let him. Had they captured the infant yet? Perhaps not, but what did it matter? He knew what the outcome would be.

The priests would strike at the child through him, just as

they had struck at him through his brother. Under guard or not, his son would die. Matopahu knew that this time *he* would be the sennit-man.

A freezing wave of fear swept through him. The priests would wrap him while he still lived. He remembered the dreams that had tormented him. . . .

Oh gods. If only he might be dead by then. Could he will himself into death before the sennit claimed him?

But what of your son? a voice whispered inside him. *If you die, he has no hope. . . .*

Aitofa stood before a crowd of Arioi, men and women, while Head-lifted tried to shout her down. Her followers stood in a circle, protecting her with their spears.

"The high chief demands your loyalty," Head-lifted called hoarsely to the people around him. "This is your duty."

"It is," Aitofa agreed. "Go to your chief. Tepua is carrying him."

"Tepua is disgraced!" retorted Head-lifted.

"She has made a great sacrifice," Aitofa replied. "A sacrifice that many highborn women of the Arioi have to make. She is no longer one of us, but she has brought us a remarkable gift." Aitofa remembered how unsettled she had been by the onset of Tepua's pregnancy. Knowing the difficulty of protecting the child, she had done everything to discourage Tepua from keeping it. But now Aitofa had no choice but to defend the son of Matopahu. The Arioi remained loyal to their chiefs—not to usurpers, but to those the gods had sent to rule.

As the crowd shouted and disagreed, Head-lifted seemed to sense that the mood was turning against him. "How can we know which one is the true chief?" he tried to argue. "Let us walk up into the hills and wait until this is over. Then we will be loyal to the one who survives."

Aitofa was astonished to hear a few cries of agreement.

"What has happened to you?" she shouted back. "Will you flee like fish from a shadow? Those who are still Arioi, come stand with me to defend the rightful chief."

*   *   *

Matopahu waited until he thought the priests had gone. Then he made a new effort to move his legs. Nothing, not even a quiver. Perhaps Land-crab's men had left him with a broken neck.

No. He had talked with men in that woeful state, and they said they could feel nothing in their legs. The gritty sharpness of pebbles digging into his thighs gave him a slight reassurance. Perhaps his problem was just weakness, or the effect of being struck on the head. Perhaps if he waited awhile longer . . .

Wondering if his eyesight had recovered at all, he forced an eyelid open a crack. In the dim light, he glimpsed a low wall built of round-faced stones. The sight sent a bolt of excitement through him. He nearly moved his head, but managed to control himself.

Now hope fluttered in his belly. Land-crab's priests had taken him to the principal *marae* of his people. His hand lay within reach of the wall, and these ancient stones held *mana*. If he could just stretch out his arm . . .

But the wall might have been standing on the other side of Tahiti for all the good it would do him. His arm lay, limp and heavy, unaffected by all his efforts to move it. His struggle was made even harder by the need to conceal it from the priests, whose voices told him they had returned. Any tremble, any uplift of the chest to gasp a breath, and they would call a warrior to club him again.

Once more, cautiously this time, he sent a demand to his muscles. Was there a slight flicker in his forearm? Did his fingers give a twitch? Yes, but very weak. His recovery, if real, was too slow to help him. The priests would see the signs long before he could make any real use of his arm.

He prayed that the men around him might move off again, but they remained, talking, until he thought he would cry out with frustration. Then someone called for attendants to carry his body to the binding platform, and he knew that his hope was gone. Arms reached under his back and legs. He felt himself lifted, carried away from the wall and into the *marae* itself.

He opened one eye a crack, saw the priests standing ready

under the chilling moonlight. The chant he feared had not yet started, but he knew it from memory.

"Bind him like a fish . . ."

He knew what was coming next. The sharp pegs and the coils of sennit lay ready. He heard a priest's impatient call.

The attendants quickened their pace as they carried him, feetfirst, past the familiar uprights of his ancestors. Just ahead he glimpsed a stone slab that made his pulse pound in his throat. If he could only think about that instead of the sennit!

The approaching upright was sacred to him as the firstborn of his line. It marked his personal place in the *marae*. More than once he had spent an entire night praying before it, begging the favor of the gods. There was great *mana* within the upright. If he could but reach out his hand . . .

For the sake of my child, he thought as sweat broke out on his forehead. A short while ago he had managed to move his fingers, but he needed to do far more. The attendants were already carrying him past his upright stone.

Now! Suddenly his arm shot to the side, his hand hitting so hard that the pain stunned him. The bearers shrieked in surprise, some releasing their hold on him, others tightening their grip. His fingers clutched and fastened on the stone as he tumbled to the side.

The priests cried out in dismay. Matopahu ignored them, concentrating on the one hand that clamped onto the upright. The rest of his body remained useless. But now he could feel the sacred essence of his ancestral gods.

He felt the power enter him, rushing from the stone of the *marae* and from the spirits that lingered around it, power that banished the weakness in his muscles. Strengthened by the contact, he grabbed on with the other hand. Pulling himself to the upright, he flung both arms about it in a desperate embrace. Now the ancient *mana* poured into him like the sea filling the lagoon at high tide. The attendants were shouting, trying to break him away from the power-filled stone. Others were calling for warriors.

Matopahu laughed. The priests' own rules worked against them now. A warrior would not dare step onto the sacred courtyard to attack him. He was safe, so long as he stayed here.

But he could not linger; he saw guards converging to block his escape. Cautiously, Matopahu stood up, breaking contact with the upright, stretching his arms and legs. The blow to his head had taken its toll. He still felt sore where the club had struck, but now he could move on his own. He hoped that he could defend himself.

He shouted praises and pleas to his gods, then pushed past the milling crowd of attendants. Looking for an opening, he leaped the courtyard's low wall. The first of Land-crab's men came charging, clubs raised, urged on by shrill cries from the priests.

With a deep roar, Matopahu wrenched the club from the warrior's grip. A kick in the gut doubled the man up, and a hard slam to the side of the head sent him spinning, blood spraying from one side of his nose.

Then two priests blocked him, but the *ari'i* swept them away with the borrowed club. More warriors were coming. He found a way past them. From nearby Matopahu heard voices that he recognized, men drawing closer, calling his name. Eye-to-heaven and the warriors from Eimeo!

Then he realized that others stood with them. As he emerged from the precincts of the *marae* he saw a host of men—warriors who had served his brother, and a surprising number of Arioi as well. They seemed poorly armed, yet so many had gathered.

Hope warred with apprehension in Matopahu's mind. He had heard the priest's tale of Tepua and a child. Now he wanted to see for himself if this was true. The cheering crowd made way for him, but the ring of warriors they revealed stayed in place, spears pointing outward.

Then he caught sight of Tepua in the center, cradling a male child in her arms. Briefly she raised the baby high so that everyone could see. Shouts of *"Maeva ari'i!"* rang from all sides.

My son!

His joy lasted but a moment; then outrage swept through him. She had lied to him, tricked him, made him think his son was dead. . . . Yet here was the child, lifted in her hands like a battle standard. He thought he could strike her down once for her deception and again for bringing his son into such danger.

Was there any hope of saving the infant? All around him he heard the loyal shouts of his supporters. Women as well as men had gathered in great numbers. First among the Arioi stood Aitofa, who had long been his friend. Many Arioi clustered behind her.

The people were rising to fight for his child. As he heard their shouts, the refrain burst from his own lips as well. *"Maeva ari'i!" The people hail you as their chief.*

But he had no words for Tepua. All that mattered now was saving his son. The fight would be soon—his ragtag band against an array of highly trained fighters. In the distance he heard another chorus of war cries.

Land-crab's men were coming. A parade of torches burned, moving closer, until he could see the oncoming mass of painted warriors, heads wrapped in bark-cloth, weapons ready. They halted in a line behind their field commander.

"Matopahu!" shouted their leader. "Who are these fools behind you? Why are they so eager to die?"

The *ari'i* strode forward to answer. "We are the people of this land."

The other man sneered. "And we are your masters!"

"Then who is *your* master? Where is the swine who calls himself your chief? Is he afraid to face me?" Matopahu heard a murmuring behind him as his supporters closed ranks. Their sheer numbers seemed enough to give the opponents second thoughts. A pitched battle now would mean disaster on both sides, bodies piled high, air filled with the mourning cries of the survivors.

There was another way to settle this. As was often done, each army could send out a champion.

"I fight for Land-crab," the commander said, his face glistening in the torchlight. "Let us waste no more words."

"And I fight for myself," Matopahu retorted. "But who will give me a proper challenge? An *ari'i* must have a worthy opponent."

The warrior grinned. "I will finish you quickly. Then these fishermen and canoe-builders can go home to bed."

"I will fight Land-crab, and no one else. That is the only battle the gods will accept. Is your chief afraid of me?"

The grin vanished. The warrior chief turned to look at his men, who moved restlessly, eyes fixed firmly on him. "Land-crab fears nothing."

"Then call your chief to battle!" Behind Matopahu the crowd raised a chorus of jeers and insults, all bearing Land-crab's name.

TWENTY-TWO

"The war canoes are leaving," Tepua announced mournfully as she peered past a stand of ironwood trees toward the shimmering lagoon. Land-crab had agreed to fight Matopahu, but had insisted on the pomp and ceremony of a battle on water. Now morning had come and the twin-hulled canoes had been launched—each bearing a raised platform between its two bows, each streaming banners of white bark-cloth.

Tepua had no time to linger. She and Eye-to-heaven were still searching in the forest for the sennit-wrapped body of Matopahu's brother. They still had a short while before the combat began.

"We must try somewhere else," came the priest's voice from behind her. "There is nothing buried here."

Tepua glanced once more at the lagoon, hearing drumming and the bray of conch-trumpets. Soon the canoes would meet. . . . Hurriedly she turned away and began to follow the priest inland.

Eye-to-heaven looked discouraged. "If the bones are hidden in a mountain cave, we are lost," he said as he followed an overgrown path.

Tepua sighed, remembering how the *ari'i* had shouted his bold challenge to Land-crab. "Matopahu seemed so full of confidence—"

"If this were just a battle of one man against another, then Matopahu would win. But the curse still holds him back—so long as the cords bind his brother." Eye-to-heaven paused. "Do you hear the drumming? Land-crab has asked his priests to perform a ritual to strengthen the *aha-tu*."

"Then hurry," Tepua said.

Eye-to-heaven pushed past hibiscus branches that swept the ground, dislodging petals of withered flowers as he went by. Tepua caught up with him as he neared another courtyard that was walled by black stones neatly fitted together. Out of respect, he put aside the *tapa* cape that was slung over his shoulder, placing it on a branch outside the sanctuary. Matopahu had worn this cape earlier, but had changed his dress to face Land-crab. The priest needed the cloth to hold the bones of Knotted-cord—if he found them.

Tepua watched as Eye-to-heaven stepped over the low wall and crouched to examine the ground. Grass and saplings sprouted from crevices between the stones. Moss was thick everywhere. "This *marae* is overgrown," she said. "If someone had dug a grave here, we would see signs."

"More than a year has passed since the burial," the priest reminded her. "This part looks cleaner than the rest. Maybe I'll find something . . ." He began to probe with a stick.

Tepua felt outraged by the *tapu* that kept her outside the *marae*. If only there were another priest to help, someone still loyal to Matopahu. Or a quicker way to find the remains of Knotted-cord. She turned toward the shore, peering past a stand of trees, and tried to see what was happening on the lagoon.

Matopahu stood on the fighting platform just behind the twin bows of his canoe. Looking down, he saw his paddlers, a row of broad-backed warriors in each hull. These men had pledged him their loyalty. They knew what their fate would be if he failed.

He was already starting at a disadvantage. This double-hull was older and smaller than Land-crab's. Worried, Matopahu eyed the towering upward-curved prows and high platform of the oncoming canoe.

As the warrior watched his opponent approach, something to the side caught his eye. Close to his own hulls he noticed two high fins cutting through the water. Sharks!

Why had they come? Did they know that blood would soon be staining the lagoon?

The fins were a slate color, without the black tips that marked common reef sharks. He could not be certain, but he thought these were great blues, sharks sacred to the highest chiefs of the land. Once, long ago, they had greeted him. Now, perhaps, they had come to honor his last battle.

Matopahu tore his gaze from the water to watch his enemy's approach. Even from a distance, Land-crab made an impressive figure. He wore the *fau,* the tall cylindrical headpiece of a principal warrior. Behind him stood attendants holding an array of clubs and shark-toothed *paeho* swords.

And Land-crab was not coming to fight alone. Close behind followed another two-hulled vessel, a floating *marae* manned by priests and their attendants. They all wore robes of dazzling white bark-cloth. On the canoe's high platform a ceremony was already in progress, offerings laid out on a table. The wind in Matopahu's face brought the boom of sacred drums.

Another sound dismayed him even more—the solemn bray of a conch-shell trumpet. Land-crab was not letting anyone forget his claim to the chieftainship. *As if the gods had actually chosen him.*

In response, men on the deck below Matopahu sounded a defiant reply. He was surrounded by the boom of skin-head drums and the hollow clatter of the slit-log *toere.*

The sound raised his spirits, yet he could not shake off the effect of Land-crab's appearance. Standing atop his platform, Land-crab had the look of a great warrior, with broad shoulders and powerful arms. His tall headpiece, covered with crimson and orange feathers, made him seem even more fearsome. Black spikes of frigate-bird feathers surmounted the top. Each movement of the usurper's head made the forward-curved front nod threateningly.

Equally daunting were Land-crab's half-circle gorget and cape, fringed with feathers so brilliant that they seared the eyes. Matopahu felt a pang of awe as he remembered kneeling in the *marae* before a feather-covered image while Oro's presence transformed the red-and-orange plumage into sacred fire. Now the usurper seemed clothed in the same divine flame, the mark of the great god in his war-loving aspect.

Matopahu's hand trembled on the haft of his war club, and a choking feeling weighted his chest, spreading weakness down into his legs. With horror, he recognized not only the paralyzing fear of the god, but also the sign of the lingering *aha-tu* curse.

As the usurper came on, the terror of his appearance seemed to spread through Matopahu's men. He heard the strident challenge of his drums falter. From the paddlers below the fighting platform rose despairing moans.

"Red Oro has been wakened!"

"This is not a man we fight—it is a god!"

The *ari'i* gathered his breath and forced a derisive shout from his lips. "If a swine wears a *fau,* he looks like a god. But when I strike it from his head, you'll see what he really is!"

At this cry, his men roared defiance. Drums boomed fiercely once more as the two war canoes drove closer. Then the vessels slowed as the raised prows almost touched, one sliding past the other so that the fighting platforms met. To his chagrin, Matopahu saw that Land-crab's platform stood a step above his, giving the usurper both prestige and fighting advantage.

"Fear me, Land-crab!" Matopahu bellowed as attendants scurried to lash the vessels together. "I fight for my brother. I fight for my people, who are starving so that you can grow fat. You are no great chief. You are a petty squabbler and a thief, using war to take what you do not deserve!"

"What are you but a sennit-wrapped corpse?" Land-crab threw back, his predatory eyes gleaming. "Have you forgotten what I did to your brother? My priests will help you remember."

Matopahu took a quick glance to the side, at the floating *marae* canoe where the priests were still chanting. He could not see what they were doing, nor could he spare any attention to look. Suddenly he felt a sharp pain at the top of his head. It eased, only to be followed by a fiercer pain, first at one ear, then the other.

This, too, passed, replaced by a new discomfort and a wave of dread. From the top of his head came a feeling of constriction, as if the crown of his skull were being wound with cord.

Like my brother . . .

No! Matopahu refused to believe that the priests could bring the old nightmare on him again. He threw his head back, expanded his chest. "Your threats cannot stop me," he called defiantly. "And neither can your priests."

Land-crab laughed. "Use your words, Matopahu. They are all you have left. Watch the last ceremony and then we will begin." He turned to the *marae* canoe. This time Matopahu followed his gaze.

Below the platform where the priests stood, two warriors held a man whose hands and feet were bound. The captive crouched, shivering with terror. Then one warrior lifted a club and brought it down on the back of the victim's head. The man slumped, lifeless. The warriors heaved the corpse up to the high platform.

"Red Oro, take your fish," the priests chanted. "A gift without blemish . . ."

"There is my offering to the god for victory," Land-crab exulted. "I grant you leave to do the same."

Matopahu felt a thick disgust choke his throat as he wondered how many other men the usurper had sacrificed since daybreak. He looked away from the grin of triumph on Land-crab's face. As his gaze swept past the priests, he could not help seeing that they were readying the victim to be suspended like a gill-strung fish.

His gut heaved; the throbbing in his head and ears reawakened with a vengeance. His hands closed on the handle of his paddle-club. It had a long shaft, and a flat-bladed end for cleaving skulls. "Soon I will make my offering," Matopahu answered. "*You* will be the fish I bring to the altar of the gods."

With a roar of rage, Land-crab snatched a weapon from his attendant. Matopahu saw the white flash of shark's teeth mounted in wood. With a quick movement, he used his paddle-club to parry the stroke.

The shock jarred him and a sudden lash of pain down his

chest made him gasp. He reeled back, bleeding and confused. How could his opponent have drawn first blood? The paddle-club's shaft had blocked the shark-toothed blade. Then he saw, as Land-crab swung the weapon up for another blow, what kind of *paeho* his enemy wielded. It was not straight, as Matopahu expected, but had a deadlier shape. From the handgrip, *two* blades forked out. The paddle-club had stopped one row of teeth but not the other.

Matopahu licked his lips, ignoring the fierce sting of the slash down his chest. Never before had he fought a man who used the forked blade.

"Do you like my Claw?" Land-crab taunted. "I use it to carve up stinking fish like you."

The usurper's next rush carried him over the low railing of his own platform and onto Matopahu's. Knowing no defense against the forked *paeho,* the warrior gave way before Land-crab's slashes. Sweat poured from Matopahu's body. Black patches danced before his vision, and the ache of weakness dragged at his arms and shoulders.

"When I finish you," Land-crab snarled, "I will set every man in the district to making sennit. My priests will bind you, then your supporters. Even your friends among the Arioi will not escape."

It was all Matopahu could do to keep from clapping his hands to his ears. The words alone seemed to bring on a new strike of agony through his head.

Land-crab pressed closer, laughing with bared teeth as one slashing blow followed another. The *ari'i* braced the end of the paddle-club against the deck and whipped the shaft back and forth to take the force of each strike. As he fought, he felt a return of ghostly fingers. Now he felt cord winding tightly across his forehead. As it passed over his eyes, a part of his sight vanished, as if his eyes were slowly being covered.

Like my brother . . . like my brother . . .

No! Squinting to fend off the encroaching blindness, the *ari'i* met Land-crab again and threw him back. Death wrapped itself around Matopahu, binding his limbs. His muscles cramped painfully and contracted, his joints refused to straighten, yet somehow he kept fighting, almost welcoming the blows as a distraction from the attack of the priests.

He felt as though he were splitting into two—the warrior still defending against the *paeho,* and the helpless victim of the curse.

Matopahu knew he had only two choices. To give himself to the forked blade or fling himself over the rail to the sharks.

And then the Claw swept toward him and he had no choice at all.

As Tepua followed Eye-to-heaven to another old *marae,* she heard a quiet rustle in the underbrush. She halted, ready to warn the priest of a possible attack. Tepua sighed with relief when she recognized the sound of a dog panting. "Te Kurevareva, why are you here?" she asked sharply. "You should be guarding Ruro." She had left her son with Maukiri, a circle of warriors, and Atoll Cuckoo, hoping that the white dog would give additional protection by warning Maukiri of any approach by Land-crab's men.

Te Kurevareva ignored Tepua's complaint and trotted at her heels as she caught up with Eye-to-heaven. "We have to search the sites in this area," the priest said, pointing to another overgrown trail.

"By the time we finish, it will be too late," Tepua cried. Then, glancing at the dog, she suddenly had an idea. "Let Te Kurevareva sniff Matopahu's cloak."

The priest stopped, and stared at her. Then, his eyebrows rising slowly, he took off the cape and held it out to the dog. "A man and his brother have a similar scent," he said doubtfully. "But I wonder . . . And the dog must not trespass in a *marae!*"

Te Kurevareva looked from Tepua to the priest, as if asking what was expected of her. Tepua took a stick and dug into the ground. She guided the dog's muzzle to the cloth, then toward the hole, repeating the lesson several times. "Something that smells like this is buried in the ground. Find it."

Te Kurevareva cocked her head, her tail lifted. Then she dove into a thicket.

The priest, muttering his doubts, walked on. "I will catch up with you," Tepua called to him. Wiping moisture from her brow, she crashed through the underbrush after the tip of a waving white tail. Shortly, she lost sight of the animal.

She stopped and called again, but Te Kurevareva didn't reappear. Driven by a feeling of urgency, she searched for paw marks in the red clay soil. The trail doubled back. Ahead she heard a yelp.

By the time she made her way across a fallen tree, the dog was gone again, and this time she found no tracks. She wandered about awhile, wondering if she should give up and return to the priest. The area was thickly overgrown, with no sign of a burial place. "Te Kurevareva, are you following a lizard?" she called in frustration.

From far off, Tepua thought she heard another yelp. Pushing through heavy foliage, she came on an unexpected sight. A few slabs of blackened coral stood upright under ancient ironwood trees. None of the other features of a *marae,* such as surrounding walls or an *ahu,* remained. How long ago had this place been abandoned? Tepua felt a reluctance to tread on what once had been sacred ground. She gave the uprights a wide berth.

Suddenly, behind her, she heard a scraping sound. Te Kurevareva was scrabbling at a hole in the base of a small mound. The dog stopped digging and looked up eagerly. Tepua crouched for a better view and then ran to find the priest.

By the time they returned, the dog had uncovered part of a buried coral slab, leaving red soil scattered on all sides. Eye-to-heaven intoned a prayer, then bent to finish the digging with the end of a branch. "Keep back," he warned Tepua. "Nothing tainted by death must touch you."

He found a heavy stick, wedged it into a gap, and tried to dislodge the stone. "Let me help," Tepua pleaded.

"You will have your chance," said the priest, almost out of breath. With a scraping sound that put her teeth on edge, he moved the stone enough to open a gap. He grunted, then tried again. This time the entire slab came up, tilted over, then dropped away with a heavy thud.

Tepua felt a shiver down her back as she dared a step

closer, until she could see the cord-wrapped bundle within. "Is this what you are looking for?"

"Yes," the priest answered. "I recognize it. I caught a glimpse of the dead man after he had been bound."

Tepua did not ask when or how. From the corpse rose a smell that was heavy with the scent of decay. A surge of emotion made her eyes fill with tears. She said, "Poor Knotted-cord. He had his faults, but he did not deserve this."

She glanced up to Eye-to-heaven, saw that the priest's eyes were also moist. "Do not touch the body," he warned again. He took Matopahu's cloak, wrapped it around the remains, then carried the bundle down the trail to a nearby *marae* that was still in use.

"Build me a fire, Tepua-mua," he said, pulling out a shell-blade knife. "As quickly as you can. There is no established ritual for this, but I must try."

Hastily Tepua found what she needed to make a fire plow—a split piece of soft hibiscus for the plow bed and a harder stick for the blade. She knelt on the ground not far from Eye-to-heaven. She saw how he was sweating, his lips moving in impassioned prayer as he slowly cut the cords that bound the bones. Her hands trembling, she began rubbing the fireplow against the bed, making wood dust that refused to smolder.

"Tapahi-roro-ariki," she cried, invoking the aid of her own guardian spirit. Then, to her relief, she saw a tiny flame rise. She fed it tinder and a few dry sticks, then larger pieces.

As she stood back, wiping soot and perspiration from her face, Eye-to-heaven turned his head at the crackle of the fire. The look of hope in his eyes warmed Tepua. He picked up a dry twig that had fallen into the *marae* and brought it out, holding the wood in the flames until it caught. Still praying, he took the torch to the pile of cut cord he had placed on a stone.

The mold-blackened cord slowly came alight. Eye-to-heaven began to chant. His body shook with the intensity of his plea. Sweat ran from his face, and unashamed tears from his eyes, as his voice rang out with solemn power.

O Ta'aroa, whose curse is death.
Take your fish.
Take the bones that are bound with your sacred cord.
But free the man who has done you no wrong.
He was cursed wrongly, with evil.

Let the cord that binds his brother be burned.
That the curse on him shall fall away.
For my sake; I who am his friend.
For her sake; she who is his woman.
For his sake; he who is his son.

On the war-canoe, Matopahu fell to his knees, clutching the rail of the fighting platform. With excruciating effort he had struck away Land-crab's slash, but the act had drained him. Now he wondered why Land-crab was delaying the final blow. Was he pausing to savor his moment of victory?

Matopahu's knees were bent and would not straighten. He was collapsing slowly into himself, drawing tight into a cord-wrapped bundle. His calves were pressing against the back of his thighs, his knees into his chest, his feet shoved back so that his callused heels slowly crushed his genitals. *O gods,* he prayed, *if this is to be my end, give me the power to meet it well.*

His head strained against an invisible binding around his jaws and throat. His lips moved beneath the sennit, forming words of prayer. Though he could no longer see, he sensed the blade coming. Somehow he found strength to lift his weapon and fend off one more blow. . . .

And then he felt a sudden heat washing over his body. A dim orange glow penetrated the covering over his face. He strained to open his eyelids against the strands of fiber cord. A gap appeared, and then another, allowing him to peer through.

Flames seemed to dance all around him, licking at his bonds. He could actually see the bits of cord charring and falling away. Was this Eye-to-heaven's doing? The curse of binding seemed finally broken!

Matopahu had no time to wonder how it had been done. Land-crab was raising his vicious weapon. The *ari'i* still ached and bled from the battle, but he felt a surge of new strength. The deadly weariness of the sennit-curse was gone. His vision was clear and his limbs quick as he brought up the paddle-club shaft to meet the shark-toothed blade.

As he parried smartly, he heard frenzied chanting from the priests, but their words no longer harmed him. With a scream of rage, Land-crab tried again, striking so hard that the paddle-club's shaft shuddered in Matopahu's grip, stinging his hands. But over the crack of weapons, and his own grunts of effort, the *ari'i* heard a sound that renewed his battle fury. It was the hoarse whistling of his opponent's breath. Land-crab was starting to tire.

On the next exchange, Matopahu whirled aside, letting the forked weapon hit the rail of the fighting platform. Teeth broke from the blade. *The thing is deadly, but fragile,* he thought. *He trusts too much in the strangeness of the Claw. He leaves his head unguarded.*

Land-crab cut low, striking at Matopahu's legs. The warrior leaped to clear the forked blade, but as it passed beneath his feet, he kicked down, catching the shaft beneath his heel and driving it toward the deck. More teeth broke away.

He lunged at Land-crab with the paddle-club, aiming swift, precise blows past the deadly sweep of the Claw. With a joyful roar, Matopahu gripped his weapon low and swung the blade end in a scything path at Land-crab's head. He heard the crack of breaking wicker as Land-crab's towering *fau* began to topple.

A great howling broke from Matopahu's supporters, and the drums thundered around him. Now it was Land-crab giving ground, wielding the forked weapon with one hand while trying to hold on to his *fau* with the other. Matopahu drove the usurper back, forced him to make a hasty retreat onto his own platform. For an instant Land-crab again took the advantage, using the greater height to reign blows down on the warrior, but battle fury swept Matopahu after his foe.

Now he was on Land-crab's fighting deck. With a crash the Claw met the paddle-club. One of the forked shafts broke off in a hail of splinters and shark's teeth. Before the usurper could recover, Matopahu aimed again at Land-crab's head and struck off the *fau*.

It was as if he had sliced off a limb, for Land-crab shrieked in anguish at the loss of the war helmet. In that moment of inattention, Matopahu swung again, bringing the flat end of his club down on the back of Land-crab's neck. The *paeho* fell from the usurper's hand and Matopahu kicked it away.

But the neck blow had merely stunned Land-crab, who heaved himself up again. His face was writhing—not in pain or defeat, but in terror. His eyes rolled like a man on the edge of madness.

He grabbed another weapon, a short club, but now he barely had strength to swing it. "Not the *aha-tu*—you will not bind me," he breathed as he backed away from Matopahu. His gaze went suddenly to the sharks, still circling in the water below. For a moment he hesitated. Then, with a howl, he threw himself off the fighting deck and plunged into the lagoon.

The leap was so unexpected that Matopahu could do nothing but watch. While the cries and drums of victory sounded all around him, the two fins converged and then vanished beneath the lagoon's waters. There was no thrashing or frothing on top of the water, only a horrifying calm and then a blooming of blood at the surface.

Still consumed by battle fury, Matopahu found it hard to put his weapon aside. He half hoped that Land-crab would rise again, but he knew that was impossible. The water remained still, reddening from beneath.

The drums fell silent. The priests ceased their chanting. Everyone around him seemed stunned by the outcome.

Matopahu's head swam with the dizzying sense of victory. For a moment he could not believe what had happened. He turned, looking at the terrified faces in the usurper's canoe. Knotted-cord's death was avenged! The *aha-tu* curse was broken!

"Bring me your banners," he shouted at last to the men who had served Land-crab. "Then cut your vessels loose and go back to shore. I have no quarrel with any of you."

As he returned to his own canoe, the paddlers below

stood up to hail his victory. "Death to Land-crab's kin," they shouted. "Treat them as he treated your brother."

Matopahu listened patiently, waiting for the tumult to die down. "It is time to stop speaking of war," he answered loudly. "Land-crab is gone. Now we must send the spirits of war back to the Room of Night, and call the spirits of peace into the Room of Day."

The men shouted back their disagreement. Again they called for revenge.

"You will see that I am right," Matopahu answered. "Take me to shore. The victory celebrations are waiting for us."

By the time Tepua reached shore again, the war canoes were coming in. Her spirits soared at the sight of Matopahu's craft, flying twice as many streamers and banners as it had before. The larger canoe behind it was stripped of decoration.

But she did not let loose her shout of exultation until she saw the *ari'i* standing victoriously on his canoe's fighting deck, his arms lifted in triumph.

"Praise to the gods!" Tepua cried.

Eye-to-heaven's sonorous voice rang out, joining with hers. Maukiri gave a raucous yell. Little Ruro, cradled in Tepua's arms, added baby laughter. Te Kurevareva filled out the chorus with a few sharp yelps.

Eye-to-heaven stood close beside Tepua. "No man could have a better *taio* than you, Eye-to-heaven," she said, her eyes moist with emotion.

"And no man could have a better woman or a finer son," the priest answered.

Te Kurevareva danced around them, her tongue lolling. After getting muddy from all the digging, she had taken a bath in the stream, and now she was white again. When she jumped up to claim her share of affection, neither Eye-to-heaven nor Tepua pushed her away.

As Matopahu's war canoe drew up into the shallows, a solemnness came over Tepua. She felt the warm weight of her child in her arms. Her eyes followed Ruro's father as he descended from the fighting deck, reflected light from the water rippling over his face. She saw that he had lost his bark-cloth turban in the fight. Now his black hair was tousled by the wind.

He came triumphantly ashore on the shoulders of his men. Overhead, a tropic bird swooped, its scarlet tail feathers aglow in the brilliant sunlight. A breeze from the lagoon blew against Tepua's cheek as she watched the crowd of warriors bring Matopahu to her.

The face of the *ari'i* was regal, noble, almost the remote countenance of a god. But something in her breast tightened when she saw the depth of hunger and affection in his eyes. Yes, he was a man, though he had battled like a god. He was a man who had a son . . . and a woman as well, if he wanted her.

He gave an order and the men set him down in front of Tepua. "Land-crab is dead," he said, his voice husky. His gaze went to the child. "My son is safe. And the curse is gone." He lifted the child so that its gaze met his. Ruro's eyes were wide open and so was his mouth. His head wobbled, but he met the attention of his father with an equally courageous stare of his own.

"Maeva ari'i!" Matopahu roared, raising his son above his head. "Hail to the new chief!"

"Maeva ari'i!" came voices from all around as a crowd began to gather. Then silence fell again as Matopahu turned to Tepua. She knew what he was thinking. He had his son now. If he wished, he could keep Ruro and send her away.

He seemed in no hurry to decide. She heard the wind rattling the branches overhead, and waves booming against the distant reef. Then the hardness of his eyes melted and he laid his son back into her arms.

Her heartbeat threatened to overwhelm her as he stepped closer, embracing her, his arms about mother and child.

A crowd stood in the shallows, men in one party, women in another. The people were fishing, but not for the colorful lagoon fish that flitted beneath the surface, nor for the eels hiding in the rocks. Aitofa, Curling-leaf, and other Arioi women helped Tepua and Maukiri pull a net of plaited coconut fronds across the bottom of the lagoon.

As the stiff net moved, it gathered small pieces of broken

coral. The women plucked these fragments from the meshes until their baskets were full. Shouting gaily, they brought their "catch" ashore.

Eye-to-heaven's powerful voice rose over the splashing of the people and the lapping of the lagoon against the shore.

Let the land be purified.
Let the defilement of war be erased.
So that evil is cleansed from the land.
So that we may abide on the soil and eat of its fruits.

The priest raised a piece of broken coral and others did the same as he chanted,

These are our offerings, great gods.
We bring you these white fish.
Let the land be made as pure as coral,
Fresh from the sea.

Then everyone rejoiced. At last, they were free of the taint of battle. The land was theirs again. The spirits of peace reigned once more.

TWENTY-THREE

Three days after the coral-fishing ceremony, an enormous crowd of spectators gathered in the clearing around the new performance house. Late-afternoon sunlight slanted in under the high roof, illuminating the platform that held stools for the honored guests. The highest-ranking men and women of the district had already taken their places. Wearing an elaborate feather headdress and ornamented cape, Tepua occupied the foremost seat, next to the one high stool that stood empty.

The celebration today was for Ruro, though he would not be present to watch. Tepua was being honored as his mother, and Matopahu as father and regent—if and when he arrived, she thought in exasperation.

Her thoughts turned to young Ruro as she had seen him just a short while before on Maukiri's lap. He was wearing a little *tapa* turban with a parakeet feather on the front. A small loincloth made of the softest white bark-cloth was wrapped around his fat stomach. Ruro was growing fast. From the size and the strength in his plump little limbs, she knew that he would attain the powerful physique of his father. But he also had the atoll heritage, which would make him as tough and sinewy as the pandanus tree.

But where was his father? The guests on the platform grew restless, muttering quietly as they waited. The Arioi stared at each other, making subtle signs.

Then, suddenly, far to the rear of the crowd, she saw a

wave of activity. At last he was coming! A swell of cries and cheers developed as the *ari'i* appeared from the direction of the high chief's compound.

He had dressed himself modestly in a simple *tapa* cloak, his head crowned only by a plaited sunshade. As he mounted the platform and took his seat, Tepua glanced at his expression of indifference. On this grand occasion, Matopahu was acting as if he preferred to be elsewhere!

While she listened to the chanting begin, Tepua tried to understand. Though he had said nothing to her, she sensed that he still resented her lies about the child. As the thrill of victory had waned, his coolness toward her had become more apparent. Perhaps this was why he showed little enthusiasm for today's celebration.

With a sigh, Tepua turned to watch the Arioi. Attending as an honored guest, instead of a member of the troupe, gave her mixed feelings. Though the Arioi honored her as Ruro's mother, she could never again participate in their rites. She must serve Oro now in other ways. She hoped that she could find alternatives.

She watched the ceremonies begin, Head-lifted strutting forward to make his welcoming speech. To Tepua's eyes he had aged greatly in only a few days. His refusal to take a stand against Land-crab had cost him much support. Soon, she was certain, he would step down and let someone younger lead the men's lodge.

A renewed Aitofa addressed the crowd. She, too, had changed, but much for the better. Now her step was light, her voice charged with spirit.

As for Pehu-pehu . . . Tepua felt satisfied that the woman would trouble her no more. Pehu-pehu had fled to Eimeo to beg her old troupe to take her back. There was no longer room for two Blacklegs in Wind-driving Lodge.

Now the chanting of the chorus began again, recounting the history of the order—the deeds of Oro and the founding of the Arioi. The obligatory performances followed, portraying tales from long ago. Tepua drew in her breath and waited patiently, sensing that everyone in the crowd felt as eager as she did for the event that would follow. Honoring

the gods and ancestors was necessary, of course, but people
had also come here to have fun.

Rumors about a surprise performance by the Arioi had
been on everyone's lips. The rehearsals had been done in
secret. Perhaps Matopahu knew more about it than she did,
Tepua mused. Perhaps that was another reason for his lack
of enthusiasm. It was customary for the performers to poke
fun at everyone, even heroes such as Matopahu.

At last, to the approval of all, Aitofa announced the piece
that all had awaited. It was to be a reenactment of the battle
between Land-crab and Matopahu. Faces brightened.
People leaned forward in anticipation. Everyone knew that
this would be a parody of the actual events.

The slit-log drums clattered wildly as the players, clad in
outrageous costumes, arranged themselves in a tableau. On
one side stood Land-crab's warriors. On the other stood
Matopahu's forces. And in the center, the two champions
faced each other.

Their weapons were enormous "clubs" stitched together
from pigskin and stuffed nearly to bursting. The fighters
were painted absurdly, with dots and streaks of red over
cheeks and bodies. The actor portraying Matopahu was the
tallest in the troupe. He waved his club as the chorus spoke
his challenge. The actor playing Land-crab was short and
stocky, with a heavy wrapping of cloth to make his big belly
seem even larger.

Tepua gasped as a new performer—a hefty male Arioi
dressed as a woman in a dancing skirt and flower crown—
sashayed onto the stage. "She" was lugging a youth garbed
in baggy diapers who pretended to suckle greedily at his
mother's breasts. The oversized infant kicked and squalled
as his mother shoved him under a massive muscled arm.
"Tepua-mua," the audience roared, while they pounded their
thighs in applause.

She felt her face burn as the hefty actor did a crude
imitation of her dancing while trying to keep the mischievous infant under control. Well, she had certainly helped
cast the sharp spear of Arioi humor at others who deserved
it. Perhaps it was right that she also feel the sting.

Onstage, "Matopahu" shook his weapon angrily at

"Tepua" while the chorus chanted his words of rebuke for bringing the child into battle. The skirted actor struggled to lift the infant in order to display him to the crowd, while the chorus spoke Tepua's answering lines in falsetto. The youth playing the infant assumed a look of idiocy, stuck his thumb in his mouth, and let his saggy diaper slip.

"Matopahu" turned to his enemy. Without preamble, the fighters began to swing their weapons wildly, soft "clubs" smacking loudly into flesh. As each man was hit, he mimed great pain, hopping about in anguish.

The audience roared its approval as the upper hand in the match went back and forth, "Matopahu" falling to his knees, then rising again to defend himself. All the while, "Tepua" kept lifting the squirming child and making grimaces of dismay.

Suddenly the lively infant slipped from his mother's grip. On all fours he scampered across the stage with his mother in hot pursuit. He capered about the two fighters, scuttling around them and then diving between their legs, disrupting the battle. "Matopahu" tripped over him and went down.

Dancing with one hand holding up the diaper, the infant seized his father's oversized club and began raining blows on "Land-crab." The club split and grass stuffing flew about the stage. Then "Tepua" joined the fray, grabbing her enemy's weapon from his hand. "Matopahu" lay on the stage and rolled his eyes while the two beat "Land-crab" around the stage.

Finally, with a bored expression, "Matopahu" got up, snatched the club from "Tepua," and with a casual blow, knocked his opponent to the ground.

At this moment, the crowd of "Land-crab's" supporters began shrieking with woe, throwing down their mock weapons, tearing off their garlands and necklaces. "Matopahu's" allies danced in triumph.

The infant continued to tear around the stage, flourishing what was left of his stolen club and eluding all efforts at capture. Ignoring the celebration and the antics of the child, "Matopahu" and "Tepua" stood glowering at each other. The battle was over, and now they were finishing their lovers' quarrel.

The chorus began to recite accusations, each more outlandish than the next. Growing impatient with the arguments, the infant bashed both parents over the head with his club and watched with delight as they too sank to the ground. Then he strutted about waving the tattered remains of his weapon. *"Maeva ari'i,"* shouted the chorus, and the crowd joined in gleefully.

Tepua stole a sideways glance at the real Matopahu beside her. He was trying to control his amusement. She saw his lips pressed together, his belly heaving. Suddenly he could hold it in no longer. When he began to laugh, the actors took this as a signal. The partners revived, turned to each other, embraced, touching noses. "All is forgiven," the chorus chanted.

In the play that is true, but only in the play, Tepua thought glumly.

Then the drumbeat quickened and the entire company of Arioi began to dance. The people in the audience rose to their feet as well. Head-lifted waved his arms and tried to restore order so that the closing chants of the performance could be said, but no one paid him any heed.

When Tepua saw the sea of dancers outside the meeting house, she knew that she could not stand by and simply watch. She flung off her headdress and cape. It did not matter if Matopahu came with her. This celebration was for Ruro.

She was no longer an Arioi in good standing, but no one could stop her from joining the crowd. With cries of greeting, the people outside made an opening for her. She suddenly felt charged with the energy she had thought would never return.

The soles of her feet tingled with delight at the feel of the hard-packed earth of the dance floor. Stepping forward and back, her knees bent, she swung her hips boldly. Matopahu remained in his seat on the platform, his feet planted, his arms folded.

She felt a sharp pang of disappointment that slowed her steps for an instant. But the joy of the dance itself was too great for her to stop. As she spun around, feeling her skirt whip against her legs, disappointment gave way to resolution. He was going to be stubborn, was he?

She remembered how she had danced for him long ago, when she was new to Tahiti. And in Eimeo she had danced to challenge him, to taunt him into fierce competition with Uhi. She had driven both men to exhaustion, but now she meant to put on her best performance ever. She meant to cast a lure so enticing that even the stubbornest cliff climber would be drawn into her arms.

Oh, Tapahi-roro-ariki, give me your spirit. Give me the strength of the shark, the suppleness of the eel, she prayed as she danced. *Let me be all that my atoll home made me.*

Oh Purea, daughter of my son in a far-distant time, give me your spirit. Give me your visions, your patience, your courage. You are the one who will risk everything on the unknown, who will rise up to see with true vision. I am the canoe that launches from the beach. You are the canoe landing on the other shore. Let me be worthy of you.

She felt the spirits come to her, filling her with power. Now she was dancing not just for Matopahu, but for herself, her son, for Maukiri who had come so far with her, for Aitofa, who had believed in her. She was dancing also for something greater—for Tahiti, her adopted land, its people, its pride, and its future.

Her hands wove patterns in the air. Her fingers seemed to move of their own will, as when she wove figures out of string. And it seemed to her that she was weaving a vision of the future, this time not with fingers and cord, but with the entirety of her being, both mind and body.

She moved in ways both ancient and new, using the motions of the dance to tell the story of her life: how she had been swept into the sea, how the gods had allowed her to survive and reach this land. She had struggled, suffered, grieved, and at last, triumphed.

The people, and even the Arioi, slowed their steps to watch. Some understood her message. Some, perhaps, did not. But all seemed to understand that they were witnessing something extraordinary.

Matopahu remained sitting on the platform, but his arms were no longer folded, and the expression of tolerant amusement had left his face. Now he was staring as if entranced, a hunger starting to burn deep in his eyes.

Oh, but he was strong-willed, this cliff climber! Strong enough to stand against the highest wind. Strong enough to deny anything, even the call of his spirit.

She flung her hair over her shoulder and laid her head back, calling out, not only with the silent voice of her mind, but with the movement of her limbs, the nearly visible images forming between her fingers. And she prayed once again.

Oro-of-the-laid-down-spear, forgive me for choosing the life of my child over obedience to your order. I cannot believe that I was wrong.

Perhaps I ask too much of such a god. Yet if my action did not offend you, show me by giving a small part of your spirit.

In answer, a shimmering brightness began to grow, not only in front of her eyes, but deep at her center. It was the crimson of the sunlight shining on sacred red feathers, and the color of flames leaping against the dark night.

As if from a great distance, she heard the cries from the crowd. *"Nevaneva,"* they said. "The spirit has entered her." She smiled to herself, pleased with the words of admiration. Indeed, she felt infused with the essence of the great god, but this was not the same divine frenzy that had gripped her before.

No, this was different. Oro filled Tepua but did not take her. His strength became hers and the dance remained hers, even through the fiery nimbus that surrounded her.

And then there was a shape moving in that fiery brightness—the form of a young god, dancing with her, laughing with her. He spoke in a voice like the rush of a wind-fanned flame.

"You have no need to ask forgiveness, Tepua-mua-ariki. You have served me well."

Her rejoicing grew until she felt she might burst with the power of it.

"Oro," she whispered, and reached out for his hand. She felt not only the incandescent touch of the god, but the solid warmth of a man's palm. Perhaps it was this touch that made the fiery halo start to fade, and the god's form shift and harden into the shape of Matopahu.

Her spirit leaped, perhaps even more than it had for Oro. The one dancing with her was the beloved quarry she had sought to draw. She looked into deep brown eyes, as molten as the god's fire. Her gaze traveled down the powerful bronzed swell of his shoulders, his arms.

"Even my pride cannot hold against you, atoll woman," Matopahu said in a low, fierce voice. "You have no need of line and lure."

She danced then for him, and he for her. Each displayed to the other in a blazing courtship driven by the drums. And when the beat ended, with a rattling flourish, they stood with their gazes locked on each other, bound together by the fevered lash of the dance that had married their bodies and their spirits.

Awed by the performance, the crowd pulled back, leaving a broad aisle open. Tepua felt every joyful face watching her as she walked hand in hand with Matopahu to the shore. The sun was low, casting a golden light across the water.

They stood together, whispering of Ruro and all their hopes for him, and of their plans with each other. The marriage ceremony would come soon. The ancestors would be brought down from their cave to witness the formalities and celebrations. But in the eyes of the gods, Tepua knew, the union was already sanctified. The gods had shown her what was to come.

At last Matopahu flung his head back and gave a whoop of sheer joy. He plunged from the beach into the water. Tepua went after him, refreshed by the coolness that swept over her. The two splashed like children in the gentle waves as night came on.

Inside the special house erected for the mother and young son, Tepua sat one night and let her gaze rest on the cozy glow of the candlenut lamp. A pleasant weariness weighted her limbs. Ruro lay contentedly asleep. By all rights she should also be deep in slumber.

When the final candlenut burned out, she drew a *tapa* robe over herself and closed her eyes. Though drowsy, she did not immediately fall asleep. Images flickered behind her eyelids, images that were faint but growing brighter. . . .

Suddenly she was once again riding the waves of Matavai Bay. She was Tepua but she was also Purea, standing on the raised deck of her regal double-hulled canoe. She felt a sharp sting of loss as she gazed out across the water.

The great ship of Tapani Vari was leaving through the pass, heading for open sea. All her pleading had failed to keep it here a day longer. Tears slid down her face, for she doubted that she would ever see Tapani Vari again. Despite the trouble he had brought, the anger he had stirred between chiefs, she had come to count the strange pale-skinned commander as a true friend.

Tapani Vari had praised her with grand words and had presented many gifts. As she watched the square sails billowing from masts that grew smaller at every moment, Purea cradled the best gift of all. The warm purring weight in the crook of her elbow was a precious comfort. Tapani Vari had given her one of the remarkable creatures she called *puhi,* an animal with the golden eyes of a god.

With a sigh of mixed grief and joy, she caressed the fur between the *puhi*'s ears. The animal turned its gaze up to her with a soft mew. Looking into its eyes, she felt a new calmness and serenity come over her, as if she were floating in a tranquil sea the same color as those eyes.

The days of trouble seemed far behind now. Yet she could still see Tutaha's livid face when he berated her for protecting Tapani Vari. . . . But in the end she had kept Tutaha from harming the visitors.

Now Purea looked up from her reverie and watched the ship passing the outer reef, flags fluttering from the mastheads as if offering a farewell salute. To watch any longer would only prolong her pain. Once more she gazed down at the *puhi,* stroking its soft belly, feeling the slight swelling there and the little teats. Soon there would be more of the delightful creatures.

The animal stirred in her arms, rubbed its head affectionately against her hand. Far more than just a gift, the *puhi* was a token of an enduring friendship. There would be many disturbing changes in the land, she sensed. Despite their good intentions, the foreigners would bring much suffering.

But the people of Tahiti would survive. She had assured herself of that much. The sons and daughters of her great ancestors would live on. . . .

Tepua returned slowly to herself. She was still filled with Purea's feelings—the warm weight of the golden-eyed animal in her arms, the overflowing affection and friendship for the stranger who had gone, the sparkling beauty of Matavai Bay.

The vision was gone and might not come again. But one day she hoped to see an infant in arms who would grow up to be the proud, strong *vahine ari'i*, a great woman of Tahiti.

I will be old and faded, a grandmother. Yet, with the help of the gods, I will be able to teach her, to prepare her, for what is to come.

With that last thought came contentment. Tepua reached out and caressed her own child. Then she drew the wrap around her and drifted into dreamless sleep.

AFTERWORD

The "discovery" of Tahiti by the outside world occurred in June of 1767. H.M.S. *Dolphin,* under the command of Samuel Wallis ("Tapani Vari"), cruised around one side of the island and eventually entered Matavai Bay. Our knowledge of what happened in the following weeks comes from the logs and diaries of the Englishmen. One can only speculate about the Tahitian side of the story.

The interactions between Englishmen and Tahitians described in this work of fiction are based on the historical records, though certain incidents have been combined for brevity and dramatic effect. The actions and attitudes of Tutaha, however, come from the novelist's imagination. History does not tell us why this powerful chief remained in the background, allowing Purea to appear to be the "queen" of the island. We do know that a strong political rivalry eventually developed between Tutaha and Purea, and that Tutaha was not shy about presenting himself to Captain Cook in 1769.

The impression that Purea made on Wallis had a surprisingly vast impact on the outside world. Wallis's accounts of this gracious "queen," along with his descriptions of her island, captured the public imagination. In France, influential writers pointed to the seemingly freer and happier way of life in Tahiti as proof that European society was unnatural, contrary to man's innate virtue. Though some of their conclusions were based on misunderstandings, there is no doubt that they helped bring on the French Revolution.

The ensuing history of Tahiti is too complex for any summary here. Suffice it to say that though Wallis claimed the island in the name of King George III, England never planted a colony there.

GLOSSARY

aahi: albacore. There were specific names for fish of different sizes, such as *aahi perepererau* for young ones, *aahi araroa* for the very largest, etc.

aha-tu: a prayer used to invoke the sennit-curse. An enemy chief or warrior slain in battle was sometimes made into a "sennit-man" by winding cord around the contracted body. Once the ceremony was completed, the curse fell on the whole family, which soon became extinct.

ahu: stone platform, sometimes built of layers in pyramidal fashion, typically placed at one end of a *marae.* This was not an altar, but a sacred resting place for spirits that attended the ceremonies.

ari'i (ariki): a chief, or a person of the ruling class.

Arioi Society: a cult devoted to worship of Oro in his peaceful aspect as Oro-of-the-laid-down-spear. In this role he also served as a fertility god.

Arue: one of several ancient districts of Tahiti that adjoined Matavai Bay.

ava: a relative of black pepper. The roots and stems were used to make an intoxicating, nonalcoholic drink. (Known as *kava,* and still popular today in the Fiji Islands and elsewhere.) *Piper methysticum.*

Blackleg *(avae parai):* the highest rank in the Arioi order. Members were distinguished by heavy tattooing on their legs.

breadfruit: the staple food of ancient Tahiti. A single tree can produce hundreds of pounds of fruit. When eaten baked, its flavor and texture resembles that of yam or squash. *Artocarpus incisa.*

candlenut: oily nut of the candlenut tree, *Aleurites molucanna.* The shelled seeds were strung on a coconut-leaf midrib and one was set afire, each nut burning in turn, to light the interior of a house.

Eimeo: the island known today as Moorea, about eleven miles northwest of Tahiti.

fai: the art of making string figures, popular throughout Polynesia; "cat's cradle."

fanaunau: Term applied to Arioi who were parents, and thus banned from participation in the activities of the sect.

fare-hua: "house of the weak." A temporary shelter where a mother and child were ritually secluded after birth.

fau: headdress worn in battle by distinguished men. The hollow crown of canework sometimes towered two or three feet above the head.

fe'i: mountain plantain. Bears small bananalike fruits that turn reddish yellow when ripe. Eaten cooked. *Musa fehi.*

gorget: a decoration hung around the neck for battle or ceremonies. Made of stiff matting, it had the shape of a half circle and was often decorated with feathers, shells, and fringes of white dog hair.

Ha'apape: an ancient district of Tahiti near Matavai Bay and the present capital, Papeete.

hanihani: caressing, love-making.

Hina: A goddess thought to reside on the moon, spouse of Ta'aroa, mother of Oro.

Hiro: legendary hero and trickster known for skill at navigation, canoe-building, and prodigious appetite.

hotu: a large tree of the Brazil-nut family. The seeds were used as a fish poison. *Barringtonia.*

ironwood: a hardwood tree with many uses. *Casuarina.*

iti: little.

maeva: hail!

mana: sacred power, which was considered capable of transmission by touch. Humans as well as objects possessed *mana* to varying degrees.

marae: an open-air place of worship, usually a rectangular courtyard bounded by low stone walls, with an *ahu* at one end.

maro: a narrow piece of cloth worn by men about the loins, made of bark-cloth or finely plaited matting.

Matavai Bay: choice of anchoring place of first European visitors to Tahiti, resulting in the development of the present capital of Papeete.

mati: a tree whose berries were an ingredient of the Tahitians' crimson dye. *Ficus tinctoria.*

Matopahu: lit., "steep-sided rock."

miro: Tahitian rosewood, *Thespesia populnea.* Considered sacred, it was planted about the *marae,* and its boughs were used in religious ceremonies.

motu: a low island created by the exposed part of a coral reef.

nevaneva: an ecstatic frenzy said to be caused by a god possessing a dancer or actor.

opu-nui: marae attendants. The name may be translated as "big-bellies" or "august stomachs," because these men ate food that had been sanctified.

Oro: Polynesian god of war. Son of Ta'aroa and Hina. One of the major gods of Tahiti at the time of European contact.

Oro-of-the-laid-down-spear: the aspect of Oro that presided over peace and fertility. In this aspect, Oro was the patron god of the Arioi.

paeho: a weapon made of a length of wood with sharks' teeth bound along one edge.

pahi: a vessel built by connecting two canoe hulls side by side with poles, usually with a platform mounted above the hulls. This type of craft was used on long voyages or for carrying large numbers of people.

pandanus: a type of palm tree that bears fruits that look somewhat like pineapples. The tough, slender leaves make highly durable baskets and thatching.

Pare: ancient district of Tahiti near Matavai Bay.

Porapora: island known today as Bora Bora.

Purea: (known in England as Oberea). The short name of Airoreatua i Ahurai i Farepua, the eminent chiefess who was thought by Europeans to be the Queen of Tahiti. At the time of first contact, there was no paramount chief of Tahiti.

rata: the Tahitian chestnut tree, *Inocarpus fagiferus.* Today called *mape.*

sennit: cord made from softened fibers of the coconut husk.

Ta'aroa (Tangaroa): generally viewed as the creator god. Considered too far removed from human affairs to be addressed directly in most forms of worship.

Taharaa: a prominent hill overlooking Matavai Bay, known in English as "One-tree Hill."

tahu'a: specialist, healer, healing priest.

tahutahu: witch-woman, sorcerer.

taio: a sworn friend, joined with another through a formal friendship pact.

Tane: a principal god of Tahiti, to whom many *marae* were dedicated.

tane: man, husband, lover.

tapa: bark-cloth, made by pounding the softened inner bark of the paper mulberry, breadfruit, or hibiscus tree. Cloth was often dyed or painted, the best colors being scarlet and yellow. Rolls of *tapa* were prized as gifts, not only for their utility and beauty but because of the amount of labor they represented.

Tapahi-roro-ariki: legendary female atoll chief (lit., "Brains-cleaving-chief").

Tapani Vari: used here to refer to Captain Wallis of H.M.S. *Dolphin,* discoverer of Tahiti in 1767. (Note that the Tahitians called Captain Cook "Toote" because their language lacked the hard "c" and "k" sounds.)

tapu: sacred, forbidden. Something that is restricted.

taro: a widely cultivated plant of Tahiti. The root, when baked, tastes somewhat like a potato. The cooked leaves have the taste of mild spinach. *Colocosia esculenta* and *Colocasia antiquorum.*

te: definite article, "the."

te'a: a sacred archery contest, "the game of the gods."

Tepua-mua: lit., "foremost flower."

Tetiaroa: atoll located about twenty-five miles from Tahiti's northern coast. A popular retreat for chiefs and their retinues in ancient times.

ti: small tree of many colorful varieties. Its leaves were used for decoration and in sacred rituals. *Cordyline terminalis.*

tiare-maohi: famous Tahitian flower known for brilliant white petals in stellate formation and delicate fragrance. *Gardenia tahitensis.*

Tupaia: a nobleman of Raiatea who served as Purea's advisor and high priest.

Tutaha: political ruler of Pare and Arue districts of Tahiti at the time of European contact (1767). Son of the Tutaha who ruled during the time of our main story (c. 1710).

umu: shallow pit used for cooking. Stones within are first heated by fire. The food is then placed between the stones and covered to bake.

Urietea: the island known today as Raiatea, located about 130 miles northwest of Tahiti. The center of the Oro cult was located here. Ruins of the great *marue* at Opoa can still be seen today.

va'a: one-hulled canoe with an outrigger float mounted parallel to the hull.

vahine: woman, wife, lover.

SELECTED READING

Adams, Henry Brooks, *Tahiti; Memoirs of Arii Taimai,* Gregg Press, Ridgewood, NJ, 1968.

Danielsson, Bengt, *Love in the South Seas,* translated by F. H. Lyon, Reynal & Co., New York, 1956.

Emory, Kenneth P., *Stone Remains in the Society Islands,* Bernice P. Bishop Museum Bulletin No. 116, Honolulu, 1933.

Emory, Kenneth P. and Honor Maude, *String Figures of the Tuamotus,* Homa Press, Canberra, 1979.

Hawkesworth, John, *An Account of the Voyages Undertaken by the Order of His Present Majesty for Making Discoveries in the Southern Hemisphere,* vol. 1, London, 1773.

Henry, Teuira, *Ancient Tahiti,* Bishop Museum Bulletin No. 48, Honolulu, 1928.

Kane, Herb Kawainui, *Voyagers,* Bellevue, Washington, 1991.

Moorehead, Alan, *The Fatal Impact,* Harper and Row, New York, 1966.

Morrison, James, *The Journal of James Morrison Boatswain's Mate of the Bounty Describing the Mutiny and Subsequent Misfortunes of the Mutineers Together with an Account of the Island of Tahiti,* Golden Cockerel Press, Great Britain, 1933.

Oliver, Douglas L., *Ancient Tahitian Society,* 3 volumes, University Press of Hawaii, Hawaii, 1974.

Robertson, George, *The Discovery of Tahiti,* edited by Hugh Carrington, Hakluyt Society, London, 1948.

Come take a walk down Harmony's Main Street in 1874, and meet a different resident of this colorful Kansas town each month.

A TOWN CALLED
✎ HARMONY ✎

__KEEPING FAITH by Kathleen Kane
     0-7865-0016-6/$4.99 *(coming in July)*
From the boardinghouse to the schoolhouse, love grows in the heart of Harmony. And for pretty, young schoolteacher Faith Lind, a lesson in love is about to begin.

__TAKING CHANCES by Rebecca Hagan Lee
     0-7865-0022-2/$4.99 *(coming in August)*
All of Harmony is buzzing when they hear the blacksmith, Jake Sutherland, is smitten. And no one is more surprised than Jake himself, who doesn't know the first thing about courting a woman.

__CHASING RAINBOWS by Linda Shertzer
     0-7865-0041-7/$4.99 *(coming in September)*
Fashionable, Boston-educated Samantha Evans is the outspoken columnist for her father's newspaper. But her biggest story yet may be her own exclusive–with a most unlikely man.